The Cuckold's Bride

A Doctor William Gilbert Mystery

THE CUCKOLD'S *Bride*

A DOCTOR WILLIAM GILBERT MYSTERY

Leonard Tourney

LUME BOOKS

LUME BOOKS

Published in 2022 by Lume Books

ISBN 978-1-83901-479-6

Typeset using Atomik ePublisher from Easypress Technologies

www.lumebooks.co.uk

But we do not propose just now to overturn with arguments either these errors and impotent reasonings or the other many fables about the lodestone, as for example ... the assertion that a lodestone placed unawares under the head of a sleeping woman drives her out of the bed if she be an adulteress.

William Gilbert, *De Magnete*. 1600

PROLOGUE

Dame Fortune turns her wheel, sometimes slowly, sometimes with cruel suddenness. Who can dispute this, save he is a great fool or born yesterday? The young English doctor was neither.

He reflected on this as the vessel emerged from the river into the open sea. He stood on the ship's quarterdeck, his hands clutching the rail, his knuckles corpse-white and cold. It was early summer, but the salt air was frigid. The sea was turbulent, and the vessel rocked and dipped in response. Only a few days before he had been happy, on the verge of advancement and a new life in London. Now he was a fugitive, accused of deception, malpractice, murder. How did this happen to him, he who thought himself to be honest, capable, and well-intended? How could everything have gone so wrong?

The vessel was a caravel with a Dutch master and crew. The shipmaster, an old bewhiskered fellow with a missing arm and bad limp, had cast a wary eye upon the doctor when he begged for passage. He had responded to the doctor's appeals in a butchered English, made him pay double what the voyage was worth, for the ship was battered and filthy and stank of herring.

The shipmaster asked no questions of the young doctor. Perhaps he was used to Englishmen fleeing their country in the dead of night. Perhaps the shipmaster had discerned the mark of Cain on the doctor's forehead, or sensed his desperation to escape and decided to leave well enough alone. The Englishman had a smooth, boyish face, was tall and thin as a post. He had narrow shoulders and soft, uncalloused hands. But what of that? He might still be a threat. A desperate man is a dangerous man, as all the world knows.

The doctor knew that even the Channel might not be a sufficient

1

wall to protect him from the great enemies he had made. There was the family of the deceased. There was the College of Physicians with its rules and regulations, its strict licensing whereby he might be expelled from his profession forever, unable to practice his art, his long years of study at Cambridge come to naught.

But foremost was Cecil. William Cecil, now Lord Burghley, the Queen's chief minister, a man of fearsome power, who might with his little finger extinguish the doctor without trial or hearing, without pity or regret, and certainly without understanding of what the doctor had done or why. This great man was now his enemy.

The wind and salt spray stung his beardless face, blurred his vision, spurred tears as he thought of his loss. Behind him, England was disappearing into a heavy fog. His previous life was vanishing as well. He must change his name, learn new tongues. He would become an exile, driven to wander. Lord Burghley had agents and spies everywhere. The young doctor would have no rest, no peace.

Compulsively, he reviewed each moment that had brought him to this pass, each misstep, each blunder, each false hope. He worked through his memories methodically. So he had been trained. It was the way his mind habitually worked, for he was a scientist as well as physician. As much as he was able, he relived each event, summoned up from his memory each exchange of words, recalled expressions on faces, seeking clues to guile, deception, malice where before, in his innocence, he had found none.

He did this over and over and despaired, for worse than his fate as an exile was the fear that he would never learn what had happened to bring this fate upon him. He would live in doubt of his own innocence. He prayed now not to God, in whom he yet believed despite all that had transpired, but to Fortuna, the ancient Roman deity, whom the poet Hesiod called the daughter of Oceanus. A fitting supplication now that he was in a tumultuous sea and prisoner of the sea god's good will. He was bound for Amsterdam, a city of strangers. But he had one friend there, a friend he knew would understand and—perhaps—help.

The doctor remembered that, by tradition, Fortuna wore a blindfold, hence her capriciousness. Turning her wheel. He knew he could not ask her to remove the blindfold, to see him as he truly was, innocent. But he could appeal to her better nature.

O *Fortuna,* the doctor prayed, *do turn thy wheel.*

2

1

Five days before his flight from England, the young doctor had looked down at the flaccid body lying upon the examination table. His patient's naked chest was sickly white and covered with coarse hairs that repelled him, but the doctor applied the black squirming creatures as he had been taught, placing six; one on each breast, two upon the man's soft belly, two lower still, just above the cloth that hid the bulge of the man's genitals. The patient, a cobbler the doctor reckoned was about fifty, breathed deeply and seemed to fall asleep as the leeches began their work. Slowly, they began to swell with blood. This sight, too, disgusted the doctor. He had been well trained for this procedure, but he had little faith in its efficacy.

His mentors at Cambridge, disciples all of Aristotle and the old Roman, Galen, were persuaded that such a treatment would draw out bad blood, restore the harmony of the body's elements, and thereby cure a multitude of ills. William had not made himself loved or admired by his skepticism, either with his learned professors or fellow students. But he had been an earnest, dedicated student and thought of himself now as a competent physician. Yet since receiving his medical degree he had achieved little success in his vocation. He was twenty-six, but knew he looked but twenty or less with his thin, sinewy body, narrow shoulders, and pale skin. His effort to grow a beard to give himself a certain clinical gravitas in the eyes of his fellow townsmen had been a failure. A few blond hairs on his chin and the mere suggestion of a mustache were not enough to inspire confidence. They were hardly enough to proclaim him a man and not a callow youth more fit to play a woman's part in some vulgar comedy than attend the sick.

In due course, the treatment was completed. His patient snored on. Carefully, the doctor pulled the swollen leeches from the cobbler's body,

3

inadvertently yanking the man's chest hairs so that he cried out in his sleep, awoke, and cursed the doctor.

"Damn you, boy, can you not be more careful? I came to you for relief of pain, not to suffer it from your hands."

"Doctor, not boy," the doctor corrected.

"Well, then *Doctor*, if you will. For I suppose a man may call himself as pleases him, whether he deserves the title or no."

The cobbler sat up abruptly and got himself down from the table. Scowling, he put on a much-stained shirt and apron, reached into a purse at his belt and withdrew a coin. He glanced at the coin and handed it to the doctor. "That's what we agreed, is it not?"

"Two," said the doctor.

Reluctantly, the cobbler made another visit to his purse. "That seems a great price to pay for so brief a treatment. Especially since the work is done by creatures, rather than yourself, who do little more than preside at the feast."

"He that *presides*, as you call it, is also worthy of his hire," the doctor said. "Two, if you will."

His name was William Gilbert, and he was called William by all who knew him. Never just Will, for his demeanor defied such informality. He was a serious young man, as dedicated to his science as a priest to his vocation. He knew that other practitioners in the town—the empirics, who were self-taught and healed from experience not formal training, the barber-surgeons who could likewise apply leeches or draw blood from a body, the apothecaries with their nostrums for every condition under heaven, even the cunning women whose practice was little more than witchcraft—all charged more for their services. He beat their price because he needed to live. That whole week he had had three patients: the cobbler with the hairy chest, an old woman with a canker sore, and a child with a cough that her mother could not stop—nor could the doctor, even with his supply of medicants. It would be hardly enough to sustain him. He could not think of marrying, of having a family, even if he were disposed to marry, to beget children, at least not right now. Living off his father's wealth, which was not inconsiderable, did not appeal to him.

William led a simple life. He ate little, drank moderately, dressed with a studied simplicity in gray or olive doublet, buttoned at the front, breeches that reached his knees, long hose generally in sad colors—gray or black—shoes that were comfortable but did not call attention to themselves with grandiose buckles. His plain linen shirt had a modest ruff collar, and on his head, he wore a flat woolen cap the same color as his doublet. It was essentially the manner of garb he had been wearing since his days at university. Not the same clothes of course, but similar. It was enough to cover his nakedness, to proclaim him no common laborer, but fell something short of announcing his arrival as a gentleman, much less a courtier. Like the rest of his countrymen, he was aware of the dangers of dressing above his station—but, most of all, he dressed the way he did because he disdained finery and ostentation and was contemptuous of his friends who aped the fashions of the day, who modeled themselves after this lord or that earl, or some other cynosure of every eye. He wanted to see, comprehend what was around him, not necessarily to be seen.

The town was Colchester, Essex, the place of his birth and his rearing, the place to which he had returned from Cambridge to practice his art, for medicine he believed was that: an art, not merely a craft. It required knowledge but also a skill with those he endeavored to heal, a perceptivity and a compassion for suffering—although he had suffered little or less in his own life, his father being well established in the town and prosperous by any estimation.

Under the shadow of a castle, beneath which were the ruins of an old Roman fort, he lived in his father's house, known by the townspeople and himself as Tymperleys, and named after an earlier occupant. The house, solid and well-timbered, was located on St. Peter's Hill between Upper Thames Street and Little Knight-Rider Street. It would stand for centuries after him, but he could not know that now.

His father, Jerome Gilbert, was a lawyer and a town official, a quiet man who was rarely at home and content to leave the management of his domestic establishment to his second wife, Jane Wingfield, a thin, acerbic woman who did not like William, or so he suspected. His birth mother, Elizabeth Coggeshall, had been of a prominent family in the area, and had died while he was young. There was also a boisterous number of younger siblings from his father's two marriages.

The floors sagged with the weight of age. The rooms were dusty and loud with young voices. His patients came to a low-ceilinged, ground floor chamber fitted out as his clinic. It was also a laboratory, for while he had trained as a physician, his greater love was natural science and more particularly the mysteries of the lodestone or magnet. With regard to the latter, he had conducted many carefully-crafted experiments that at Cambridge had earned him among his fellow students and some professors the cognomen, *Doctor Magnetic*.

He knew that the name was meant to belittle, to mock his obsession, and yet he did not resist or resent it. He knew well that he might have suffered worse nicknames, greater obloquy. His college at Cambridge had been no monastic retreat of learned scholars. It was rife with undisciplined and undisciplinable youth, many from noble families, arrogant and prideful, some as young as twelve and thirteen, as he himself had been when he first entered those solemn precincts. Many of his fellow students spent as much time boozing and whoring as they did attending lectures or studying the classics by candlelight. Some were as ignorant and unteachable as savages. Most were so, in his estimation.

The cobbler gone, William returned to his work. On another table in the low-ceilinged chamber sat what he called his terrella or little earth, a ball-shaped lodestone of curious workmanship representing the whole planet itself, which he held to be nothing less than a huge magnet, the core of which was iron. In contrast to ancient authorities most of his contemporaries venerated as persons whose wisdom was beyond question, he trusted not authority but his own experiments. These he made and dutifully recorded in Latin that they might be studied eventually by other scholars throughout the world, Latin being the common tongue of learned men everywhere.

He delighted in the thought of magnetism and its invisible power of attraction and dreamed of possible practical uses and its relationship to the stars and planets themselves. Jane, his father's new wife, thought it all a distraction and urged him to put it aside. "What does it profit you—or us—in this house, that you have no patients to cure of their ills and complaints because you busy yourself with these foolish rocks?"

"They are not foolish," he said, although he had learned it was futile to argue with his stepmother. She was a good woman, but unlearned and opinionated, a dangerous combination. "This is philosophy, science," he told her. "Of value in and of itself. Besides, it's not as if the townsfolk beat upon the door for my services."

"They might, were you to broadcast them abroad as do your rivals in the town," she returned with confidence that her argument was unassailable.

"I'm not given to such *broadcasting* as you call it. I'm not a hawker on the street corner selling my wares."

"T'were better that you were," she said. "You would profit more from it." She left the chamber in a huff.

It was an old and futile battle. His stepmother's practicality was annoying, and yet William understood it. He simply disagreed. Science to him had practical purpose, but the search for knowledge had to be free ranging. It could not be pent up or confined, made dependent on utility, lest its vision be limited and the true scope of nature—the work of the Supreme Artificer—be neither understood nor appreciated. To William, it was God's will that the world and its workings be understood, yet it was not the Maker who was charged with discovery, but man himself.

That evening, William walked out of the town in the fading light. He crossed the fields and looked up at the heavens. For him, it was a familiar pastime at the end of day. He knew the names of all the stars, the constellations, the mythology they embodied, even the human nature they dictated. He understood the earth rotated around the sun as taught by Copernicus. He imagined each of these heavenly bodies—doubtless rocks aloft as was the earth in this celestial display—each equipped with its magnetic poles. Not just luminaries on a flat surface but at various distances from the earth. He knew at last that it was all by divine construction and sustained by divine will, but he knew too that he, like all mankind, was invested with power to discern and to find out the mysteries of God, the secrets and mechanics of creation.

Yet, he must also survive. His stepmother was right about one thing, at least. His present life in Colchester was unsustainable. He was not content to live off his father's wealth, or to do his science in his father's house. His future, he imagined, would lie in London, sixty miles to the south and east.

But by the time he returned home, his resolve had weakened, and he lay upon his bed and soon fell asleep, dreaming of leeches and their black, tumescent bodies sucking upon his own white flesh.

2

The next morning, William sat at a desk cluttered with books and papers, measuring the magnetic force exerted between his lodestone and a carpenter's rusty nail. He measured carefully, taking into consideration the size of the lodestone and of the nail, which he had uncovered in his father's garden. He was curious as to the degree to which the rust upon the nail might diminish or enhance the magnetic force, for he had a new nail, clear of rust and exactly the same size, to use for comparison. He was gratified when the measurement differed. It proved his hypothesis. Rust had a corrosive effect, reducing the ferrous material of the iron.

All this he recorded dutifully, like a monk in his cell writing his meditations. Yet a person of religious bent might have turned William's experiment into a homily. The magnet, God; the corrosion, sin. The mutual attraction reduced thereby. William was content to note the physical fact. He would leave spiritual analogues to the Anglican clergy, or to the Puritan ranters who stood upon street corners to prophesy doom or call sinners to repentance.

But all this was interrupted by a gentle knock at the door and the appearance of his stepmother. "You have a patient, William, a gentleman by his dress and manner. If he does not have a full purse and a generous disposition, I will miss my guess. I pray you treat him well. Do not be modest in stating your fee, a fault I have often observed in you. Trust that the gentleman can well afford it. I know money when I see it. His very clothes proclaim it."

William felt more annoyance than excitement at the prospect of an undoubtedly well-paying patient. He had planned to spend the morning on his experiments. Now, he was called to work of a different kind. At that moment he was not thinking about money.

"The gentleman would not say what condition he suffered of," Jane added.

"Bid him come through, then," William said.

The tall, imposing figure who entered was indeed by all appearances a gentleman—from his fine leather boots to the woolen cloak and high-crowned hat he wore, he presented the very image of not only a gentleman, but an aspiring courtier. Then William recognized the face. It had been several years since he had seen his visitor last, but it was not a face easily forgotten. It was too handsomely featured, with its aquiline nose and square jaw—a young Greek god in doublet and hose.

"Orlando Kempe, if I am not deceived," William said.

"Doctor Magnetic?"

They both laughed and shook hands warmly.

"Pray God, you are well, my friend?" Kempe asked.

"I am well enough off," William answered, too proud to admit otherwise.

"And prosperous enough?"

William laughed again but did not answer. He invited Kempe to sit down. He had not seen Kempe for two years. Now if his dress were any evidence, he had done very well for himself since. They had not spoken or written in the interim, and William found himself jealous not so much of Kempe's fine boots and cloak as of his neatly-cut black beard, giving him the mature, dignified look William coveted.

"May I hazard a guess?" Kempe grinned. He stretched his long legs out in front of him in that casual pose favored by London gallants. "You lack business in this town. You are beset with rivals for your skills and live among folk who prefer the charm and the herb to your knowledge of anatomy and physiology. If they need an amputation, they resort to the barber, who can slice flesh as readily as shorten locks. If they need an emetic they appeal to the old woman at the end of the street, or worse, a false, money-grubbing apothecary who plucks weeds from the ditch and sells the same as miraculous cures from the Americas. The clergy address other matters, although some of them dabble in medicine to the great hurt of the ignorant multitude. And I have quite forgotten the astrologers with their tedious charts and even more dubious calculations. Your considerable talents are wasted here, my friend."

"Perhaps," William said. He glanced at his magnets, the nails, his notebook and the experiments he recorded. The shelf of books—Aristotle, Galen, and Matthioli's *Materia Medica*. "It takes time. To build a practice, to instill confidence."

Kempe leaned forward. He had taken off his fashionable hat, and his dark wavy hair that framed his handsome face and fell to his shoulders furthered the impression of prosperity. But he looked concerned and said, "Is Time then your mistress, that you may play with her at your leisure? Look, William, I came here not merely to see an old friend, though I suppose that is motive enough, but to make you a proposition that if it is agreeable to you, God willing it may advance you to a happier state."

"How happier? More patients, you mean?"

"Well, yes, but let us say patients who pay not only well, but lavishly."

"Lavishly? Because it is London and not Colchester?"

"Because, William, it is the seat of the court, the Queen's circle of lords, ladies, hangers-on and a multitude of the rich, landed gentry, merchants whose wealth rivals those of princes, and foreign potentates who come to visit our happy land and spend their treasure as though it had no end."

William frowned. "Do you think because I live in Colchester, I'm not aware of the attractions of the City? My father is a man of substance in this town. A town official. He has business in London from time to time and takes me with him. I have seen what there is to see there. Most importantly, I do know what opportunities await a physician who succeeds there."

His friend raised his palms in mock submission. "Peace, William, I don't wish to insult you or your town."

"God forbid, Orlando, for it is the place of my birth. When I die, it shall be writ large in my epitaph."

Kempe laughed. "Oh, my friend, you do think of the future, do you not? But what of the interim, in which we all exist and have our being?" His friend's voice dropped to a conspiratorial whisper. "Look, William, do I seem impoverished to you, in want, at a loss for work?" He leaned back so that William could estimate the cost of his doublet, which had silver buttons, and his silk hose that William estimated must have cost him plenty. Kempe fingered his hat, which was peaked and feathered, not flat and simple cloth like his own. Kempe's ruff collar, not white but saffron, was a good six inches in width all round, starched straight up. It was a bizarre effect that William liked not at all. He would not have worn such clothes even if he could afford them.

"No. To be honest, you are the very picture of prosperity," William said. "I reckon you wear half your annual interest on your back. Do you have a wife, children?"

"None as yet," his friend answered, smiling whimsically. "But I have prospects."

"You always did, if memory serves," William said. "Fortune has smiled on you, Orlando, there's no denying it. But pray, don't tell me you came here to rub my poverty in my face?"

Kempe laughed. "On the contrary, William. As I have said, I am here to do you good. Hear me out then. I have a patron, a certain Sir John Parmenter. His daughter has but three months past married an older and even wealthier man who seeks a physician for his wife. The position is yours if you want it, and I do hope you do, for it would benefit us both."

"How benefit us both?"

"Well, obviously you, for it would be the end of your work here and bring you within an hour's ride of London. As for me, should you succeed, I have credit with both gentlemen, Sir John and his son-in-law, whose wealth by the way is considerable. He's a silk merchant. In his dotage."

"His name?"

"Thomas Fanshaw," Kempe said, warming to his theme. "I tell you, William, that when you enjoy the patronage of a wealthy man, you are made as a doctor. Patients come to you in droves. I mean not just the common sort, but persons of rank. Persons who have the Queen's ear. Persons whose names you would recognize were I disposed to talk familiarly about them, which I am not. I have my own house in the City, servants and, in sum, I do very well for myself."

"I am overjoyed to hear it," William said. "I congratulate you on your success."

But it made William feel no better about his own fortunes.

As Kempe talked on, William remembered more of their shared past. They had met at Cambridge where both aspired to become doctors. Kempe was ahead of William and was five or six years his senior. Kempe's father was a vicar of a small church somewhere, as had been his grandfather, but Orlando Kempe had little interest in the church. He had avoided the prescribed rituals when he could, and spoken disparagingly of most of the sermons he was forced to hear. He had often complained of his father's poor circumstances and declared his determination to rise above them. It did not surprise William that, driven as Kempe was, he should have by his own account at last succeeded.

11

William remembered, too, a certain scandalous episode involving a young girl. At Cambridge, Kempe drank, roistered, and wenched within an atmosphere more bacchanalian than academic. But the affair with the household servant got him into serious trouble with the girl's employer, who evidently lusted after her with equal fervor. Thus, Kempe had to deal not merely with an outraged employer, but a vengeful rival for the girl's affections. So went the gossip around the college.

William did not like gossip. He did not gossip himself, or pass on what he had heard. Yet he had learned Kempe's history from persons in position to know.

William could not remember how the matter turned out, although shortly thereafter Kempe left Cambridge. William had heard he had continued his education at some university abroad. Italy, he thought.

His friend was still talking about himself, about his house, his garden, his new London friends. William had to interrupt him to bring their conversation back to its point.

"I am most grateful, Orlando, for being thought of, although I trust London is full of learned physicians that you need not come all the way to Colchester to find me."

"As I said, old time's sake—and also because of the peculiarities of the case of Fanshaw's wife."

"What peculiarities might those be?" William asked.

"Ah, those I will leave Master Fanshaw to disclose. As I have said, I am nothing if not discreet."

"Tell me more, then, about your Master Fanshaw," William said.

"He's an old man, near seventy I should think. Made his money in silk, and plenty of it, money I do mean. Started small, ended large, like many of his class these days, when our prosperous gentry have more wherewithal than the nobility. Has no scruples that an honest man could name. Rich as Croesus. Indeed, some lords of the realm are but beggars compared to him. He has a house full of servants, a stable full of mounts a prince might covet, and he has friends in very high places—as in William Cecil, Lord Burghley, the Queen's chief minister."

"And his wife?" William asked.

"Fanshaw married again after many years as a widower. Her name is Alice. She is young, twenty-one or two, a very Venus in my humble opinion. You shall see for yourself, and if I lie in overpraising her you may beat me

12

roundly and I shall not object. Her father, my patron, is a knight of the realm, a Sir John Parmenter. A very old family but somewhat decayed. Alice is of a delicate constitution, given to strange fancies and impulses. And something more—"

"Yes?"

"She's with child."

"And?'

"Fanshaw fears for her life—and the life of his son."

"Fanshaw knows it's a son his wife shall bear him and not a daughter?"

"He is absolute on that point. When you meet him—and I hope you shall—do not contradict his prophecy. He had it from some astrologer in the City, in whom he has great confidence."

"And you think I should apply for a position as his wife's doctor?"

"Apply?" Kempe laughed. "Nay, not *apply*. The word suggests you have competitors for the post. Trust me, you do not. The position is yours, should you want it."

"By what means?"

"I am well thought of by Fanshaw. I was Alice's physician prior to the marriage and have known her family for some time. I mentioned your name to him. I spoke briefly of your qualities, your learning and interests. He bade me talk to you straightway."

"You might have recommended another of our friends, men of equal merit and attainment," William said. It was not that he was not interested in his friend's proposition, but that he did not want to appear overly so.

"You are too modest, William, by far. I know you. You have exceptional talents as a doctor. Few can match your learning. Few know as much about the body, its parts and particles. And as I have said, Fanshaw has excellent connections in the City and at Court. Why, in no time at all you will be beset with patients. I mean by ever so many men and women of rank and distinction, who will hear of your service to Fanshaw's bride and want the same for themselves. And all will pay generously in gold and silver, not chickens and fruit and vegetables from their garden, as rural householders are wont to do."

Kempe took a deep breath before continuing. "I tell you, London is a veritable encyclopedia of disease, not only that which is native to us English, but disease that is imported through the countless persons who

13

come unto us from other lands. You will never want for work, or for patients, and they will be of the highest quality."

There was a pause in the conversation. His friend waited patiently, a thin smile on his face. William thought about what Kempe had said. It was indeed what he had wanted—not only to make enough to live, but to thrive. To thrive not only to escape his present state, but to have precious time and space to continue his experiments, to discover the full scope of his interest in magnetism and its place in the divine scheme of things. He liked helping people, even the common sort, but was there anything wrong with helping oneself? To be a physician was not to take a vow of poverty. Undoubtedly, the mighty and powerful of London needed his help too.

Besides, he reflected, his science was neither understood nor appreciated in Colchester. His stepmother's thinking was typical. London would be different. He had his own friends in London, friends who like him were devoted to understanding the natural world—botanists, metallurgists, astronomers, chemists, even alchemists. Some had trained at university, others were amateurs, but dedicated, skilled. Like him, they performed experiments, took notes, exchanged discoveries with other like-minded men—and some women—not only in London, but across the waters as well.

"When can I meet this venerable gentleman?" William asked.

"Tomorrow afternoon."

"So soon? Are you serious?"

"You know me, William. I am nothing if not serious. Do you not remember the reputation I enjoyed at Cambridge? For seriousness, I mean."

They both laughed at this, since quite the opposite was true.

"How soon can you be ready to leave?" his friend asked.

"For London?"

"No, for the moon, you simpleton."

"Within a few hours," William said, feeling a sudden charge of excitement.

"Make it less, my friend. Half an hour, no more. Look outside. I have come well prepared for a speedy journey, the two of us. It's a fine day so the weather will be no impediment. You do ride, do you not?"

"Of course. Who does not?"

William stood and walked to the window. At the gatepost, a mare and a gelding stood companionably grazing on some blades of dry grass. He could tell that the saddles of each were finely tooled, probably Spanish leather. The mounts of gentlemen, not those of mere farmers or townsmen, or the hirelings available at the blacksmith's. His friend had come prepared, indeed, and even his mounts proclaimed his new-found prosperity. They also evidenced Kempe's assurance that William would find his proposal attractive and that he would not be returning to London disappointed.

"But how did you know I would go with you? How could you be so sure?"

Kempe paused before answering. It was a long pause, as though Kempe had been taken by surprise by the question and needed time to frame the answer. Finally, he said, "Because we are both alike, William—ambitious, always looking for the main chance. Never content to turn our backs upon Fortune's gifts."

In truth, William did not see himself that way at all—at least, he didn't think he did. He was still young, as busy discovering who he was as discovering the properties of the magnets he studied. Still, he was not disposed to argue with Kempe. What could he lose in following his friend's advice?

His father, when William told him, encouraged his son. "Go with your friend," Jerome Gilbert said. "See this Master Fanshaw, who I trust will do right by you. Find your fortune in London, if it be God's will. Nothing ventured, nothing gained."

It was a saying his practical father often repeated when counseling his son.

But his stepmother was alarmed at the thought of William's departure. She protested vigorously. "Why, William, will you leave me in such a state, with your father to care for, your brother and sisters?"

"My father can well afford your keep, all of you. Besides, he has given me his blessing."

"Still, the children's needs are great, and they will become greater."

He stepped forward and put his hands on her thin shoulders. It was a rare gesture of affection and solace—rare not because William did not feel these impulses, but because his stepmother ordinarily was resistant to any such tokens from him.

She began to weep piteously. "You may well promise, William, yet you cannot be sure what fate awaits you in so great a city, filled as it is with the rabble of the earth, foreigners, soldiers and the vermin that sail the seas."

"Shame on you, Stepmother," he retorted. "Her Majesty would hardly be pleased to hear you slander her brave sailors so. For they do protect us from Spanish devils and other enemies of England."

His stepmother was not consoled. She continued to argue against his leaving for London, but to no avail. William was resolved. His future was in sight, and he knew he must go toward it, like a moth toward the flame, undaunted by uncertainties.

3

It was nightfall of the second day when William and Kempe reached their destination. An infrequent and not entirely competent rider, William was stricken with weariness and buttocks and thighs so sore they seemed afire.

Their journey had been interrupted by a stay at an inn in Chelmsford, where Kempe drank a prodigious amount and regaled William with stories of his former patients and their conditions. He spoke rapturously of his years in Italy, the customs of the Italians, which he ridiculed, what he called their excessive religiosity and superstition, and the viciousness of Italian politics. He spoke of the women he had pursued while there, his conquests, and his views of Italian girls, whom he said were far superior in their amorous skills than were the English, whom he scorned as a pallid, frigid lot. He had also served the Duke of Turin as a physician to his soldiers and had performed ever so many amputations and healings of wounds made by sword and ball.

Kempe had little more to say about the Fanshaws, or the golden opportunity their patronage might afford William. When William asked, Kempe merely urged him to be patient and assured him that all questions would be answered by Fanshaw himself in due course.

Fanshaw's house lay north of London, beyond the city walls and into the countryside. "Still it is most convenient," Kempe said. "No more than an hour's ride to Holborn. Master Fanshaw hates city smells, and therefore chose more wholesome air."

"Indeed, the air is sweeter here," William agreed, and then looked beyond where in the early evening a goodly manor house appeared. Presently, they came to a gate, above which was written *Maldon House* and a Latin inscription *carpe omnia*: "seize everything."

It was a fitting motto for a successful silk merchant whom industry and good fortune had blessed, William thought, and an impressive house—not a nobleman's seat with its aura of medieval glory, but a more modern brick house with central clock tower, many windows, and a portico that bespoke its owner's social importance. Here would enter Fanshaw's wealthy guests. Here would he receive them in this undeniable demonstration of his social position. Sartorial finery and impressive masonry—the twin emblems of Tudor achievement. Neither meant much to William, but he was well aware how much they meant to his countrymen in general.

"Will I see Master Fanshaw tonight?" William asked.

"Possibly," Kempe said, "but more likely in the morning. Like all old men, he retires early."

"And his young bride?"

"She keeps to her bed," Kempe said. "Worried about the child in her womb and other afflictions and preoccupations as you will soon discover. I think the morning will serve well enough to meet the family, get the lay of the land, so to speak. I have spoken so highly of your attainments they will welcome you with open arms. Trust me in this."

"Should we return then tomorrow? Shall I find an inn for tonight?"

"Nonsense," Kempe said. "Fanshaw's house has a dozen bedchambers or more. Your lodging within is already arranged. I'll see you to the door and wish you farewell, at least for now, my friend. I sleep tonight in my own bed, in my own house."

A tall, dour manservant answered.

"Jenks, this is my friend, Doctor Gilbert," Kempe said.

Jenks looked at the young doctor; surveying him suspiciously, William thought.

"Show him to his room," Kempe said in what was more an order than a request. "Your master expects him."

"I have been so instructed, Doctor Kempe," Jenks answered.

Kempe gave William a fraternal pat on the shoulder. "Until tomorrow, William. Sleep you well. You stand on the threshold of your good fortune. I pray you have joy of it."

Jenks bore a brace of candles, and he led William deep into the house, through several drawing rooms and then up fancifully adorned stairs, the newel posts of which were crowned with marble statues of naked nymphs. At the top of the stairs was a spacious landing, adorned with paintings of various sour-faced personages that William assumed were Fanshaw ancestors. He was disabused of this notion when Jenks, seeing him take note of the paintings, volunteered the information that these were not Fanshaws but Maldons, the ancestors of the previous owner of the house, who, having owed a great sum to Fanshaw, surrendered both the house and its contents to settle the debt.

From the landing, William followed the butler down a long passage on each side of which were doors he assumed were bedchambers. He knew the floor above would house the servants, and it was gratifying to him that he was not to be deposited there—for although he wanted a patron, he did not want or need a master. He had not spent years at Cambridge to end up a household tool.

They came to one of the doors, which Jenks opened. He motioned to William to enter.

"When will I see Master Fanshaw?" William asked.

"After breakfast, Doctor," Jenks said. "My master knows you are here. He looks forward to speaking to you."

"And I to him," William said.

Jenks lit the lamp by the bed, which was a large, canopied four-poster fit for a gentleman or even someone higher. The window was covered by luxuriant silk drapes, the walls adorned with mythological figures depicted in a wild variety of amorous postures, some of which were scandalous, But then William had seen more graphic displays in the houses of churchmen, who seemed tolerant of nudity and licentiousness as long as it was safely ensconced in the old world of Greek and Roman myth. He wondered if the artwork reflected Fanshaw's taste or the previous owner's. Given that the Maldon family portraiture still hung in the house, he assumed it was Maldon's.

Jenks said, "Good night, Doctor Gilbert. Is there aught you desire before I leave?"

William looked around the spacious chamber. He had never slept in such a room, never even seen one so commodious and well-furnished. Certainly, there was nothing like it in his father's house. He told Jenks he lacked nothing. Except for a clearer idea of what his duties should be, but that was a question only Jenks's master could answer.

He had supposed that after the long and tiresome journey sleep would come easily, but he lay awake for a longer time than he expected. Kempe

19

had fed his head with the glorious possibilities of his new life. William now imagined a veritable parade of high-born patients, women and men, coming to him for cures and remedies, expressing their admiration for his knowledge and skill, overlooking his unimpressive appearance, his boyish awkwardness, and paying him handsomely for his services that he, like his friend, might live in a handsome house with servants, enjoy a spacious garden, and have leisure to continue with his scientific studies. But now he lodged in a strange house, and in the morning to come, he would meet a very rich old man with a young wife, whom his friend had described as a veritable Venus. A Venus big with child, Kempe had said.

William decided that though her husband be old, yet he evidently was capable of fathering a child at that age. That was a wonder, but not unheard of. Had not Abraham fathered Isaac when the eminent patriarch was a hundred years old? And William had heard of a man in France who had welcomed his first child when he was eighty-five and his wife but a few years younger. The first of these was deemed a miracle by the faithful. The second, he supposed, contrary to nature. But then who knew what nature was capable of? Or for that matter, Frenchmen? Every day men were discovering new and wondrous things in the world, chief of which was the internal workings of the body, the mysteries of procreation being among them.

He finally fell asleep. It was light when a knocking at his chamber door awoke him. It was Jenks. Not supercilious and suspicious of him as the night before, but respectful and solicitous, a transformation that put William more at ease.

"Master Fanshaw will see you at ten o'clock, Doctor. He insists on punctuality, which he often declares is the first of the cardinal virtues."

William was tempted to correct Jenks, the first of the cardinal virtues being faith, and punctuality not mentioned at all. But he resisted. He was now, he believed, in the good graces of Fanshaw's servant. Why poison the well so early in the morning on the first day of his employment?

Jenks insisted on helping him dress, which help he had not needed since he was a small child, but again he thought it unwise to resist. "The master doesn't take breakfast," Jenks said. "He regards it as a most unhealthful practice, provoking the bowels before they are fully awake."

"I suppose it depends on what is taken at breakfast," William replied, as he put on his shoes and buckled them himself. "Or the quantity of what is taken." He had not heard of this doctrine before, the avoiding of food in the morning, but then each day one heard some new salutary practice commended. Most of it being absolute rubbish, at least to William's mind.

Jenks made no response, which pleased William, since he did not care to debate the point further—certainly not with Jenks, and most definitely not with his master. William made a mental note to avoid the topic at his interview to come.

4

William was relieved to discover that Fanshaw did not force his dietary dogma on his household. Or at least, not on his guests. William ate alone in a large chamber with a ceiling adorned with nymphs, ornate silk wall hangings that continued the classical theme. Two solicitous serving girls fussed over him. One, rosy-cheeked and buxom, was especially attentive to his needs, and he was sure she tickled his ear while he ate slices of ham, butter and bread, and apple jelly.

But then he might only have imagined it. His experiences in life thus far had kept him generally apart from women his own age. He was not accustomed to their ways and wiles, except for those of one particular girl, of whom he often found himself thinking. He had known her in Cambridge. But she was far away from him now. He was not likely to see her again, much to his regret.

He finished eating, wiped his mouth on a linen napkin of fine workmanship, and felt much at ease with the world and himself. He did not remember when he had last eaten so well, or so much. He was normally a picky eater, easily satisfied with what was put before him, and commonly eager to move to the next thing in his life rather than gourmandize or linger at table in idle talk. But today, he believed, would be a memorable one; a day of new beginnings when some of his fondest aspirations would materialize before him. For that, he required—nay, he deserved—a full stomach.

"Doctor Gilbert, you must come now. The Master awaits you," Jenks said, reappearing suddenly.

He followed Jenks again, this time to another wing of the mansion; he now realized that Maldon House was constructed in the shape of the letter H, having been built in King Henry's time when such a design flattered the monarch, who ruled by divine right and the brutal power of his will. The butler opened the door for him, and William entered into a bedchamber, much larger than the one he had occupied the night before, splendidly furnished, aromatic with herbs, and dominated not by the bed, which was only a little more elegant than the one he had slept in, but an enormous hearth with a black marble mantle and surround. This was adorned with delicate carvings of various woodland creatures, satyrs and nymphs, gods and goddesses, and he knew not what other denizens of the old world.

He was distracted from these observations by a movement in the room. He turned and saw rising to meet him a heavy-set, square-jawed old man. William knew this must be Thomas Fanshaw. Fanshaw had heavy brows and a wrinkled face as lined as a map. Kempe had said the man was seventy or thereabouts. William thought he looked every year of it.

William made a slow, deliberate bow, what he thought a man of Fanshaw's wealth deserved. "Master Fanshaw?"

The old man nodded and pointed toward a chair opposite him. "Sit down, Doctor Gilbert. I have heard much good of you and am eager to know you better. Let us visit a while."

What Fanshaw called a visit, William would later remember as an interrogation. It began with a most uncomfortable scrutinizing of his physical person. Had Fanshaw's eyes had the capacity to see inside William, they would have, so long he stared, as though William were a horse or sheep at market and Fanshaw was determining its worth.

Finally, Fanshaw said, "Dr Gilbert, you seem very young for someone of your reported attainments."

"I am twenty-six," William said, trying not to sound defensive. His boyish appearance was a sore point with him, and his sensitivity had been intensified by Fanshaw's scrutiny.

Fanshaw nodded. His lips curled into a slight smile. William thought perhaps he was remembering when he was that age, what he did then, what he had done since. Fanshaw had certainly accomplished much since, if this grand house were any indication. Kempe had said Fanshaw had made his money in silk, which meant he was an importer of that valuable commodity, but he also seemed to be an investor or a lender of money, which William knew might be an even more lucrative practice. In either case, Fanshaw had the look of a shrewd businessman, not easily duped, and demanding in his expectations. As inexperienced as he might be with women, William was not inexperienced with men of Fanshaw's nature. There were men like him in Cambridge and in Colchester, and William had also met wealthy merchants in his visits to London with his father. They were not a class of men he particularly esteemed, although his awareness of their power earned a grudging respect in his eyes.

Fanshaw shifted in his chair and reached for a cup at his right hand. He sipped a bit of the liquor, wiped his lips with a napkin. William waited.

"This is very good wine, Doctor. Will you drink with me, sir?"

William declined politely. Evidently, Fanshaw's abstemiousness in the mornings did not exclude liquid refreshment.

"As I think Doctor Kempe explained to you, your chief duty here will be to see to my wife. She is with child and suffers from frequent cramps and sometimes delusions and visions."

William said, "The cramps may be morning sickness, which can be difficult for some women. There is medication to relieve such discomfort. But tell me, what manner of delusions and visions?"

"Of a ... religious nature," Fanshaw answered, taking his time as though he was looking for the right phrase. "Since our marriage three months ago, she has taken a strangely pious turn where she was not so before. She reads religious tracts, books, wears ever a cross about her neck. Now she has a confessor, a Father Julian Mottelay, whom you will meet in due course, for he does these days spend more time with her than do I."

Fanshaw said this bitterly. He turned away from William, lost in thought.

"You were going to describe these visions," William said.

"Yes, various saints come to her. The Holy Mother. I know not the details. You may ask her herself. Her descriptions are confused."

"Can you tell me more about your wife's history?" William said.

"Her name is Alice," Fanshaw said. "She is the only daughter of Sir John Parmenter, of whom you may have heard. The marriage was as much an advantage to him as to me in marrying a young woman of singular attributes, since I was able to save him from certain financial difficulties. She is my third wife. The wife of my youth died in childbirth before she was twenty. My second wife, Augusta, betrayed me. I will spare you the details. While they may be of a certain prurient interest to you, they are painful for me to remember, much less relate. I do not know whether she

24

lives still or no, and could not care less. The marriage was annulled by the Bishop of London at great expense to me. I have no children until now. I mean the child in my wife's womb."

William thought about this for a moment, then said, "I will do all in my power to help your wife—and your child—to health, sir. As for her religious visions, that may be for her confessor to deal with. My purview is the body, not the soul."

"Yes, quite so, Doctor, but I have a concern beyond what I have said thus far."

"Sir?"

"First, tell me, are you a man who can keep a confidence?"

"Upon my oath, sir, I can and do and will."

Fanshaw frowned. "I have had those serving me over the years who have sworn likewise and yet forsworn to my detriment. And to their detriment as well, for above all things I prize loyalty. I do hate a servant who tells tales out of doors, who listens at keyholes that he may entertain his friends with his master's miseries and foibles. Worse that he should spy to gain advantage, preferment."

"You may trust me implicitly," William said.

"Very well. I say all this because I am about to disclose to you certain personal matters that if they were talked of outside this house I should be greatly offended."

"I will be the soul of discretion, sir. Nothing that you say to me will be conveyed to another person save you permit it or instruct me otherwise."

"Then you must know, Doctor, that while Fortune has smiled upon my business interests, I have not been so lucky in love. My first wife, Elizabeth, a grocer's daughter, died along with her baby. We had been married but a year. I waited a dozen years before marrying again. By that time, I had accumulated enough wealth to deserve a woman of rank, the younger daughter of a gentleman. Her name was Augusta. She was a great beauty and, at last, turned out to be a great whore, for she betrayed me with a friend—nay, with more than one friend. I caught them in the act, Doctor. She was shameless. She taunted me with it. She did not deny it. I could have killed her for that, but was prevented by her escape. To where? In faith, I know not. Abroad, I think, perhaps Italy, for in addition to her lovers she was besotted with things Italian. That's a bad sign, don't you think, Doctor?"

"Sir?"

"Her infatuation with things Italian," Fanshaw said.

"Just so, sir. The Italians have a somewhat mixed reputation. But I think your wife's adultery was a worse sign, treasonous as it is to the marriage state."

"Indeed it is, and for that reason I am particularly sensitive to betrayal."

"I understand, sir."

"Such sensitivity might be easily dismissed as mere jealousy, a man's fear of being cuckolded, you know. Those by jealousy possessed are figures of fun, are they not, standing jokes, matter for comedy?"

"Yes, I suppose they are, sir," William admitted.

"Which brings me, Doctor, to my present wife. You must know that I love my wife, the age difference between us making my feelings for her all the more intense and exquisite. Yet I must admit my own weakness therein, that of which I have spoken. Jealousy, I mean. I fear I have married an adulteress, and that fear ever wars with my hope that she be honest. Do you understand my conflicted thoughts?"

William said that he thought he did. Fanshaw took a deep drink from his glass. For a long moment, the two men sat in silence. Fanshaw had leaned forward in his chair and given William another searching look; trying to read his soul, William supposed, or at least looking for some understanding or shared experience. William recognized this, though he had never suffered this dilemma himself. He said, "May I ask, Master Fanshaw, why you fear your wife that now is, has been unfaithful?"

The old man sighed. "Because of her condition."

"Her pregnancy?"

For a moment, Fanshaw said nothing. He stared at something on the wall, one of the many ornately woven wall hangings. But William knew he wasn't looking at any image, but trying to decide whether to disclose something even more deeply personal. Then Fanshaw spoke, and William knew he had been right.

"Her pregnancy, yes. Coupled with my own impotence," Fanshaw said. He leaned back in his chair, seemed to forget about the wall, and dropped his eyes.

William waited. He did not know what to say. Fanshaw continued.

"Since our marriage I have been, what shall I call it? Incapable. You see, I lack not the desire, but the performance. Our marriage was never consummated. When my wife told me she felt a stirring within her, languished sick of a morning, and her belly began to swell, I confronted her. I told her I didn't believe I was the father of this child. I reminded her of my ... incapacity."

"And what did she say to that?"

"She denied all but insisted she had known only me. She acknowledged that there had been certain difficulties in our mating but said that once, when I was well drunken, on our wedding night it was, I did the deed with her and with that single instance planted my seed within her. She wept without ceasing at my doubts and suspicions and took to her bed. It was then she began to experience her dreams and visions and cry out for a priest to shrive her."

"And you agreed ... I mean, to the priest?"

"Her family are Papists, although quietly and prudently so. I knew this when I married her. Then, as I have said, she was indifferent to religion. But all that changed. I am a doting husband, Doctor, and when she said she wanted a priest to attend to what she called her spiritual needs, I secured one. A priest of her church, I mean. Father Mottelay was priest to her family. I invited him here under the guise of being a secretary of sorts to me. You know how dangerous it is to harbor a priest of the Roman church. That I undertook to do so for her sake testifies to my love for her, does it not?"

"I do think it does, sir," William answered. "Since another man might have refused her wish, and with some justification given the dangers you describe."

"How can I know whether the child is mine or some other's? That is my question."

"I know not, Master Fanshaw. I suppose when the child is born, your likeness, minted upon the babe's face, might give evidence of your true paternity and erase those doubts and fears that now possess you."

"Pray God, they might," Fanshaw said, sighing and rubbing his wrinkled forehead. "And yet, I have learned there might be a better way."

"A better way?"

"Doctor, have you heard of Barodius?"

It was a name vaguely familiar to him, but William decided to say no.

"He lived many centuries past. He wrote a book of poems about plants and their virtues. Also stones, rocks, and their special properties. There was a story he told about iron rocks."

"Magnets," William said, remembering now what he had dismissed as myth. "That magnets can detect an adulteress."

"Exactly, Doctor Magnetic."

5

William's heart sank at Fanshaw's words. *Doctor Magnetic*. What he had been maliciously called at Cambridge. Now he realized why he was here. Not to attend the sick, but to apply his expertise in magnetism. And not for his patient's health, but to determine her fidelity.

"It's a myth, sir," William said when he could find his voice. "No better than an old wives' tale."

"I have it on good authority that it is not a myth but true science, as you would call it," Fanshaw said.

William wanted to ask what authority Fanshaw meant. He did not. He was now almost at a loss for words.

Fanshaw continued. Melancholy before, he now seemed sanguine, filled with energy and almost religious enthusiasm. "Doctor Kempe tells me that you experiment with magnets, investigate their powers. Tell me, Doctor, have you ever performed an experiment with a magnet's capacity to determine a quality within a person, like infidelity, or some other moral flaw?"

"I have not, sir," William answered. "That has not been the aim of my work. I am interested in the operation of the lodestone, to give it a more proper name, and its strength and application to, say, navigation and understanding of the celestial sphere."

Fanshaw seemed to mull this over, but only briefly. Perhaps he had anticipated William's objection. He said, "Then is this not an opportunity for you to perform such an experiment? Are not man's moral nature and amorous impulses of equal importance as these other things?"

"Well, they are not unimportant, sir," William conceded.

Fanshaw said, "I am told that these magnets, these lodestones as you call them, embedded in a blanket and pressed upon the naked body, by

29

their virtue cause a swelling of blood and inflammation within the woman's womb should she be an adulteress, whereas if she be chaste no such effect occurs. She experiences, rather, a pleasant sleep of innocence. Her flesh remains unmarked. Her virtue confirmed. Some call this inflammation the Devil's mark, and some say it causes the adulteress to cry out and confess her fault, whereupon the inflammation subsides."

William hardly knew how to respond to this. It was nothing he had ever found in his reading, heard tell of, or imagined in his heart. It sounded like the most preposterous fabrication—a wild concoction of fables and myths—but he knew he must watch his words with Fanshaw, temper his response. He could not denounce the very idea in blunt language, however much he wanted to.

He took a deep breath, composed himself and said, "I have never heard of any of this, sir. So I cannot say if it be true or just an old fable to discourage errant wives from taking lovers and teach them to be wary of magnets."

William smiled when he said this, hoping Fanshaw would see some pleasure in his wit. Fanshaw did not. The old man's jaw was set, his thick lips pursed.

"But you cannot say it is not true?" Fanshaw said.

"In faith, sir, I cannot say so. Yet it seems most unlikely to me."

"Why so?"

William said, "There is, in truth, iron in the blood, which as all the world knows the magnet attracts. But I doubt a magnet or magnets exert power sufficient to draw the blood out, or if it had such power, I know not why it should detect infidelity in a woman, or in man for that matter. The body is one thing, the mind and soul another. You may ask your priest about that. I am sure he will concur. Body and soul may indeed converge in ways all our learning has yet to discover, but for now, they do appear separate spheres, having little or nothing to do with the other. Thus, a good man or honest women may be the picture of health in body but steeped in sin. Similarly, an honest spirit may dwell in decaying flesh and bones. We do see this every day in the aged—righteous in their years, though the body fails under the inevitable weight of time."

Fanshaw said, "I grant you your principle, Doctor. But tell me, does not body, mind, soul all converge in the adulterous act? Can adultery be committed save the body acts unlawfully? And can the body act unlawfully and the soul of the transgressor not be tainted thereby?"

Fanshaw waited for an answer. After a moment, William said, "With respect, sir, I am a physician, not a theologian. I deal with the body, not the soul."

"Well, Doctor, I am no scholar," Fanshaw continued, "yet it does seem plain to me that there is a connection between mind and body and therefore blood may tell a moral tale even as it compels an immoral act. We do say of sin that it proceeds from hot blood—violence, lechery, fornication, adultery. Do not all these vices proceed from, relate to … *implicate* the blood?"

To William, the answer was no, yet he felt pursuing the point would gain nothing for him. He had not expected his interview with Fanshaw to turn into a philosophical debate. But somehow, it had. Fanshaw might be old and unlearned, by jealousy possessed and arrogant, but he was shrewd and manipulative. It was no wonder he had succeeded so well in his business affairs, no matter how unhappy his marriages were.

Fanshaw sat back in his chair. He was studying William again, a smile of triumph on his aged face, as though he had won his point. But in William's mind, Fanshaw had not. And now he bristled at the thought that he had been somehow tricked, a victim of misrepresentation. His services secured not as a doctor of physic but as a kind of magician, for surely, he felt the discernment of a faithless wife to be beyond the power of mere iron, as powerful as that wondrous metal might be in capacity to direct, and if anything were confirmed it would be by some supernatural power beyond his own control or comprehension.

William fell silent, waiting for the full unfolding of Fanshaw's logic. These were weighty questions he would have gladly debated at Cambridge or some other place where men stood on equal ground, but before this old man of wealth and power he felt besieged and vulnerable.

Fanshaw pressed on. "Is there no theory of magnetism by which this discernment you describe could be plausible? Come, Doctor, by your friend's account the testing of hypotheses is as familiar to you as a sailor's craft or a cobbler's shoe. I ask only that you put the power of your magnets to the test. You are a skilled experimenter, are you not?"

William felt himself being worn down. He knew it. He hated it, but at the moment he could do nothing about it. It was not the superiority of the old man's reasoning that rattled him. It was the strength of his will.

"I am so skilled, Master Fanshaw."

"Well, then ..."

William hesitated. It seemed another instance of his doing something that did not comport with his own beliefs—like applying the damnable leeches to the cobbler's chest to bleed him of malign humors. He had done that to his shame—for the pittance of his fee and because he had been prevailed upon by a patient convinced a blood-letting would do him good. Complying with this new assignment savored of the same sort of betrayal of his calling, a violation of his honor.

"I would pay you well for this service, this experiment, Doctor Gilbert. And your having conducted it, I would want you to continue in the service to my wife until she is well, and the child delivered. Beyond that, I have many connections with persons in the City who I am sure would appreciate your skills at physic."

"You would want me to attend her even if she is proven to have betrayed you?" William asked, astonished.

Fanshaw leaned forward again. His gravelly voice fell to an intimate whisper. "If my wife has cuckolded me, I do not want to broadcast my betrayal to the public ear. I would rather keep her adultery, and my humiliation, private. Believe me, Doctor, I would rather have her at any cost than lose her. I will reconcile myself to her sin and encourage her repentance, even as Christ did the woman taken in adultery. I will secure her promise of fidelity going forward and raise the boy as though he were my own. That is, if she is proven false to me."

William needed to think before he answered. Had he heard the old man rightly? He would have gladly asked Fanshaw to repeat himself, but he knew that would imply the incredulity that he indeed felt. Perhaps, Fanshaw had spoken truly. But if so, he wondered at Fanshaw's devotion. What husband, finding a wife false to him, condones the behavior, keeps the bastard as his own, moves forward as if nothing happened, Christ's example notwithstanding? William expected rather outrage, the casting away of the transgressor, perhaps even the murder of her and the child she carried. There were times when Christian forbearance seemed a species of insanity, a violation of reason as well as custom. William wondered if this were not one of these.

Fanshaw must have read his thoughts. He said, "I can see you wonder at my charity, Doctor, my willingness to forgive and forget. But my love for my wife is stronger than my injured honor. Besides, I want only to know the truth, Doctor. It is not her betrayal that maddens me, but the uncertainty of it with which I cannot live."

Abruptly, Fanshaw stood up, surprising William with the alacrity of his movement. He had seemed before not merely old but decrepit. Now a more vigorous Fanshaw emerged. A vigor that matched the power of his will. William arose too.

"Perhaps if you were to visit my wife," he said.

"Sir?"

"She knows you're here and wants to meet the man who can cure her of her maladies. Do you attend upon her, then give me your decision as to whether you will determine the power of your magnets by testing them on her, or return to—where is it you're from?"

"Colchester," William said.

"Ah yes, Colchester. It is in Essex, is it not?"

"Yes, sir."

"Where you hitherto practiced."

"Yes, sir. Briefly."

"Come, then, Mistress Fanshaw awaits you. You may examine her and see how she fares, how fit she is to give birth safely. I would not have her die in childbirth as did my first wife, Doctor Gilbert. You do understand me, do you not?"

William said he understood perfectly.

Fanshaw led him to an adjoining room and then to yet another, each splendidly furnished with finely crafted wall-hangings and the heavy oak and mahogany tables and cabinets then in fashion. They came to a door on which Fanshaw knocked almost timidly, as though the chamber beyond were holy ground or a queen's chamber one entered at his peril.

Fanshaw turned to William and whispered, "She is doubtless with her confessor at this hour. He's a meddlesome fellow, very pious—but with a lecherous eye, if you ask me. I am of the Roman church myself, Doctor, but I trust no priest, neither in the pulpit nor the bedchamber."

"Yet you suffer him to be with your wife alone," William said.

"It's as she wills. Though I do not trust her completely, yet I am too besotted with her to deny her anything. You shall understand when you see her."

Fanshaw knocked a second time when no answer came and then a third. Finally, a soft, musical voice was heard bidding them enter.

6

If not Venus, as Orlando Kempe had described her, still Fanshaw's bride was the most beautiful woman William had ever seen. She lay upon her bed in a silken shawl adorned with little roses and leaves, while her long, golden hair lay about her white shoulders—extending almost to the end of her slender white fingers. Her face was perfectly formed, with a delicate nose, wide-set eyes of cerulean blue, and red lips of a sensuous fullness that William had rarely seen in English women. Her skin, as much as he could see, was flawless, alabaster, so had she been dead she would have more resembled a marble effigy upon a catafalque than flesh and blood.

Then he became aware she was not alone. Seated in the corner of the chamber was a long-legged, thin man of thirty or so with dark eyes, a pointed beard, and neatly-trimmed mustaches in the Spanish fashion. He was dressed in dark colors with white ruff collar, and by the total effect and the small book in his hand—a prayer book, no doubt—William surmised this was the priest Fanshaw had disparaged.

"You are my new doctor, I believe?" she asked in a pleasant voice, as she took the measure of William with a curious but not unfriendly gaze.

"I am William Gilbert, dear lady," he answered, with a short little bow. "Doctor William Gilbert."

This chamber too amazed him. Somewhat smaller than her husband's, it was adorned with a large crucifix above the bed and several paintings: William took these to be saints by their suffering countenances and haloed crowns. There was also a faint odor in the room, incense or some medication she had taken. It was not perfume. The room seemed more a chapel than a bedchamber.

"This is my friend, Father Mottelay," she said, pointing to her confessor, evidently unconcerned that his identity as a priest be revealed. This was undoubtedly the man Fanshaw had described. If he had a lecherous eye William could not discern, but the air of Papist piety was evident enough.

The priest regarded William with a curious stare. William thought perhaps the priest thought of him as a rival, given that the line between physician of the body and that of the soul was not always clearly drawn.

"I will see my new doctor alone, Father Mottelay."

The priest stood, responded with a stiff bow, and slipped from the room.

Alice Fanshaw motioned to William to sit by the bed, in a chair the departing priest had probably occupied before William's entrance. He sat and looked at her again. This time her skin seemed not so splendiferously white as pale and somewhat sickly, as though she lacked blood in her body. He noticed on her belly the slight protuberance that signaled her imminent motherhood.

"Your husband tells me you are with child."

She nodded and smiled radiantly. It was a winning smile that involved her eyes as well as her mouth, and William could well understand her husband's attraction to her.

"And how far are you along, madam?"

"Three months, I think," she said. "Master Fanshaw and I have been married but three. We were blessed almost at once. I do think I conceived on the very night of our wedding."

William looked at her again. She seemed much farther along than that but said nothing to contradict her estimation.

He hesitated to examine her, but he knew that was what he was expected to do, what he should properly do. He was, after all and at least for the time being, her attending physician. Trembling a little, he asked, "May I?"

"Of course, Doctor," she said.

He rose from his chair and approached her bed. She parted the silk covering, revealing underneath an even more translucent material. This she pulled aside to reveal her naked midsection and the swollen belly he had discerned earlier. He placed his hand upon her and gently probed. "Is that tender to my touch?" he asked.

"A little, Doctor."

He leaned over her and placed his ear against her belly. He could hear nothing. No heartbeat. Nothing, not yet.

"May I, Mistress Fanshaw, examine you further?"

36

She blushed and nodded, turning her face away from him.

He ran his hand down beneath her smock to her groin, felt the warm, wet opening. His fingers penetrated easily. She would have no trouble with the birth, he thought. Her body, except for its extraordinary pallor, seemed healthy. He had not in his short career examined many women, but he had examined some, and what he felt within her body was more consistent with a woman who had given birth previously than not. Under other circumstances, he would have asked her directly. Now, he did not dare. Neither her husband nor she had mentioned anything of an earlier marriage or earlier childbirth. He knew he could be wrong about his suspicions. But even had he been certain, he would not have asked her.

He covered her and walked over to a basin he had seen on the other side of the chamber. He washed his hands with a scented soap and dried them on a towel hanging nearby. Another doctor would have wiped his fingers on his apron or handkerchief, but William was fastidious about cleanliness. He turned back to where Alice Fanshaw lay watching him.

"Have you found anything untoward?" she asked tentatively.

"No, you should have no trouble giving birth," he said.

"Heaven be praised," she said, smiling.

"How have you been feeling, generally?"

"I am sometimes sick in the morning."

"Quite common," he said. He lifted her hand to feel her pulse. It was rapid, but he thought that might be the result of her unease about his examination of her. Her wrist was warm and delicate.

"Are you eating well?

"Yes."

"Sleeping well?"

"Not always."

Her answer pulled him up suddenly. "And why not, madam?"

She paused and looked away from him. "I have dreams."

"As do we all, madam. It is natural. Even sleep abhors an idle mind."

Another pause. She said, "I do not think your word describes them."

"My word?"

"*Natural.* They are sometimes quite frightening."

"Can you describe them?"

"They happen sometimes when I am awake."

"You mean a daytime vision?"

37

He asked her what she saw in these visions, expecting something consistent with what her husband had called her recent religious conversion. But there were no saints, no Holy Mother, no threatening, hooded monks. Nothing that he might have imagined or associated with religious delirium.

"I see myself as a child, as a young girl. I see things I have done in my past."

"What sort of things, may I ask?"

Now her face turned away from him again and took on a reflective expression. "To my parents, I was not an obedient child. I did things not becoming my station or the faith in which I was raised. I call out for help, for light, for someone to save. No help comes. I wake shaking. I feel I am being punished."

"By God?"

She nodded. Her eyes welled with tears. "And there's something more, something more fearful."

He waited for her to say it.

"I feel I am doomed."

"Doomed?"

"To die young, to die soon. In my dreams I sometimes see myself. I am young, as I appear now before you, and I am dead, lying on a bier. I am incapable of movement. I am in a fixed state, and I realize I will remain so, forever."

"Do you have these dreams often?"

"Every night. Doctor Kempe gave me a potion to make me sleep."

"What potion?"

"Valerian root, I think. Mixed with a little wine."

"Valerian is commonly prescribed by our physicians," William said. "But it hasn't been effective?"

She shook her head sadly.

"Then stop taking it. No good comes from taking anything into the body that helps neither the body nor the mind."

"Father Mottelay has been a great consolation to me," she said, staring toward the door from which the priest had left the room.

"Yet his ministry has not given you peace at night," William said. "You continue to dream these dreams, these nightmares that alarm you."

"Perhaps it is no less than I deserve." She looked searchingly at him, as though she wanted him to confirm her harsh judgment, or perhaps

38

refute it. But he could do neither, knowing so little of her history and not yet prepared to trust completely anything that her husband had said, or anything she said to him now. Besides, he was, at the moment at least, her doctor, not her judge.

"That's a sad view of yourself," William said.

"It's a sad view I have, Doctor Gilbert."

They sat silent for a moment, then she said—in a somewhat different voice, a kind of conspiratorial whisper—"You know, Doctor Gilbert, I understand why my husband asked you to be my physician."

"Madam?"

"As I am sure he told you, he suspects the child I carry is not his, but another's."

He dared to ask, "And is that the truth?"

"The truth?"

"Is the child not his?"

She paused, then said, in a louder voice now, "I swear by God, the Holy Mother, and all the angels in heaven that I have known no man save my husband, Thomas Fanshaw."

Her declaration was more an oath than a statement.

"He said he was incapable," William said. "He said he lacked the procreative power."

She blushed, then said, "My husband, as you have seen, is somewhat older than I. He has had some difficulty in our bed, but on our wedding night he, having celebrated our nuptials overmuch, was able to do that which since then he has been unable to do."

"I see," William said, admiring the delicacy of her description.

"I also used something else?"

"What would that be?"

She reached beneath her pillow and pulled out a strange, rootlike object. The root resembled a man with two branches entwined like human limbs.

William knew what it was. Half the housewives of Colchester had such an object. It was mandrake root. Mandrigora. From time out of mind used for its aphrodisiac powers and ability to encourage pregnancy. It seemed to William just another fable, but such figures were widely commended by apothecaries and common folk and highly prized for their supposed efficacy.

"Who gave you that?" William asked.

"A friend."

She put the root back where she had gotten it and said, "I do know that my husband has asked you to put me to some manner of test—to confirm my fidelity. Involving magnets, I believe."

It took him a moment to recover from this surprise. He had not supposed Fanshaw would have revealed his plan to his wife, but then why should he not, given his claimed predisposition to forgive and forget? On the other hand, perhaps Kempe had told her. Yes, William thought that likely. Kempe would have known Fanshaw's true intent from the beginning. Why else would he have recommended William as the conductor of the test?

"I have not yet agreed ... to conduct such a test," William said.

"Oh, Doctor, but you must," she cried, grasping his hands.

Her touch alarmed him, and he almost withdrew his hands from hers. He had not expected this, nor did he understand it. There was a desperate look in her eyes. For a moment, he was rendered speechless. That she should desire such a test was as incomprehensible to him as her husband's willingness to forgive should she somehow fail it. Finally, he said, "But why would you want to submit yourself to such a test?"

She took a deep breath of resignation, or perhaps annoyance that he was slow in understanding her need. "So that his jealousy might be assuaged and his trust in me restored."

"To be honest, Mistress, I don't know whether magnets can be used to discern fidelity in a wife. There's a myth to that effect, which your husband believes. But I cannot understand how my magnets, no matter how powerful, can do anything to confirm or deny what your husband suspects and fears."

"But that's all the better, Doctor," she said, her desperation giving way to a hope. "If I am not affected by your magnets then my fidelity is confirmed, is it not?"

William said he supposed it was.

"What harm then, in appeasing his desire?" she asked. "I have known doctors and apothecaries too who prescribe for their patients simply because the patient demands it—if it do no harm. Is that not true, Doctor?"

William admitted it was, conscious he was himself among the doctors she mentioned.

"Oh, do let me take your test, your magnets, Doctor. I shall thereby be found a faithful wife. His mind will be at ease. He will trust the child I bear is his child, and he will love us both, even as is proper in the eyes of God."

He could not deny her reasoning, although he doubted her account of her husband's drunken state reviving his procreative powers. In his experience, drunkenness was much more likely to unman than to invigorate. As for the mandrake root, it was no more than a silly doll revered by the ignorant and those that longed for love or a child. It was, at best, a harmless toy. Yet William suddenly found himself wanting to please this woman. Perhaps this was the power Fanshaw had spoken of, the beguiling power of her beauty, her sweetness of voice and expression. Or perhaps he merely felt sorry for her—a young bride married to an old and bitter man, a beautiful woman haunted by dreams, anxious to be trusted and loved.

"I beseech you, Doctor, put me to your test. I warrant you I shall not fail it. I shall be vindicated in my husband's eyes and in yours. So shall I enjoy peace in this house where there is none now, and you will rise in my husband's esteem. My husband, as you know or will soon learn, can be very generous. And he will be very grateful to the doctor who has put his mind at ease and been so solicitous of his wife's needs."

She released his hand—but not the expression of appeal in her eyes, which remained fixed upon him.

"I have yet to decide what to do, Madam," William said. "I don't even know how to design such an experiment, or what the ancients who advanced such a notion meant when they said that magnets could reveal faithlessness in a wife."

"But I am told you know more about magnets and their power than anyone in England. Certain it is then, that you can devise such a test, if any doctor in England can."

She held him in a steady gaze. It was a look that brooked no denial. Yet he still resisted. The strangeness of her request, of her husband's need, had not been in the reckoning when he agreed to meet with the Fanshaws. But now this was where he was, on the horns of a dilemma. He did not like it, but lacked the will to deny her request outright.

"Let me think upon it."

It was what he had told her husband.

But her response was as though he had agreed to her request. She beamed with pleasure and gratitude. "I pray you do think upon it, Doctor, and think well, with compassion for my husband and me. You are my

41

only hope to confirm my husband's trust in me and restore our mutual love. You are as well the only means to give my husband peace of mind. His doubts torment him. I can see it in his face. I hear it in his voice. It breaks my heart to see his misery."

7

William's conversation with Alice Fanshaw had settled nothing. His path forward was uncertain. Her husband had asked him to return to him after William had spoken to Fanshaw's wife, and he was about to do so when from out of the shadows of the corridor a tall, slender figure appeared. It was Father Mottelay.

"You have completed your examination of Mistress Fanshaw, I trust?" the priest asked.

"I have, sir."

"And you find all well with her?"

"Hardly, she suffers bouts of sickness connected to her pregnancy and certain perturbations of the mind."

"Perturbations of the mind? And you think to treat that with your pills and things?" Mottelay asked, skepticism written large on his face.

"Her treatment I am yet to determine," William said.

"You understand, do you not, Doctor Gilbert, that the lady's malaise proceeds from a spiritual condition, not a physical one," Mottelay said, in what was more a statement than a question.

"I have no such understanding, Father," William said. "My examination of her was cursory. And it was private as well. She talked briefly of disturbing dreams. I said they were not unusual. All have dreams that instill fear." William did not like the priest and was not about to discuss his patient's condition with him.

"She is a most sensitive lady at the threshold of her repentance for sins committed in her youth," Mottelay said. "Her mental afflictions proceed from a heart burdened by transgression, not weakness in the body." Mottelay added this with a confidence that William found more than a little annoying.

43

William would have liked to know what sins the priest spoke of besides the suspected adultery. Yet, though not a Catholic himself, he knew enough about the confessor's role to know that Mottelay was under a vow of silence with regard to anything Alice Fanshaw had confessed to him.

"That may be the case, yet the lady is also with child," William said, "a physical condition wherein my own services may be required. Moreover, her husband is old and subject to afflictions incident to age."

"Speaking of age, you seem very young, Doctor," the priest said. "I trust you have the qualifications for your office?"

"I am a graduate of Cambridge, where I received both a bachelor's and master's degree as well as my doctorate in medicine," William said, cursing himself for yielding to the temptation to boast, an impulse he detested in others.

"And were I to attempt to verify these claims, I trust I might not find you a pretender to these honors you claim?"

"You would find all I have said true," William said. "And I do not boast. I simply offer facts to refute your suppositions. But I would know under what authority you inquire into what is private and personal? You are not the master of the house, or the lady's husband. Do you have some commission from Master Fanshaw of which I am unaware? Are you the gatekeeper of his affairs, or his wife's?"

"No, but I care deeply for her," Mottelay answered. "I would in no way see the lady abused."

William shot back, "Abused? I am a doctor, sir, not an abuser. My function is to heal and comfort."

"Yet some doctors do abuse their office," Mottelay said.

"That may be so, but not this doctor."

William had grown heated in this exchange. Both men stood within a foot of each other, the priest, being older and taller, having something of an advantage. Yet William stood his ground. He had not sought this contentious rivalry. It had found him, and he blamed the priest for it.

For a few moments the two men stared each other down, like schoolboys daring the other to strike the first blow. But then the moment passed. Mottelay backed away and raised his hands in a gesture of conciliation. William felt inclined to leave abruptly as a show of disdain for the priest. Then Mottelay said, "We seem to have gotten off on the wrong foot, Doctor."

"So it would seem," William replied curtly.

"Shall we begin again, then?"

"If it please you, sir."

"If your concern for Mistress Fanshaw is genuine as you claim and I am prepared to believe, then if we cannot be friends because of our conflicting roles in life—you a doctor, I a priest—we can at least be confederates in her salvation."

"Salvation?"

"She is vulnerable in body—and in spirit," Mottelay said. "Let us help her, each in his own way."

William looked at the priest. Haughty and contentious before, Mottelay now seemed a softer version of himself. William, not easily riled, sensed the atmosphere of hostility had blown away.

"Agreed," William said and extended his hand.

Mottelay took it and smiled pleasantly. "Let me escort you to Master Fanshaw's chamber, Doctor. Maldon House is like a maze where a man may wander for a month before finding his way out."

"Lead me then, Father Mottelay, and I will follow," William answered, trying to match his companion's conciliatory tone—although in his heart, his annoyance at the priest's haughtiness had only begun to cool.

8

William might have found his way back to Fanshaw's bedchamber on his own. He had a good sense of direction and almost perfect memory for physical details. Nonetheless, he thanked the priest, who in parting wished him well—as though he knew more about why William was at Maldon House than he should.

William saw that Fanshaw had traded his nightgown for pearl-studded satin doublet and hose that he might have worn to some public occasion; a change that made him look younger and less the invalid. Indeed, he seemed almost vigorous, and not a little threatening. He stood very rigid, fixing William with the steely gaze of an inquisitor.

"Well, Doctor, what have you decided? Will you serve me, or return to your practice in Colchester?"

Until his confrontation with the priest in the passageway, William's answer might have been the latter. Then, he was still bothered by his doubts about his magnets and their powers. But he had wavered in Alice Fanshaw's chamber under her seductive appeal for help, and in the passageway the lady's confessor had stirred within him a competitiveness that had pushed him over the edge.

"With your approval, I'll stay, sir."

"Excellent. And you will put my wife's virtue to the test?" The old man asked.

William said he would, and gladly.

A wave of satisfaction and gratitude passed over Fanshaw's face. He breathed a sigh of relief, as though what was to come had already been achieved. He asked: "This test, as we have called it, what form shall it take? "

"The very form you suggested, sir. The magnetic blanket."

"Surely it will not cause her any harm?"

"Physical pain? No sir. I see no reason why it should."

"I then take you at your word and will rest content that no harm shall come to her. I tell you again, Doctor, that my hope is that your magnets confirm her honesty. For I would have an honest wife, a son who is my own, a son to inherit when I die. It would be the crown of my old age."

William said he understood perfectly.

"You will of course live at Maldon House. I want you to be near at hand. After the test, you will see to the health needs of my wife and child as well as myself. And as I have said, I have friends at Court who are ever seeking medical services. Especially from well-trained young doctors like you."

"I will need to return to Colchester to obtain my magnets."

"You shall have a horse and cart, and a man to go with you—nay, Doctor, you shall have two."

Fanshaw rose slowly from his chair. William did likewise. William bowed and turned toward the door.

"Oh, Doctor Gilbert?"

"Yes, sir?"

"Have you forgotten something?"

"Sir?"

Fanshaw was smiling broadly. "Stay, Doctor, I have another word to say. You are an unusual doctor indeed, for you have not mentioned your fee. I do not think you provide your most valuable expertise gratis. Good service must have its reward."

Fanshaw turned to the table by him and opened a small coffer that sat upon it. From it he pulled a silk purse. "I think you will find this satisfactory," he said, handing the purse to William. "Consider this as payment for your ongoing services to my wife—and for your discretion as to its outcome. For you must promise that you will not reveal to another soul what your magnets prove, whether they condemn or exonerate. That will be for me to learn, none other. Except you, of course."

William promised. He said he would swear an oath upon it.

"Your word, Doctor, shall be sufficient," Fanshaw said.

Fanshaw nodded toward the purse to indicate that William should open it. He did, then worked to conceal his amazement, which he thought might make him seem greedy or overly surprised.

Inside the purse was a plenty of gold and silver coins. Had he been alone, he would have immediately counted out the sum, driven by mere curiosity to learn how much he was enriched thereby.

He tied the cords again, clutching the purse in his hands. Kempe had said Fanshaw was generous. Fanshaw's wife had said the same. They had been right. Should William tell his skeptical stepmother of this bounty, she would think him delusional or, worse, a liar. His heart raced with excitement. This was far more than he expected or needed or believed he deserved, but he could hardly refuse it. Even before this reward for his anticipated service, he had promised to stay. He could not break his promise.

Before setting out for Colchester, William sent a letter to Orlando Kempe, thanking his friend for recommending him to the Fanshaws. Although William still felt uneasy about the validity of the test he was to administer, he was happy at his future prospects. Fanshaw would be a demanding employer, he knew, but attending to the beauteous Alice Fanshaw was not without its appeal, and while he suspected she might indeed be a faithless wife who had given birth to a bastard child and conceived a second before her marriage, he thought whatever test he contrived to prove that fact would undoubtedly fail.

And what if it did? If it failed, Fanshaw would rest content believing his wife innocent, the child his. Such a result would not guarantee marital happiness for either, but that was their business, not William's.

9

"I see your fine-feathered friend has led you astray with his grand vision of your prosperity in London. Pride doth indeed go before a fall, William my son."

Thus spake his stepmother as he came in the door at Tymperleys. "I trust you must be satisfied with our local sick and dying to earn your keep, since you will not avail yourself of your wealthy father's goods."

"No so," he replied with no little satisfaction. "The Fanshaws have secured my services—for his wife, who is with child, and for him, since he's an old man and must of necessity suffer aches and pains incident to age. There's the promise as well of patients among Master Fanshaw's friends. I've come home only to obtain items I will need in my new practice."

The look of triumph on his stepmother's face was replaced with sullen disappointment.

"Would you have a blanket I could use, something thickly-textured and not over-used?" he asked her before she could leave him.

She wanted to know what for.

"For some medical purpose. You would not understand," he said, trying not to be too haughty or abrupt in his response but impatient to get on with the work at hand.

She looked at him doubtfully and went upstairs.

He passed into his chamber and opened a chest in which he kept his magnets. He had dozens of them, of varying sizes and shapes, which he had acquired from a half dozen countries, some at considerable expense. He chose eight, each about the size of a Spanish doubloon, and put them on his worktable, arranging them first in a line.

"Will this do, Doctor?" his stepmother asked behind him. She glanced at the magnets and made a snorting noise, then handed him a folded blanket.

He remembered it. His mother had knitted it with her own hands, in a pattern she said was her mother's, and had been her mother's mother's before her. He had not seen it in years, and he suspected that his father's second wife had hidden it away along with other family heirlooms that she associated with the first wife, and therefore disdained.

"Yes, that will do," he said, although he would have preferred another blanket. He consoled himself with the thought that he would get it back after Alice Fanshaw's use.

When his stepmother left him, he laid the blanket out and arranged the magnets, imagining where Alice Fanshaw's body would lie and placing them so that their position corresponded to her breasts, her heart, her navel, and her loins. He reasoned that if the magnets would have any efficacy at all, they must be associated with those body parts most actively engaged in illicit love. Perhaps those intimate parts reflected a heightened sensitivity in an adulteress, which the magnets had power to detect, even as Fanshaw had claimed.

Then he began some stitchery of his own, embedding the magnets so the blanket seemed adorned with little bumps, barely detectable in the woven fabric.

Within the week he had returned to London, or at least its outskirts. He had respectfully declined Fanshaw's offer of a chamber in his house in favor of a room at a local inn called the Prince's Pride. Ultimately, he wanted his own house, as his friend Kempe had, where he would be master and which he might furnish as he pleased. To be a physician in residence was too much like being a household servant. The idea did not appeal to him. The money he had received already from his patron he reckoned was more than sufficient to lease a suitable habitation. Not a mansion like Maldon House, but a comfortable cottage in the neighborhood with sufficient rooms on the ground floor for his patients and laboratory, a spacious garden in which to grow vegetables and herbs, perhaps an orchard as well. He wouldn't need to depend on greedy, unscrupulous apothecaries and their mislabeling of their leaves, barks, and oils.

It was night when he came to the inn, the blanket secure in his satchel, along with various other instruments he anticipated using. He lit the oil lamp in the chamber. It was a small room, barely furnished beyond a narrow hard bed, but it was enough—at least for now. He read a treatise on magnets by a French correspondent, deciphering the Frenchman's Latin with ease. It was cold in his chamber and there was no fire. He took the magnetic blanket from his bag and wrapped himself in it. He had never experimented with the power of magnets to heal or to comfort, much less detect marital treachery and as he lay enshrouded, he monitored his own body's response. He felt nothing but the added warmth—and the memory of his dead mother—before he fell into a profound sleep.

In the morning, William was about to set out for Maldon House when he encountered the innkeeper, a big red-faced fellow with a bulbous nose and a harelip. The innkeeper invited him to sit down with him and tell him who he was and where he went. The man did not apologize for his curiosity about strangers. He said he made a practice of knowing who men were that he might be their friends, or enemies. He said he was also careful of strangers who might have ill intent—vagabonds, burglars, highwaymen, Papist spies.

William assured him he was none of these, but a physician, planning to set up a practice and looking for a house to live in.

"Well, you're a young doctor indeed by the looks of you, sir, but I trust you will have patients enough, especially amongst the womenfolk, whoever enjoy a handsome young gentleman looking after their particular needs." The innkeeper winked lasciviously.

"I already have a patient who undoubtedly will occupy all my attention for the time being," William said.

"Oh, do you now?" said the innkeeper, "And who might that be, Doctor? Mayhaps I know him."

William thought there was no harm in answering the innkeeper's question, but when he mentioned the names of Thomas and Alice Fanshaw, the man's expression darkened. He took a deep drink from the glass he had brought to the table.

"You know Master Fanshaw and his new wife, do you?" William asked.

"Oh, Doctor, there's not a man or woman round about who does not. He is the wealthiest personage of this part of the county. Though he has neither rank nor title, there are lords of the realm who are beholden to him. He lends them money when their vanity and pride have made them needy. You are the doctor for his new wife, the young fair one?"

"She is my patient, at least for the time being," William answered, careful not to say too much.

51

The innkeeper stroked his jaw, which was fringed with a sparse red beard. He had a faraway look in his eyes. "My father, now passed, was the baker to her father and thereby knew the family well. Her father is a knight, lives in a big house not far from where we sit. But he was a poor knight, made poorer by having been robbed of certain jewels of great price—among other misfortunes."

"Sir John Parmenter?" William asked.

"The very same, Doctor," the innkeeper replied.

"Other misfortunes, you said?"

"Fanshaw's bride, Alice I think her name is, was the knight's only daughter. She was a wild one in her youth, as my father told it. Ever pursued by young men and generally glad to be caught by them, to her mother and father's disgrace and shame. When she was thirteen or fourteen, they sent her away for almost a year. They said she went to live with her uncle in Norwich. Maybe she had an uncle in Norwich, maybe she didn't. But I do think few that knew her had any doubts about the reason she was sent off."

At this, the innkeeper gave William another wink of his eye and made a gesture suggesting the rotund belly of an expectant mother.

"There was a child?" William asked, thinking of his examination of Fanshaw's wife and his suspicion that she had given birth before.

The innkeeper shrugged. "Whether it was born alive, lives still, or was murdered to hide her disgrace, God knows. The family, the Parmenters, are Papists. It's an open secret thereabouts. Papists—which I trust you are not, sir?" He looked at William suspiciously.

William said he was not a Papist.

The innkeeper seemed relieved.

"Well then you know Papists have strange practices, yet not so strange that they could suffer their daughter giving birth to a bastard."

"Who was the father?"

"Sir John Parmenter was her father."

"No, I mean the father of her child," William said.

The innkeeper shrugged again. "He might have been a half dozen young men of the neighborhood; men of her station or some local lad itching for a roll in the hay and made happy by the lady's ready compliance."

"I do wonder if Master Fanshaw knew of his wife's history when he took her as his bride."

"Mayhaps it made no difference to him," the innkeeper said. "Thomas Fanshaw is no saint himself. The Parmenters have improved their state by their daughter's marriage, as has their daughter's state improved for, married well, she is now respectable where before she was a thing of naught. So do them above us sell their children for gain and lose much honor thereby. But who am I to judge, being as I am a mere innkeeper?"

In other circumstances, William would have disdained as unprofitable and unseemly this indulgence in local gossip, which the innkeeper obviously relished in the telling. Now, however, he had a vested interest in knowing more about his patron and his patron's wife and was clearly getting information that he would not have received from Fanshaw, nor his wife's confessor, bound as the priest was under the seal of the confessional.

"Tell me more about Master Fanshaw," William asked.

The innkeeper looked around him as though he were concerned about being overheard, although by now William and he were quite alone in the room. Then he leaned into William. His voice fell to a whisper. "Well, Doctor, as I have said, he is wealthy beyond belief. And a hard man when he is wronged as well. If you betray his trust, consider yourself dead."

William felt a chill in his bones when the innkeeper said this. He knew Fanshaw was a hard man. He had seen that at once. And a jealous one. That Fanshaw was murderous was another matter altogether.

The innkeeper refilled William's cup and placed his elbows on the table.

"Fanshaw's bride is his third wife," the innkeeper said.

"I know that."

"His first was—I forget her name. They say she died giving birth, which caused him great grief, for the child, a son, was lost as well."

"That too I have heard," William said.

"His second, Augusta, was famous in the neighborhood for her red hair. I, Doctor, as you can see, have red hair as well, but hers was famous for its length—and full like a cloud it was. All women envied her. She was a fair beauty, like the wife he now has, but she proved false to him at last."

"I understand she left him. He had the marriage annulled, he told me."

"Oh, Doctor, I know not of formal matters. He may say she left—and imagine she lives somewhere afar off with her lover, but I suspect one of these days she will be found in some nearby wood or field, or at Maldon House, a rotting corpse. If you know what I mean."

"I do *not* know what you mean," William said.

"I mean, Doctor, it's a rare husband that can abide being cuckolded by his wife. Some would cast the faithless bride out of doors, but others provide a grave in a secret place and then tell some story to explain her disappearance."

"I see," William said.

The innkeeper's lurid tale disturbed William, even more than the unsavory traits the man had ascribed to Fanshaw. But then he considered that the innkeeper might enjoy exaggerating Fanshaw's traits. It would be a good joke on this credulous young doctor, to fill his head full of terrors and bugbears that might be nothing but figments of the innkeeper's fertile imagination. William resolved not to be taken in, if that is what the innkeeper was doing. This was one man's opinion of the Fanshaws. William could not be certain that any of what the innkeeper said was true.

"Do you really think he would have killed her?" William asked.

"I would not put it past him. He's a dangerous man, Master Thomas Fanshaw. What he does not do himself now that he is old and decrepit, he can assign to his minions."

"His minions?"

"Not just household servants. He has friends, friends in the City, friends at court. Persons who owe him money and would more gladly repay in service to him, though it be against man's law and God's, than pay in hard coin."

William thought about this. Fanshaw had told him of his readiness to forgive his new bride her adultery, should she prove to be unfaithful. The innkeeper's story, if true, contradicted all that. And yet even William had been skeptical of Fanshaw's profession of Christian charity should his new wife prove false.

From somewhere upstairs a woman's voice called out. It was a shrill, commanding voice.

"That would be my wife," the innkeeper said, making a woeful face. "She won't leave me alone for a minute. Are you married, Doctor?"

William said he wasn't.

"You are fortunate then, sir. With good luck, you shall stay single, for a man married be as good as buried." Savoring the rhyme, the innkeeper laughed wildly on his way upstairs. On the landing he stopped and looked back down at William. "Good night, Doctor, sleep well. And I do wish you good fortune with the Fanshaws. You'll need it, I warrant you."

William made no answer. It seemed the innkeeper didn't require one.

Besides, William was still thinking of what he had just been told about the Fanshaws. Truths, lies, exaggerations, who could know? But the innkeeper's stories troubled him.

What had he got himself into with these people, this silk merchant and his bride? More important, if something went wrong, how could he get himself out?

When he was a boy, he had disobeyed his father's warning that a local pond was deeper than it looked. In response to a friend's dare, he had waded in and quickly found his father was right. Suddenly, he was in over his head. He was unable to swim. He struggled for breath beneath the dark water until he found his footing again, then walked beneath the water until he reached the shore, gasping for air, his eyes filled with tears, his cheeks suffused with shame.

His friend who had challenged him called him a fool for accepting the dare. William had never forgotten the humiliation, nor the brush with death.

10

William's doubts about Fanshaw plagued him all the way to Maldon House. He had taken Fanshaw's money. He had given his word, both to Fanshaw and to his wife, that he would conduct the required experiment. He had invested all hope in the future they offered him. But now he was afraid, not merely of the experiment which he thought likely to prove nothing, but of his involvement with a dangerous man, a man who might be a murderer.

When he came to the gate of Maldon House he stopped and looked at the long path up to the door. His heart raced, and he felt sweaty and hot, though the day, being in early June, was seasonably cold and damp. He paused for a while and took great breaths to calm himself. He reasoned that he might make some plausible excuse for resigning his position—a previous commitment, a death in the family, a legal entanglement. Flimsy excuses, even to his ear. He doubted Fanshaw would believe any of it. He knew he might simply say the truth, that he had had second thoughts. That the experiment was distasteful to him. That his duty as a physician was to heal, not harm, which would certainly be the likely case if the experiment worked and Alice Fanshaw's infidelity was 'proved'.

These things ran through his mind when suddenly he heard the sound of horses coming up behind him. He turned, and saw Fanshaw himself with another gentleman advancing apace. Seeing him, they reined in their mounts and rode along beside him.

"Good morning, Doctor Gilbert," Fanshaw called.

William responded in a weak, dry voice that must, he thought, have betrayed his fear. Fanshaw sat confidently on his mount like a much younger man than the person who had spoken with him in the house.

"This is your daughter's doctor," Fanshaw said, addressing the man who rode beside him. This man was younger than Fanshaw, with a neatly cut beard, broad forehead, and startling blue eyes that Alice Fanshaw had obviously inherited. "Doctor, this is Sir John Parmenter. He's come to see how his daughter is bearing up in her confinement."

Parmenter gave William a cursory glance, as though he were a groom come to take the horses into the stable and not a learned physician worthy of some regard, especially in light of his being the caretaker of his daughter's health. William had experienced this haughtiness before by those above him, and it rankled. He had no great hatred of the hierarchy of classes that was as embedded in his country as firmly and eternally as the rocks beneath his feet, but he believed the arrogance and pride of the aristocracy was no benefit to man, but a hindrance to learning and good governance.

But suddenly, Parmenter spoke. "How does my daughter do, Doctor? Will she bear the child and live?"

"It is more than likely she will, Sir John," William answered. "She is a healthy young woman in every respect. If it please God, she will thrive— and her child as well."

"My son, you mean," Fanshaw said, with the same degree of certainty about the child's sex as he had expressed to William at their first interview.

"It may be a maid or man-child," Parmenter said, turning to Fanshaw.

"By God, it will be a man-child," Fanshaw declared in a booming voice, as though commanding it to be so.

William followed as the two men rode toward the house and then to the stables, where a groom emerged to take their horses. They walked toward the house. Parmenter left them alone to seek out his daughter.

"Master Fanshaw, may we talk?" William asked.

"God willing," Fanshaw said pleasantly, eyeing William with a curious gaze and taking his arm with a surprisingly strong grip for the old man he was. "Come with me, Doctor. I have words for you, as well."

Fanshaw's library was a gloomy, spacious room with heavily adorned walls and a dark coffered ceiling that seemed fated at any moment to collapse and crush whoever was below. A fire blazed on the large, ornate hearth, the designer of which seemed concerned that there be no space on the side panels or mantle unadorned. To William's mind the room was designed to intimidate, rather than accommodate, its occupants. Not a library as he knew them, a comfortable retreat smelling of old tomes and inviting learning and reflection, but a throne room with Fanshaw as its king. Having been unnerved before, William was now more so.

"I have had some second thoughts, Master Fanshaw," William began even before the two men sat down.

There, he had said it. It was what he hoped he had courage enough to say since his conversation with the innkeeper, which he had come to think was more likely a true picture of Fanshaw and his wife than idle gossip or an entertaining fiction.

"Second thoughts? You mean you've changed your mind?" Fanshaw asked, searching among papers on his desk.

"Well, yes, sir."

Fanshaw looked at William and smiled grimly, as though he had anticipated William's second thoughts. "Come then, Doctor, do speak your mind freely. Even as I have unburdened myself to you previously, confessing those things I have never told another man, nor would."

"I have reservations about the experiment's ... validity," William said after a moment's hesitation.

"Indeed, so you said before, yet you agreed to do it, those reservations notwithstanding. I paid you your fee, did I not?"

"Which I would happily return to you, Master Fanshaw," William said, hoping that would end the matter—but somehow knowing it would not.

For a moment, Fanshaw said nothing. His silence itself caused William to shift in his chair uneasily. The old man's brow darkened. He said, "Doctor, I believe I have said enough for you to know how important it is to me that I determine my wife's fidelity. I told you how cruel and burdensome uncertainty is to me. When first we met you told me you had some doubts about the ability of magnets to achieve a hidden knowledge of a woman's soul. I do think I answered those doubts, with weighty testimony of other, older authorities. I do not understand why suddenly you've changed your mind. Perhaps you can explain that. I do hope you did not betray my confidence by discussing my wife's case with anyone else. Your discretion was a condition of our going forward together."

"Never would I do that, Master Fanshaw," William said. "But on reflection, I did wonder if I were the best person for your needs. There are many other physicians you might have called on. My friend Orlando

Kempe, for example. He's familiar with my work. He might as readily serve you in this and thereby your wife might be free of the discomfort of a new and unfamiliar doctor."

Fanshaw shook his head impatiently. "Doctor Kempe recommended you as knowing more about magnets and their power than any other doctor or learned man that now is in England. Your expertise, not his, is what I want and need, and to be direct with you, Doctor, it is what I must and will have. You have taken my money and given your word of honor, and you shall not turn away from it. Besides, Doctor, I must tell you that Mistress Fanshaw was most impressed by your visit with her. She told me you were a sensitive doctor, careful not to offend when you did your examination of her. She said she looks forward to your … ministrations. She has confidence in you. That's no small thing, is it, Doctor?"

William agreed it was no small thing, a patient's confidence in her doctor. William tried to avoid Fanshaw's glare, but it was impossible. He felt the old man's eyes penetrating his skull.

Then Fanshaw stood abruptly from his desk and fixed William with a hard stare. William's heart pounded in his chest with such violence that he feared Fanshaw would hear it. This then was the Fanshaw that the innkeeper had described, commanding and ruthless. Given to sudden impulses and violence. William quickly considered his state. If the experiment proved nothing, he might provoke Fanshaw even more. To some degree, now, in complying with the man William could hardly incur a worse fate than his backing away, which at that instance he desired to do with all his heart.

For a long moment there was silence between the two men. Then Fanshaw smiled and said, "Is it more money you want, Doctor? Of some other emolument?"

"It is not about money," William said. He did not dare tell Fanshaw what it was really about, what the innkeeper had said, what William felt in his heart.

"You doubt yourself then?"

"No, sir."

"You doubt your science?" William felt his resolve failing him.

"No, sir, I trust my science, both its possibilities but also its limits."

"And are there indeed limits? How, Doctor, can limits be known unless they are put to the test? You, Doctor, are the great exponent of experimentation, the critic of the ancients who you say merely repeat each other and accept nonsensical premises without proof. Here is an opportunity for you to be consistent with those principles, to set aside presuppositions as you call them. If the experiment fails, it fails. It is God's will. But if it proves your magnets have the power that I believe they have, then all's well that ends so. My doubts will be settled, my wife's chastity will be vindicated, and you, Doctor, will have done no less than what I paid you for. Think not, therefore of the outcome. Do not fear it. Have the courage of your convictions."

The courage of your convictions. For a few moments, William did not answer. He could not. He acknowledged to himself the logic of Fanshaw's reasoning. He felt the pull of it, and since the easiest thing for him to do at the moment was to concede Fanshaw's point, William said, "Very well, I will proceed with the test."

Fanshaw smiled broadly and placed both hands on William's shoulders, as though he were a priest giving a blessing. "You've done the right thing, Doctor Gilbert. You have been wise."

But William felt he had done the wrong thing, and yet he must go forward.

Fanshaw returned to his chair and motioned William to sit down again. The two men faced each other across the desk.

"Now, Doctor, tell me again what you will do with your magnets."

William had brought his satchel with him into the chamber. He reached down and pulled out the blanket. "I have powerful magnets sewn into this blanket. Your wife will envelop herself in them. Come morning, if she is affected on those body parts most incidental to lascivious acts, you will have the answer you seek. If not, then she is either innocent of adultery, or the magnets have no effect at all."

"What do you mean *affected*, when you speak of her body?"

"Magnets attract iron, as I told you. Iron is an element in the blood. One might expect to see inflammation in her breast, stomach ... private parts."

Fanshaw nodded his head. "I would not have her harmed unto grievous sickness or death."

"There is no chance of that, Master Fanshaw," William said. "At worst, nothing will appear upon her. She will have but a restful sleep and awake refreshed."

"Be about it then, Doctor," Fanshaw said. "But do not tell my wife what the experiment aims at. Make up some story about the blanket being good for a woman with child. I'm sure you're capable of so small a deception in the cause of scientific discovery—and for the good of your patient."

William said he was capable, but there was more fear in his belly than conviction.

11

William climbed the grand staircase to Alice Fanshaw's bedchamber; but before he could knock, the door opened, and her father appeared. Parmenter took his arm. "I want to thank you, Doctor, for helping my daughter. Her mother had difficulties with childbirth. The sickness that plagues some women of mornings plagued my wife until the very day Alice was born. Evidently, my daughter inherited that same fault. She has just told me how grateful she is for your attendance upon her, how you eased her fears about a number of things."

"A number of things?" William asked, thinking certainly she would not have revealed to her father her husband's suspicions about her infidelity, or the test about to take place.

But Parmenter was talking about something more innocent. "You know, the general fitness of her body for childbirth. Because of her mother's difficulties it was inevitable that she should fear for herself—and for the child, of course."

William said, "Certainly, being this is her first child, her pregnancy might alarm her regardless of her mother's history."

William was alert for any sign in Parmenter's face of acknowledgment that his daughter had given birth before. But he saw nothing. Parmenter looked calm and confident.

"Indeed, Doctor. I told her you were here. She awaits you within."

"Very well," William said, almost regretting that there didn't seem more to be said to this seemingly careful father, notwithstanding his willingness to sell his daughter for financial gain, or so the innkeeper's story went. Although William knew, too, that such practice was commonplace, and that for every marriage incited by Cupid's bow, there were a hundred moved by greed or ambition, the nuptial pair mere pawns of parental calculation.

And so he knocked, heard the now-familiar voice of his patient beckoning him to enter, and prepared to meet his fate and hers.

Alice Fanshaw lay abed as in his first visit, although she seemed more frail and wan than she had the day before. She started, as though surprised that it was he and not someone else. William thought she might have expected her confessor. Or maybe even her husband.

"How do you do, dear lady?" he asked.

"I do well enough, now that my morning sickness has passed."

"I am pleased to hear it."

"I'm ready," she said, glancing at the satchel he'd placed on a chair.

He nodded and reached into his satchel for the blanket. He pulled it out and showed it to her.

"That's finely worked," she said, looking at the blanket admiringly. "It's not a gift I ever had, doing such work. I would have learned, but for my mother's saying it was for common folk to learn, not for gentlemen's daughters."

"I imagine you had other gifts to offer," he said, and then realized she might have misinterpreted his words as a slur upon her. Yet he thought it unlikely that she suspected he knew more of her history than she had revealed to him, which was little if not nothing.

"Tonight, before you sleep, remove all your bedclothes and wrap this blanket about you as you would any ordinary blanket."

He showed her the little mounds where the magnets had been embedded. "These place over your breasts, this over your heart, this over your navel, these above your loins. It's important that they be placed exactly as I have said. The magnets will exert power over the iron in your blood."

"There's iron in my blood?"

"Among other elements of nature," he said.

She looked at him imploringly, her eyes suddenly fearful. "Will it be painful?"

"Painful? no." He said this confidently. Had he not wrapped himself in the same blanket the night before and awakened without ill effect?

"I trust you, you know?" she said.

"And so you may, dear lady."

He wished her well. He told her he would bring her something to ease her morning sickness.

63

"And the test, the experiment. How will I read the signs, the evidence of my innocence?"

"There probably will be no signs at all. If there are, your husband will read them."

"Pray God, he reads them aright, for I tell you, Doctor, I am falsely accused by him—and by others, I suspect. The child I bear is his and none other, conceived upon our wedding night. Tonight, I am going to confess all to Father Mottelay. He has urged me so to do, that my sins may be forgiven through the blood of Christ our Lord and the Holy Mother's intercession. But when I confess, I will not confess to what I never did do, and that is betray my husband."

She said this resolutely, even defiantly. William thought, perhaps she speaks truly, despite her history.

Or perhaps she is only a very good liar—a liar to him, a liar to her confessor, a liar even to God.

"Do you just as I have required of you," William said. "All will be well."

"Pray God, it may be so," she said. She smiled at him, but he detected more fear in her countenance than confidence.

He promised he would return on the next day and bid her goodnight.

Julian Mottelay appeared as William was leaving Maldon House. The two men nodded to each other in passing, but did not speak. William was glad for that. He was not in the mood for casual conversation, and he definitely did not want to answer more questions about Alice Fanshaw's condition.

He still felt fearful and uneasy, but he consoled himself by thinking that this time tomorrow the magnets would have done their work, or not. After that, his relationships with his employer and his wife would be far less complicated and dangerous. It might even be possible to end them, since the service for which he had been in truth hired would have been completed.

When he came to the inn, the innkeeper was waiting for him. The innkeeper had a condition, he said, and wondered if the good doctor might look at it. The inn was busy, especially the taproom.

"Very well," William said. "Come up to my chamber."

He had no expectation that the innkeeper would pay him for his medical advice or treatment, if that was necessary. But then he felt he owed the man. It was the innkeeper who had alerted him to the danger presented by Fanshaw, told him the story of Fanshaw's wife and that of her father, Sir John, the poor knight enriched by selling his daughter to an old man.

"I think it be a mere rash, or so my wife says, and it will go away. But it has not gone away yet. Do you think blood-letting will help? I don't want to be cut, but I do hear it said that leeches are better. They suck out the blood, which I am told they thirst for."

"I have no leeches with me," William said. "Besides, I doubt what you have requires a blood-letting."

William looked at what the innkeeper had called a rash. It was red and crusty and spread across the man's broad chest from his shoulders to his navel. William had seen this affliction before. "Do you have some mint in your kitchen, or sea salt, or vinegar?"

"I think not," the innkeeper said.

Then William thought to ask, "Has your wife a mandrake root?

"My wife does have one," the innkeeper replied, sheepishly.

"Grind it up into a poultice," William said. "Apply it three times a day. But take care that you eat none of it, for it may make you sick unto death. The rash should go away. It will take some time, maybe a week or two. Have patience, which is often the best medicine."

"I'll do it, Doctor."

"And forget about the leeches," William said.

12

William woke at dawn but lay abed for an hour, thinking about Alice Fanshaw and the experiment. By now, he thought, his magnets would have either worked their magic or failed to exert any effect. But he decided not to rush to Maldon House. There would be time enough for him to discover how things had fallen out, for good or ill. Besides, he did not want to suggest that he was anxious about the outcome by arriving too early, although anxious he was. It would not look good to his new employer or to his patient. He wanted to project an image of confidence and competence, not insecurity and desperation.

He went downstairs, breakfasted, then returned to his bedchamber. He wanted to finish his book in peace and planned to set out for Maldon House at noon. He tried to concentrate on his reading, but his mind quickly returned to the experiment and its consequences. He would read a sentence or two, and then its content would be replaced by an image of Alice Fanshaw, or her father, or his blanket, or the innkeeper's stories of Fanshaw's earlier wives and their fates. Soon he gave up and began to pace. But within the hour he heard heavy footfalls on the stairs outside his bedchamber. The door, which he had not bolted behind him, burst open like a gunshot. It was Kempe. William leaped from his chair.

"For heaven's sake, Orlando, what is the matter?"

His friend's face was white, almost ghastly.

"I have news," Kempe said. Already William knew it could not be good.

"Alice is dead," Kempe said hoarsely. "Alice Fanshaw is dead and still wrapped up in that blanket of yours."

It took William more than a few moments to take this in, determining that what had just been spoken was not some dream of his or figment of Kempe's imagination.

"You saw her body?" William asked, trembling, his voice dry as dust.

"I did," Kempe said.

"And what did you see?"

"Her torso was black and blue as though she had been beaten."

"And what did Fanshaw say when he saw it?"

"He cursed, called her whore, then railed at you for murdering her before he could."

William wondered if Kempe could hear his pounding heart. But if he noticed, he said nothing.

Kempe continued, "Fanshaw lays his wife's death at your door, as does the lady's father and her Papist confessor. All speak in one voice, condemning you. I rode quick pace from Maldon House to bring you the news. I had gone there to see you, thinking you were still there, but found the whole house in an uproar, the lady dead, Fanshaw mad with grief and anger, and the priest joining in your condemnation."

William sat down heavily on the edge of the bed as though his shoulders bore a great weight. Kempe remained standing, leaning with his back to the door. William's mind swirled. He tried to clear his head. That he should be blamed by husband and father might be put down to the wildness of grief that ever struck out wherever it might. As for the priest … William supposed it natural enmity and rivalry, despite Mottelay's offer of friendship and cooperation.

"As God is my witness, I did nothing that would cause her death," William said. "True, I commended to her some nostrum to relieve her pains, but that would cause no harm, certainly not unto death. It is a well-accepted mendicant used by doctors and apothecaries everywhere."

"It's the blanket, William," Kempe said. "It's the blanket. The priest, Father Mottelay, has told Fanshaw the blanket and its magnets are the Devil's work and you are the Devil's agent."

"Ridiculous," William scoffed. "The blanket, the magnets, they have nothing to do with the Devil, or indeed with any supernatural being or creature."

"The lady's husband and her father incline to agree with him," Kempe insisted. "Fanshaw himself is more furious than grieving. He believes that you betrayed him and your oath with your damnable blanket. He is calling it malpractice—worse, even murder."

"Did he say anything of the blanket's purpose, the discovery of his wife's infidelity?"

"Not a word about that," Kempe said, "especially in the presence of his wife's father or the priest."

"But this is idiocy," William declared. "And the priest's accusations are the rankest superstition. The blanket was made by my mother. The magnets are harmless. Why, I slept with the blanket upon my own body the night before without any malign effects. That it should cause death defies belief."

"I tell you only what I have heard from Fanshaw himself," Kempe said. "Fanshaw rages and threatens vengeance and complains to everyone who will listen not only of your incompetence but your evil intent toward him and his wife—and the child of her womb, now dead as well."

"Evil intent?' William cried. "Why, in God's name? What evil intent might that be? I have known the Fanshaws but a week. Before that, I did not know Thomas Fanshaw from Adam. There is no reason I would wish anything for them but good days and better health. He secured my services as his wife's physician. What evil intent do they imagine? By Christ, there's a child dead as well. It could not survive its mother's loss. Am I a monster, a King Herod, that I should kill the unborn—and without motive?"

He looked up at his friend, desperate for some kind of affirmation of his innocence.

Kempe pressed down on his shoulders to calm him.

"Be steady, my friend. Calm yourself. Of course, I don't believe a word of this, William—and certainly not Father Mottelay's babbling about devils. He resorts to the supernatural because it is his stock in trade, his daily bread. What do you expect him to say, he who can say nothing else but drivel? He knows nothing of physic. He knows nothing of the law. His business is the soul not the body."

"What do father and husband believe?"

Kempe paused, took a deep breath. William feared another baleful disclosure but had steeled himself for it.

"They believe you might be an agent of one of Fanshaw's enemies, a man called Peter Maldon. It was he who owned Fanshaw's house before and lost all in the settlement of a debt. Maldon hates Fanshaw, and the feeling is mutual."

"But that he should want Fanshaw's wife and child *murdered*—it's beyond belief."

"Some are just that evil, William," Kempe said. "You do see too much goodness in the world and are blinded to evil all about you. You have ever been such, my friend, and now finding yourself in the midst of such moral turpitude, you stagger and falter."

On another day, William might have taken offense at this casual description of himself as a naïve innocent, but now, beset as he was, on all sides it seemed, he could think only of the charges against him, and he was thankful for what consolation Kempe offered him.

"Besides," William said. "I do not know this Peter Maldon, and I very much doubt he knows me at all. Why would I, a doctor of physic, be involved in some quarrel between strangers to me?"

"Fanshaw declares that you *do* know the man, and were physician to him."

"Not true," William said. He almost laughed at the ridiculousness of it. But this was no laughing matter. The fear that had begun to grip him before, now was worse. Now, a motive had been attributed to him. Though it was false as hell, it had a plausibility about it. Vengeance was a common motive for crime. One heard of it all the time. Avengers regularly used others to exact their vengeance. He imagined a jury weighing the evidence, the word of a wealthy merchant with good connections at court against his own word, the word of a young doctor.

"Fanshaw says he has evidence of your relationship. That you took a goodly sum from Maldon to murder his wife."

"I took nothing from a man I have never met, nor would I take money to murder anyone."

"He has evidence, Fanshaw says."

"Which he has concocted, if he has it at all," William returned, not just confused, but angry now. "I swear before God and the angels of heaven that I have never known Maldon or had aught to do with him."

"He was in this very inn last night."

"What?"

"You might have seen him. Below, at the bar."

William remembered the crowded taproom. Several dozen men standing about hoisting beer tankards and talking animatedly. He recalled no particular face or form, just faceless men, tradesmen, small merchants, not laborers or countrymen, certainly no gentry, as Maldon is.

69

"I went directly to bed last night. I noticed no one, heard no names. Besides, why would Maldon spend time in this shabby place? That it is called the Prince's Pride does not make it so. We neither met nor plotted," William insisted. "And that's the long and the short of it. I have told you that I do not know the man."

William put his head in his hands and felt tears welling up, shaming him before his friend. "Please tell me, Orlando, that I am dreaming all this, that this is a nightmare from which I will presently awake, or that my very presence in this inn is but a dream, and your visit to me, and the Fanshaws themselves, a dream or delusion. For I would rather be a madman than a murderer."

William reached out for his friend's hand to affirm the reality of what he had just heard.

Then he said, "I must go to the manor, examine the lady's body. Perhaps I can discover the true cause of her death and thereby free myself from these baseless charges."

"That would be unwise, William," Kempe said. "You would be exposing yourself to Fanshaw's wrath and making matters worse. It is likely by this time he has called the constable, perhaps even sent notice of your crime to his high-placed friends in the government. William Cecil, Lord Burghley, for example."

"The Queen's chief minister?"

"Word is that he and Fanshaw are fast friends and confederates in many an undertaking," Kempe said.

William's heart almost failed him. He looked about the chamber, fearful that even now his pursuers would burst in and seize upon him. They would bind him, drag him from the inn, do what they willed with him, torture him, hang him. His vision of disaster paraded before his heated imagination, all in a second.

"You will not only be disgraced but face prison, if not worse," Kempe said.

William knew what worse was. Hanging, since the authorities might give credence to the priest's outrageous accusation of witchcraft. But he knew too that there was an even more immediate danger. William remembered what the innkeeper had told him about Fanshaw's violence, about the possibility that his former wife's body was secretly buried somewhere on Fanshaw's land. Perhaps Fanshaw would not wait for the strictures of the law or an investigation that might clear him of blame, but take the law in his own hands. William might not be a murderer, but he was persuaded that Fanshaw was, or at least was so inclined.

William realized that his friend was giving good counsel. The last thing he should do is return to Maldon House.

He might never leave it.

Kempe must have read his thoughts. He said, "William, you are free now, but it's only a matter of hours, if not minutes, before Fanshaw and his men come for you. They know where you are, don't they?"

"Yes, they know."

He had told Fanshaw where he would be staying when he declined his invitation to live at Fanshaw's house. At least William had acted wisely in that decision, no matter how foolish he had been in others. Had he been resident there at the time of Alice Fanshaw's death he would already be in bonds, futilely defending himself with Alice's dead body before him and Thomas Fanshaw in his face, implacable and bent on revenge.

"I must leave here," William said. "Now. Home to Colchester, my father's house."

Kempe grasped his arm. "Not Colchester, William. Trust me, Fanshaw will follow you there. He knows that's where you're from. He will bedevil you there and your family too, on some pretext. Go abroad, that's my counsel. You have little choice. It's your life that's at stake, not just your profession. You can practice medicine abroad, play with your magnets, live your life out as a free man, marry, have children. Maybe even return to England safely when the two old men are dead, which I do pray will be soon, for now I do hate them both. In England, Fanshaw alive has a long reach, but he may not be able to follow you abroad."

"But where abroad?" William asked himself as well as his friend.

"Italy isn't bad. I completed my medical studies there. In Turin. I have friends that could help you establish yourself. You were always an excellent Latinist, William. You could learn Italian in a month, nay—a week."

But language difficulties were far from William's mind. "May I use your horse?"

"It's yours."

"I'll take a ship. I'll send you a message where the horse can be found."

"No, sell it, my friend. You'll need the money. Now, make haste. I'll stand guard outside the inn and direct them away should Fanshaw and

71

Sir John arrive before you're clear. I'll tell them you've already fled—to the west, Wales or Cornwall."

William might have laughed at this, had he not been so sick at heart and full of dread. Kempe rushed downstairs to stand guard. William gathered his things. As he did so, he thought of his mother's blanket. It was one of his few mementos of what had been a happy childhood. He would never see it again, not now that it was in possession of his worst enemy and doubtless on exhibit as a murder weapon.

He wrote a note to the innkeeper and left some money—Fanshaw's money—to pay for his lodging. He would leave most of his belongings behind. They would simply weigh him down. The innkeeper could do what he willed with them; keep them for himself or give them to the poor.

He came to the stable where Kempe's horse was, saddled and mounted. He decided to head for some coastal town where he could find a ship. He waved to Kempe as he rode through the inn's gate, grateful that there was no sign yet of his being pursued. He had already decided not to go to Italy. He had taken counsel from his friend on some matters and was grateful for it, but he thought that, instead, Amsterdam might be his destination. It would be a less tedious voyage, and while he knew no one in Italy, he did have Dutch friends who might help him. Of that, he was sure.

13

William spent his first day in Amsterdam walking about the city, taking in the public buildings and the private houses of rich merchants, the orderly gardens and the shops featuring not only Dutch-made goods, but products from all over the world. It was his first venture abroad and despite his agony over what he had left behind in England, he felt pulsating excitement run through him. He felt safe and free.

Amsterdam was smaller than London, and newer. The houses and shops stood shoulder to shoulder as they did in any English town or city, but he observed a great deal of stonework, even in private houses, and he was told by a stranger who spoke passable English that the citizens of Amsterdam were building stone houses because of the great fires that had swept the city a generation earlier. The air was clearer in Amsterdam than in London, too, the streets cleaner, the people happier, or so they seemed, despite recent wars and invasions. He noticed with approval the abundance of flowers, especially tulips, but being near the sea the city's air smelled of salt and fish. He did not mind. In another life, he might have been a mariner bent on discovering strange lands and unknown seas. The thought appealed to him, although not enough to deter him from his chosen pursuit—a pursuit that now seemed threatened by his newly-minted enemies.

Upon disembarking the vessel, he had found an inn, much like the one where he had recently lodged in England. Its name, in Dutch and therefore incomprehensible to him, was blazoned on a sign dangling from the entrance like a hanged man. It depicted a jolly, ruddy-faced burgher holding up a tankard of ale overflowing its cusp. His bedchamber was near the top of the house, small but tidy, and his bed—although narrower than a typical English bed—was adequate for his lean body. He slept until late in the morning that first day, and awoke finally to remember why it was he was in Amsterdam and a fugitive and not in Colchester or London.

During the afternoon he walked along a quay and looked out at the harbor. It was full of ships of every size, a marvelous testimony to Dutch mercantilism. He stood there gazing beyond the horizon in the direction from which he believed he had come, wondering if he would ever return. Suddenly, he heard his name called out in a voice thick with a Dutch accent.

"Doctor Weinmeer, how good to see you," he said to the barrel-chested Dutchman advancing toward him, all smiles and his big hand extended.

"Taking the air, are you Willem? By God, what are you doing in Holland? Have not the English enough sick and dying that you bring your practice here?"

Pieter Weinmeer was, like William, a physician and scientist. They had met at Cambridge where Weinmeer had sometimes lectured. Of all his mentors there, Weinmeer was the most learned, most curious, and most dedicated to the pursuit of knowledge. He had grown homesick for his native land and returned to Holland the year before William had finished his studies. He had intended upon choosing Amsterdam as a refuge to find Weinmeer but that they should have so conveniently met, William considered a sign, if not from heaven, at least from a more abstract but benevolent universe where good fortune came when needed.

"Why are you here, Willem, and where are you staying?"

As much as William admired and trusted Weinmeer, he was not prepared to tell him why he was in Holland. Where he was staying was an easier answer.

"At an inn, two streets over. I don't know its name, but its sign is a very corpulent gentleman satisfying a great thirst."

Weinmeer laughed. He said something in Dutch, a guttural explosion that William knew he would never be able to produce himself. Then Weinmeer said, "It means a good fellow, you know, one who you would enjoy drinking with. But why are you living in an inn, such a place for abandoned souls? You must come to my house. My wife and my daughters will remember you from our happy days in Cambridge."

"If they were that happy, I suppose you and your family would have stayed," William said, allowing himself to be led along.

"Oh, I missed good Dutch cooking, Dutch air, and the sounds of my native tongue. Besides, I have my greater family here, aunts, uncles, my own *vader* and *moeder* still living and in my house here. But you must

74

forsake your inn and come dwell with us. This inn, it is not a bad place, but you are amidst strangers. That is not good. It will be an honor to have you, since of my students you were the most brilliant."

William felt his face redden at the compliment. "But I do think that would be inconvenient for your family, being as it is so large."

"Don't be foolish, my boy, my family is large but my house in Amsterdam is far larger. The owner before me was one of the greatest merchants of the city, and as you know, Holland—unlike England—is governed not by titled gentlemen, but by rich burghers whose first duty is not to the commonweal but to feather the nest of themselves and their friends. When I returned from England I bought his house for a pittance, for the merchant had lost most of his wealth in a bad investment in the India trade. His wife left him. His friends abandoned him. Then he fell sick and died."

"Then I thank you for your goodness, Doctor. My room at the inn is small as a dog's kennel, and I know no one else in the city, at least no one as well as you."

"Come then," Weinmeer said. "Our cook, who rules like a queen in our house, commands us all to sit at supper no later than six o'clock or she complains and pouts. It must be near that now."

At that moment, church bells struck five around the city.

Pieter Weinmeer's house was in the typical Dutch style—stolid, magisterial, proclaiming its owner's wealth and prestige in a city ruled by rich merchants. Its many-paned windows shone in the afternoon sun. William followed Weinmeer through a mahogany-framed entrance as wide as a cart into a spacious hall, on the walls of which hung paintings depicting life in the city, a pleasant change from English portraiture which ran to grizzled ancestors with stern, imperturbable faces. These paintings were so life-like that William could almost believe that those depicted lived and breathed and might at any moment descend from their frames and accost him to inquire what business he had walking amongst them.

A pleasant, ruddy-faced woman in her forties appeared from an adjoining room. "*Ach God in hemel,* if it isn't young Willem Gilbert, sorry I do mean *Doctor* Willem. Is it really you?"

"It is really I, Mistress Weinmeer."

Weinmeer's wife ran toward William with open arms. She was a large woman, with heavy breasts and wide hips, and she nearly smothered him in her embrace. She smelled of some strong perfume, overlaying a more familiar aroma of cooking oil and sweat. Then, behind her, William heard the voices of children. One voice he remembered especially from several years before. The Weinmeers had a daughter named Katrina, to whom William had tried to teach English when the family lived in Cambridge. She had proved an apt student. By the time the family returned to Amsterdam she was speaking English as though she were native born, a skill he attributed more to her intelligence than his superior teaching skills.

"Supper will be ready in a half-hour," Mistress Weinmeer said, although her announcement was more sung than spoken. "Come, you men, wash the dirt from you and sit you down. Cook has prepared a dish which will delight you beyond your science, so-called." She looked at William. "It is good Dutch fare, like you will remember when you visited us in your school days at Cambridge."

Katrina Weinmeer was now sixteen or seventeen, William judged, long-limbed, fair haired and rosy-cheeked. One would not have called her a great beauty, but she had a pleasant oval face, wide-set blue eyes, and skin an angel might have envied. She was naturally cheerful and curious and had obviously inherited her physician father's wit. It wasn't until supper was over—and it was more feast than supper since the Dutch, William had observed, were even heartier eaters than the English—that he had the opportunity to talk to her privately.

"William, I am much gratified to see my English teacher again. You are welcome to Amsterdam. I pray you, forgive my grammatical mistakes. I have had little opportunity to practice since we returned to Amsterdam. All here is Dutch, Dutch, Dutch."

"I should not expect it to be otherwise," William said. Besides, your English is perfect, and grammatical mistakes are small matters in the larger scheme of things."

"Will your visit be a long one?" she asked.

He told her he didn't know, and then followed her toward the adjoining chamber, a kind of parlor where they took chairs and sat silently regarding each other as though neither knew what to say next. Although while in England they had become not only student and teacher but also friends, the awkwardness on his part at least now proceeded from his recognition that she was more woman than child—and he no longer a reputable medical student but an accused murderer and fugitive.

"Perhaps you have come to converse with my father?" she said at last, looking a little disappointed.

"Yes, I have some medical questions to discuss with him."

"Medical questions?" she started with alarm. "I do pray you are not sick with some strange illness that you journey so far for treatment."

"No, I am for all I can know healthy enough. I have no complaints. I meant certain procedures I have heard your Dutch doctors have perfected that we English would gladly learn and practice."

She looked relieved. She smiled brightly. "That's a long journey when letters exchanged might have served as well."

He caught the reproach in her voice. He remembered he had promised to write to her. He had not. He thought about her often, but when he sat down to write he could not think of what to say that did not sound foolish or presumptuous. He said, "But I do prefer face to face, like most, and am impatient with the mails, which in my country grow increasingly untrustworthy."

"I see," she said. But William saw his failure to write had not been forgiven.

Pieter Weinmeer entered the room, saw them sitting together, and said, "Well, I see the young have gathered together as they will and should, leaving us that are old to doze at table."

"I was just asking William about the length and purpose of his visit," Katrina said, as her father advanced toward them.

"Do not you be so rude, Katrina," Weinmeer chided her. "Willem will think we want to be straightway rid of him."

Katrina blushed and then insisted that quite the opposite was the case. She turned to look at her father. "Not so, Father. I am most glad to see our English friend again, dear William … although out of due respect I should address him as *Doctor Gilbert* and not so impertinently as *William*."

"You may freely call me by my Christian name, if I may call you Katrina rather than Mistress Weinmeer."

"You freely may," the girl answered, and then, evidently seeing that the two men were eager to begin their discussions, she wished them both goodnight and passed out of the room.

William and Weinmeer stood looking after her. "Do you find my daughter much changed, Willem? Has she not, as you might say in English, bloomed since Cambridge?"

"She has indeed, sir."

Weinmeer dropped his voice to a whisper. "You know, she has already received two proposals for her hand, both by young gentlemen with more money than brains. I have supported her refusals. She's too intelligent a girl for that, and neither I nor her mother wish to push her into a loveless marriage just to get her out of the house and produce a flock of grandchildren. But come into my study. I want to know everything about your current experiments. I assume you still perform them?"

"I do, sir," William said, trying not to think of the Fanshaws, although it was impossible for him not to.

"Very good," Weinmeer said. "Then I am all ears to learn how you progress."

William tried to satisfy Weinmeer's curiosity about his magnetical experiments and demonstrations, even though he had no lodestones with him and had to use common rocks Weinmeer fetched from his garden to illustrate his points about magnetic attraction, what he called coition, and field of force. William was thrilled at the opportunity of sharing his ideas with someone sympathetic to his experimental methods. Indeed, Weinmeer was quite comfortable with William's independence of thought and congratulated him on it.

"Willem, you must put all of this in writing, else it will be lost. I see you as the author of an impressive book—a veritable tome of scientific learning in regard to the magnet and how the whole world, our dear mother earth, is a magnet, with what you call poles, north and south. I do believe it will refute the old ideas about our planet we have inherited from Aristotle and taken as gospel truths, though none be tested or verified by experiment."

It was also William's dream, the idea of a book, but he knew he was not ready, nor might he be for years to come. He knew his understanding of magnetism, as he called it, was far ahead of that of other scholars of his time, but he knew also there was so much more to know and understand. The practical applications of magnetism—for seafarers, especially—had already been demonstrated in that miraculous device, the compass. Yet he knew there was much more that could be done with magnets, even though their power might fail at proving infidelity in faithless brides.

"Thank you, Doctor Weinmeer. I may in due course compose such a work, God willing. But when I am ready, which I do not think I am now."

"Perhaps you're right, my boy. But look you to that end, will you?"

William assured him that he would.

"It would be gratifying to me to be able to say I knew such a distinguished scientist and author when he was young," Weinmeer said. "Now, before bedtime, may I ask you one question more?"

"About magnets? Gladly."

"Not about magnets or magnetism, but rather this. Tell me, Willem, are we friends, true friends?" Weinmeer leaned toward him and patted his knee.

"Sir?"

"You heard me."

"I would like to think so," William replied, mystified by the question. "Having been welcomed so generously and accommodated, I would think it easily assumed that we were friends, and good ones."

"Accommodating you in our house? That is but common courtesy extended to a weary traveler," Weinmeer said with a dismissive wave of the hand. "I would have done likewise to any, save he be a dangerous enemy and present a threat to me and mine. Which I hasten to say, you are none. But today when I asked you about your reason for coming to Amsterdam, you did not answer directly. I knew you were evading my question. Tell me then the truth, Willem. Your evasion suggests you are in trouble of some sort. That you are fleeing England, not just visiting Holland. I sensed that as well in our talk at table. I may be an old man, but still I am not deaf or blind to the difficulties of another, even when they do not make themselves known in the body, which I can treat for its infirmities."

William, still seated, looked down at his hands. "You are indeed neither deaf nor blind, sir. I am running away from England, if the truth must be told, and I suppose it must—at least to you, sir, for as you say, friendship demands an openness betwixt us."

"Tell me all, Willem. And do not fear condemnation or censure—if that is what you're afraid of."

"It's a brief story, but a complicated one," William said.

"As many a story is," Weinmeer said.

"May we wait until the morning? I promise you I will tell all then, honestly and truly. In the meantime, I assure you that you are not hosting a criminal in your house or one who would present danger to yourself or your family, whom I do swear before God I love as dearly as my own life."

"I need no such assurance," Weinmeer said, slapping his big hands on his knees. "I know you, Willem. I know your heart as well as your head. Let it be in the morning, then. After a good night's sleep. But after breakfast as well. I cannot think on an empty stomach, and I want to give full attention to your story. Perhaps this old man can help in some way. We shall see."

William lay awake for a long time before falling into a troubled sleep. He had been given a room in the house near other bedchambers where he could hear muffled voices of the obstreperous Weinmeer brood, and once, he thought, the voice of Katrina, beseeching her siblings to be quiet so as not to wake their English guest. She spoke in Dutch, yet he imagined that was what she was saying. It would be like her.

14

In the morning it rained in the city. Rain steamed down the windows of Weinmeer's study, making strange streaks that reminded William of some of the diagrams he had drawn to illustrate magnetic force fields. Weinmeer was already at his desk, a large square table piled with books, papers, and medical instruments. He greeted William and then folded his hands on his belly and waited for William to speak. Clearly, he had forgotten nothing of the conversation of the night before, or William's promise to reveal why he had really come to Amsterdam.

William began his account with the appearance of his fellow student, Orlando Kempe, and the offer to become physician to Fanshaw's wife.

"I remember this Kempe, I think," Weinmeer said. "A tall young gentlemen, very handsome. I think he came to the house once, looking for you. We invited him for supper, but he said he had an appointment at the college and could not stay."

"Yes, he came once with me when you had a gathering of students at your house in Cambridge," William said.

"Well, it is good that he arranged your advancement," Weinmeer said. "A young doctor needs a step up. When I began my practice, I too was helped by colleagues and fellow students. I owe my present state to their interest in me. It is the way of the world, is it not? We lift each other up and benefit mutually."

William told Weinmeer about the pregnant bride, his examination of her that led him to think she had given birth before, and her acceptance of the magnetic test so as to prove her innocence.

"She insisted the child was her husband's?"

"Yes, despite his inability to perform the act, which he does admit, although not cheerfully."

"How did she explain that?"

"That in a drunken stupor on their wedding night he became capable, which event he forgot."

Weinmeer laughed. "Drink is likely to cause forgetfulness, as many a Dutchman and Englishman too will attest, but unlikely to stimulate the organ of generation beyond making a large quantity of urine. Did he believe her explanation?"

"No, hence the test. Fanshaw is a man jealous by nature and experience. He probably would have suspected her betrayal even if his procreative powers were intact. His wife was a beautiful woman, young enough to be his granddaughter."

"Ah," Weinmeer said, "an old man and a young wife. A perfect recipe for misery. Take heed, Willem. If you marry, marry young—and choose a wife your own age, or a bit younger. You will be happier in the long run and the short."

William said he would take heed, but he wasn't sure if and when he would marry. "I have so much to think about right now. Courtship takes a quantum of leisure, and I have none."

"Well, my boy, when you have found the right woman, you will in the same hour find time enough to court her. Trust me. I know from my own experience. But tell me, this power of magnets to discern infidelity, you say came from some myth about magnetic powers?"

"And attested to by some ancient authorities."

"Willem, we both know well what such testimonies may be worth without verification. Most pronouncements of the ancients are tissues of myth, rumor, and wishful thinking. But you are the master of magnets, Willem. What say you, have your magnets such power?"

"I thought not," William said.

"But this Fanshaw persuaded you to do the experiment on his wife, your doubt of its efficacy notwithstanding?"

William felt shame as he admitted this. Had he sacrificed his integrity as a scientist? Had he sold his soul for a purse full of gold and silver? Weinmeer's silence and thoughtful stare after his admission suggested that he had.

"It was in the nature of an experiment," William said, hoping to mitigate his disgrace. "I did not positively know that magnets could not discern moral turpitude. It is widely believed that iron is an element in the blood."

"So I believe," Weinmeer said. "Among a great many other elements as yet to be given a name."

"Fanshaw himself suggested the experiment," William said. "I hypothesized about the result, wove magnets into a blanket for the lady to wrap herself in. The idea was that if she was guilty of adultery the magnets would draw the blood to the surface of her skin, especially above those organs most implicated in the adulterous act."

"Humm," Weinmeer said. "It has a plausibility about it, does it not? But I suppose the proof is in the blanket, is it not?"

"The woman died." William said.

"What?" Weimer exclaimed.

"She died of it, or so it is believed."

"But how could that be? How could a magnetized blanket kill her?"

"I don't know, sir. But I am blamed and cursed by Fanshaw, by the dead woman's father and mother, and even by her confessor, a Papist priest named Julian Mottelay. They have gone to the law and beyond."

"Beyond?"

"Fanshaw has powerful friends. William Cecil, Lord Burghley, for example. My medical career is at an end, at least in England. Moreover, my life is in danger, not merely from the law but from Fanshaw himself. Rumor has it that he has murdered once and by disposition will murder again."

"To avenge the death of a wife who doubtless betrayed him with another in the first months of their marriage?" Weinmeer looked unconvinced.

"I think before the marriage. He loved her beyond reason, or so he claimed," William said.

"Ah, that is unusual, but not without precedent," Weinmeer reflected, looking toward the window as though recalling friends afflicted with the same disposition.

The men sat silently for a few moments. Outside the rain continued to stream down the windows. The streaks no longer reminded William of his drawings but of a collection of worms grotesquely entangled and dripping with poison.

"Too bad you could not examine the woman's body," Weinmeer said.

"I cannot imagine Master Fanshaw permitting me within a mile of it," William said. "He is convinced I murdered his wife with my magnets.

83

And, more, he believes I did so on behalf of the previous owner of his house, whom Fanshaw displaced to settle the man's debt to him. This man, Peter Maldon, hates Fanshaw. He thinks of him as a usurper, both of property and even ancestry. The portraits of Maldon's ancestors still hang upon the walls. Fanshaw pretends they are his."

"Fanshaw has no ancestors of his own?"

"Not to boast of. He comes from common stock."

"Does he have any evidence of this connection with you and he who he displaced, this Peter Maldon?"

"None, sir. I do not know Peter Maldon, this displaced gentlemen. Not even by reputation. Fanshaw's belief is a lie."

For a moment Weinmeer sat in silence. He turned his head to look out the window. The rain had stopped. Then he turned back to William and said, "You must return to England, my young friend."

"Return? You can't be serious," William answered, shocked by this suggestion.

"Oh, I am very serious," Weinmeer said. "These high persons who are your Master Fanshaw's friends will not hesitate to track you down, wherever you flee, if matters are as grave as you believe. Your only hope is to prove your magnets are not responsible for the lady's death. Otherwise your guilt, confirmed by your flight from England, will be assumed beyond question."

William shook his head. He could not believe the counsel his old friend had just given him. It seemed little short of madness, to put himself so readily in harm's way. Granted, Lord Burghley had a long arm and would undoubtedly oblige Fanshaw by sending his agents to fetch William home again. But he could not imagine himself enduring another voyage and then sneaking like a thief into London. And to do what? To examine a corpse, to look again on that perfect face and body? To ask questions of witnesses, if there were any? And all this assuming that he was not seized the moment he stepped upon English soil. And how should he do this? By wearing a disguise or a false beard or adopting a faltering gait to imitate an aged and thereby harmless inquisitor? Or, beardless as he was, dressing as a woman that none should suspect he was the notorious Doctor Gilbert?

"Well, think upon it," Weinmeer said. "I have given you advice, which you may take or leave. Whichever you choose, you are still my dear friend, and I will do whatever I can to help you. Stay with us in the meantime. Think of our home as yours. The children are fond of you."

"And I of them," William said, although he was thinking then particularly of Katrina.

15

Weinmeer had told him to go home, to face his accusers. But he was afraid. And yet the thought of perpetual exile from England, from his family and friends, from all that was familiar to him gave him no peace. In the days following, he came to see his escape from danger a naïve fantasy. Weinmeer was right. It was only a matter of time before Lord Burghley tracked him down.

It was well understood that Burghley had spies and agents throughout Europe. Walking about the city, William frequently heard English spoken. Were these simply merchants traveling abroad on their business, or were they Burghley's agents, perhaps already seeking him? Kempe had assured him that if he were asked by Fanshaw, he would say Gilbert had fled to Wales or Cornwall. Even Kempe didn't know that William had chosen Amsterdam as a place of refuge instead. Still, he was fearful, always watching his back, always alert to curious stares. He had even bought some Dutch clothing so as to be less conspicuous in the streets when he chose to walk abroad, which he did less and less. Finally, he concluded that if he were always to live in fear he might as well do so in England, the country he knew best where his Englishness would be inconspicuous, the language and customs his own, and where his great enemies had no reason to expect his return.

In addition to all that, he missed his vocation. He was a physician. He was a scholar of the natural world. Weinmeer had taken him on several occasions to attend to the Dutchman's well-healed patients, mostly rich burghers for whom even minor ailments required a doctor of physic, whereas in his own country even a person of comparable wealth might have rested content—and received healing—from some garden herbs, the virtue of which the household cook knew from her grandmother.

But he did not want to merely follow the attending physician, to be an assistant. His years at Cambridge had prepared him for more than that.

No, exile was not the life he envisioned for himself. Slowly he realized that there was no help but that he should return to England and somehow clear his name.

As he prepared to do what he must do, he found consolation in Katrina. His friendship with her now was much different to what it had been before, when she was but a child and he her English tutor. He felt a powerful attraction to her, as though he were a nail and she one of his magnets. He felt his soul going out to her, but at the same time he knew that his own dangerous position could put her at risk as well. As for her, she showed genuine friendship but little sign of welcoming attention beyond what good manners demanded. Her father had told him that she had suitors whom she had rejected. Why? She was of marriageable age, and her father had not described these gentlemen as being unworthy as to wealth or station or character. Instead, her father had faulted their intelligence, or lack of it. But then Pieter Weinmeer was brilliant. He might have faulted any man for lacking what he had in so much greater abundance. Besides, that was her father's assessment. What was the cause of her reluctance?

One day he learned, but not because he had asked her directly. Rather, he had asked her why she and her family had returned to Amsterdam. She answered. "It was because of me."

He heard the catch in her throat when she said this, saw her eyes swell with tears.

"You? Your father said he missed his family."

"He did, but in truth the fault was mine. My father never knew the cause, only that my mother insisted she wanted to come home again. My father, as you know, is a strong man, full of authority, the kind of man of whom it is said he rules with an iron hand, yet not so, my father. You have seen how solicitous he is to my mother, how her every wish commands him."

William agreed. "He is the soul of courtesy to her. But you said you were the cause of your family returning to Holland."

They were seated in the garden. It was laid out in the Dutch fashion, very neat and orderly, in long rows with red brick walkways.

"William, I know you are running away from something in England. What it may be, I do not know, but I'm not so dull of brain as to not recognize the signs. I too ran away from England because of something … something that happened to me in Cambridge."

He waited, aware that he was about to learn perhaps the source of her reluctance to marry. He sat silent on a bench with her, tempted to take her hand but somehow knowing that such a move on his part might be misconstrued, or at least discourage her from saying more. Besides, she might think his gesture too intimate. They were, after all, friends, not lovers.

"I was attacked there," she said matter-of-factly. "I was fifteen, and I was attacked."

For a moment he could not speak. This was not what he expected to hear from her, and the image her words conjured up in his head after the first tremor left him speechless.

"Who … who attacked you?" he asked when the silence between them became unbearable.

She spoke softly, deliberately, in a tone different from her usual voice. "Two men," she said. "They wore masks. Carnival masks. I think they were students at the university. They dressed like young gentlemen, not like simple countrymen. I had gone walking with one of my English friends into the country to enjoy the air. The two of them came out of the woods and fell upon us before we were aware. My friend ran away. I tripped and fell. They pulled me back into the trees and there—."

She stopped. Her eyes welled with tears again. He had no need to hear the rest. The event seized his imagination, as though he were a direct witness, and he felt outrage welling up within him. Katrina took a deep breath, smiled faintly, and went on.

"I told my mother what happened when I returned home. I had to tell her. What might she think otherwise? My gown was torn and filthy from where they threw me down. I was bleeding. My face was bruised, and there were marks about my neck and on my face where they restrained me." She paused, wiped her eyes of tears. "One of them possessed me first, and then his friend. I fainted at last. Yet before I did, I heard them laughing and bragging to each other how they had enjoyed the Dutch girl and how they might do so again now that she was no longer a virgin."

William took her hand. It was soft and dry. "Did you also tell your father?"

"I made my mother promise that he should not know. I was afraid what he might do by way of revenge. I didn't know who the men were. There was no witness to what they did, save heaven. How could I have received justice, for they might well have said they only gave me what I wanted from them, that I agreed to it? I was a simple girl, a foreigner. Who would take my word over two young gentlemen doubtless of good English families and superior education? Besides, had my father sought revenge he might have put his own life in danger. When he saw the bruises on my face, I told him I had fallen whilst walking in the country, which was true, yet only in part. He doesn't know to this day why my mother insisted that we leave Cambridge."

Her tears fell freely now. He felt at that moment like a priest hearing a confession, not of a sinner but the victim of sin. Strong emotions welled up within him. They were emotions unfamiliar to him. But then so was this situation.

"You didn't tell your father. Why do you tell me?"

"Because I am ashamed, and my shame makes me unworthy of any man. You must know this, William, before our friendship, which means more to me than you now know, moves to something more."

His heart caught in his throat when she said this. Had she been feeling all along what he was feeling; that their friendship might become something deeper, more intimate? Had she not just admitted the same?

"Shame? Wherefore should you feel shame?" he asked. "The fault was not yours."

"Because, were I good and honest—."

"But you are both," he protested.

"God would not have permitted it."

"That's nonsense, Katrina. You have no reason to be ashamed," he said. "The fault is not yours, but theirs. Yet I see why you returned home to Amsterdam. You were no longer safe in Cambridge. Doubtless the two would have carried out their threats. You were easy prey—young, unprotected, a foreigner, one always vulnerable in a strange land. And I think you speak truly about the difficulty in finding justice for yourself. It would have been their word against yours. Your reputation would have been ruined in the telling of the ordeal so that in the town you would have been put down as a …". He hesitated to say the ugly word, as common as it was. It was too cruel a slander.

But she said it, with the directness he had learned to admire in her. "A slattern, a wanton, a…."

"No," he insisted. He covered her mouth with his palm, that she

89

should not speak it. "None of these. Not at all. You were innocent. You are blameless."

She said nothing when he removed his hand.

"But you say you have no thought of who it was that did this?" he asked.

She shook her head. And then she said, "But one thing. One of the men called me the Dutch girl, which means I was to them no stranger but one they knew of before. They knew from whence I came."

"Cambridge is a small town. It is difficult to go unnoticed."

She said, "I think they knew me. I feel it, William." She continued, "I tell you this story that *you* might know me, William. What I am in truth, not what I appear to be. I want you to know me."

"I want to know you," he said.

"And more, I want you to know that I, too, am a fugitive. I do know the feeling, William. But although I have tried to flee the place of my hurt, my mind dwells still on the event. It is the stuff of my dreams. I am unable to go forward, to make plans, to be happy. I might as well still be in Cambridge for all Amsterdam helps me to forget. Or forgive."

"Forgiving them might be more than any woman is able to do," he said. "More than she should need to do."

Suddenly, she turned to him with alarm. "You won't tell my father?"

"No. Upon my word."

"It would crush him if he knew," she said.

"Then he shall not know from my lips," William said.

William stayed another two days in Amsterdam. He conversed with Katrina many more times, but never about her ravishment or the men who did it. Along with her father's counsel, he also took hers—not given to him directly as her father had done, but implied in her own effort to live with her shame. Exile would resolve nothing. Wherever he was, he would always be himself. He would carry his own personal history around with him until his life ended, carry it like a great burden on his back.

Later in that week of his exile, he arranged passage to England, this time on a worthier vessel. He bid goodbye to each member of the family that had taken him in and treated him as a son. But before that, he had found Katrina alone in the Weinmeer garden where she had revealed her secret to him. It did not seem to him enough that they should merely say goodbye, as he had done with her younger brothers and sisters, or even as he had done with Pieter Weinmeer and his wife.

"I shall miss you, my dear friend and tutor," she said. "But I will think often of you whilst you are gone from here. Whatever trouble you are in that drove you hither, I do pray you may endure it well and come off victor in all your difficulties. I do not know what these are, these difficulties. My father would not say, though I do know he knows and keeps your secret as you do mine."

"I did not wish to burden you," he said. "It would not be fair to you, especially now. I don't know when I shall return to this pleasant place."

Or if he would or could, he thought.

"You don't like Amsterdam?" she asked.

"It is a paradise to me."

"Then why leave, William? Why leave?"

"Because I must earn the right to enjoy it," he said.

He reached down to kiss her lips, but she shrank from him, as though he were tainted with that same taint as her despoilers. He might have spoken to her of love, but he knew it was still a word that neither of them was ready for.

16

The Dutch shipmaster put William ashore near Gravesend, near the mouth of the Thames. From there he walked the twenty or so miles to London. It was a long day's journey, but he was fit and practiced in walking like most young men of his years. Besides, it gave him time to think and to plan, for a sense of danger was ever present in his thought and the difficulties before him kept accumulating in his imagination like some unnatural growth a surgeon might excise.

He found lodgings in an inn outside the City, and set about writing a letter to the innkeeper whose gossip about the Fanshaws had chilled his blood and which at one time he had supposed mere fiction. It was too dangerous to return to the same inn. It was too close to Maldon House. But he needed to know where Alice Fanshaw had been buried. If Fortune favored him, Alice would not have been buried on Fanshaw's property, where William's access to the body would be difficult if not impossible. He imagined, rather, an isolated churchyard in some rural village rarely visited by the living and therefore vulnerable to his search. His friend Kempe had mentioned something about Fanshaw's common roots. That almost surely meant some town or village remote from London. But which? There were hundreds of lonely cemeteries in England, one attached to almost every church, where the obscure dead slept largely ignored by the living and where therefore he might gain a discreet access to what remained of Alice Fanshaw. The idea of disturbing her grave was repugnant to him. But what else could he do if he were to discover how she really died?

And this, then, was the part he imagined the gossipy innkeeper to play. The hostility the little man had expressed toward Fanshaw assured him, at least somewhat, that he might again find him a useful informant. The man had told him that his father had worked for Sir John Parmenter. The innkeeper's father would be aware of where Alice Fanshaw was buried. As a long-time retainer, the innkeeper's father might even have attended the funeral.

William wrote the letter. In it, he did not say where he was or why he wanted to know, but asked the innkeeper to find out where Alice Fanshaw was buried. He paid a servant at his London inn to bear the letter to the innkeeper, asking the man to wait for the answer and return forthwith.

It was the night of his second day in London that the servant returned with the innkeeper's response. Scrawled in a barely legible script was a single phrase: *St. Mark's Maidenstowe.*

William had heard of Maidenstowe. It was a small village in Hertfordshire, not a day's ride from the Fanshaw manor house. He knew nothing of Fanshaw's origins save that they were humble, yet he knew that the enriched who built great houses to celebrate their good fortune also built tombs and monuments to their humble ancestors afterward as though offering a hand up to their less fortunate forebears.

The next morning, he hired a horse and set out. He arrived late in the evening to the village, to find it a poor place in a broad, wooded valley. The church, St. Mark's, on the crown of a hill overlooking the village was a stone edifice in the Norman style with a stub of a tower, as though they that built it ran out of the will or money to complete the work. Now it looked as forlorn as the village itself, which consisted of a single narrow street, rows of ill-kept half-timbered houses on each side, only a few shops, and a stone cross on the high street, a monument to something or someone. He had not taken time to look. There was a tavern, as indispensable to the village as the church, and an apothecary's shop, which he suspected constituted the village's medical establishment.

The door to the church was open, the interior empty, except for some equipment of plasterers and painters repairing the ceiling. The religious imagery associated with Papistry had been removed, leaving the walls and altar bare except for a stone crucifix. The churchyard was to the side of the church and enclosed in a stone wall with a lychgate, a small, roofed structure, at the entrance.

He tied his horse to one of the posts supporting the roof of the lychgate and passed into the cemetery. Amid a scattering of yews, elms, and beeches were many lichen-covered funereal monuments and crosses, tipped at odd angles as though weary of standing upright. Sprinkled among the trees were a few family tombs. Each of these he examined with some care until he came to what seemed a newer edifice with the name *Fanshaw* inscribed above the iron-spiked gate protecting its residents from casual visitors. The door was secured with a heavy padlock. Within the shadowy interior he could see several biers or shelves upon which rested stone boxes. These, he assumed, were the Fanshaw dead. The corpse of Alice Fanshaw would surely lie there, too.

He was alone in the churchyard and supposed whatever he might do there was unlikely to be observed. He was about to try the strength of the lock when he heard a voice behind him.

"Good day, to you, sir. Do you seek out some dead of yours?"

The voice had startled him, and he turned suddenly to see an older man who by his worn cassock, folded hands, and pious expression he guessed was the vicar of the church.

"Yes," William said. "I was looking for the resting place of Mistress Alice Fanshaw."

The vicar of St. Mark's beamed with pleasure at being of use. He was a small, ruddy-cheeked man—in his fifties, William judged.

"Why, you do stand before it, sir. This is the place of the lady's interment, indeed. Why, it has been but a fortnight since she was laid to rest here. I do grieve for her poor husband. How sad to lose a young wife—and they but three months yoked. May I ask, sir, if you are of the family?"

"I once, sometime ago, had the honor of being her physician," William said, deciding he might as well tell the truth about that. "I have come to pay my respects, to honor her memory."

The vicar said, "They say she died but might have lived, had he who was her doctor when she died had not practiced some manner of deviltry upon her body. I am told she was with child too, so her tomb contains two bodies in one."

The vicar smiled with satisfaction, as though he approved of the economy of space achieved in the interment.

William asked, "Did you know the family, Vicar?"

"Ah, indeed, Doctor, I do. I knew them from the time Master Fanshaw first prospered in his business. He was born in Maidenstowe, you know. His family lived here from time out of mind. I knew his second wife, Augusta. She was a wicked woman, Doctor."

"A wicked woman?"

"Indeed, sir. She slept with many a gentleman who was not her husband and ran off with one of her lovers, never to be seen again."

"And the third wife, Alice?"

"Oh, I never knew her or saw her, sir. The family arrived here with the body in a cart covered with a finely wrought coverlet. Very pretty and decorous given her station. It was a sad day, but Master Fanshaw was strong, sir, as strong as I have seen a widower be at the grave of his young wife. He shed not a tear but looked on stonily as though he meditated not upon her death but upon him who caused it."

"This other doctor, you mean?"

"That is my meaning. It's a shame when those we pay for services rendered give evil rather than good, but then there are many who claim to be doctors who are naught more than charlatans and mountebanks. Of these I have known more than a few in my life, but I trust God will judge them in the life to come."

"I pray He will, sir," William said. "But you were talking about Master Fanshaw."

"Yes, sir. The young Master Fanshaw who grew up in this very village I never knew. His youth was before my time. But he is known as a hard man. It is said he was so in his youth by those who were alive in those days. But perhaps you would like to be alone here to mourn the lady?"

"Just a while," William said, trying to make a sorrowful face. His heart was beating rapidly. He wondered if the vicar could detect his unease, or the lie he had created.

"Then I will leave you to it, Doctor," the vicar said, and he walked back toward the church.

After a few moments, William turned to see that the vicar had not gone, but stood watching him from the church porch, on which he appeared as a small black figure overpowered by Norman stonework. William wondered if his story had been believed. The deceased's former doctor travels from afar to pay his respects. It seemed a poor excuse for his visit, even to him. Perhaps the vicar suspected that William was the doctor who had caused her death, not some earlier doctor quite innocent of her demise. And yet the vicar had shown no sign of suspicion but seemed content to reminisce about the Fanshaw family and sermonize on the evil that men do.

Well, he could hardly break into the tomb and inspect Alice Fanshaw's corpse with the vicar looking on. He waited a while, thinking the vicar might go inside the church, but he did not. Finally, William walked toward him, asked if there was an inn in the village.

"Oh, there was once, but it stood empty for years and then burned to the ground, struck by lightning. God's judgment on sins committed within, I think. But it would be my pleasure to be your host, if you will allow it, Doctor. Consider it an act of Christian charity."

"Charity I will gladly accept," William said agreeably, deciding that sleeping in the open offered little prospect of a good night's rest.

"Then kindly follow me, sir. By the way, may I ask your name?"

"My name is Kempe, Doctor Orlando Kempe."

The lie had proceeded from his lips without thought or hesitation, an impulsive act that was unlike him. What on earth had made him give the name of his friend as his own? But then it did make sense, at least a kind of sense. Kempe had been in truth the "earlier doctor" William claimed to be. Besides, he did not want to give his true name. The vicar may have somehow learned it. Perhaps from Thomas Fanshaw himself when he buried his faithless bride and happened to drop the name of the traitorous physician he blamed for her death.

The vicar was staring hard at him. He seemed puzzled, confused, but then he shook William's hand and said, "You are most welcome here, Doctor Kempe. Yes, welcome indeed. My wife and I rarely have guests, our only child being grown and gone. I am the Reverend Arthur Smith, vicar of St. Mark's. My wife of twenty years is Joan. But let me show you the way to the vicarage."

William retrieved his horse and followed the vicar.

Beyond the church was a modest cottage that William surmised was the vicarage. It was surrounded and largely concealed from view by an impressive stand of trees of mixed variety but all contributing to an atmosphere of gloom and neglect. Here he was introduced to the vicar's wife, a woman in her late forties or early fifties with a bent back and the pinched expression of one in constant pain. "This gentleman, good wife, is a learned doctor from London, Doctor—"

William realized the vicar had already forgotten the false name, which he thought was just as well, thinking it might presage his forgetting his entire visit, which would serve his purpose too. The vicar went to his wife and whispered in her ear. Then he returned, smiling.

"Kempe, Orlando Kempe," William said.

"Yes, quite so," the vicar said. He turned to his wife. "I have invited him to spend the night with us before he returns to his home in London."

The vicar's wife looked at him strangely, as though she was both unaccustomed to visitors and afraid of them, then looked back at her husband, who nodded to her. William wondered if she was well. She seemed afflicted and somewhat confused.

The vicarage consisted of the cottage and several outbuildings that looked like workshops or stables. Glimpsing into one of these he found a place to secure his horse for the night and noticed an array of farm implements and tools. He took note of each.

The cottage itself was like the village, weary with age and with a thatched roof in need of repair and several boarded-up windows. But it was warm inside. A generous fire burned in the kitchen and William was immediately invited to sup with them. The meal was simple. Heavy oat bread with sweet butter and a kind of bean soup. At once he remembered the lavish meals in Amsterdam, the jocund company of Pieter Weinmeer's wife and children. Well, he would not be proud but thankful, he decided. His stomach would be fed but also his grave robbing tools supplied. All that remained now was to keep his purpose secret from his hosts.

During supper the vicar prattled without ceasing, gossiping between mouthfuls with a kind of joyfulness. He said he was born in the village and that the Fanshaws were one of its oldest families. "Thomas Fanshaw was not always what he now is, that is a gentleman of great wealth and stature. God's truth, his father Gabriel was no more than a blacksmith. A common person who could not even read or write. If he came to church, it was a kind of miracle, though laws of him who was king then commanded it. He was a mean, cruel man by all accounts, who would violate the Sabbath and drink dry the tavern at the end of day. This was all before my time, but such stories continue to be told in the village, long after their subjects are gone."

Both vicar and wife laughed at this list of improprieties as though they almost took pride in them.

"And he was most cruel to his wife, Thomas's mother, beating her whether she deserved it or no," the vicar continued.

"She never did deserve it, husband," the vicar's wife interjected. "She was a good, virtuous woman who suffered much from her husband's wrath and jealous fits, a pure and virtuous woman as the scriptures speak of them."

"He was a jealous man indeed," the vicar added, nodding to his wife.

William thought about Thomas Fanshaw, also a jealous and violent man. Were such moral traits inherited like unto physical ones, as he himself had inherited his father's height and thinness? It did not seem an unreasonable thing to consider.

"Of course his son, Master Thomas Fanshaw, had good cause to be jealous of her that was his second wife," the vicar's wife said. "Why, she was no better than a whore, though her blood they say was good and surely better than his."

"And no one knows what happened to her?" William asked.

"No man knows, but they say she had a lover who was of high station and the two of them went off together," the woman said.

"They say she changed her name as well," the vicar added, with an expression suggesting that this too was a grievous offense, perhaps even worse than adultery.

"As well as such a woman might," his wife said, her lips pursed in disapproval.

"I'm surprised Master Fanshaw didn't pursue his adulterous wife," William said. 'Most men would, especially those who are rich and can well afford the pursuit."

"Oh, I suppose he was glad to see the back of her," the vicar said, concluding the subject.

William said, "I thought Master Fanshaw was of the Roman persuasion. Surely, this village is of the Queen's religion."

"The village is, Doctor, every born Christian, and Master Fanshaw was of our faith, but has since I regret to say fallen prey to Papist views, and poisonous views they are."

"Yes, very poisonous," his wife said.

"I trust you are not of that hateful sect, Doctor?" the vicar asked. The man looked worried.

William said he was not.

After supper, the vicar went into an adjoining room and brought back a book that for its size William assumed to be the Bible. He placed it on the table before him. He opened it somewhere in the middle and began to read. It was the Geneva Bible, the text that William had learned when a boy—and he recognized the passage the vicar now recited. It was the Twenty-Third Psalm. The vicar was a good reader with a well-modulated voice. When he had finished that psalm, he began another. William realized that a guest in the house was no warrant for changing the older couple's daily routine. He sat patiently, not listening so much to the reading as thinking about what he was to do later that night and how he was to do it. Across from him, the vicar's wife sat with her eyes closed, in prayer or meditation he first supposed—until she suddenly snorted, and William realized she had fallen asleep. Her own snoring had awakened her.

The vicar looked up from his reading and cast a reproachful glance at his wife. "Well, I do think that is sufficient for tonight, my dear, the Lord be praised."

He turned to William. "Doctor, you must be weary, having journeyed so far this day."

William said he was indeed weary, although the truth was, he was far from it. He felt, rather, a stirring in his blood, a sense of danger, thrilling rather than fearsome. He knew then what he had to do and how he was to do it.

At last, the vicar took a candle and showed him to his room, which was hardly larger than a closet and appeared to be adjacent to the chamber of the vicar and his wife. A straw-filled mat lay on the carpetless floor. There was a single, rather tattered, blanket but no pillow or bolster. A small window looked out into the night.

At supper he had remembered the lavish table set by his Dutch friends. Now he recalled the soft down, clean sheets, and warmth of a Dutch bedchamber. Well, so much for that. He was in the very place he wanted to be now. Where he needed to be.

17

Later, he heard the loud snoring of his host coupled with that of his wife, a raucous duet that would have prevented sleep, had he desired it. The time had come. He rose from his bed, slipped on his shoes. He took the candle and slid into the narrow passageway. He trod softly, as softly as he could, opened the door which the vicar had forgotten to bolt, and passed out into the night.

It was cold and damp. The moon, nearly full, might have made his walk toward the churchyard easy enough, but he needed the candle for another purpose. On his way, he stopped into the workshop he had eyed earlier, found the tool he needed, and then proceeded to his work. He went forward with confidence, knowing that if somehow his movements were detected, he could always claim he had gone out to the privy, which was but a few dozen yards from the vicarage.

He walked quickly through the monuments of the more humble dead to the tomb of the Fanshaws. The padlock hitherto preventing his entry yielded with a single stroke of the hammer he carried, though he immediately regretted it, so loudly it sounded through the otherwise silent darkness.

He pushed open the iron gate and entered. He did not close it behind him. Now he had a full view of the stone biers, which were arranged against the east and west walls in three levels, affording space for six coffins. At the end of the chamber there were another three shelves, unoccupied— waiting, he supposed, for other Fanshaws when they should pass. He shivered. However cold it was outside, it was twice that inside and he felt a chill to his bones and a dampness in the air that seemed laden with disease, perhaps the very disease that had taken the life of some of those who reposed here.

As a physician, he was inured to death. Nor did he fear threatening spirits. But he had always felt uneasy in confined spaces. The interior of the tomb was such a place. What if the iron gate shut behind him, locking him within? He would have to call out for help, alert the vicar and his wife, betray his mission and struggle to explain just why he was where he was at such an ungodly hour. He could hardly claim he had confused the tomb with the privy. He shook off the fear as being childish. Still, he left the gate of the tomb ajar.

He had expected the odor of dank stone and decaying flesh, but what he sensed was more like cinnamon or some similar spice, a surprising sweetness. He thought it might proceed from some nearby plant or herb, sending its aroma into the night. Whatever it was, it pleased his sense of smell and helped him anticipate the more offensive odor he knew would come.

Holding his candle aloft, he examined the names on each coffin. He came at last to the one he sought. He put the candle down and opened the coffin lid. It opened easily, as though not only permitting inspection of its contents, but inviting it.

By candlelight, Alice Fanshaw seemed asleep, her beautiful face framed by the linen shroud that covered her head, exposing only the delicate features of her face and a slight suggestion of her white throat. Her small white hands were folded across her breasts. Her fingers clutched the crucifix he had seen her wear when he first visited her in Maldon House.

Though a young doctor, he was accustomed to the dead and felt neither fear nor revulsion in touching her cold forehead or lips. As a student at Cambridge he had excelled at anatomy. He knew the interior mysteries of the body as some know the faces of their beloved, every wrinkle, blotch, or wen. He knew the human heart as a literal object, not a metaphor. The lungs that pumped air, the languorous pathways of the blood beneath the skin. He had performed a hundred autopsies on the dead, sliced the flesh with a butcher's skill and plucked from their seats ever so many parts invisible to the eye. He had with him a surgeon's blade in a little sheath hidden within his shirt. He was prepared for whatever needed to be done. He would know whatever could be known as to how Alice Fanshaw met her end.

Her lips parted slightly, as though she still breathed. Then, he pulled the shroud that covered her down from her face and off her shoulders. Beneath, she was naked. He saw now what Kempe had seen and reported to him at the inn, saw where the bruising stained that perfect flesh. It had practically covered her torso, although now it was faded, a remnant of how it must have appeared when her body was discovered. This, then, is what had provoked her jealous husband's rage. The proof that the magnets had worked, the proof of her infidelity.

Or so Fanshaw had believed.

Now William could smell the decay of that body. But that did not repel him, either. His attention was fixed on something else. It was a puncture wound hardly larger than a pea beneath the swell of her left breast. It would have been almost unnoticeable at the time of her death. At least to the casual observer. Now the flesh had parted and made it more evident to his experienced eye. The puncture would have penetrated the heart. She would have bled internally, probably slowly, until she was dead. Looking closer, he saw it was a wound made undoubtedly by a long, round blade. Perhaps a pick or some saddler's tool, like the ones he had seen in the vicar's stable, or a poniard perhaps, its tip hardly larger than the circumference of a pea. This then, was the indisputable proof. His blanket, the magnets, were not at fault, although he never believed they were. He was almost relieved that he had no need to perform the autopsy that he had planned. Alice Fanshaw had been violated enough. She had been cruelly murdered.

He was covering the body again, relieved that his work was so readily and easily accomplished. Then he saw something else. He had missed it before. Beneath Alice's body was the fringe of another garment, a garment of green and silver, although faded and tattered. What was it? He reached down at the side of Alice Fanshaw and grasped the fringe. He pulled at it, recognized it to be the sleeve of a woman's gown, and then pulling it harder saw at the end of the sleeve a hand, not of flesh, but of bone.

He saw now there were two bodies in the coffin: Fanshaw's bride and another woman's beneath. He rolled Alice Fanshaw onto her side, taking care in doing so as though the disturbance was disrespectful and might wake her to protest the indignity of her young doctor's bedside manner.

The body beneath, more raw white bone than flesh, had been dead for years by its condition. It was clearly a woman's body. The face was still covered with a veneer of yellowed flesh, the eyes hollow sockets, the long teeth, hardly human, exposed to their roots, the mouth gaping as though her life's last act was a cry of agonizing pain or protest. He saw too the cause of her death. A severe blow had cracked her skull. He pitied her, whoever she had been. But then, suddenly, he knew.

It was the hair that had caught his attention. It was, as it must have been when she lived, a vibrant red and it streamed over her shoulders extending almost to her waist.

He knew this must be Augusta Fanshaw, the second wife of Thomas Fanshaw.

The innkeeper at the Prince's Pride thought Fanshaw's second wife had been murdered, speculated that her body would in time be discovered in Fanshaw's field. He had been right about the deed, wrong about the site. Given her present resting place, it was unthinkable that anyone but Thomas Fanshaw was responsible for her death. Fanshaw had built the tomb and, according to the vicar's account, he alone had placed Alice's body in its stone coffin, a privilege he had reserved for himself. Now it was clear why. The wives he had not fully possessed in life, he possessed in their deaths.

He laid Alice's body back where it was before, careful to cover her body with the shroud, so it now covered the remains of the second Mistress of Maldon House as well. He replaced the coffin's lid. Now, all was as before.

He knew the coffin would be opened again. This time with witnesses to see that Alice Fanshaw had been indeed murdered. But not by him, or his magnets.

William extinguished the candle, closed the gate behind him, and passed out into the night. Moonlight would be enough to see him back to the vicarage. The great body of St. Mark's, with its truncated tower, loomed before him, a quiet reproach for his sacrilege. For wasn't that what it was, disturbing the dead with his probing, his motive notwithstanding? And what of his own responsibility for Alice Fanshaw's death? Her jealous husband may have murdered two of his wives, but had not William himself participated in the act, in providing a convenient cover for the deed? He had willingly participated in the charade, made promises and taken his fee. Though he had done so in woeful ignorance, at least part of the blame for Alice Fanshaw's death must fall upon him.

Depressed and suddenly exhausted, William let himself back into the vicarage, pausing at the threshold to listen. The raucous snoring had stopped. The house was as quiet as the tomb he had just violated. He bolted the door behind him and tread softly across the floorboards to avoid their creaking and entered the chamber that had been provided for him. He threw himself onto the bed and covered his eyes with his hands to obscure any light from his window.

He could still smell the stench of decayed flesh. It was in the air about him. It was on his hands. In the morning, would the odor of death betray his secret mission to his hosts? Would they somehow sense what he had been about in his nocturnal wanderings? The vicar had shown little curiosity about William's motive for visiting the Fanshaw tomb. Rather, he had seemed grateful to have someone's interest in an inhabitant of his churchyard. Glad to have someone to talk to who was by his voice and demeanor an educated man. Balm of Gilead for his loneliness. Someone who might appreciate his prattle about the town's most famous son.

William was half asleep when he remembered the padlock. He sat up, broad awake, as though he had heard a scream in the night. The lock had surrendered easily to the blow of the hammer. But what a careless fool he had been! He had forgotten to replace it on the shackle. It was lying upon the grassy verge of the tomb, along with the hammer from the vicar's workshop. He could see it in his mind's eye, clear evidence of an intruder's presence. Would he have time and opportunity to replace the lock and hammer in the morning without being seen? And even if he did, the hammer had done its work. Just replacing the lock where it belonged would not be enough to disguise the illicit entry. Concealment of his deed would depend on sheer luck, on Dame Fortune—and he had already concluded that she was an undependable ally in his efforts to discover truth and free himself from blame.

18

William woke early, before light, seized by a terrible fear. At once he recalled every detail of the night before. The flood of memory was almost more than he could bear; the horror within the coffin, the awful deception practiced upon him by Fanshaw, his own guilt. It took some time before he came to himself, cleared his head. He must, he knew, attend to the immediate business of his leave-taking. He must conceal evidence of his invasion of the tomb. He must determine what he was now to do about what he had learned, what he now knew to be the truth.

But already he could hear the muffled voices of the vicar and his wife in the chamber next to his. He wished it had been otherwise, that he had risen first, stolen forth into the churchyard and replaced the padlock, mounted his horse and hied back to London while the old couple snored on, ignorant of his mischief. The blow of the hammer had destroyed the lock for practical use, but he supposed if he hung it on the shackle the damage would not be noticed—perhaps not until Thomas Fanshaw should take his place there along with his ancestors. Along with his murdered wives.

William had not undressed except for his shoes, which were muddy from his walking through the long grass of the churchyard. These he put on and walked out of his bed chamber to find the old couple in the kitchen, sitting at table and whispering to each other—so as not to wake him, he supposed.

"The good doctor has risen," the vicar announced when William came into view. "And doubtless would not mind a hearty breakfast before returning to the City."

"I would not put you to so much trouble as to feed me a second time," William said, while the vicar's wife busied herself setting the table for three and ladling into a bowl a thick, savory pottage.

Over her shoulder, she said, "Doctor, do eat this, for though you travel by horse, yet will you find your journey less tedious with a full stomach. Is that not right, my husband?"

"Amen," replied the vicar, pulling a chair up to the table and motioning William to join him.

William resigned himself and sat down. He decided he might as well be agreeable. The vicar and his wife had provided for him a bed, and thereby opportunity and means to accomplish his purpose. He was indebted to them for that, though he prayed they would never know it.

He ate a half dozen spoonsful of pottage and drank a cup of goat's milk while the vicar resumed his gossip about the Fanshaws. Most of this repeated what the vicar had said the night before and what his wife had affirmed, but William made no effort to remind him of that. Both seemed unnerved. They fidgeted and fussed, and kept eyeing him as though they expected him at any moment to leap from his chair and assault them. Garrulous the night before, they were more so now. He wondered again if they somehow knew of what he had done and found and for that reason feared what he might yet do.

Having finished eating, he thanked the old couple and went out into the morning air. It was cold and the sky was gray. Would it rain? The ride to London would not be pleasant, but at the moment he had one final thing he must do before leaving. The vicar had followed him outside. He reached for William's hand. William shook it. The vicar's grip was surprisingly strong for an older man, but then he remembered Thomas Fanshaw. He was old. But he was strong, and he was dangerous.

"May God bless you, Doctor. And do have a safe journey to the great city of London, which I do hope one day to see with my own eyes."

"Thank you, Vicar. But may I pay my respects at Mistress Fanshaw's resting place one last time?"

"Of course, Doctor," the vicar said. "I'll accompany you."

William assured him that wouldn't be necessary. "I have troubled you enough, you and your good wife. Surely you have tasks to do about your house, a sermon to prepare, or some person in the village to console."

"And so I do, a sick member of my flock. I quite forgot it. Thank you, Doctor Kempe, for reminding me."

"My pleasure, sir," William said, surprised that the old man whose memory seemed faulty had nonetheless remembered the false name William had given him.

Alone now, William walked down to the tomb. He quickly found the broken padlock in the high grass and slid it onto the latch. A curious eye could easily see the lock had been broken, but it would be a careful and determined eye, not a casual observer. He found the hammer where it had fallen and snatched it up. He would have returned it to its place in the shed, but that was impossible now. He tucked it inside his cloak. There had been more than one hammer in the shed. Perhaps the vicar would not miss this one. William would cast it into a ditch or hedgerow on his way to London.

He took a final look at the church and the vicarage beyond. The vicar had not moved from where he had bid William goodbye. His face, William thought, bore an inscrutable expression. Of bemusement? Of fear? William couldn't tell. Had the man seen him pick up and replace the padlock, conceal the hammer? William couldn't tell that either.

He breathed a sigh of relief as he passed through the lychgate. He had discovered the truth of Alice Fanshaw's death and more. He found his horse tethered to a post near the shed. He mounted. Armed with knowledge, he was now left to decide what to do with it.

19

He had been right to worry about the weather. He had no sooner set out from Maidenstowe than the rain began to fall, first in a light sprinkle, so common in England in the summer, then in a torrential downpour that turned the road into mud and made travel slow and torturous. He did not return to his London lodgings until nearly midnight, bedraggled and thoroughly soaked. Once in his chamber he tore off his wet clothes and fell into his bed. He did not take time to light a candle, preferring the solace of darkness and the oblivion of sleep.

He dreamed, inevitably. Why should he suppose it would be otherwise, given what he had seen and what he now knew? As exhausted as he was, he woke every hour or two in a kind of delirium. He struggled to close the lid of the coffin in which Fanshaw's wives were entombed. The dead women were struggling to rise as though it were the day of Resurrection. They glared at him with ghastly, accusing faces, especially the second wife whose face was more white bone than flesh. It passed through his mind that he had done nothing to her that she should blame him. But for Fanshaw's last wife it was another matter. There, he acknowledged, was a fault—not that it had been he who had punctured her heart, but he had provided a concealment for the act. That he had done so in ignorance did not mitigate. He had undertaken a medical experiment for greed, ambition, and desire to please his patient, a beautiful woman for whom he felt pity. None of that gave him cause to feel blameless before God or man.

When he finally awakened, he burned with fever. His bare chest and shoulders were damp and hot to the touch. His pulse raced. There was a pitcher of water in the room and he drank from it, dampened a towel, and wet it to cool his body. He considered telling the innkeeper of his condition but decided against it, not now at least. No need to alert the man to the mysterious stranger in the upper room whose illness might sound an alarm to all within and bring the authorities to see who was sick and of what. Was it the plague, perhaps? They might suppose this and cast him out into the street. In a season of plague, compassion was ever in short supply. At the very least, they would want to know his name, his business in London, his place of origin. They would discover who he was and why he fled.

For three days he mostly lay in bed, sleeping or studying the blackened beams of the ceiling. He suffered more delirium, envisioning things that were not. On the second of these miserable days he secured the attention of a boy passing in the street below and gave him money to fetch food and drink to be brought to his chamber. Nothing heavy, but rather gruel and soup and bread and a little cheese, which he forced himself to partake of, knowing that a weakening constitution would not help mend him. On the fourth day of his confinement, he began to improve. The fever had gone but left him weak and unsteady. His appetite had returned, but he was hesitant to go abroad in the City, at least not yet.

There was in his chamber a cabinet with shelves. One of these he used as a writing desk. He began to write in a notebook he carried with him to record his observations or ideas for experiments. Before he left Amsterdam, Pieter Weinmeer had beseeched him to write when he returned to England, reporting all that he undertook to clear his name. Weinmeer had made him promise. William in turn had secured Weinmeer's word not to disclose the letter's contents to anyone, not even to Katrina. Especially not to Katrina.

And so he sat down to write about his visit to Maidenstowe, sparing nothing as to his discoveries or his suspicions. He wrote in great detail until he had filled a dozen or more pages of the notebook, then tore them out, folded and sealed them. He wrote Weinmeer's name and the word *Amsterdam* in a careful script on the outside. Weinmeer had told him that there was a Dutch immigrant living on Lime Street who regularly posted letters from London to Amsterdam. Weinmeer had assured William that the man was competent and trustworthy, and that William should have no fear of his missive failing to reach its destination.

William added a postscript to Katrina. Since her father would read it, he decided to make nothing more than a polite greeting between friends. They were, after all, nothing more—and surely nothing more in her father's eyes.

The boy who had fetched food for him, and whose name William learned was Adam, now came each day to see to his needs. He gave the boy the letter to Weinmeer and the directions to the Dutch postmaster, along with what he supposed the post might cost. He said Adam could keep what was left over. The next day he changed lodgings to an inn on a nearby street but kept Adam as his personal servant. He still had most of the money Fanshaw had given him in advance for his services.

Although he still felt weakened by his bout of fever, he felt now strong enough to continue with his plan, which was to find his friend Orlando Kempe. Kempe had helped him escape Fanshaw's wrath. Kempe had believed him. William trusted that his school friend might do the same now that the picture of Thomas Fanshaw's perfidy was fully drawn and the evidence was at hand. From Kempe he would find out how matters stood at Maldon House and with the Parmenters. From Kempe he would receive counsel as to how he should proceed in defending himself, armed as he was now with his new knowledge.

Kempe had said his house was on Lime Street, a close-knit neighborhood in the City favored by wealthy merchants, physicians, apothecaries, and delvers into natural history, plants, animals, insects. Whatever God, the Supreme Architect, had made. His father had taken William there on one of Jerome Gilbert's rare visits to London. He had pointed out to William some of the fine houses with their spacious gardens, most visible through chinks in walls for privacy's sake. Kempe had never told him which house was his, although he had described it to William in great, self-congratulatory detail as evidence of his newly-found prosperity. William was confident he could find it. Lime Street was a winding street, but short. Besides, a passerby might tell him what he needed to know.

And that was what happened. A finely-dressed woman, doubtless some rich merchant's wife, accompanied by two young girls he supposed were her daughters, kindly pointed where he was to go after William had created an impression of physical suffering that persuaded her that he might need the services of Doctor Orlando Kempe. "Whether he be good or bad, sir, I cannot tell, since I have not sought his services, but I do know where he dwells."

William followed her directions and came to one of the smaller houses on the street, much less grand than his friend had described, but nonetheless a solid house that looked newly built of sturdy timbers and brick. It rose several stories above the ground floor, where there was a sign announcing his friend's name and a caduceus, the intertwining serpents signaling the medical service he performed.

William did not approach the house immediately but stood watching to see who entered and who departed. For the first hour that morning he saw no one enter. But the second hour he saw a woman, modestly dressed, knock on the door and go in. Shortly, she came out again. While he watched, he saw no one he recognized, but then did not expect to. He was after all a stranger in the district and the neighborhood was famous for taking in immigrants and refugees, especially those who brought wealth with them or otherwise could distinguish themselves. But he could not be sure that passersby did not know him, did not seek him—hence his hesitation to approach openly. After all, Kempe was known to be William's friend. Would not Kempe's house be watched, should William dare return to England?

He waited until dark, and the street became quiet. He had noticed a garden wall attached to Kempe's house, low enough for him to scale under cover of night and make his way into the house. He had no instinct for burglary or trespassing, but necessity drove him to it. Breaking into the Fanshaw tomb had been but practice for this new violation he intended.

Scaling the wall proved more difficult than he had supposed but he did it, scratching his hands and arms in the effort. Within was the garden and then the house and a postern door which was surprisingly, but helpfully, unlocked. He walked in, and found himself in an empty kitchen, but heard voices from an adjoining room. He was approaching to see who was within when he felt a hand on his shoulder and himself turned suddenly around to face the very man he sought. It was hard to know which was the more surprised. Kempe was holding a staff in his hand with a heavy metal knob. By his expression, he had every intent to use it on William.

"By heaven, William, I thought you were a thief and was about to brain you. What are you doing here? I thought you were in Italy. Why this foolhardiness in returning to England?"

William raised a finger to his lips. There were servants in the house. He could hear their voices. He trusted Kempe, but no one else.

"And what happened to your hands?" Kempe asked, noticing the scratches.

"I scaled your garden wall."

Kempe laughed. "Instead of knocking on my door? Would a simple knock not have been easier—and safer?"

111

"I did not want to be seen. Are you being watched?"

Kempe didn't answer. "Come with me," he said, and they passed into another room and then a second, which was a library with a large table as a desk and books on shelves, and a large, straight-back chair beside a hearth in which no fire was laid. "This is my inner sanctum," Kempe said, taking the chair. "We can talk here. My servants are forbidden to disturb me when I'm within. I terrorize them regularly, you see, with instructions on how they should behave and if they do not, well, I am the master of the house."

"I'm sure you do terrorize," William said, settling into a chair opposite of Kempe's and looking about him. "I see you do live very well."

"Not as well as I did. After the unfortunate death of Mistress Fanshaw—"

"I think you mean the murder," William interrupted.

Kempe looked surprised. "I mean no such thing. It was an accident, just as you said."

"It was murder, my friend. I have discovered the truth."

William related his experiences at Maidenstowe, his visit to St. Mark's churchyard, the discovery of the deadly wound that must have been the true cause of Alice Fanshaw's death.

Kempe said, "I cannot believe you were so bold. To go to Maidenstowe, a wretched place, to put yourself at such a risk. You are a fool, my friend, whatever else you might be. And you stayed overnight at the vicar's house? Did you tell him your name?"

"I gave him your name"

"My name?" Kempe cried. "But why should you do that?"

"I was afraid to give him mine," William answered. "I feared he would know I am the one accused of her death. It was an impulse. A sudden inspiration, you might call it."

Kempe shook his head. He looked at William. "I don't believe you."

"It's the truth, Orlando. Alice Fanshaw was murdered."

"I mean, I can't believe you did what you did."

"No. Why not? A man can give his name however he wishes."

"Not the name but going there in the first place. Exposing yourself to capture."

"I felt no threat from the vicar or his wife."

"Not from them, but from Fanshaw. How could you know but that he was there at the same time as you, come to mourn his dead bride and find you at her tomb? He would have killed you on the spot."

"I think it unlikely Fanshaw would be that devoted to his dead bride's memory, given he is by your report convinced she was unfaithful. Besides, there is something else I found."

He told Kempe about the other body beneath Alice Fanshaw's, the decayed remains of Augusta Fanshaw.

"Good God," Kempe cried. "You mean the wife thought to have run off?"

"She did not run off—at least, not far," William said. "Her skull was crushed. No accident that, but murder plain and simple."

"I don't think there's aught plain and simple about murder," Kempe said. "This is very hard to credit, William. Fanshaw is a jealous man and a violent one when crossed, but that he should murder his wife—."

"*Wives*," William corrected him.

"If the lady's body was decayed, how did you know it was she? I mean the second Mistress Fanshaw?"

"By the color of her hair."

"Red. A burnished gold?"

"It crowned her skull."

"That would be she, without a doubt," Kempe said. "She was famous for it."

"You knew her, then?"

"Knew of her," Kempe said, looking away. They said she turned heads of great and small and was ever being pursued by men not her husband." He looked back at William. "From all this then you conclude that Thomas Fanshaw murdered both of these women and that the bloody bruise he construed as evidence of Alice's adultery was caused by some pointed instrument or tool?"

"Yes," William said.

"But both the women?"

"Why else would he bury both together, but as a monument to their guilt?" William said.

"Then the mystery is solved." Kempe said.

"But not yet proved. In the public mind, I am still to blame, a murderer, an incompetent, deprived of license and my reputation in ruins before I had chance to make one."

Kempe sighed heavily and frowned. "I, too, am undone, William. Fanshaw has complained to my patron, Sir John, who has abandoned me because I commended you. I am followed, I think, each day because of my friendship with you. By Lord Burghley's spies, I think. I tell you, I rue the day I came to your house in Colchester to tell you of what I supposed was a gift of Fortune."

"Not any Fortune that I would wish for either of us," William said. "I don't fault you for that, Orlando. Or telling Fanshaw about my magnets, for which reason he secured my service. You meant well. But Fanshaw had plans of his own. He deceived us both."

"Do you not want revenge for these wrongs?" Kempe asked, in what was almost a whisper.

"Not revenge," William said. "Justice, rather. Justice for the women dead. Justice for you and for me. Exoneration from blame. Peace to live and thrive in England without fear of Burghley's spies or Fanshaw's wrath."

Then Kempe said, "All good ends to strive for, William, but stay for a moment and think. Fanshaw is beyond the hands of any justice. He is more than rich, and as you know he has powerful friends that would rather you suffer than he. Besides, let me be plain: his two wives were whores. If your experiment did not reveal the truth of Alice's adultery, certainly Fanshaw knew it well enough without the experiment. The old man is impotent. He even complained to me of it, sought remedies, none of which worked. Her story about the revival of his powers whilst drunk was nonsense. Alice Fanshaw was faithless, and that's the end of it. Does she deserve our pity? I think not. Who loves a faithless bride, or labors to excuse her fault?"

"Fanshaw said he did."

"Indeed, as much as he loved his previous wife, she who shares Alice's coffin."

"Therefore, I should do nothing, but slink back to Amsterdam and grow poppies?" William asked.

"Better an exile than hang," Kempe said. "Any other course of action is futile."

"I think you commended that course to me before I went to Amsterdam."

"I did so for your good, William. For my love of you, for no other reason. Think upon it, it saved your life. Fanshaw would have shown you no mercy. Perhaps now his anger has cooled, and indeed, I do think he

114

may not be long for this world. He's old. How much longer can he live? Alice's father likewise. I warrant you that when they're gone, no one will remember what you did or did not do. By the way, why Holland and not Italy, as you told me?"

"It was nearer at hand. Besides, I had old friends there."

"Ah, the Weinmeers, Pieter Weinmeer from our Cambridge days?"

"The same."

"I do remember him," Kempe said, laughing loudly. "A stout old fellow looking every inch the Dutchman. I found his lectures boring and his accent impenetrable. It was always a wonder to me that you could listen so long to him or comprehend his execrable English."

William ignored this dismissal of his teacher and friend. It was Kempe's caustic humor, which prevented him from saying much good about anyone other than a few. William was honored to think himself included in that select company.

William laughed. "You thought all our learned faculty boring, Orlando. Confess it."

"I do confess it—and proudly," Kempe said. "The instruction was much better in Turin. As were the Italian women." Kempe laughed.

"They took me in, treated me as his son, "William said. "I told Weinmeer what had happened to me. He said I should come back to England, clear my name. He said there would be no peace for me as a fugitive."

"Did he? Such counsel is easy enough to give if you are not the one sent back into the lion's den. With all due respect to your Dutchman, my own counsel is that you take the next ship back to Amsterdam, or wherever you will. Indeed, think Muscovy or far Cathay. The farther from England, the better. Your exile will not be forever. As I have said, the old men will die soon and your so-called malpractice and murder will be stale news. Do not fear. Have patience in your suffering, so said the ancient philosophers as I recall."

For a moment, Kempe was silent. Then he said, "Weinmeer had a daughter, did he not?"

"Yes," William answered.

"I have forgotten her name."

"Katrina."

"A pretty maid, I recall."

"Quite pretty," William said.

115

"Has she married?"

"No. She has had suitors," William said.

William was not prepared to confess his love for the girl Kempe had called a pretty maid. It was one of the things he reserved to himself. Kempe was a friend, but not *that* good a friend, or at least, not yet.

They talked far into the night, his friend pleading with him to be sensible, William more determined than ever to stay and clear his name.

Finally, Kempe said, "Very well, then, cut your own throat if you must. Strange, I do not remember you so stubborn at Cambridge, but quick rather to agree and concede when there was contention."

"Recent experience has made me bolder," William said.

"More stubborn," Kempe said.

"Call it what you will," William answered.

"Well, then, do tell me your plan."

"My plan?"

"How you propose to make all know Fanshaw murdered his wife and blamed you for it? It seems an impossible task to me, but then what do I know, whose advice you have scorned from the first."

"Not scorned," William said. "You advised me to flee England, and so I did."

"And my advice stands, but since you will not be ruled by me, I will stand a constant friend to you still and help you in your holy quest any way I might."

"Spoken like a true friend, Orlando."

"Know that I am that before all," Kempe said. "Then granted that you shall be staying and pursuing Fanshaw, which I will contest no longer, I advise you to write down all you discovered at Maidenstowe and give it to a friend, that some other party might know and perhaps testify on your behalf."

"A friend like you, you mean?"

"Well, yes, but not necessarily."

"I did write a letter to Weinmeer yesterday. I did precisely what you advised."

"Good, good. But then Weinmeer is not an Englishman. I do doubt a stranger as he is and was whilst here could provide a fit witness in any English court."

"You then shall receive my account within the week," William said.

"Look, William, where do you lodge whilst here?"

He gave the name of the inn.

"I believe I do know the very place. But be my guest at my house."

"Thank you, but no. You asked me if I had a plan, and so I do. And it is business I must be about."

"And what would that be?"

"Alice Fanshaw's confessor."

"That tedious fellow, yes," Kempe said, frowning. "He is much to blame for her descent into religious hysteria at the end. That the old man suffered him to come and go at will and converse with her privily was a wonder. Why it would not surprise me if Mottelay were not the bride's lover and the father of her child. If so, he would not be the first man of the cloth to do the deed of darkness with one of his parishioners. I would sooner trust the devil than a priest."

"The truth of that we may never know, since the bride is no longer with us to name her paramour," William said. "The priest may know more about her. I do mean what she did and Fanshaw did."

"He will not betray his priestly duty, the seal of the confession, save he is a renegade Papist, which I do doubt," Kempe said.

"It's not her sins I wish to uncover, for I can guess them well enough. I do believe she was untrue to her husband—and that she had an earlier lover. She had given birth before."

"Your magnets told you that?"

"Not the magnets, but I did examine her before her death, with finger and eye. I do suspect she had given birth before."

"You are sure?"

"My examination suggested that to me, coupled with what I learned from others about her past, her youthful indiscretions, which caused her father and mother much distress and grief. You were her doctor when she lived with her parents. Certainly you must have heard rumors, seen things, inferred things."

"Well, I did," Kempe said. "But I knew nothing of her having a child, only that she had been wild in her earlier youth. I did not see it as my part to probe her secret life, but to keep her well, which I did do until she married and became religious. So, what can you learn from the good father then?"

"He came to the house after I left for the night," William said. "He may know her mind after, or her husband's mind and acts. He may have witnessed what Fanshaw did or heard something about what he intended to do."

"I don't know where Mottelay is, nor do I care," Kempe said. "I have heard nothing of him since the lady died and was buried."

"I'll find him," William said.

"Well then, good luck to you, William. I doubt he will tell you anything that you do not already know, if he speaks to you at all. He's a cold fish, if you ask me. Smiles once in a fortnight and passes his time counting his prayer beads. Still, if I can assist in any way, remember I am your friend. Besides, I am in your debt."

"What debt is that?'

"For getting you in this stew of misery in the first place."

Kempe prevailed upon him to leave by the front door of the house, rather than by scaling the garden wall again. He said at this hour the street would be deserted. All on Lime Street would be asleep or at least minding their business within doors. This time, William accepted his friend's counsel.

He stepped out the front door into the blackness of the street. Just before, he had looked carefully from the right to the left. No one. He waved to Kempe, who stood on the threshold to see him off. William walked quickly. Somewhere in London a house or houses were afire and a thick, acrid smoke covered the sky. Someday, William imagined, a learned artificer would find a way to illuminate human habitations, not with fire but by some other means. The night would lose its dominance of the day. Man would come and go, read and write, at any hour, defying the dark. It would not be magic. Science would make it happen. He believed this as much as he believed anything.

He arrived at the stroke of midnight at his inn, where he encountered an old bewhiskered porter with a lamp complaining that the gentleman was very late in his return and was thereby an inconvenience to the whole house.

"How can that be? The whole house sleeps, does it not?" William asked.

"If it does, it's a miracle, sir, because of your knocking. At this hour, all Christians are abed or at prayers."

He gave the porter something for his inconvenience—and for the good Christians whose sleep and prayers he had disturbed. His father had

118

once told him it was always wise to keep on the good side of servants. They might be a great help in times of need. Certainly, they were a great hindrance in trouble.

The next morning, the same porter saw him preparing to leave the inn.

"I forgot to tell you, sir, yesterday a man came to ask after you."

"What man was it?"

"He did not say, sir, but asked for you. You are Master William Johnson, are you not, sir?"

It was the false name he had given to the innkeeper. William hesitated to answer. His heart beat rapidly. Was this then what he had feared, an imminent arrest by some official of the law?

"The man said he had a letter for Master William Johnson. He spoke a strange manner of the Queen's English. I have the letter here, sir."

It crossed his mind the letter might be from Weinmeer. Could the post travel with such speed between the two countries? Two days to cross the Channel. The same number of days to return. Weinmeer had said the Dutchman who was postmaster for correspondence between England and Holland was wondrously efficient, that mail bags passed on ships each day and were delivered promptly, that there was no postal service in all the world that traveled with such speed.

He looked at the letter. It was addressed to his false self. It was not Pieter Weinmeer's writing, which he had seen many times and could recognize easily.

It was Katrina's.

The letter was brief, and before he read the first word a wave of disappointment passed over him that it was not longer. He read it slowly, prepared to savor each word.

Dearest Willem,

I was regretful that you left so suddenly, most especially after our talking in the garden and so rudely to you I behaved. My father told me that you had some special business to do in London and therefore your visit to Amsterdam was foreshortened. He would not tell me what it was, if it involved some danger to yourself or some good fortune you were eager to partake of. I believe he knows but will not tell. I respect his silence. I have imposed the same

119

burden on you, my secret. Yet I do wish you very well, whatever
you do, wherever you go. And I pray daily for your safety.
  Your friend and pupil,
    Katrina Weinmeer

He read it through several times before folding it up and putting it in his notebook. Then he removed it—and, without unfolding it, brushed his lips against the coarse paper Katrina had touched.

20

He had been bold in declaring to Kempe his purpose to find Julian Mottelay, though he knew himself that such a quest would be difficult. Papist priests ministered to their flocks in secret, usually disguised as family friends, distant relatives, or tutors; sometimes as clerks or secretaries. The penalty imposed if they were captured was severe, sometimes prison or exile, often death. He was not even sure Mottelay would talk to him, were he to find him. They had taken an instant dislike to each other and then reconciled, or so William thought. But then Kempe had told him of the slanders made against him by Mottelay after Alice's death, the absurd and malicious accusation of witchcraft.

The more he thought of some future conversation, perhaps even collaboration, with Mottelay, the less likely it seemed. Perhaps Kempe had been right about the hopelessness of his finding Mottelay. He could not really ask around the city for a Papist priest. He could not ask Fanshaw where Mottelay was.

But he did have another person who might help him. He had not shared that person's name with Kempe. His friend would have been beside himself with laughter. William imagined Kempe's response. "I never supposed you to be such a fool as to think you could approach the dead woman's father, Sir John Parmenter, when he is fully convinced that you and your magnets caused his daughter's death. He would drag you without ceremony before the magistrate or kill you outright and claim self-defense for cutting your throat. And who would believe otherwise? He is a knight of the realm. You are ... a mere doctor."

But that was exactly what William determined to do next.

He might not know how to find a Papist priest in London. At least he knew where to find Alice Fanshaw's bereaved father.

William knew the Parmenter's manor house lay not far from Fanshaw's, or far from Maidenstowe. He knew it would be relatively easy to find some herdsman or farmer who could point the way. As for Sir John, William had spoken to him but twice. He remembered a lean-bodied gentleman with a pointed white beard who upon introduction and a curt nod paid scant attention to him, although Fanshaw told Sir John that William was to be his daughter's physician. Later, meeting Parmenter outside his daughter's bedchamber, William found the knight more amicable, even grateful for William's helping his daughter. Alice's father felt differently now, by Kempe's report. Confronting Parmenter would put William at risk, but someone in authority needed to know how Alice died and why. Someone in authority needed to see the evidence against Thomas Fanshaw.

Yet perhaps Sir John already had his suspicions of his new son-in-law. Fanshaw's jealousy was well-allowed, his hot temper likewise. Parmenter must have known of his new son-in-law's reputation when Fanshaw petitioned him for his daughter's hand, when the bargain was struck, the bride's youth and beauty her only dowry, the aged husband paying off his new father-in-law's debts. And certain it was that Parmenter knew of his own daughter's sordid history. Knew of the bastard child. Knew of the dubious paternity of the child in her womb. William reckoned Alice's father would have known all of that.

That Fanshaw might kill Alice were she unfaithful to him would surely be within the compass of her father's imagination, if only as a remote possibility. How could it be otherwise, save the knight were blind or stupid?

And, therefore, William concluded that, were the grieving father on his side, Lord Burghley might give credence to William's accusation against Fanshaw and rescind the warrant for William's arrest. His bride's tomb might be opened again, disclosing the evidence of her murder and the murder of her predecessor in Fanshaw's bed.

What would be difficult and perilous was the first encounter, the first, tentative steps. William would have to secure Parmenter's attention and then his forbearance while William told his story and offered the proof.

William left his London lodgings and set out again from the City for the country. When he arrived at his destination, he found new lodgings, using the same false name he had used in London, William Johnson, a name too common to be memorable.

He paid for his bedchamber at a small inn, which he knew to be within a dozen miles of Parmenter Hall, and then went downstairs to where there was a tap room that also served food. He ate a little of his supper and a half glass of ale and wondered again whether Kempe had been right about the foolishness of his getting anywhere near Alice Fanshaw's grieving and enraged father.

He was about to go up to his bedchamber again when he saw a familiar figure approaching him. He could hardly believe his eyes, for such coincidences he believed did not happen in the normal course of living but seem contrived by fate or by God in heaven dictating what was to be.

"Doctor Gilbert, I believe."

"Father Mottelay?"

The priest put a finger to his lips. Without invitation, he sat down at the table opposite him. "I beseech you, doctor, to speak soft. My particular vocation isn't known here, at least not in the village. You understand, I think, what it means to be under the eyes of the law. In England these days a priest is not thought better than a common criminal or spy—or, say, a doctor who murders his patient. They are all one—to be apprehended, tried, and probably hanged. A seemingly inevitable and proper progression in the eyes of some."

Mottelay looked around as though to see if they were being watched. The room was half empty. Other occupants seemed too much in their cups to notice anything. The two men sat looking at each other. The priest smiled grimly. "I was passing along the street and, glancing in the window, saw you sitting by yourself. Believe me, I was as amazed to see you as I suppose you are to see me. I thought you fled to Wales or Cornwall, or some other godforsaken place. Your friend Doctor Kempe told us that."

"And so I did, for a while," William said, deciding to keep his Amsterdam sojourn to himself.

"A short while indeed," Mottelay said. "And have now returned. May I ask why? Are you so guilt-ridden that you wish death as absolution for your crime?"

"I committed no crime, Father Mottelay."

"*Master* Mottelay, if you please. You help us both in keeping my true identity to yourself. I would not have my religion known in this place." The priest looked around him nervously.

"I shall," William said, "If you do likewise. Obviously, I have no need to hear my name on the town's lips."

The priest thought about this, then he said, "Agreed."

"Agreed," William said.

"So I ask you again, Doctor, why are you here and not hiding out in some pleasant place—say France or Italy? The weather there is better I assure you, the people strange but not unfriendly, and they have as much need for your services as do English folk."

William took a deep breath and recited what he had said to himself many times since leaving Amsterdam. It was a personal creed now. He would have blazoned it on his chest had he the courage. At least his lips could declare it under these dangerous circumstances.

"I have come home to clear my name, my reputation, my honor as a doctor. I have come to speak to Alice Fanshaw's grieving father, to explain what happened, how I am not to blame nor are my magnets for his daughter's death, and to secure his help."

The priest nodded his head. He beckoned the tapster to the table they now shared and ordered a drink, gesturing toward William's glass. "And refill this gentleman's as well."

When the tapster returned, the priest took a long appreciative sip, wiped his mouth with his long sleeve, and leaned close to William. "I will tell you, Doctor, that which will surprise you."

"How surprise me, Master Mottelay?"

"I am not amongst those who find fault with you or your magnets," Mottelay said, looking very serious.

For a long moment, William stared at his drinking companion. These were not words he expected to hear from the priest, and he was not sure he could believe them. Kempe's report of Mottelay's slanderous accusations still echoed in his head. The charge that he had used witchcraft to kill Alice Fanshaw was particularly outrageous. One did not forget or forgive such a slander, at least not easily.

"In truth, you do?" William said. "May I ask why? For all others are convinced I am to blame, and most especially her husband and her father. And I am told you did blame me before, accusing me of doing the Devil's work."

124

"I never said such a thing," Mottelay said.

"I have it from a trusted source."

"Then your trust may be misplaced, Doctor. I swear on Christ's tomb that I never made such an accusation—against you or against any man. I do believe the Devil exists, but also that he is blamed for much that is man's own folly and devilry."

William looked hard at the priest. Mottelay seemed to be sincere, but William knew he could easily be taken in. It was a fault in himself he recognized and lamented. He trusted too readily, and often to his detriment.

Mottelay took another drink. He smiled coldly. "Doctor, believe it or not, I am not without respect for your science. All of it has its place in the healing of the body. But I never believed that your magnets could do what Master Fanshaw claimed. Fidelity is a moral trait, not physical. Its diagnosis is a matter of spiritual discernment."

William said, "And you discerned, spiritually, that the lady had been unfaithful, that the child she carried was not Fanshaw's but that of one of her lovers?"

"Ah, were I to tell you that, I would violate my sacred oath, the seal of the confession. That I will not do, Doctor. And therefore you may surmise what you will about what I know or do not know about the lady's virtue. But to be plain, I never believed your magnets killed her. I saw the body on the morning of her death."

"What did you see?" William asked.

"The area of her flesh from groin to breast was a vast bruise, as though all the blood had been sucked from the heart to coagulate beneath the skin. Given her beauty in life, it was an ugly death, horrid to view and contemplate, regardless of her sins. Her husband took it for a sign your magnets had done their work, detected her crime, but her death therefrom was not in his reckoning. I was there while Fanshaw raged—not only at his faithless wife, but at her faithless physician who had not warned him that she might die of your experiment. He hated her sin and wanted her punished. By him, not by death. He felt cheated, you see."

"And her father?" William asked.

"He cursed you, too. Fanshaw did not tell him the purpose of your ministrations. To him you were merely helping her through her pregnancy, not applying a test of her chastity."

They sat quietly for a moment, neither speaking, but William's mind was a chaos of thoughts, some new and not the least that in this annoying priest he may have found a friend, or at least an ally. But he remained guarded. Cambridge had been no academic Eden, free of duplicities and conspiracies. But this, the world beyond, was worse. Who could be trusted in such a world as this was?

"Tell me, sir priest. I am much amazed to find you here," William said.

"Why amazed?" Mottelay answered. "Before I became confessor to Sir John's daughter I ministered to his household, pretending to be his secretary when in truth I brought him and his house the holy sacraments. By such devices, we priestly ministers of the true religion survive in this country as it now is."

Mottelay frowned when he said the last, as though denying great Elizabeth's divine right to rule and reign. William reflected on what he had heard of the Romish priests who, according to most of his fellow-religionists, infested the country and were thought responsible for treasonous acts as well as the propagation of an alien creed.

"You knew, of course, that the Parmenters are what the government and its church are pleased to call recusants," Mottelay continued. "I would prefer a better name for those who reject the common heresies of our day. Heresies that lead their followers carefully down to hell."

"You returned then to your former post when she died?" William asked, eager to avoid religious wrangling in which he had little interest.

"I did. Fanshaw, as you know, is a reluctant convert to our faith. I say *convert* with much hesitation, for I think he feels nothing for our religion but converted only that he should have Alice Fanshaw as his wife. He suffered my presence for her sake, as he suffered her return to true religion in her last days. When she died, I was no longer needed. Nor wanted. I did not wait to feel Fanshaw's boot against my backside. Her body wasn't cold before I returned here."

It was now late, and William was weary from his day's travel and uncertain what to do next, given this unforeseen meeting with Mottelay. But when he began to excuse himself to go to bed, the priest begged him to stay a little. He said he had business to discuss with William that might be to their mutual advantage.

"I am here under a false name," William said. "Call me Johnson. William Johnson."

126

"And so I shall," Mottelay said. "But listen, you did say earlier that you were here to secure Sir John's help. What manner of help from a man who has cursed you for killing his daughter?"

"Help in prosecuting the true murderer," William said.

During his youth, William had not thought of himself as brave or courageous. He had preferred a quiet life of predictable outcomes. He was averse to risk. But the past several weeks had wrought a mighty change in him. He had risked coming back to England, risked discovery in opening Alice Fanshaw's coffin, risked meeting with Orlando Kempe. Now he contemplated the greatest risk of all, attempting to persuade a bereaved father that he was innocent of his daughter's murder.

And he wondered how far he could trust this priest. He looked at the man's face. He had the earnest, well-meaning expression of an honest man. He decided to take a chance. He said, "I believe Thomas Fanshaw murdered his wife in cold blood. I believe it was not the magnets that drew blood from her, but a pointed object stuck beneath her breast that caused her to hemorrhage so. A sharp-pointed knife or other like instrument."

"The lady's death, not a mishap, not malpractice, but murder then," Mottelay said.

"Murder, sir."

The priest considered this. He sighed and drained his glass. He called the tapster over for another. He said to William, "Fanshaw is malevolent enough, jealous enough to do that. But what proof have you? A simple accusation isn't enough. Sir John will give no heed to you without proof, and he may well seize upon you and deliver you to the magistrate, or worse to Lord Burghley, who Fanshaw claims owes him a favor and will repay by punishing you."

"I have proof, proof absolute," William insisted. "Enough to convince any man with an open eye and mind."

Mottelay said, "Tell me then. Give me your proof that I may become a believer in this theory of yours and advance your cause with Sir John. He trusts me, I think."

William laid out his evidence, aware that Mottelay might not believe him, but thinking that it was at least good practice for his ultimate presentation to Parmenter. He started with his visit to Maidenstowe and the tomb of Alice Fanshaw. He told the priest he had been shown the family tomb by the vicar and then how he had stolen forth by night to break into the tomb and look within her coffin.

"I saw her body, where she lay dead. I saw the wound beneath her breast. A small puncture. It would have ruptured her heart. Hence, the blood beneath the skin. The bruise you observed. And there was something else, the important thing."

"What important thing?" Mottelay asked.

He told the priest about the decayed body, the body he knew was Fanshaw's second wife, the body that had been concealed in the family tomb because Fanshaw had killed her, too. Faithless wives both of them, entombed together as a testament to a husband's indignation and outrage at being betrayed. How else could the bizarre burials be interpreted but as a kind of jealous madness?

"You found her beneath Alice's body?" Mottelay asked, his disbelief evident in his eyes.

"Yes, the two together," William insisted. "As God is my witness. I saw it with my own eyes."

Mottelay was silent for a while. William did not know what to say next. He had said what he wanted to say. He had offered his proof, which was his word—at least, that was his only proof for now.

Then, Mottelay said, "You reason that if Fanshaw killed his second wife and concealed her, he killed Alice as well?"

"Is that not a reasonable conclusion?" William asked, surprised that his deduction should be questioned. "The tomb is his family's, built since he became rich and could afford to build it as a tribute to himself in the town where once he was a poor boy. The vicar presided at the funeral, the burial. He said Fanshaw carried Alice's body into the tomb by himself. He was her sole undertaker. He would not be helped by any servant who might see what evil his master had done. All this I learned from the vicar. Fanshaw knew what was in Alice's coffin, and he would not have it seen for all the world."

Mottelay said, "Were we to go there now, to the churchyard at Maidenstowe, we would find the very evidence you affirm?"

William said they would. He said he would swear to it.

"Upon what oath?" Mottelay asked. "You do not seem a religious man, that you should swear by God or Christ, or the Holy Book."

William said, "I swear by all I believe is good in the world, the creations of nature's God, the stars that give evidence of His glory."

Mottelay looked at him thoughtfully, without speaking. William knew the priest was experiencing the same uncertainty that had made William hesitate in disclosing his evidence of the murder.

"Very well, Doctor," Mottelay said, at length. "I will speak to Sir John. I will put it in his mind that another explanation for his daughter's death exists and should be put to the test. I think he will consider that. Sir John is not an unreasonable man. Not like Fanshaw, whose anger is so much a part of him that it will not pause in its pursuit of you, either abroad or here in England."

"And Sir John's curse?"

"On you? Ah, Doctor, curses come and curses go. A man may curse many a thing in his lifetime and make peace with it at last. Let's pray that this is true in your case."

"If it is not, then I am lost," William said. "For his hatred may prove the end of me."

"Pray it will not fall out so," Mottelay said. "Look, I will test the water. If it boil, you shall not jump in. If it becomes tepid or cool, then you shall swim safely to your port."

William laughed. "By this mix of metaphors, I trust you give me hope that you are a good advocate of my cause."

"Oh, Doctor, I will be an excellent advocate for you, though I lack the poet's skill to keep my metaphors in tune."

"You know, Father Mottelay, when we first met, I didn't like you. I freely confess it. I thought you arrogant and supercilious."

"Indeed, Doctor? Then I will confess I liked you even less," Mottelay replied good-humoredly. "I found you gifted with the same qualities. More, you did to me seem green in your trade."

"You mean my *profession*," William corrected him. "Medicine is not a trade. No more are you a tradesman as a priest. But tell me, sir, do you like me better now?"

"I do, and I must say it is not only because I sympathize with your plight. It is rather because you seek a good thing."

"A good thing?" William asked.

"Justice—for the faithless wife, her sins notwithstanding. For yourself, your youth notwithstanding."

William said, "And for Thomas Fanshaw, for a murderer must also face justice—either in this world or the next."

"Give me a day or two, Master Johnson, as you desire to be called in this place. Stay close in the inn, that you be not seen. I'll return, I promise you, and God willing I will have good news."

"Good news?"

"An invitation to Parmenter Hall to disclose to Sir John your weighty evidence. I warn you, though, he may want to see your evidence for himself. With his own eyes."

"I will show him, and gladly," William said. "You and he shall learn that what I say is true."

"It may take me a week to persuade him to hear you out," Mottelay said.

"I am nothing if not patient," William said.

"Meanwhile, since I am doing you a service will you do one for me—in your professional capacity?"

"You're in need of a doctor?" William asked, hoping that the priest did not want him to use his magnets for any dubious purpose.

"Not I," Mottelay said. "A young friend, whose family grieves over her state and old family remedies and our town physician and apothecary have failed to heal. This is a young girl, but five or six, a lovely child much beloved by those who care for her. They are tenants of Sir John, a peat-cutter and his wife, and live on Parmenter land, but far removed from the Hall. You might visit there without fear of detection from Sir John or any of his household."

"How far removed from here?"

"Three miles I would judge, not more. It's an easy walk. You could do it in less than an hour and it would be better for you than being holed up here. I will, like a good pilot, mark your course to the farmstead. You shall not go amiss, I warrant you."

William paused to think about this. He was relieved that the service was medical. At least he could do the work for which he had been trained. But Mottelay must have seen his hesitation.

The priest said, "If your visit to them is successful, that is. If you succeed in healing the child, you will advance your own cause with the Parmenters mightily."

"How so?" William asked.

Mottelay continued, speaking slowly and thoughtfully. "Sir John and his lady wife have a special interest in the child. If it is you who provide the cure, it will convince them of your innocence all the more. Gratitude is an asset in any negotiation. You shall see for yourself if you are as wise and perceptive as you think you are."

"I don't understand," William said, ignoring the allusion to his pride, for which earlier the priest had taken him to task. But he did feel that there was something more to Mottelay's request than had thus far been revealed. William was uneasy, and despite the good fellowship that had developed during their conversation, his trust in Mottelay was still tentative, like a hypothesis pending proof.

"You may trust me to act on your behalf, both in this service I have asked of you and the service I will do you with Sir John and his lady," Mottelay said.

The priest smiled broadly, drained his cup, and rose to go. He signaled to the tapster and paid the charge of his drink and William's supper. "I will go before you and tell them that a Doctor Johnson, a learned graduate of Cambridge University, is sojourning here, has heard of their daughter's case and, his bowels moved to pity, does offer to treat her gratis."

William laughed. "No cost? You are free, sir priest, with my time and talents. Besides, will that not make them suspicious, such an offer? What doctor cures without pay for his service? William remembered it was a question Fanshaw had asked of him at his first interview.

"I think not. The Digbys, which is their name, are more likely to suppose your fee is being paid by their landlord. They will not hesitate to accept your offer of help or question your motives for so doing. Don't worry, Doctor. The more I think upon it, the more confident I am that it will work to your advantage."

"And is Sir John Parmenter so generous with his tenants?"

"In the case of this family, yes. Their name is Digby, as I have said. Jonah and Joan Digby."

William repeated the names.

"Think, Doctor, your reward will be in heaven for your service, as is my own."

"Pray God we may both be rewarded before that time," William said. "I am loath to think I need die before I am paid."

21

He slept late, until nearly seven of the village clock, dressed, went below to breakfast, and was approached by the innkeeper, a fat, slovenly fellow with wiry hair and a filthy apron.

"Here, sir, Sir John's secretary, Master Mottelay, left this note for you."

William opened the paper that had been folded in two and bore the name of Johnson on the front. Within was a roughly-drawn map, directing his way to the Digby farmstead. He forgot about breakfast. He fetched his horse from the inn's stable and set out at once.

It was a fine clear day, for which he was grateful, remembering the ordeal of his travel from Maidenstowe back to London only a week earlier. Today, he followed the priest's map and found himself and his horse on a dirt path that crossed flat, fenny land, with marsh grass and sedge. He saw to his right and left occasional farmsteads of a mean, dilapidated sort, sheep and cattle at graze and occasionally ponds of still green water. At last, he came to a rise and having reached its highest point he looked down to see a somewhat more prosperous dwelling that, according to Mottelay's map, was his destination.

This cottage was small but looked well cared-for, with a roof of freshly cut thatch, a single, stone chimney, shuttered windows and a door painted bright red, so that it gave a somewhat welcoming prospect. At the side of the cottage were long rows of peat, cut into brick-like squares, and a cart loaded with them as well. William was hardly within hailing distance when he heard a deep-throated voice from within the house. The shuttered window opened, and a man's head appeared. "Would you be the doctor, sir? Would you be Doctor Johnson?"

When William said he was, the owner of the voice strode from the door of the cottage and walked over to greet him. "I be Digby," he said. Digby was a man William surmised as older than he by four or five years, with massive shoulders and muscular thighs. He wore a simple countryman's smock tied at the waist and had a square, brownish face. Shaggy black hair emerged from beneath his flat cap. As William identified himself, a woman came from the cottage. Digby said, "And this, Doctor, be my wife, Joan."

Joan Digby looked to be about her husband's age, but where he was muscular and dark she was plump, with fat cheeks, mottled skin, and wide-set eyes that gave her face the guileless look of one who saw no evil in the world but only good.

"Master Mottelay told us all about you, Doctor," she said. "You have come to cure our dear Perdita. A doctor from the village could do no good for her, but Master Mottelay gave us to understand that you are very familiar with conditions like unto hers."

Since the priest had not said what their daughter's condition was, William did not know how to respond to this. He said, "I will do what I can for her."

After this he tied up his horse to a post next to the door and followed the peat-cutter and his wife into the cottage. There, he found himself in a single room with a hearth at one end, a rudimentary kitchen and a rough-hewn table and several stools. The other end was concealed by a heavy cloth partition. Here, he assumed, the family slept. He was about to ask where his patient might be found when two ragged children of an age he judged to be four or five came tumbling into the room after their parents, giggling and hitting at one another. They stopped when they saw the stranger among them, and their mother pushed them out the door again, bidding them to go play—for the doctor had come, she said, to make their sister well again.

"Perdita's in here," Digby said gravely, frowning as though the child's fate were already sealed and William had come to give her last rites. The peat-cutter drew the curtain separating the rooms to reveal a single large straw pallet with a sheet drawn over it. A crudely woven blanket was cast aside. On the edge of the bed lay his patient, on her side, her legs curled up so that her knees touched her chest.

The two rowdy children, boys, exiled now to out of doors that the doctor might work, were the very image of their father. Indeed, it was easy for William to see how the features of the father had been replicated in the children, for as young as they were they already had a sturdiness that promised they would in time follow in their father's footsteps and cut peat in the fen, dwell in a humble cottage, and beget children like unto themselves.

But Perdita was different; not merely by reason of her sex, but because of a natural fineness of feature already evident, even in her sickened state. Her unkempt hair was gold, her eyes blue, her skin translucent. Indeed, he no sooner looked into her face than he could not help but see a resemblance to Alice Fanshaw. William knew imagination could be a mischievous trickster, and perhaps he was being played for a fool now. But if this child before him was not the offspring of Alice Fanshaw, then he himself was nothing at all.

The girl eyed him curiously but did not respond to his greeting. Did she fear this strange young doctor, or was she incapable of speech?

He took her shoulders and lifted her into a sitting position. She did not wince, by which he inferred that her bones and sinews were sound enough. But it was plain she was not well. She was listless, and her skin felt hot to his touch.

"How long has she been like this?" he asked the mother.

"For two days, three days," Joan Digby said. "She were healthy and strong and ate like a horse. Now she does not rise from her bed or eat, but will take a little water."

William had no idea what was wrong with this child.

"Where do you hurt, child?"

She pointed to her belly.

"Does it ache there?"

She nodded and looked up at him piteously as though she expected him to wave his hand and make her well again. Other than her complaint, she seemed a healthy, well-nourished child, her skin clear and without the blotches signaling a more devious ailment such as plague or pox. She had been healthy and active in the days before, her mother said. What had poisoned her? Suddenly, he was struck with a memory of another sick child he had tended in Colchester with a similar malaise. A neighbor's daughter had fallen sick from some contagion from the family's well. The cause was discovered when the well went dry and upon digging the man found therein the rotting corpses of dead animals. Dogs, if memory served.

He thought to ask, not the child now, but the mother, "What did she do, I mean before she was afflicted?"

"She played as a child does, Doctor."

"Like unto her brothers?"

He heard the father laugh softly behind him. Digby said, "Nay, Doctor, when she plays, she plays alone. Not with her brothers. I suppose she fears their taunts and slaps."

Joan Digby said, "She has interests of her own, Doctor. Her brothers roughhouse, dig peat and throw great chunks at each other. Perdita is ever roving the fens, collecting flowers and small creatures she keeps in a covered bowl. You may see it if you wish, Doctor, though I doubt it has anything to do with what ails her so."

"I will see it," William answered.

Joan Digby walked over to the corner of the room, reached down, and brought to him a covered bowl. She removed the cover to show him the contents. Within was brownish water and within that William could see swimming creatures that reminded him at first of the leeches he so much detested, but upon closer examination he saw they were a creature of another species, finned and eyed and apparently thriving in this confined watery world. Were they a strange manner of fish? He did not know.

"Them are what we call peatbats," the mother said, "for they abide in the fen water hereabouts, though other folk call 'em by different names. Our daughter loves the creatures. Who can know why? You can't eat 'em, so why save 'em? I ask her, but she loves 'em. She studies 'em. They are like her pets, they are."

"Where does she collect them?"

Digby made a face suggesting he thought the question strange. "About a mile beyond our gate there is a pool of water, very brackish. You would not want to drink the water or take aught from it, but it is the girl's way."

"To drink the water?" William asked, appalled at the thought.

"Nay, Doctor, but to take the peatbats from it."

"I see. Was she at this pool on the day she first fell sick?"

"She was, Doctor," Joan Digby said.

"Do her brothers ever go there?"

"I think not. We can ask them, if you wish, but it is unlikely. They have no interest in water creatures."

"Show me the place."

"You want us to take you to the pool?" Digby looked perplexed. His wife did as well. William could read their minds. What manner of doctor

135

was this, who showed more interest in a fenland pond than in his patient languishing in bed before him?

"I'll take you, Doctor," Digby said. "You just follow me, but don't expect to come back with your shoes dry. This be fenland for sure, for God made it so. Every second step is water."

"It will be alright, Digby," William said. "Don't worry about me. Go on. I'll follow."

It seemed further than a mile, the walk to Perdita's pool, and he was glad when Digby said, "Here it is. See it down there, Doctor, just beyond the verge of those green rushes."

And there it was, a pool of brown water covering no more ground than the Digbys' cottage, with rushes all about, so that he wondered the child could get down to it to capture what these people called her pets. The idea of Perdita, aged six by the priest's account, wandering about in so remote a location, dipping into such water, troubled him. Her curiosity about the creatures did not. He mingled regularly with men—and some women—who like him were curious about the natural world, collected specimens of every kind, corresponded with each other, excited by every new discovery and willing to share it. London's Lime Street, where his friend Kempe lived, was such a place. Why shouldn't this present place be likewise? Every scientist was once a child and most, he suspected, were so inclined in curiosity and discipline from their earliest youth.

He got as close as he could to the pool and then drew closer, pushing his way through the thick rushes until his shoes sank in the moist earth. He looked down into the water and saw a shadow beneath the surface. It was an object, a thing, not moving. Given the murkiness of the water it was a wonder to him that he could see it. This strange thing, appearing like some great amphibian that would presently emerge, wake from its slumber, and crawl toward him threateningly.

"There's something there," he said to Digby, pointing to the shadow.

"Aye, Doctor, 'tis the pond that's there."

"No, more than the pond," William said. "Something floating just beneath the water. Come and see for yourself if I lie."

Digby came to where William stood, moving deftly through the rushes as William had not.

"Do you not see it?" William asked, hoping that the peat-cutter would answer that he did, for William feared he might be seeing things, even as he imagined Perdita might be Alice Fanshaw's lost child, a thought he could not get out of his head.

William was relieved when Digby answered that he *did* see something, and knew not what it was, though it was indeed something that he would not expect to see in a pond, at least not a pond in his part of England.

It was a dead man.

22

William watched as the peat-cutter stripped to his waist, waded resolutely through the rushes, and then sank slowly into the water. The pond was deeper than William had supposed, how deep and noxious he could not imagine. Digby was up to his neck in it. The peat-cutter approached the body, cradled it in his arms and then turned to make his way slowly back to the verge. He grunted in carrying it to William, and laid it down gently like some terrible offering, like a cat bringing a dead rat and dropping it at his master's feet.

Digby whispered, "Blessed Jesu, 'tis Master Gresham."

"How do you know him?" William asked, looking at the dead man.

"He was Sir John's gentleman, his steward, sir. When Sir John wants to talk to us, he sends a message by Master Gresham, or Master Gresham comes himself. He's served at the Hall as long as I can remember. We haven't seen him for a week or more."

William judged the man to be thirty or thirty-five, smooth-faced, fully and well clothed, his face composed and unwrinkled. It was a scholar's face, or maybe a cleric's, with a sharp, delicate nose and thin lips. He could not have been in the water for many days, William thought, although he had heard that peat water might have some preservative effect.

The man's pale blue eyes were open, unclouded. The pale lips slightly pursed, as though he were about to speak. From the corner of his mouth dangled a piece of sedge that William at first thought to be some creature, perhaps a worm.

William looked more closely at the dead man's shoulders and chest. He saw no sign of wound or bruise to suggest a violent death. Perhaps Gresham had simply drowned—but then, why would he? Surely, he would not have gone into the pond willingly, to swim or to fish or to find local fauna, peatbats, as Perdita had done. The water was brackish and unwholesome. His body must have been put there by someone, but for what reason? No English person disposed of their dead so casually, without rite or proper burial. It would have been sacrilege. It was a suspicious death, then, unlikely to have been an accident.

Something prompted him to examine the body more closely. He carefully removed the dead man's upper garments, exposing his hairless chest, and found what he was looking for. It was a small puncture mark below the dead man's left breast. It was the same manner of wound that had marred the perfect flesh of Alice Fanshaw, and it had achieved the same mortal result.

Behind him, Digby asked, "Should I go fetch my cart, Doctor? I can carry him back to the Hall in it. Sir John and his lady will be most sorry to learn of Master Gresham's death. I know they thought much of him, though he were only a servant. And he was a great favorite of their daughter Alice, she who is now herself dead as we have heard."

"A great favorite?" William asked. "She knew him well?"

"Oh quite well, Doctor. Or so I have been told by them up at the Hall."

"Yes, fetch your cart," William said.

"Will you be coming too, Doctor?"

William said he would remain by the body.

It was a good while before Digby returned, but it gave William time to think of how this death might be related to Alice Fanshaw's. At first, while he found the presence of the dead man curious, he saw no common bond. But now he did. There was the similar wound, made perhaps by the same weapon or instrument. Alice and this secretary were close, according to Digby. Might he have been the father of her child? If so, he would not have been the first servant to copulate with a member of his master's family and get a son or daughter thereby.

But there was another thing to consider. Perdita had been drawing her creatures from the depths of the pond. Perhaps she had drunk from it, either purposely or by accident. A decomposing body released malevolent gases that could poison the living. He had read of such things. Sometimes whole towns or villages fell victim to the pollution, like the child of his neighbor in Colchester. Was this the cause of Perdita's sudden sickness, which had struck her but none other in her family?

He circled the pond and found on the side opposite the body a path where Perdita might have approached the water. He thought he saw marks there where she would have planted her knees to lean over and look for the creatures that beguiled her. He imagined her doing so, filling her little bowl. He was relieved. She would not have seen the horror beneath the surface from that place. The thought of a child seeing such a sight disturbed him, even though in his world children were rarely spared the ugliness of death. Parents took their children to public executions, hangings, bear-baitings, and dog fights. Children were present at duels and brawls and often at the bedside of a parent or sibling dying in unspeakable agony. Still, he was relieved for her sake. Yet although invisible as it was to her, Gresham's corpse would have had its effect, poisoning the water. Poisoning her.

Digby returned. William helped the peat-cutter lift the dead man into the cart. He rode back to the peat-cutter's cottage with the corpse. He was growing used to the smell now, although Digby had wrapped a scarf over his nose and mouth. Digby said he needed to take the body on to the Hall. He said again how much the Parmenters thought of Gresham, how saddened they would be by his death. He was more family member than servant, he said again.

"Master Gresham was very dear to Sir John. He will want to see him, even as he is now."

"You go," William said. "I want to examine your daughter again."

"She won't die, will she, Doctor?"

"I think not. Have hope, Digby. Say your prayers."

Digby gave a sigh of relief. "Sir John and his lady would be most unhappy if anything were to befall that child. And unhappy with us for letting it happen," he added.

William found Digby's wife sitting by Perdita. Her husband had told her about Gresham, she said. She had seen his body in the cart and was in great distress of mind, shaking her head and declaring what an evil world it was when a good man might be drowned dead and his body left uncared for. William agreed it was a dreadful thing, but did not say the death was murder. He thought the woman had enough to contend with as it was.

When she was more calm, he said: "Tell me how Perdita's been."

"Well, Doctor, as I've said, she won't take food, complains of her belly aching, and, oh yes, she had the runs."

"You mean she had a loose stool?"

"If that's what they call it. It smelled foul and was all watery. Poor wretched child."

"And the doctor you had here to see her before me?"

"Doctor Simkins. Well, sir, I don't think he's a real doctor, but he would have us in the village call him so for his dignity's sake."

William asked her what she meant, although he could guess and guessed rightly.

"He learned his craft from pure experience, I mean. He never went to school, as I understand you did, nor had any—what do you call it?"

"License."

"Yes, sir, I think it is a license he lacks. He says often that all he knows about healing he learned at his mother's knee and by an old book of herbs he has."

"What treatment did he prescribe?"

"Why, sir, he wanted to bleed her. He said her sickness proceeded from an imbalance in what he called the humors. He used other big words I've never heard of."

"I am sure he did," William said. "And did he bleed her?"

"Oh no, Doctor, I wouldn't let him touch her. A wise woman from the village came and gave her some syrup but she vomited it up as soon as she tasted it. The woman got angry at that and said Perdita would die soon because she refused her medicament. She said the devil was in her and that's why she vomited it up, the syrup."

"Did this woman say what was in this syrup?"

"No, Doctor, I asked her, but she said it was a concoction of her own and she didn't want any other person to know how it was made."

"Bleeding her would have made her worse," William said. "As for the syrup, God knows what it might have been, either for her benefit or hurt. Where do you get your water for drinking?"

"There's a spring just beyond the pasture," the woman answered.

"Does she ever drink water from the pond where she catches these creatures that she's fond of?"

"Well, I think she might, sir. On a hot day, she might. I mean who would not if he's thirsty? Our water is good here. None of us gets sick of it."

"Unless there's a dead body floating in it," William said.

The woman covered her face and began to weep. "Blessed Jesu, sir, what's to come of us? Oh God, sir, Sir John put us in charge of 'er and now she's dying. What will he think, and the lady as well, who so dotes upon 'er and calls 'er pretty names."

"Perdita isn't your child, then?" William asked, although he already knew the answer.

The woman clasped her hands to her face and sighed heavily, "Oh, I have said too much, Doctor. I have spoken out of turn. My husband will be angry with me, and Sir John as well."

William put his hands on the woman's shoulders. "Don't fear. Your secret is safe with me. I have no interest in your lord's business or family matters. That you spoke will be our secret, just the two of us."

Joan Digby looked relieved. But William wanted, needed, to know more. He led her out of the cottage into the air. He did not want Perdita to overhear, though she seemed asleep.

"Sir John put the child in your charge, from what age?"

"Why, since she was but a babe."

"And her true mother?"

Digby's wife gasped. She hesitated before answering. William knew this was a deeper layer of mystery. But then she said, "Sir John's daughter, Alice. She was but a child herself when she gave birth. The family sent her off to her uncle's house far to the north while she was carrying the child. There was no thought of getting rid of it. Lady Parmenter would have none of that. She's a very religious woman, you know. She said the child was a gift of God. It was, after all, their blood grandchild, and they have none other."

"Do you know who the father is?"

"Oh, Doctor, God knows who he may be. Alice was a wild child, and I fear the truth is that she had more than one—what shall I call 'em?— boys and young men to sue for 'er favors. But she was far too young for such things as she did, and certain it is that she was too young to marry."

"Though not too young to take a lover," he said.

"A sad truth, sir. The girl would not be ruled."

"This man who died, whose body we found. Your husband said he was a servant at the house."

"Yes, Doctor, his name was Gresham, Simon Gresham."

"And he had been Sir John's servant for many years."

"Yes, sir. As long as my husband and I have been married."

"Your husband said that he and Alice were friendly."

"Oh, I doubt it was anything improper, Doctor. When she were a child, I do mean Alice, Master Gresham looked after 'er. Lady Parmenter was often sick and unable. When she got with child, I mean Alice, not 'er mother, it was Master Gresham who took 'er up to the north country to stay with her uncle and aunt. And it was he who brought the babe to us, here. Master Gresham arranged it all. He knew we wanted children but could not have 'em, though my husband and I tried enough. He told us the child were an orphan, the parents dead, but we knew right well what child it were and who the mother were. That wasn't much of a secret. She is 'er mother's glass, if there ever were one. Master Gresham said Sir John wanted the child cared for. He said Sir John would pay the cost of it."

"And you accepted, you and your husband?" William asked.

"We were twice blessed, I thought then, Doctor. We wanted a child of our own, and we needed the money. We are poor, sir. We do not profit, Doctor, otherwise. Taking the babe helped us, then and now. I pray you do not judge us harshly for what we did then."

"I don't judge you," William said. "But you are sure this Gresham is not Perdita's father? Such couplings are not unheard of in great houses."

The woman thought for a minute. "My husband imagined he might be so, but I do not, Doctor. But then what happens between man and maid when they are alone so regularly, well, sir, maybe I can't be the one who says he's not Perdita's father. He comes, or came, regularly to see her here. He said his duty was to make report to his master, Sir John, of how the child thrived, and to discover whether we were good parents. I think in time they would have taken 'er to the Hall and said she was some cousin or such. Some person worthy of the Hall, a Parmenter. Then after we had her but six months, I myself got with child, twins, sir, as you have seen. 'Twas then we knew we had done the right thing."

"The right thing?"

"Taking Alice's child for our own, Doctor. Because we did, we was blessed with those boys you've seen. Our service to Sir John was rewarded by heaven."

"When was the last time Gresham was here?"

"Why it has been at least a week, sir, maybe two. Five days past, Sir John sent a servant around to ask if we had seen 'im. The servant said

Master Gresham had not come home again and there was concern at the Hall that he might have been robbed along the road, or had some other mishap. Such things have happened, Doctor."

"When Gresham came to visit you, what did he do?"

"Do, sir?"

"I mean with the child."

"Well, Doctor, sometimes he would bounce 'er on his lap, and sometimes he would sing a pretty song to 'er. Master Gresham had a tolerable voice, and he was very loving, sir, more interested in 'er than one would suppose a person to be who had no relation to 'er, but only because she was the granddaughter of Sir John and he owed 'im a duty, which he did faithfully perform."

"Did he ever speak to you about Alice?"

The woman thought for a minute. Then she said, "Why no, sir, I don't think he ever did."

"Did Alice ever come here to see her daughter? "

"Not since her marriage to old Master Fanshaw."

"Do you think Master Fanshaw knew about Alice's child?"

"Oh, I shouldn't think so, sir. No, I shouldn't think so at all. He would have been angry if he did and may not have married 'er. What gentleman wants a wife who is soiled, as Alice was? With her child begot by God knows who? Her father and mother put her out as a virgin, pure and undefiled. But she was not so. No, Doctor, I doubt her new husband knew anything about 'er history or that there was ever a child of her body."

"She's a beautiful child, Perdita," William said.

"She is indeed," Digby's wife said. And then she shook her head sadly. "Still, she is fatherless for all that. A bastard, really, though she be fair as fair can be."

They went back into the house. The girl had fallen asleep on her side, her body curled with her knees raised to her chest. Her forehead was beaded with sweat. Her breathing was shallow, her pulse rapid, fluttering like a sparrow's wings.

William said to Joan, "Bathe her face and chest in fresh water to cool her. Be sure she drinks plenty of water, clear water, more than she wants, nothing stronger. Her fever will pass. Feed her soft foods only, a boiled egg, a piece of flesh, chicken or duck. She will not die, I assure you, but let no other doctor or wise woman attend her. No drawing of blood, either by knife or leech. The man who may be her father has poisoned her—not by design, but in his very dying. But the contamination will pass. Trust me."

"Oh Doctor, I do trust you," Joan said. "But please, I pray you don't tell my husband what I have told you of 'er. Let him think you believe the child to be of my own body and he the father, as is put out in the village."

"I'll keep your secret, I promise," William said, thinking that the keeping of other people's secrets had now become a way of life for him.

He promised to return the next day.

23

When William returned to the inn, the innkeeper handed him another note from Mottelay. It said that he had begun his work of reconciliation, which he prayed might come to fruition soon. He urged patience. He trusted William had found a way to help the child.

William thought about the priest and their newly-forged relationship. What should he call it—a compact? An alliance? How should he know? He was sure, however, that Mottelay knew Perdita was Alice's child. Mottelay had been a resident of Parmenter Hall before the Fanshaw marriage, intimate with the family and therefore knowledgeable of family affairs, perhaps even while Alice was with child by her unknown lover. Why hadn't he told William but let him discover it for himself, which William might not have done at all? Had Mottelay known about Gresham's disappearance and death? Was this part of a larger plan yet to be revealed? And would such a plan benefit the both of them, or only Mottelay?

William was still thinking about that question when a knock came at the door. William rose to answer the summons, but before he could the door opened and Mottelay appeared.

"I have only just read your message," William said as the priest entered without invitation and sat down heavily upon the bed.

"I am come now on more pressing business, Doctor."

"What manner of business, Master Mottelay?"

"Digby brought a dead body back to the Hall, shortly after I sent the message you hold in your hand. He was Simon Gresham, Sir John's steward. Both Sir John and his lady wife are inconsolable. He was indispensable to the family affairs, especially Sir John's business interests."

"All this I know," William said. "He was his master's factotum, his secretary, his steward."

"How did you know that?"

"Because I found his body. Digby was with me and told me who Gresham was. I told Digby not to mention my part in the discovery, but to say he found the body himself."

Mottelay said, "Wisely done, Doctor. Sir John might have thought you had murdered the man yourself. It would have complicated my efforts to make peace betwixt you both. As to Gresham, he was more family friend than servant. He kept accounts for Sir John, conducted business, private business, some of which even Lady Parmenter was unaware of. You could say he was a trusted advisor."

"I do hope Digby didn't tell them I had a part in finding him."

"Of course not. As I have said, that would spoil all," Mottelay said. "I am still at work paving the way that your story should be credited. Your part in discovering Gresham would do nothing less than make them more suspicious of you."

"Well, it was an inadvertent discovery, although a beneficial one," William said. "I thereby learned, I think, what had sickened the child. The dead body's pollution of the water where Perdita was wont to go. I do not doubt that she drank from it. Or perhaps only dipped her hands in it."

William thought of the girl's father, who had gone into the pond to retrieve the corpse. Would he be his next patient?

"Will she recover, do you think?"

"I believe she will. Her present pains will pass, unless this village doctor—"

"Simkins?"

"Yes. Unless he bleeds her. There's a wise women of the village that tried to force some medicinal syrup on her. She vomited upon taking it, vomited on the woman. She needs healthy liquids, mainly fresh water and plenty of it, chicken broth, soft-boiled eggs. No more drinking pond water."

"Simkins is an old fool," the priest said, shaking his head. "He bleeds his patients for every condition under the sun until they are worse for the cure than for the condition itself. He once prescribed the ground up skull of an unburied corpse as a cure for Sir John's gout, whereupon Sir John sent him packing. You see now why I asked you to attend her. We are in the wilderness here, Doctor, and ignorance is king thereof."

"So, Father Mottelay," William said. Let us speak of Perdita. I know she is Alice's child. Why didn't you tell me when you sent me to cure her?"

Mottelay smiled at the question, a response that surprised William. "Well, in truth," Mottelay said, "I thought you were observant enough to see the resemblance between mother and child straightway and thereby put two and two together. Look, Doctor, I am under a heavy obligation to keep what I have learned in Alice Fanshaw's confession a secret. I would have violated that obligation had I told you she had had a child out of wedlock before she married Fanshaw. But if you discerned that yourself, which I knew well you would, then her confession had nothing to do with it."

"Reasoned like a good Jesuit," William said. "But I will tell you, sir priest, something that you don't know beyond the fact of Gresham's death. He was murdered, not drowned as Digby and the Parmenters believe. And not only murdered but killed by a weapon or device like unto that which killed Alice."

"Murdered? Are you sure?"

William told him about his inspection of the body, how first he saw nothing untoward in his appearance until he removed his doublet and shirt beneath and saw the tiny wound, as unnoticeable as a mole or wen, but as deadly as Alice's injury had been.

The priest pressed his hand against his forehead as though in pain. "But are you sure, Doctor? You haven't mistaken his death's cause? You found him floating in the pond. Might he not simply have drowned?"

"He may have drowned, but first he was rendered helpless by the wound, so it is all one. Gresham did not die a natural death, nor did he take his own life."

Mottelay said, "No, he wouldn't have done that, take his own life, I mean."

"There is, then, a link, a ligature, between his death and Alice Fanshaw's. Tell me more about Gresham and Alice."

The priest said, "This that you call a ligature is no more or less than this—that Gresham came to be employed by Sir John sometime during Alice's tenth year. He sometimes acted as Alice's tutor, for he was well educated. At one of the Cambridge colleges, I think."

"Which college?"

"I don't remember. St. John's I think?"

"That's my old college, but I don't remember him there. Perhaps he was before my time, or only briefly there. Let boy or man pass a week in college and he boasts of his matriculation to the end of time. Alice's lover—I asked Digby's wife if she thought Gresham might have been he. They were close, she said."

148

"What did Joan Digby conclude, about Gresham and Alice?"

"That he was not the one."

"I am of the same mind," Mottelay said.

"Why are you so certain?"

"Because Gresham was drawn to boys, not girls. It's no secret at the Hall. It is for that reason that Gresham was entrusted with Alice's care. No, there is nothing that Alice had, either then or now, that he should delight in her body and get her with child. But I am surprised Joan Digby disclosed anything to you about Alice Fanshaw. She is a simple, good-hearted creature if there ever was one, and she and her husband were bound by direct order of Sir John not to reveal Perdita's true parentage."

"I drew it out with some effort," William said, "then promised her not to tell her husband she told me anything about the Parmenters."

"I can tell you another thing about Gresham. It's something you may learn yourself if I succeed in making peace between you and Sir John."

"Which is?"

"When Alice first knew she was with child she ran away with her lover and took with her a strongbox in which there was a goodly amount of gold and silver that Sir John had secured from various investments in the City. Gresham was sent after them. Of course, Sir John wanted his money back, too. Perhaps more than he wanted his daughter, who had always been a vexation to him."

"And did Gresham catch his prey?"

"Alice only. Not her lover. Not the money."

"Alice never revealed the father of her child?"

"Some boy from the village, she said. She said her lover had abandoned her and taken the money with him. Lady Parmenter was so grateful for her daughter's return that she convinced Sir John to let the matter go, to write the loss of his money off as he might a lost wager. Then, before Alice began to fully show her condition, Gresham took her up to Norfolk to a relative's house where she gave birth in secret. The rest you know. They gave the child, Perdita, to the Digbys to raise, at least during her early childhood."

"A boy in the village, her lover, some farm boy or apprentice black-smith?" William was almost disappointed. "The two of them conspired to steal her father's money?"

"So much for filial duty," Mottelay said. "I could tell you stories about that, Doctor, when you are at leisure to hear them. You will thereby turn as much a cynic toward filial duty as have I."

"Gresham seems then to have been a faithful servant," William said.

"By all accounts, he was."

"But what about his disappearance? Did Sir John do nothing about it when his steward just vanished?"

"He did. He sent out men all about the county asking for him. They searched for a week or more. Sir John finally concluded that Gresham must have fallen ill somewhere, died somewhere. He couldn't believe after all those years that he would just leave service. Gresham had no family living. Few, if any, friends in the village."

"No enemies that would want to do him harm?" William asked.

"None that I know of. And I ministered to the family for the last few years, I think I would have known."

"I suppose you wouldn't say whether Alice, in her confession, revealed to you the name of this boy from the village, or the name of her more recent lover, assuming as we do the father of her more recent child was not her husband."

The priest frowned, looked at his hands, then up at William.

"You're right, Doctor, I wouldn't say. I will not say. I will not even say whether the names of either man or boy was mentioned or a part of her confession. That is between her and God now."

The two men fell silent, then William said, "Tell me you're moving forward with my cause. I don't want to grow old with this uncertainty and this danger."

"I assure you I am moving forward, Doctor. When do you visit Perdita again?"

"In the morning. I promised the Digbys I would return tomorrow and attend to the child. Pray God, she is getting better."

"I tell you it will help your case with Sir John more than you know. I am softening him up, if you know what I mean. And when he is soft enough, I will commend you to him for restoring his granddaughter's health. He will then think the better of you. Do trust me on this."

24

As promised, William returned to the peat-cutter's cottage in the morning. This time he walked, being as it was a dry, fair day with not a cloud in the sky. But before he could see the sick child he was met by Digby. Digby told him he had done what William had asked of him. Digby had received a shilling for bringing home Gresham's body. It was an ill wind that did nobody good, William thought.

William had not told Digby of the wound he found in Gresham's chest. It was not information he felt compelled to share with the man whose discretion he was not ready to trust. Much less, share indirectly with Sir John Parmenter. There would be time later to reveal to the Parmenters the grim truth of the murder and see what Sir John and his lady would make of it.

"How did the Parmenters react to your finding their secretary dead?"

"Why, they were first much amazed, Doctor. But then they grieved, sir, as much as you might expect, Master Gresham being so long in their employ and so faithful in every way. Why, he was almost like a son to Sir John."

"They were that close, were they?" William asked.

"Oh, close as could be. I would say they were more friends than master and servant.

William thought about the two murders—Gresham and Alice. The similarity of the wounds suggested a similar instrument. Suggested, not proved, not as yet. And, of greater weight to him, it suggested the same murderer. Suggested, not proved, not as yet. The secret was in ferreting out the link between the two. Something more than just the household tie. Something more sinister and worthy of a murderer's malice.

Digby led him into the cottage. Perdita was upright, sitting by the fire where Digby's wife was cooking something. Color had returned to her face and her lips. Joan Digby had combed the girl's hair and it now flowed around her shoulders, so that the resemblance between Perdita and her dead mother was even more striking.

He spoke to her. "How are you, pretty maid? How are your creatures this morning?"

He had seen the bowl, the brown water, and the peatbats swimming about, happily unaware that they had been removed from their native place. Or so he imagined.

"They are well enough, I think, Doctor," she said. "But sometimes they don't live beyond a day or two."

She spoke in a soft, shy voice and looked at him as though he would demand that she throw her pets away. She repeated what she had said about the brevity of these creatures' lives. She said, "You're a doctor. You know things."

"I know some things, not all things," William said.

"Do you know why their lives are so short?"

He did not. Who did? But he wondered how Mottelay would answer such a question. He would probably assign it to God's will, the duration of a creature's life. Or find the answer in some ancient Father of the Church who had written of such mysteries. God's will. It was as good an answer as any he had. He knew that there was a great chain of being. God was at the apex, His angels beneath. Then came man with creatures of lesser intelligence—and by extension spiritual worth—below. He suspected Perdita's creatures were near the bottom. Their brief lives need not be longer, because they had little to do. What use might they make of raw time? Yet he knew the same could be said for man. Was anyone's life long enough? Alice Fanshaw's had been abruptly cut off, her unborn child's life extinguished before it began. But Perdita deserved a simpler answer.

"God's will," he said. Perdita smiled and nodded. Evidently the answer was enough for her.

"Is she drinking water, fresh water?" he asked her mother.

"Oh, she is, Doctor, though I must force it down her. She's such a willful child."

Like her mother, William thought, but did not say.

"Does she eat?"

"Sparingly. I made her pea soup. She ate a bit of bread, but only a bit."

"Very well," he said. "Save the bread for later when her stomach is up to it. But she looks better, much better. I will be back tomorrow. I'll return until she's as well as before. Don't worry."

He took a look at Perdita. She was busy with her creatures. She was the very image of a young scientist. It pleased him to think about that. God willing, her life would turn out better than her mother's—and longer.

25

Perdita continued to improve over the next few days. By her mother's report, she was a healthy girl at the outset of her sickness. William was thus not surprised she recovered at such a pace. In the meantime, he heard nothing from Mottelay. No notes, much less an appearance. This worried him. What did the silence mean, that Mottelay had given up on him?

Meanwhile, he wrote two letters, one to Orlando Kempe in London, the other to Pieter Weinmeer in Amsterdam. Kempe had asked for a written account of his discovery of the evidence against Thomas Fanshaw. William provided it in a missive that took half the day to write. The letter to Weinmeer was easier to compose, less detailed, and was more a narrative of recent events, his friendship with the priest, and his patient Perdita, whose true maternity he disclosed. He thought Weinmeer would take interest in Perdita's case, for he knew the Dutch physician often treated the children of rich burghers of the city, although a child poisoned by a decaying corpse was admittedly no common thing.

To Weinmeer's letter he added a postscript for Katerina. It sent his good wishes for her health and inquired into her current reading. In truth, he cared little about her reading, but he knew she would interpret his query aright. Despite the awkwardness of their leave-taking, they had both moved beyond where they had been before. He was no longer her tutor, she no more his pupil. He would have said more in a separate letter to her, but he knew her father's mind was set on a suitable Dutch husband for his daughter. That is, a wealthy burgher but respectful of Katrina's intelligence, not a poor English fugitive with an uncertain future. He did not want to make an enemy of Weinmeer by seeming to distract his daughter from her father's ambitions for her. And yet, he could not deny his heart, which yearned for her, night and day.

He decided to make one last visit to the Digbys. In so doing he would fulfill his promise to Mottelay that he restore Perdita to health and to the Digbys that he would return until she had recovered. He had no thought as to what might happen next.

That morning he chose to ride rather than walk. He found the Digbys working in their small garden. He tied his horse to a post, called out a greeting to the couple, and went inside. He was surprised to find Perdita gone from her usual place by the hearth and was on his way out to the garden when he saw a group of horsemen fast approaching on the road. He counted four riders, then recounted. There were five.

At the head of this band was a person he recognized, and at once his heart leaped into his throat. It was Sir John Parmenter. With him at his side rode Julian Mottelay. The other men, following after, by their dress he thought were probably household servants.

He turned at once and walked hurriedly across the fen, toward the village from whence he had come. He had no time to secure his horse for his escape. Besides, it would have only called attention to his flight. If he were lucky, he would not be noticed. When he reached a slight rise in the terrain he paused and looked behind him. He saw that the men had not dismounted but were talking to the Digbys. He saw Joan Digby point in his direction. They had seen him.

He began to run. He ran for a hundred yards or more over the wet, yielding earth, his heart pounding in his chest, his face wet with sweat. Behind him, he could hear the galloping horses.

But even as he ran faster, he knew escape was futile. He would not escape. He might run all the way to the village, but he would be caught and be brought back to answer for his flight, which marked him guilty even in its very desperation. Moreover, there was no cover on the fen, no hole to hide in or tree with luxuriant growth to conceal him.

He slowed to a walk, his chest heaving. He dared not look behind him. But he could hear the horses at full gallop. Then his pursuers were upon him, surrounding him, the hot breath of the horses blasting him in his face.

He looked up to see Parmenter glaring down at him. "Good day, Doctor Gilbert. Taking the country air, are you?"

William was too winded to answer. Parmenter continued, his face hard.

"Master Mottelay here tells me you have healed the child, for which I am in your debt. She is a sweet child, and it would grieve me were she to be taken at so young an age. He also tells me that you have declared your innocence of my daughter's death and that you proposed an intriguing theory by which you were not responsible, but rather her husband. He says you have proof."

William was still breathing heavily, but he managed to say in a voice that did not sound like his own, "I have such proof. My magnets had nothing to do with her death, nor did they prove she had committed adultery."

"Adultery?" Parmenter said.

So Mottelay had not told Parmenter about Fanshaw's suspicions of his young wife or the purpose of the magnetized blanket.

Parmenter ordered his men to draw back, and they did. Parmenter looked menacingly at William. "I thought the magnets were to improve her general state, to ensure her child's safety. Are you saying, Doctor, that her husband suspected my daughter was unfaithful to him?"

"He did."

"And the treatment was a proof thereof?"

William said, "It was an experiment. Master Fanshaw suggested it. It could have done no harm to her."

"Well might you speak of harm, Doctor Gilbert. My daughter died as a result of your experiment." Parmenter's voice was cold and controlled. It made William even more fearful that Mottelay's efforts to conciliate the grieving father had failed.

"Not by my hand, I swear it, Sir John," William said. "Your daughter was stabbed to death with a pointed instrument, not rocks, not magnets. I found the wound beneath her breast. She bled internally. I say again, the magnets had nothing to do with it."

"You went to her grave and inspected her body? Without my permission or the permission of her husband?" Parmenter asked in a tone suggesting this invasion of his daughter's privacy was a worse offense than her murder.

Until now, Mottelay, who had not withdrawn with the other men and had remained by Parmenter's side, had been largely silent. But then he said, "He speaks the truth, Sir John. I believe him."

"You also have seen this evidence the doctor speaks of?" Parmenter said, looking aside at the priest.

"No, Sir John, I have not seen. Still, I trust the doctor has. I do not think he would lie about this. Were he a murderer he would hardly have come to this place and serve so well in making the child whole again. His honorable service speaks volumes of his innocence."

Parmenter turned from the priest to look at William. Suddenly his expression changed. He had spoken quietly and evenly before. Now, he cried out shrilly to the men with him. "Seize this man, bind his hands. Fetch his horse from the cottage and put him on it."

William looked at Mottelay. He saw the priest had not expected Parmenter's sudden fury any more than William had. Parmenter's men dismounted and rushed toward him before he could speak another word in his defense. In the next few seconds, he was bound and gagged.

26

The little company rode toward Parmenter Hall at a slow, steady pace. There seemed to be no hurry now. It was what William had feared even before leaving Amsterdam and daring to return to England. And now it had happened. It had happened because he had put his trust in the priest and because, in his pride, he thought his capacity to persuade his enemies that he was innocent would prevail over their vengefulness. Orlando Kempe had been right. Getting involved with Mottelay had been foolhardy. Now William was paying the price.

The leather strap tore into his wrists and restricted the flow of his blood so that his hands were numb. Along the way, no one spoke to him. His captors hardly spoke to each other. His guilt seemed a foregone conclusion. What came next in this dark comedy? The magistrates' court? Lord Burghley's condemnation? Perhaps hanging as the final act?

Parmenter Hall sat upon a slight incline and was a stately brick and timber house. It had the stolid, intimidating dignity of a house William imagined a knight of the realm might live in. There were outbuildings toward the rear of the manor and, beyond, dense woodland, all of which William assumed was part of Sir John's domain. Now, William would be prisoner here, at least for the time being.

The main door of the house stood open. And there, as though barring their way in, was a tall, stern-faced woman dressed in such finery as to make William sure this was the lady of the manor, Elizabeth Parmenter.

"Is this the doctor, then?" the woman asked, looking at William as though he were a common malefactor.

"He is the very man," her husband said triumphantly.

He had to be helped down from his horse where one of Parmenter's men unbound his wrists and removed the gag from his mouth. Another steered him down a central hall with a high decorated ceiling and entrances to other chambers on each side of him. Despite what he had heard before about Parmenter being a poor knight, Parmenter seemed well enough off. The house was richly furnished, the house well populated with servants who eyed him curiously as he passed, and when they arrived at the gallery, a long room with a bank of tall windows giving a pretty prospect of the woodland beyond, he was ordered not to speak unless he were spoken to, and to answer every question put to him under pain of death.

Here he was commanded by his guard to sit, with the lord and lady facing him. Mottelay drifted in from another part of the house and stood in the corner, watching. William tried to read the priest's face. Was it smug satisfaction that all had gone bad? Sorrow that he had failed to persuade Parmenter that William was innocent? William couldn't tell.

Elizabeth Parmenter spoke first, which surprised William, for he expected his interrogation to begin from the mouth of her husband, who had clearly taken upon himself the role of chief prosecutor. Lady Parmenter asked about Perdita. About his diagnosis of her sickness from consuming water from the pond. She would have learned that from Mottelay. From the priest she would have learned as well that William was the doctor who had aided Perdita, made her well again.

William told her about Perdita's earlier doctor and wisewoman and their failed ministrations. He described his theory of her illness, what he had prescribed as a remedy. He gave an optimistic report of her condition and foretold her complete recovery. As he did so, he glanced once or twice at the lady's husband, hoping to see some yielding in him. He saw none. He was still the object of Parmenter's detestation, for all the aid he had given the man's ailing granddaughter. Parmenter might have been grateful, but it was not enough to overpower his distrust and hatred.

Lady Parmenter seemed to soften, however. She asked him about her daughter, Alice. About the magnetized blanket. He told the same story again, word for word, because it was true and because he had rehearsed it in his own mind a thousand times. She listened without comment, even when he mentioned the reason for the experiment. Unlike her husband who had expressed umbrage at the accusation of his daughter's adultery, Elizabeth Parmenter took it in her stride. It wasn't until William accused her former son-in-law of Alice's murder that her manner changed.

"Fanshaw," she said as if the very name disgusted her.

"I have evidence," William said.

"It is easy enough to blame another," her husband said, scowling at William. "To claim evidence no one has seen but he. I ask you what manner of evidence is that?"

He had put this question to his wife, but she made no answer. She continued to fix her gaze on William.

"What manner of evidence, Doctor?" she asked. "Tell me the evidence, Doctor Gilbert. Tell me why you believe Thomas Fanshaw murdered my daughter. Wherefore should a doting husband, such as he was, do such a monstrous thing?"

William breathed deeply. He knew he needed to choose his words carefully, but already he suspected that in the room, this stern-faced woman might be more amenable to his narrative than her husband had proved. He said, "Thomas Fanshaw may have doted, but he was also a jealous man, my lady. He had been betrayed by an earlier wife. He told me this at my first interview. He feared your daughter might be carrying another man's child. He was himself impotent, or so he believed."

"And was that true? I mean about his … impotence?" Parmenter asked.

"I had it from his lips, Sir John. Why should he lie? Your daughter explained herself by telling Master Fanshaw he was restored to full manhood after a night's banquet, the marriage feast. It was an improbable story, and he did not know whether to believe her or not but feared the uncertainty more than the knowledge of the truth. He had heard I studied magnets and their powers. He sought me out to perform the experiment. And so I did."

"And did your so-called experiment prove my daughter faithless?" Lady Parmenter asked.

"Fanshaw thought so," William said. "And sought to avenge himself upon her. I have since found evidence that he murdered his earlier wife as well, she before your daughter. He would not be a cuckold for all the world. That he found himself twice so, made it all the more unbearable to him."

Elizabeth Parmenter turned and walked to the window. She stood, a solitary, brooding figure, staring out at the verdant woodlands that surrounded the house. Behind her, her husband started to say something, but she shushed him with a wave of the hand.

She turned back to William. "My daughter was unsteady in her affections, by which I mean she loved much and to her hurt. The girl you saved

160

in the cottage, Doctor, was Alice's daughter, our granddaughter, by an earlier match unhallowed by the Church."

William did not say he knew this or how. He would not betray Joan Digby. But the lady of the manor had obviously not finished.

"I never wanted Alice to marry Thomas Fanshaw. He's a brutish old man. I did not know of his jealous nature, or anything about his earlier wives, save that he had them. Alice's marriage was my dear husband's idea, to restore the family fortunes." She paused to cast a baleful look at Parmenter. "I never liked the man. My God, he was my son-in-law, yet older than I by twenty years or more."

Her husband said nothing in response to this. William suspected Parmenter had heard this complaint before, perhaps many times. It did not surprise William that Parmenter had nothing to say in his defense. The Fanshaw marriage had been no work of Cupid's bow. It had all been about money from the very first. And almost surely about hastening a marriage to cover a second unhallowed pregnancy.

Parmenter pointed to William and said to his wife, "You must know that this so-called doctor invaded our daughter's tomb and had no permission so to do, either from us certainly or from her husband, who though he may have been a devil, nonetheless he was her husband by canon law and in the eyes of God."

Lady Parmenter turned to William. "Is that true?"

William said, "I wanted to know how your daughter died. I wanted to know the truth. Which could not be known unless the body was examined." He continued his account as before, describing the wound he had found, explaining how it would have been fatal. Explaining how the terrible bruising might have convinced Fanshaw that her guilt was proved. He also told her about the decayed corpse of the second wife, also a wanton—at least by report.

"Great God in heaven," Elizabeth Parmenter exclaimed, her face twisted in horror and disgust. "Great God in heaven. What evil is this and what sacrilege! It sickens me to think on it. The whole thing revolts me."

"We have only the doctor's word for this improbable tale," her husband said. But it was a weak protest, and his wife was having none of it.

"Don't be a fool, husband," his wife said, glaring. "Let us put the doctor's word to the test rather than debate fruitlessly. We will go to the churchyard in Maidenstowe where Alice rests. Let the doctor show us himself the wound in her breast, the corpse beneath, all evidence to prove her husband's foul murder. Let us see with our own eyes if what the doctor says is true."

For a few moments Parmenter made no reply. His eyes blazed with defiance, but he seemed afraid to counter his wife's proposal. Finally, he said, "Very well, let us go, but you shall find nothing there this man swears to."

He looked at William with contempt.

"And let us also summon our daughter's former physician, whom we know and trust," Elizabeth Parmenter said.

"Orlando Kempe," William said before her husband could.

"Make all preparations," Lady Parmenter said to a servant who during the conversation had come into the room. "Let us leave as soon as Doctor Kempe can join us. He can advise us whether Doctor Gilbert is correct in his assessment of the cause of our daughter's death or not. I will know the truth, but not by Doctor Gilbert's word alone."

She turned to William. "My daughter was a troublesome child. Beautiful as she grew to be, she was ever disobedient and lascivious. When in recent weeks she summoned Father Mottelay to be her confessor, I had some hope of her redemption, which as a good Catholic I do believe in. As to Thomas Fanshaw, I will not hold my tongue. I do despise the man, and I was ever against the marriage."

She paused and turned to give her husband another disdainful look. Then she said, "Fanshaw is born of coarse common blood and has made his fortune through devious means. All who know him would agree. He is not beyond murder to have what he wants. But we shall presently see your evidence, Doctor Gilbert. And Doctor Kempe will confirm it, if he can and will."

"I do swear, Lady Parmenter, that Thomas Fanshaw is a murderer and that there is proof of it," William said.

Then, Elizabeth Parmenter became suddenly reflective, as though she were speaking now to herself, forgetting there were others in the room. "Thomas Fanshaw married my daughter because he thought her beauty a great prize to raise his state amongst his friends. He may have loved her. That I do not know, nor care now. Beauty fades. I had it once myself, but now, Doctor, you see how worry and disappointment have marred my visage and made me what you see before you. All your medicines and potions cannot cure what time has wrought. Is that not true, Doctor Gilbert?"

She asked this sadly, knowing evidently the answer.

William had to be honest, and he was. "No, madam, no physician, no matter his skill, can cure what time will do. We all fall victim to it, at last. It is God's will, not our own as to the span of our lives or the conditions of our older age."

He expected he would spend that night in some dismal dungeon or stinking outbuilding, a close prisoner waiting for the constable's men to come for him. Instead, he was left unbound, now under the protection of Lady Parmenter, and lodged in an upstairs chamber that one of the Hall's high-born guests might have deserved.

Before sleep, he reviewed the conversation in the gallery below, which had begun in terror and ended, miraculously to him, in a seeming deliverance, or at least the happy prospect thereof. In sum, he had discovered in the few days previous much more than was now being discussed or acknowledged. Was that a good thing, or a bad one? Having the choice, he decided that it was a good thing. The case of Alice Fanshaw was complicated enough. His true goal was to free himself from the false accusation. These other matters pertaining to her history or the murder of Simon Gresham might prove at last to be relevant to that, but for the present his plate was full.

The marital discord of the Parmenters had, surprisingly to him, benefitted his cause, driving a wedge between husband and wife that seemed to put Alice's mother on his side. He was also cheered by the thought that by the next day, his friend Kempe would join them on their journey to Maidenstowe. Then he would have a new ally, who could both attest to his character and the harmlessness of his magnets. A friend who could confirm the cause of Alice Fanshaw's death. Who better to render a second opinion?

Fortune had turned her wheel again. This time in his favor.

27

For all the next day, William was a virtual prisoner in his chamber, during which time he was brought food and provided reading material, in this case a Roman prayer book, which he read more out of curiosity than devotion. For all this, he lived in hope that, his evidence presented, Fanshaw's guilt would be proved, and he absolved.

Then in the evening, he was invited to come downstairs to sup with the household. Here he sat in the midst of portraiture of Parmenter ancestors—for, unlike Thomas Fanshaw, the Parmenters had been landed gentry for generations, honored with titles, gifted with lands, and enjoying marital ties with good families.

At table, Elizabeth Parmenter talked freely of her daughter's childhood. William learned that it was characterized with one escapade after another, many of which brought shame upon the family and considerable expense. She did not speak again of Alice's first pregnancy, the purloined chest of gold and silver, nor did she mention Perdita, her granddaughter. She did, once or twice, allude to the dead secretary that had been her husband's factotum and so loved and regarded as to be held almost a member of the family. She and her husband seemed to assume that Gresham had met with foul play, since an accidental drowning was unlikely and suicide out of the question. Country roads were dangerous roads. At every turn there might be some cutpurse or brigand lurking.

She said that Simon Gresham had been a tutor for their daughter, but later advanced to secretary as he demonstrated an ability to manage her husband's practical affairs. "Besides which," Lady Parmenter observed, "it is not necessary that a girl be greatly educated, her mind filled with facts and useless things. What she needs to know, she may learn readily from her mother's example." Lady Parmenter said this with pride, raising her chin, and looking to William for his approval.

William thought it politick to agree. But he thought of Perdita. She had no tutor to educate her, no fit example of womanhood in the peat-cutter's wife, yet the child was busy educating herself—and unless William was mistaken she would become learned in her own fashion, though she read and wrote no Latin, perhaps not even English yet.

Sir John was not at table. Lady Parmenter said he had gone to London on business and whilst there to fetch Doctor Kempe. She said, with luck, he would return with the doctor within the next few hours. She said she had no doubt her husband would be able to persuade Doctor Kempe to come. "Doctor Kempe is the soul of courtesy and has ever been a friend of this family."

William decided it was best to keep his own friendship with Kempe to himself. That way, he thought, Kempe's opinion would be judged to be more objective, unstained by any personal loyalties Kempe might have to his old university friend.

After supper, Lady Parmenter invited him to pass his time in the library of the house, which was extensive and included a cabinet of curiosities, collected he learned by herself rather than her husband, who she said was interested only in his horses, card games, and what she called *pleasures of the flesh*. She did not specify what fleshly pleasures these might be. She didn't have to. William could imagine.

"My husband is a crass, unlearned man," she confided. "The books you see here were obtained by Gresham and are for show. The Parmenters have been around since William the Conqueror, but he cares little for that. I do, however. His indifference to the finer things of life our daughter inherited. Along with her unseemly wantonness."

Her voice dropped to a conspiratorial whisper. "My husband has been unfaithful to me many times, Doctor. Sometimes with servants in this house, both male and female. Yet I have suffered it, with Our Lady for my present help. He may burn in hell for all I care. He shall deserve it."

She made the sign of the cross and regarded him coolly as though she suspected William of the same offenses as her husband.

William didn't know how to respond to what he was being told. An expression of sympathy for her suffering seemed called for but he was unsure how it should be phrased, given how intimate this revelation was.

He smiled thinly and nodded. Spontaneous eloquence was never his strong suit. He was a slow, deliberate writer, and in speech he often found himself tongue-tied when the subject was so intensely personal as now.

He was surprised but pleased when she left him alone there, amid the volumes Gresham had collected, for show as she had said. He examined them in their new bindings and then in the corner found something that attracted his attention even more than the books.

This cabinet of curiosities was like unto many he had seen of late in the homes of wealthy Englishmen and foreign residents of England as well. Such collections had become a fashion, stimulated by geographical exploration and the expansion of trade. William recalled that his Dutch friend Weinmeer had one such cabinet, full of seashells and sea-bird eggs and other oddities he had collected along the shore and in the flat lands of his watery country.

He had heard that Queen Elizabeth had one too, supplied by her admirals and mariners who delighted in bringing rare gifts from every part of the globe to please Her Majesty's fancy. He thought it a wonder that the monarch of his country was so imbued with an intelligent interest in geography and nature, while other kings and princes took little interest in such matters, but all were fixed upon their own glory, their wars, their marriages and alliances, their prerogatives of office.

The Parmenter cabinet was a tall, exquisitely carved piece with five or six shelves and glass doors, etched with elaborate design, so that the objects within were only dimly seen. Within he could see contents that included antique weaponry; axes, knives, and one short sword he suspected might be of Roman origin, by its design and patina of rust. He saw a helmet that an old Saxon warrior might have worn and some jewelry, crudely made but doubtless of equal antiquity.

There was also a collection of narrow, pointed knives he knew the Italians called *stilettos*. Some of these had needle-like points, and he immediately thought of the wounds in the breasts of Alice Fanshaw and Simon Gresham. A stiletto might have made such a wound, and yet he supposed there were a hundred different tools and devices, even some medical instruments, that might have done the same. It seemed a strange collection to have been gathered by a woman, these weapons of mayhem and murder. But then he decided Elizabeth Parmenter was no ordinary woman, and he

166

felt again a surge of gratitude that she was his benefactress for the time being and not, as her husband, an obdurate enemy.

It was clear to William that in gaining her support, he had lost even more ground in her husband's estimation. Her dismissive comments to Sir John, made in front of a stranger, her calling her husband a fool, could have only offended and made her husband even more determined to find William guilty as charged. Clearly it was not a happy marriage, not even before their daughter's coupling with a man Elizabeth Parmenter despised. In all, William had found himself more at home in the humble surroundings of the Digby cottage than in this dark, intimidating house with its warring lord and lady.

He had not heard a knock at the door. Now he raised his eyes to see Julian Mottelay looking down at him with the same inscrutable expression his face had worn the night before, when the priest had stood in the corner while William was questioned by the Parmenters. In fact, William was happy to find himself alone with Mottelay. The priest owed him an explanation. William was eager to hear it.

"I see I have disturbed your study," Mottelay said. "I am most sorry for it. This is an excellent library. Sadly, the books are largely wasted on this family, although you will oblige me by not telling them I said so."

The priest's cool composure angered him. It was as if nothing untoward had happened, not his being seized, bound, gagged, conveyed against his will to Parmenter Hall, accused, abused, at least verbally. Is this what Mottelay had wrought, what he had achieved through his attempt to soften, as he had called it, the Parmenters?

William looked up and said, "You promised me, sir, you would win Sir John to my cause. If he is won over, then pray tell me what you meant by such an expression, for he has greater hate for me now than ever he did before. He had me bound and dragged here against my will as you yourself witnessed. Even now, in the comfort of this chair, I am a prisoner. Were I to try to leave I would be stopped, bound and no doubt gagged again, and probably end up somewhere in the deepest bowels of this house, not sitting in this most commodious library."

Mottelay sat down and placed his hands on his knees. He looked contrite and, William thought, humbled. He regarded William kindly before he answered, and he waited to speak as though choosing his words carefully.

"You will perhaps not accept an apology from me given your circumstances. I understand that. But like you I was beguiled by Sir John's first response, wherein he seemed more than accepting of your account, called Fanshaw a villain and devil, and promised to speak fair to you when you twain should meet. Seeing him so receptive to my defense of you, I told him where you were. When we rode off to the Digbys to find you, I thought all would be well."

Mottelay paused. William urged him to continue.

"I will tell you the truth, Doctor. I was saddened to see you so abused, and I was shamed for my part in it, though I do swear upon my faith, I never intended anything but to advance your cause. As I have said, I was deceived as much as you by Sir John's calm demeanor."

William studied the priest's face, then said, "Very well, Father Mottelay. I accept your apology and your explanation of these unexpected turns. I'll hold no grudge. It would do neither of us good. Let us move forward and put what friendship remains betwixt us to a test."

"What test, Doctor? I assume it does not involve your magnets."

"I assure you it does not."

"Then I pray I may pass your test, for I swear I never meant you aught but good."

"Tell me then who fathered Alice Fanshaw's child."

The question was out of his mouth before he knew it. Not because he believed the priest knew or would tell the answer, but because it gnawed on him powerfully. Perhaps, William thought, it was the key to everything that mystified him about these murders. There was a long pause at this before the priest answered. The answer when it came did not surprise William.

"I can't tell you."

"What of the father of her first child, Perdita's father? The boy or man she ran off with? The man who took with him the chest of silver and gold?"

"I cannot tell you that either."

"Because of the confession's seal?"

"Because she never revealed it to me in the confession."

"I thought her purpose was to shrive herself of all her sins."

"So it was, though not completely. She always stopped short of her full confession."

"Might it have been Simon Gresham?"

The priest hesitated, then shook his head. "I have told you about him, his proclivities."

"Yes, but still ..."

Mottelay shook his head. "No, it could not have been Simon. The Parmenters kept her under lock and key when she returned until the day of her marriage. Not even Simon had access to her after that, at least not without one or more of her parents present and watchful."

"Look, my priestly friend, I hold her husband guilty of Alice's murder. I saw the hidden wound beneath her breast. But I also saw the wound that killed Gresham. Done by the same hand and weapon, if I do not mistake. If so, I need to know what Fanshaw and Gresham had to do with each other, that he should want him dead as well as his faithless wife."

"That is a mystery, then, I cannot dispel, though I wish I could—to satisfy your curiosity as well as my own," Mottelay said. "Fanshaw visited here in the course of wooing Alice and negotiating with her father. I remember them talking together at least once."

"Talking about what?"

"I don't know. I was rarely privy to Gresham's business. He dealt with Sir John alone. My duties were religious, not commercial."

"Was he a Papist like the rest of the family?"

"He was, but not zealous. Like Sir John, more in name than genuine faith. He was more likely to swear by the saints than venerate them. All came to Mass in chapel when I performed it, knelt and crossed themselves, consumed the host, drank the wine. Prayed, I think, to God. Or perhaps they only shut their eyes. Who can know? Only Lady Parmenter believes sincerely. And Alice, after her repentance."

"Her repentance was occasioned by what?" William asked. "Lady Elizabeth spoke freely of her daughter's youthful indiscretions. I was surprised to hear such private matters disclosed to me, a stranger suspected of her daughter's murder. I almost believed that her candor was motivated by a desire to punish her daughter, broadcast truth from the housetops."

"That may indeed be Lady Parmenter's motive. She's a bitter woman, as disappointed in her daughter as in her husband. As for her daughter's change, it would seem at first view some manner of miracle, like Paul on the road to Damascus. One moment he is an enemy to all who profess Christ. The next he is the sincerest, most devout of converts, a changed man in a flash of light."

"Do you think the pregnancy might have changed her?" William asked.

"I doubt it," Mottelay said. "Perhaps she was merely growing weary of her sins, as though they had become more tiresome habits than pleasures. I can tell you it was not the marriage to Fanshaw, which, at first, she resisted and said she would rather die than be wed to a man as old as Methuselah."

"Then why did she agree to the marriage?"

"Her father urged it. Nay, he commanded it."

"Parmenter needed the money?"

"He was deeply in debt."

"How so?"

"It was the Queen and her extravagant progresses through the country where she does love to mingle with her subjects familiarly. Good Queen Bess they call her who do not have to bear the cost of her. She stayed here a week during the summer last, she and a hundred or more knights, servants, and hangers-on. Parmenter was stuck with the bill for a prodigious quantity of food and drink, banquets every night for all and sundry, all for the honor of hosting the Queen. And, of course, royal entertainment, which these days comes at the cost of a king's ransom. Sir John had to borrow hundreds, thousands to pay for it all, went a-begging to every money-lender in London, Jew or gentile. He faced bankruptcy, ruin, disgrace. The marriage seemed a way out for him, but also for his daughter."

"Because Alice was already pregnant, faced with another disgrace." William said.

"But you said nothing to Fanshaw about her earlier pregnancy?" Mottelay asked.

"It was not his business to know such things about the woman he married," William said.

"You showed wondrous discretion," the priest said. "You might have been a priest, were you of a different mind."

"Discretion is part of my calling," William said. "I do hate a physician who gossips like an old woman at market. A patient should expect her doctor to keep mum about her personal matters. We are not bound as you priests may be, by oath and sacred covenant, the seal of the confession and all that, yet we do have ethics that seal our lips."

"Just so," Mottelay said, smiling. "And I am most glad to hear you say so, for were you my attending doctor, I would hope you would not disclose, were I in some delirium, the multitude of my sins, though I confess them."

"Trust me, Father, I would not do so, not for all the world."

"Well, it would seem we often read from the same page, Doctor, though you be a heretic and I a devoted Papist, as it pleases you to call us."

"I have no appetite for religious controversy," William said. "Although it becomes increasingly difficult to avoid in this time and place. My god is the god of nature. I know him through His creation. I study Him in rocks, in the leaves of plants, in the powers of my magnets. He is the Supreme Artificer, the god of iron and steel, earth and water. Which creed is that? Protestant? Catholic? I know not and care less for such categories, which to me do more to inflame passions and provoke wars than instill obedience to the Prince of Peace, whom I also honor."

"Eloquently spoken, Doctor," Mottelay said. "You see in me a priest of Rome who will rest content that you believe what you will. I will not try to convert you to my faith, since the faith you have will I trust lead you to heaven without the intercession of any church, mine or Luther's. Let us shake hands and be friends again. I long to know you better and in a more tempered season would desire to learn of you about your magnets, the world on which we ride, and what exists below the surface of things."

William felt the firmness of the priest's hands, which were larger than his and strangely calloused as though he worked with his hands rather than his head and heart. William said, "And for my part, I will gladly teach you what I have learned through diligent study. I warn you, though, it may contradict the learned Fathers of the Church, at least those who wrote of natural things. What I know I have learned more directly, through experiment."

They talked an hour or more of these matters; of William's science. The priest listened carefully, and sometimes asked questions, which William answered, aiming to be clear and concise and accurate. And so pleasant it was for William to speak freely of what he loved that he nearly forgot where he was and why he waited, still a prisoner of the house and under the threat of arrest.

"Will you come to the Maidenstowe tomorrow?" William asked.

"No," Mottelay said. "I don't like cemeteries. I am depressed by them, to tell the truth. But also, I haven't been invited. I would have no purpose there, save perhaps to console her ladyship in her grief. But I should leave you now to your books. It would do neither of us good if Lady Parmenter found us conspiring together, or any of her household. Go with your God of nature, Doctor, and have faith. You are on the threshold of your deliverance from these difficulties."

"God willing," William said.

28

Within the hour, William had fallen asleep over his book. He dreamed he was back in his Cambridge college, in the large and imposing chamber where the mysteries of anatomy and physiology were taught. His professor, a wizened old man with a long white beard, had secured a cadaver for their study and was holding up, before a half dozen students of whom William was one, the heart of the deceased. It was both a wondrous and monstrous thing to behold, the human heart, which seemed to William to be still beating, although it had been freshly plucked from the dead man's chest.

The learned lecturer beckoned William to come forward and take the heart. This William did, feeling the leathery muscle that seemed to move in his hand as though, released from the prison of the chest, the organ had come to life again. Then William looked down at the body of the cadaver. The face was uncovered. Earlier in the dream it had been the face of an old man. Suddenly it became the face of Alice Fanshaw. William cried out and dropped the heart.

He woke himself with his outcry and rubbed his eyes to clear them from sleep, and to help him remember where he was, and why. His heart was beating rapidly. It took several minutes before he calmed himself enough to think clearly. He understood that his vision was a dream, no reality that threatened him. Then, he heard a soft knock at the library door.

He said "come," and a servant stuck his head only within, as though his master had forbidden him to enter. He said, "Sir John has returned and brought with him the other doctor, sir. He wishes you to attend on him."

"Very well," William said, realizing that this servant was one of the men who had captured him before but whose placid, differential face now belied their brief but violent earlier confrontation. He wondered if all could suddenly change, and this same servant could seize and bind him again. Could all comity he had more recently enjoyed in Parmenter Hall be but a dream, an illusion, like the dream he had just had?

He shook himself and put that fear from his mind in anticipation of seeing his friend again. He stood just as Parmenter and Kempe entered the library.

Sir John Parmenter gave William a sour look and shoved Orlando Kempe forward, as though he were presenting a gift to his unwanted and despised guest. "Here's the doctor," Parmenter said. "For all the help he can give us here—or give *you*, I should say."

Parmenter strode off in a great show of disdain, leaving William and Kempe together.

Kempe came forward and embraced William. He whispered, although there was no one around to hear, "William, my friend, I am much in amazement. How did you do it? It is truly a miracle that this knight has not put you in the hands of the law, nay, even of Lord Burghley himself. I warned you against approaching him. I feared it would make matters worse. But here you are, safe and sound it appears."

"Neither safe nor sound, Orlando. At least not yet," William said.

"Tell me where matters stand, then," Kempe said. "Hold back nothing, for I would know fully what my duties are here. Sir John has told me little, but bade me come with him and I, owing you a debt of friendship, did not refuse."

"I told you in London that I sought out Father Mottelay, and in my letter that I had found him."

Kempe nodded. "You did indeed, and I was much amazed. I despaired of your ever finding him, given that his ministry is an offense to the law itself."

William explained how Parmenter had suddenly turned on him, denouncing him as a murderer, despite Mottelay's best efforts on William's behalf.

"Well, then, if Father Mottelay was unable to win Sir John's over, no one could. He is a most subtle Jesuit with considerable skills in diplomacy. Should he go to Rome, he will, I warrant, within the month sit upon the right hand of the Pontiff, if not God Himself."

"You give him too much credit, I think," William said with a laugh. "Yet he is a good man, and will help us."

"But tell me, William," Kempe said. "Sir John and his manservant came knocking upon my door whilst I was still in bed. He said I was needed at the Hall and that I should come straightway. He said his lady wife was in sore need of my help and that I must prepare to put myself and my art of physic at his disposal here for several days or more. He said Lady Parmenter would pay me handsomely for my service and named a princely sum as my reward. And thereby you see me here, ready for whatever I can do."

"He told you no more than that?"

"Nothing."

"Nothing about me?"

"Nothing," Kempe repeated.

"We are off to the churchyard at Maidenstowe," William said. "That is what this is about, why you have been summoned. You are to be witness to what I found in the tomb; the two bodies, the wounds, the evidence of murder. You are to provide a second opinion. Both Parmenters have faith in your judgment."

"Then Parmenter is willing to at least look at the evidence against Fanshaw," Kempe said.

"His wife commands it," William said. "But for her, I would be already in prison. I must tell you, Sir John has not been won over to my side. Indeed, he trusts me less and is more dedicated to my ruin than he was before our meeting. It is his wife, rather, who is my champion. She hates Fanshaw as the Devil himself and is prepared to think the worst of him. She will accept for proof of his murdering impulse very little, though I have a great abundance of proof I believe, some of which you are unaware since it has appeared since last we met. As for the compensation you will receive for coming here, I wish you the joy of it. As my second, you will deserve every penny and my eternal gratitude as well."

It was too late in the day to set out for the churchyard at Maidenstowe, and all made an early night, especially Kempe, who said he was quite undone by the ride from London. "You were never I remember much of a horseman," William said, laughing as they bid each other goodnight.

"Nor you, my friend, if I remember right. You had saddle sores aplenty though the distance be no more than a hundred yards."

"And there you lie, sir," William retorted good-humoredly. "It was two hundred yards I rode before the sores drove me to distraction."

William fell asleep at once, but awoke hours before dawn. He hated it when this happened, for then he would lie awake, tossing and turning, imagining the worst outcomes and falling into a melancholy that he rarely if ever experienced by day. As a remedy, he began to think about what was to come. His desired result was now within his grasp—exoneration in the eyes of the Parmenters and the promise of their help in securing the prosecution of Thomas Fanshaw. When Alice Fanshaw's coffin was opened, they would see for themselves. All doubts would vanish and, as Mottelay had promised, William would be vindicated.

29

The Parmenters and their party—William, Kempe, and three menservants—had left early, but they stopped along the way to take shelter from a summer storm that rained upon them for an hour or more until the road—a poor thoroughfare in the best of times—had turned into a river of mud. Everyone was soaked and in bad humor, but what was there to be joyous about? However the journey ended, it would be of no benefit to the grieving parents. Alice, their daughter, was dead. If William proved his innocence and Fanshaw's guilt of her murder, she would still be dead. Sir John and his lady would merely be changing one subject of their enmity for another. And it was unlikely their mutual grief would bring them together in any meaningful way, since but for Sir John's insistence that Alice marry Fanshaw, she would be alive and well. William was sure that was how Lady Elizabeth would see things.

When they resumed their journey it was a solemn progress. Sir John and his wife had little to say to each other, Sir John having objected to the expedition all along, and his lady wife discomfited by a hard saddle of which she complained bitterly. Kempe, usually loquacious when in William's company, also seemed subdued and turned inward, although William thought a lively exchange between the two, sharing memories of university days, would have confirmed the closeness of their friendship and invited the Parmenters' suspicions. He decided that Kempe was right to keep him at arm's length. In medical consultation, which in a way this was, objectivity was everything.

By this time, William's hope for a speedy exoneration was beginning to fade. Why did he feel so, when all logic suggested otherwise? His proof was dispositive, he thought. The evidence would be plain on its face, as his lawyer father might say. The two bodies, both murder victims, their place in the Fanshaw tomb—to William the evidence spoke for itself, not only spoke but cried out, implicating Fanshaw as author of both murders.

It was late afternoon when the truncated tower of St. Mark's church appeared, and the road—which had been more a wheel-rutted path for a mile or two—turned down into the valley where Maidenstowe lay, like a human settlement fast on its way to extinction. There was suddenly a general expression of relief that the journey was at an end. Behind him, William could hear Sir John's men chattering among themselves, pointing to the village's one tavern, as if the delights of drink were the sole object of the journey. But it was a desolate prospect. It had rained hard in the village too, and no one seemed to be about as the company wound its way up the hill to the church.

The vicar was not at home, only his wife, who upon seeing Sir John and his lady was all aflutter and could barely speak. Finally, she made them understand that the vicar was off visiting a sick parishioner but would be home soon. She did not seem to take note of William being with them, for which he was grateful. This was hardly the time to explain the false identity he had used, especially with the real Orlando Kempe by his side.

"We have come to pay respects at the tomb of Mistress Alice Fanshaw, who was our daughter," Sir John said almost defensively, as if he expected the vicar's wife to deny him the right of such a visit.

"Well enough, Sir John. I can show you where she lies. But would you prefer to wait for my husband, the vicar? He will return straightway. The poor woman he visits is blind and in her dotage. His visits with her are brief. He is not sure she's even aware of them."

"No need to wait for that," Sir John answered curtly. "Our business will be quickly done. We shall have no need of the vicar." He took William's shoulder with a firm grip. "Do show us the way, Doctor, if it please you."

Parmenter seemed in his own element now, among his men, not in a house dominated by his wife, who seemed content in this instance to let her husband take charge. Elizabeth Parmenter looked tired and out of sorts, displeased as always with her husband and probably annoyed that William's quest for justice necessitated this ordeal of travel, as brief a journey as it was.

William led the way up the hill to the churchyard, where they wound their way through tombstones and high wet grass until they came to the place they sought. The clouds overhead had cleared. The sun shone

178

brightly on the gravestones. Sir John noticed the broken lock on the tomb gate almost instantly and examined it as though he had newly discovered the break-in; and this was damning evidence, even though William had confessed it the day before.

It had been decided earlier that only Sir John, Kempe, and William would open the coffin. Elizabeth Parmenter had declared that she wanted to remember her daughter as she was in life, not see her as she now was, a pitiable corpse. "She has gone to heaven," she said with stoic reserve. "Through the merciful intercession of Our Lady. It is enough for me to know that." Much less did she wish to see the desiccated remains of Thomas Fanshaw's earlier wife, a woman she never knew and about whom she cared not at all.

William pointed out the coffin, and Orlando and Sir John shifted the lid from its place. At once there was an exhalation of odor that caused Sir John and Orlando to draw back and cover their noses. William too was repelled but he did not draw back. His eyes, rather, were fixed on the coffin's interior.

It was empty. All that was left was the unmistakable smell of death.

After a moment, Parmenter said, "This, Doctor, is your weighty evidence? Or have you mistaken the coffin? I see that there are others here. Perhaps you have erred in identifying this one?"

"I have not erred," William responded in a hoarse, constricted voice. He was aware of Kempe behind him, shifting lids of other coffins. Kempe worked at this desperately, discovering some were empty, others holding skeletons of former Fanshaws whose remains had been exhumed from dirt, to be reinterred now that Fanshaw was rich.

Kempe completed his search, then opened his hands in a gesture of helplessness.

Sir John glared at William. "I perceive that you have either lied to us about these bodies, or have removed them to another place to prevent us from detecting your lies. What are you, Doctor, a man of physic or a despicable grave robber? I pray you tell us, that I and all here may know what manner of man you truly are."

Parmenter did not wait for William's response, which in his own shocked awareness William had yet to frame, but called to his wife, "Elizabeth, come within. Have no fear. Our daughter is not here, nor any other woman long dead and wormy. We have made this tedious journey today

179

for naught, save to convince you perhaps that this man who claims to be a doctor is a liar and graverobber. It is not enough that he murdered our daughter but offends us the more in the theft of her body."

Lady Parmenter entered, looking confusedly first at her husband and then at William. There was no hatred of William in her eyes, but they were cold and frightened, as though presently, the body gone, the ghost of her daughter would appear. She looked into the coffin and then withdrew and began to sob uncontrollably. "Oh Alice, oh Alice," she wailed. "What have they done with you?"

To William, it was a horrible scene, and for a time he forgot the precariousness of his own state. He was inclined to comfort the woman, but held back as he must. Between him and her the enraged husband stood like a wall. William glanced down at the sword at Parmenter's side. Would he use it? Would Parmenter now achieve the vengeance he had sworn?

Elizabeth Parmenter composed herself. She looked up at William inquiringly, as though the question that came from her was a quite ordinary one. "What have you done with her, Doctor? I do not ask about the other body, the body of that ... woman, for I doubt now it ever was. But I saw her husband place Alice properly in his family tomb, and she is not here."

"I do protest; I entered as I have said before," William cried. "But I left the bodies as I found them, as God in heaven is my witness. And their condition was as I have said, as well. Alice bore a wound in her chest, made not by my blanket of magnets, but by a pointed object, a needle, a poniard, I know not what it was. It was a wound I found as well on Simon Gresham's chest when I dragged him from the pond."

"What wound upon his chest?" Parmenter demanded. "I never heard or saw any wound upon his body."

"Did you look for it, Sir John?" William asked.

"Are you saying my secretary was stabbed?"

"I am so saying, Sir John," William returned, with what he hoped was enough conviction.

His assertion had drawn Elizabeth Parmenter's attention. She was now staring at William with an incredulous look.

"You say this now, this talk of a wound," she said. "Why not before? Instead, you were silent when you spoke of Simon. I ask you again, why now? Is your purpose merely to distract us from this present offense to God and nature, that you should bring grieving parents to their daughter's grave only to taunt them with an empty tomb. What manner of doctor are you? What manner of man are you?" She looked at him with disgust.

Until this point, Kempe had said nothing. Now he intervened. "But stay, Sir John. You have blamed Doctor Gilbert for removing your daughter's body. But what if the remover were another person with some devious purpose? Perhaps the vicar, when he returns, can tell us if any other man came to this tomb, expressed unusual interest, wandered around the graves unattended and seeing the gate to the tomb unsecured, did mischief there? Her husband, perhaps? If he is the murderer as Doctor Gilbert claims, might he not wish to hide the evidence? Is it not impossible that he might have buried her elsewhere and the earlier wife's body as well? Stranger things have happened. No heart is as devious as a murderer's heart. His ways are hardly intelligible to us who live honest lives."

William felt a surge of gratitude for his friend's sentiments. It was a defense he had not thought to present himself, and of course, Kempe was right. If the bodies were gone, if the evidence was gone, who better motivated to hide it than the murderer? But that would require that Fanshaw knew of William's return to England and his efforts to clear his name by examining Alice Fanshaw's body. That was an obstacle to this new theory, but not an unsurpassable one. He knew Fanshaw had spies, or at the least had spies available to him through his friendship with Lord Burghley. If Thomas Fanshaw had known of William's visit to the churchyard, he might have moved heaven and earth to conceal the evidence. What a little thing for him it might have been to secure some hireling to invade the tomb as William had done and carry the bodies hither, burying them God knew where in some other grave in the churchyard, or beyond in the dense wood where none could find them. What mattered it to him, who despised both wives as traitors and whores that they should rest finally in some obscure, unmarked grave, the ignominy they deserved?

Parmenter said, "You provide a brave defense of your colleague, Doctor Kempe. How you doctors stick together like glue. It does amaze me. When one sinks, the other plucks him up. But I tell you I will have none of it—nor, I promise you, will the law. Your friend here is already under suspicion of murder, for fleeing the country, and I know not what other crimes he may have done in secret. Now grave robbing and sacrilege may be added to his offenses."

"I am guilty of none of these," William said, nodding to Kempe. "I thank Doctor Kempe for his defense of me, but I may defend myself against all these unjust charges. My magnets had no virtue within them to kill your daughter or expose her adultery. It was an experiment that failed. I should never have performed it, but I did, and all these troubles proceed from that error, for which the fault is mine. Thomas Fanshaw killed your daughter. He did it with some manner of knife or pointed instrument. I believe the same instrument killed Simon Gresham."

"Fanshaw had nothing to do with Gresham," Parmenter cried. "My God, he hardly knew the man. If you're saying Fanshaw murdered them both, then you must explain Fanshaw's malice toward a man he hardly knew."

William was about to answer this—to say that Gresham had been the intermediary in the marriage negotiations, as Mottelay had reported—but was prevented by Parmenter's shoving him against the wall of the tomb. "Damn you, sir," he shouted. "You are either a liar or a madman. I pray you tell us which it is, for you are destined thereby either for the rope or for Bedlam hospital where they do keep madmen like unto yourself."

William had struggled to maintain his innocence. Now, he was struggling equally to defend his sanity. He looked at Elizabeth Parmenter. She was regarding him as though he were indeed mad, as though her husband's accusation somehow proved it. She had been his defender before. But he knew now he had lost her. Now she was of her husband's mind. As vengeful as he. Not that she hated her husband less, but she hated William more.

For a space, there was silence in the tomb. William could hear his own breathing and the breathing of the others but nothing else. No one seemed to know what to say next. To William, it was like a field of battle when all ordinance had been expended. Finally, Elizabeth Parmenter, haggard and tearful, broke the silence.

"I beseech you, Doctor. If your heart is not stone, if you are a man and not a devil, have compassion for a grieving mother who would see her daughter decently laid to rest, and not discarded in some loathsome den or other hiding place."

William said, "Lady, I have great pity for you in your distress. Believe me, I know how you must suffer, having lost your daughter twice, as it were. But I swear by all I hold sacred in this life that I am not he who removed her body, nor ever would I do such a thing. I am a doctor. I have sworn an oath to respect life, to save life where I can, to be honest in my dealings with my patients, to—"

"Oh, these are cheap words, Doctor," Parmenter interrupted. "Cheap words to candy over your offense that it taste sweet, rather than the poison it is."

Then Kempe spoke. "Consider this, Sir John. I present you an alternative, which I pray you hear out. Doctor Gilbert here may have only imagined what he saw in the coffin. I mean your daughter's husband may have buried her elsewhere. The condition is not unheard of. "

Parmenter looked skeptical. Kempe pressed on. "I knew a man in Cambridge who one day saw his dead wife walking down the path to his house. You understand that she had been dead and buried for a month. It was no ghost, he saw, but rather a vision of what he desired to see, his beloved wife come alive again. It was a desire so strong that the eye obeyed the will. He saw what never was or could be again, she being dead. So does the brain of man play trickster on us all."

"And this has happened to you, Doctor?" Parmenter asked, turning to William, his voice rich with disbelief and scorn.

"Well, no, Sir John, I must confess it has not."

"I know it has never happened to me that I should see what was not," Parmenter said. "Wife, has it ever happened to you?"

Elizabeth Parmenter said, "Not that I remember, and if it ever did, I should walk all the way to Bedlam hospital and have myself interned there until I were sane again. I give no credence to these dreams and visions which the heretics claim to receive in their opposition to the Holy Church, if it is that manner of delusion you speak of."

It had been a desperate effort on Kempe's part, but neither of the Parmenters were having it, and the argument offended William, for although he was thankful for his friend's intersession, he did not appreciate being cast as a delusionary, a near neighbor to a religious fanatic. That was too much of a price to pay for getting out of the trouble he was in.

"I see you have found what you sought, gentlemen."

At this new voice, they all looked toward the door of the tomb. It was the vicar, back from his pastoral care. The man looked from one person there to another, made a little bow to Elizabeth Parmenter and identified himself. He greeted William by his true name, which surprised and puzzled him.

"I saw your company gathered about the tomb and came straightway here. You are most welcome. How may I help you, good sirs?"

"We need no help, Vicar," Parmenter said. "Indeed, I do think our business here is nearly done."

"You visited us before," the vicar said, nodding toward William.

"I did," William said.

"And now again, how pleasant."

"The body of our daughter has been removed," Parmenter said. "We believe this man, William Gilbert, has done it."

The vicar gave a look of alarm and walked over to the coffin. He peeked in and then looked at Parmenter. "She's gone," he said.

"That's clear to all of us," Elizabeth Parmenter said. "And we believe this man, this so-called doctor, has taken her."

The vicar looked at William. His eyes narrowed with suspicion. He said, "This villain was here before. And I did notice sometime after that the lock was broken on the tomb but knew not whether he had done it or some other malicious person. He told me he was once a doctor for the dead lady and had come to pay his respects. We fed him and gave him a bed for the night."

"He lied to you. He is—or was—the doctor most current of our daughter and is the man who killed her," Parmenter said.

Now the vicar looked horrified. "I have had a murderer for a guest in my vicarage?"

"It would seem so," Parmenter said. "But do not abuse yourself, Vicar. You are not the first he has deceived. I doubt you will be the last."

William said, "Tell us, Vicar, was there anyone that visited after me? Some other person who might have asked the whereabouts of the Fanshaw tomb? Were you aware of any disturbance of the tomb beyond the broken lock, or any noise or other disturbance that might have signaled a graverobber's work?"

"None," the vicar said, shaking his head. "Few come here these days, especially strangers as yourselves. You were the last and only visitor, Doctor. No one has touched the door of the tomb, much less entered it. You were the last by my understanding to look within the tomb, and you did that, I must assume, by dark of night when no one was around to see what you did or did not do there. Indeed, Doctor, you kept your visit to the tomb a secret from my wife and me and gave us a false name as well. I do not know the motive for your secrecy. Perhaps you can explain, if not to me, then to these gentlemen and gentlewoman here."

"I think I have heard enough," said Elizabeth Parmenter with a voice colder than William had heard before. "This good vicar before us has an honest countenance and bears powerful witness to your perfidy, Doctor Gilbert. Husband, have this man restrained a second time, and let us go home. I trust there is enough light for us to see our way if we do not tarry."

"That we shall do, wife," Parmenter said. "And between now and the time he is turned over to the magistrate, I trust he will confess both his murder of our daughter and the concealment of her body."

At that instant, William found himself seized from behind and a leather strap again wrapped tightly around his wrists. Parmenter's men had come forward and obeyed the command they had waited for all the day. He realized it was, after all, the reason for their being there.

30

He knew struggle was useless; as useless as further protest. He understood now that he had never really been at liberty with the Parmenters. What Orlando Kempe had said of him was true. Delusional, Kempe said. But the delusion had not been William's vision of dead bodies that never were, but of hope that somehow he could overcome the hatred of his enemies. It was more than a weight of evidence against him. It was their enmity and malice and a perverse kind of glee that the primal fault was totally his and no other's.

He looked at the vicar and saw no sympathy there in the man's smooth, imperturbable face. William could not blame him. Why should the vicar think him innocent, he who had deceived with a false name and false story, who had indeed been guilty of breaking into the tomb without right or privilege? He looked to Kempe, not for help now, but for some face, if not friendly, at least less condemning. He found it. Kempe looked at him pityingly, but William would have preferred contempt to pity.

Now he was being led away, down the path to where the horses had been tethered by the lychgate. He looked across the churchyard to the Fanshaw tomb. No one had thought to replace the lock. But why should they, now that the tomb of Alice and Augusta Fanshaw was empty? He was helped up, not courteously, onto his horse's back. He was no better than they themselves in the minds of Parmenter's men. A learned man but nonetheless a fool, for who but a fool would get himself in such a predicament?

He heard the riders before he saw them. He looked toward the end of the village where the first houses were, the end the Parmenter company had entered an hour before, and coming through the otherwise empty street were more than a dozen horsemen. These were not gentlefolk with their liveried servants and train of packhorses. It was an armed company, for even at this distance he saw they wore heavy leather jerkins; some had breastplates and helmets and at least two of them bore pikes with banners flying as they rode. William knew this was more than a county constable's recruited rabble, drawn from the taverns to support law and order in the hinterlands. These were serious officers, trained and commissioned, doubtless veterans of many a campaign. He already had a presentiment that they had come for him.

"You have come in good time, Captain," Parmenter called, when the troop was upon them.

"As you directed, Sir John," the man Parmenter called Captain said, regarding William suspiciously. "For we have long sought this man."

By which William understood that the arrival of this troop was no accident. Parmenter had arranged it. Arranged it even before setting out for Maidenstowe, that they should all meet at the Fanshaw tomb, empty of its bodies and William already in bonds.

But then William was distracted by something else, someone else. One among the newcomers he never expected to see.

Thomas Fanshaw himself.

He who commanded the troop was not Thomas Fanshaw, who was standing before him now with a cruel grin but a tall, jowly-faced officer of fifty or so with heavy brows, a ferocious beard, and a military air. His name, he said, was Broward or Bearward. He spoke with a thick Devonshire accent, so that William did not hear the name clearly, but then it made little difference to him what the man's name was. Broward or Bearward could have had any name. It was his office that mattered, his present business and his authority to execute it.

In a booming voice he announced that he acted under authority and direction of the Lord Burghley. "I am the captain of his lordship's personal guard."

"There is the man you seek, Captain Broward," Thomas Fanshaw said, pointing to William. "Doctor William Gilbert."

Since he was bound and closely guarded by Parmenter's men, the identification of himself as the fugitive sought seemed somewhat unnecessary to William. Also somewhat redundant was Broward's direction to three of his men that he take William into custody at once, replacing the leather straps that had been used to bind his hands with iron manacles of a type he had seen applied to the most violent and dangerous of criminals.

His chin raised and in what sounded like a practiced voice, Broward recited, "William Gilbert of Colchester, Essex, you are hereby arrested under proper authority for medical malpractice resulting in the death of Mistress Alice Fanshaw, wife of Master Thomas Fanshaw, of fleeing lawful jurisdiction, and of falsely accusing Master Thomas Fanshaw of his wife's murder. All these matters you must answer for before the Queen's Bar, until which time you shall be imprisoned without bailment."

The formal indictment continued in a legal language William did not comprehend and only half heard. Later, he would remember only the first few sentences, which were the gravamen of it and sufficient to define his crimes. He was not asked whether he was innocent or guilty of the charges. Somehow, he knew it would make no difference what he might say, at least not now, and manacled and surrounded on all sides, he concluded silence provided more hope of present safety than angry protest. Certainly, he was not prepared to give Fanshaw the lie. Not at this moment. Like the other men in Broward's company, Fanshaw was armed with a sword and dangerous.

Both companies, Burghley's and Parmenter's, dismounted. Elizabeth Parmenter went to sit upon a flat slab of a monument that was shaded by a broad-leafed tree. There she fanned herself and protested the appearance of Broward's troops, not because she wanted to defend William but because it annoyed her, this clamor and commotion. She was not used to this manner of experience, she said. She wanted to go home. She bitterly regretted not bringing a maidservant as an attendant—but no one, and especially her husband who somewhat reluctantly left to attend to her, was listening to this complaint. A little later she would go into the vicarage to have the vicar's wife attend her.

Fanshaw had announced that he wanted to see the family tomb, for he had heard it had been desecrated and he demanded that if it were true, the charge of grave robbing should be added to the other charges against "this incompetent and pernicious fellow, this so-called doctor."

Although willing to go peacefully, William, stung by this charge, was dragged along toward the tomb, with Fanshaw in the lead and Broward, Parmenter, and Kempe following.

Fanshaw burst into the tomb as though expecting it to resist him, even though the iron gate had been left ajar from the earlier visit. William was pushed in by his particular guard, a stout man of William's own age who looked himself eager to be gone from this place of death. William suspected the rough handling to be an effort to suggest a reluctance on his part to face evidence of his crime. Parmenter and Kempe remained outside, either because there was too little room for a larger group or because they wanted not to expose themselves to the unpleasantness a second time.

"Her body is gone," Fanshaw said, matter-of-factly, peering into the coffin when the lid was once again shifted aside. "I laid my wife here myself. Bore her to her resting place in my own arms. In death she was light as a feather."

Fanshaw raised a hand to his brow and wiped his eyes as though weeping. But William saw no tears. He was not surprised. Fanshaw's gesture was a performance for the benefit of those around him. William knew that. It was a bad performance. The hypocrisy disgusted him, but it appeared to have the desired effect on Broward, who patted Fanshaw's shoulder in a gesture of consolation and urged him to bear up: " …like unto a man," he said. "Doubtless your good wife's soul is in heaven, Master Fanshaw, where she sups with the saints and angels."

But Fanshaw would not be consoled. He continued to play the role of grieving widower.

He glared at William accusingly. "Was it not enough, Doctor, that you killed her, but you must also desecrate her body by removing it from its resting place? Was it not enough? Tell me where you have taken her, you dog." Fanshaw lurched toward him, reaching for his neck, but Broward sprung forward to intercede.

"Stay, Master Fanshaw. Do not yourself violate the law, in whose hands this miscreant now is."

Fanshaw steadied himself. William thought the man's anger had been genuine, not like the false tears he shed for a wife who betrayed him with another. He said, "And you accused me falsely of my own wife's murder, which thing I would never do for all the world. For I did love her with all my heart and soul."

This pronouncement did not ring true to William either, but since they were the sentiments a grieving husband was expected to express, William saw no signs of disbelief on the faces around him.

Presently recovered, Fanshaw stood erect and stared at William as though he were some strange marvel on the earth, a creature unlike ordinary men

189

in his want of human decency or respect for the dead. He said, "On the morning of my dear wife's death, I came into her chamber where she lay upon the bed. Her face was white, deathly white. She did not wake or stir, even when bidden. I removed the blanket you had given her to find her naked beneath and her flesh bruised all along the course of her body. The magnets you recklessly applied had sucked up her blood. They had taken her life. I found her dead, Doctor Gilbert. It was not my doing. She was already dead. Your treatment was the cause. And thus, you murdered my wife and the child she might have born unto me had she lived. You are answerable, Doctor, for two deaths, not one alone."

William noticed that Fanshaw had said nothing about his own request that William use his magnets, nor about their purpose. But he understood Fanshaw's silence. If Fanshaw admitted his wife's infidelity, he proclaimed himself a cuckold, which he had declared he would never do. He would also be confessing that he had a motive to kill her, even if he did not.

Broward said to William, "You came here earlier to find the body of this gentleman's wife, broke open the tomb to see the fruit of what your mischief had done, and then returned to remove the evidence of your crime. Tell us now what you did with this poor woman's body."

"I did nothing with it," William answered. "I examined it only and when I left, it was where it lay when I first entered this tomb. If my intent were to steal it, why not do it when first I discovered it? Why should I have made a second visit?"

Apparently, neither Broward nor Fanshaw thought William's question worthy of an answer. Perhaps because of the assumption that questions were a prerogative of legal authority, not of accused men whose questions deserved no answers.

"I did nothing with it," William repeated, "save when I examined her to determine why she died and found a puncture wound beneath her breast that had not before been seen."

"What wound?" Fanshaw exclaimed. "I saw no wound. You lie, sir. You lie."

"Magnets have not the strength to extract blood from its natural course," William said.

"Well, you see they did have such strength, as many ancient writers attest," Fanshaw answered hotly. "Besides, if she were indeed stabbed, perhaps *you* did that to her. If you can sew your magnets into a blanket, you might also wield a knife deftly. You have a surgeon's delicate hand, I see."

"I am neither surgeon nor barber," William said. "As for what you call *ancient writers*, they do attest much that is nonsense and never was. But to your point, Master Fanshaw, why would I harm your wife? What wrong had she done me that I should take her life? I had no malice toward her, nor she toward me, as far as I know. Our few conversations were pleasant, cordial."

Fanshaw looked to be on the verge of saying something more but restrained himself. At this point William did not care. He was exhausted and beginning to feel darkness overtake him. He decided to tell all he had seen on his first visit to the tomb. How could his situation be worse?

"I found upon my first visit another body in your wife's tomb. Your wife Alice laid upon it."

"What body?" Fanshaw said. William saw no surprise in the man's eyes, but sudden fear.

"I do think the body of your previous wife, she before Alice, much decayed but identifiable by her hair, which retained its red color. The wife who, you claimed, ran from you to some remote clime and has never been heard of since."

"That's ridiculous! That's false as hell!" Fanshaw shouted, his protest deafening in the closed space of the tomb. "My second wife lives still, I know not where. Besides, how do you know but that she died of a natural cause, or from some sickness or by accident? You are, sirrah, a criminal if not a madman. Is there no end to your lying?"

Abruptly, Fanshaw turned to Broward. "Captain, this miscreant has abused my reputation enough. I cannot bear it further, nor should I have to. Do your duty, sir, before I take the law into my own hands. I have a sword and I am not too old to use it in defense of my honor and the honor of my dead wife."

"Your earlier wife died from a cracked skull, a blunt object," William said. "A single blow would have been enough."

William's declaration brought another explosion of denials and curses from the grieving widower. It took several minutes for Broward to calm Fanshaw, which he did by grasping his shoulders and shaking them as though the old man were an unruly child. The effect was amplified by the fact that Broward was much taller than Fanshaw, younger and stronger.

But Fanshaw was not acting now. William's accusation had touched a nerve, and although William had not declared that Fanshaw was guilty of his second wife's death, the implication was clear and Fanshaw knew it.

"We have stayed too long in this morbid place," Broward said, when Fanshaw seemed calm again. He looked sternly at William. "You must come now with us, Doctor. Further talk is useless. Save all defenses and extenuations for your trial, where you may tell your story, and pray to God for mercy on your soul, for the evidence against you is strong as the manacles you wear."

Then, Broward ordered the churchyard to be searched. He said perhaps the dead woman had been reburied nearby. It was worth taking time to search, he said, for it had happened before when a grave was robbed. He said its occupant would be cast aside in some ditch or hallow to save the robber the labor of reburying it.

After that the search commenced. William watched as Broward's troop and Parmenter's smaller company began at the Fanshaw tomb and then extended outward in concentric circles, looking for signs of freshly dug earth or a body hidden behind some moss-covered cross or slab.

The search lasted more than an hour by William's reckoning and extended into the nearby woods that were midsummer-thick with foliage. It was futile, the search, William knew that well enough, for whoever had gotten rid of the two bodies—he knew Fanshaw would not have done that by himself—could have well anticipated the search for the remains. Perhaps, he thought, the bodies would never be found. It was too easy to rid oneself of a dead body in country such as this was, remote from dense human habitation and replete with fields, isolated glens, and greenwoods that were thick and dark and unwholesome.

During this time William was still manacled and still watched over, but his particular guard, evidently unworried that his charge might bolt, sat upon one of the gravestones eating an apple and humming, lost in some pleasant fantasy, William surmised, and not attentive to his prisoner. Kempe, not involved in the search, approached William. The two men sat down together amid the gravestones.

"Have courage, William," his friend said. "All's not lost. Lord Burghley is a just man, as are our English judges. This is not Italy, where to be accused itself is to be straightway tortured, hanged, or poisoned. The charge of murder may fail, and you will be sentenced only to a charge of negligent malpractice."

"I will try to console myself with that," William said, doubtfully. "It would be a fine prelude to a successful medical career in London. But I tell you, friend, that I no longer am hopeful. Did you join in the search for the bodies?"

"No," Kempe said. "That's Fanshaw's business, not mine. Besides, stumbling around in the woods for Alice Fanshaw's corpse is not my idea of a pleasant afternoon. I went to talk to the vicar and his wife."

"Why?" William asked. "They hate me as much as Fanshaw does. I misrepresented myself to them using your name, abused their hospitality, robbed their churchyard in the dark of night, or so they believe."

"I assured them that you committed no murders," Kemp said.

"You didn't tell them that I was delusional?"

Kempe laughed. "No, that was a story for the grieving parents. I'm heartily sorry that it didn't persuade them. I was desperate to help you, and the idea came up in an instant, much like your using my name instead of your own when you first visited here."

"Well, then what did you tell them of my case?"

I gave them the account you had given to me and swore it was true. I told them I knew you, had known you for a good while, and that you were honest and a Christian."

"Thanks for that, my friend, but did they believe you?"

"I think they did," Kempe said. "Especially when I told them my own father was a vicar. I even told them his name and the vicar said he knew my father and knew he was a good, decent Christian who would never lie and was not likely to beget a son that was any less trustworthy. I think the vicar and his wife are in your camp now. At the very least, their minds are open to the possibility of your innocence."

And then Kempe spoke of his London patients. He was enjoying great success in his practice, especially with women, whom he said had a wide range of conditions men did not and were more eager for his ministrations than their husbands and fathers, who saw stoic endurance as a mark of manliness. "If a woman has a twitch, she will seek counsel of doctor, apothecary, surgeon, wise woman, even a witch. If a man breaks a bone he will bear it a year before seeking a doctor, that he be not shamed for weakness. I tell you, William, all the money to be made in medicine comes from women."

While his friend rambled, William half listened, his responses reduced to monosyllables. How could he happily reminisce when so much good of his life was now lost to him, or enjoy stories of his friend's successes when he had none himself to boast of? It was true he had saved Perdita, the Parmenters' granddaughter, but who else recently? Of what use was he?

William said, "Orlando, do me a favor for friendship's sake."

"With all my heart," Kempe said.

"I have a pittance upon me tucked in my shoe. I shall need a good deal more if I'm to be imprisoned. My satchel's at the inn. You know it. I have a goodly sum in a hidden pocket. When you find out what prison I have been taken to, I pray you bring it to me. There is also some clothes within, some books, and a notebook I cherish. Do that for me, for friendship's sake."

"Trust me," Kempe promised. "I will come and see you wherever they take you."

For another hour the search continued, the searchers now so deep in the greenwood that William could no longer see them, although from time to time he heard the men call out to each other, and once a cry of pain and a curse as one struck his head on a low-lying branch. Slowly, one by one, the searchers returned, weary and disappointed, for Kempe told him that Fanshaw had offered a reward to be given him who found a body first, but it must be the body sought—his dead wife's—and not some other corpse thrown away.

William found Fanshaw's reward offer grimly ironic. For who amongst them all had more interest in Alice Fanshaw's body never being discovered than her husband, who needed evidence of the wound never to be seen? William felt now as he had felt earlier—that he was a player on a stage, surrounded by other players none of whom meant what they said or had the emotions they expressed, but all was false as hell.

Broward said, "A man might spend his life looking for a hidden grave and die without finding even a wayward button of him who is sought for." Then he berated William's guard for allowing him to speak with Kempe. "This is no time for gossiping with the prisoner." He cast a suspicious glance at William and spat on the ground. "Prisoners will manipulate you every time and win you over to their cause, be it ever so indefensible."

Broward said he knew this was true from sad experience.

As they made their way back to the horses, the vicar appeared. Seeing such a new and larger company of armed men he now looked not merely curious, but alarmed. "Save you all, gentlemen," he called out. "May I do you a service?" Then, recognizing Thomas Fanshaw, he ran toward him, grasped him by the hands, and said effusively, "Oh, Master Fanshaw. God save you, sir. It is good to see you again, sir. Welcome back to the village of your birth."

"And what was my wife's resting place, but is no more," Fanshaw answered bitterly. "You keep a loose tether on the bodies buried here, Vicar. How many have you lost over the years? Pray tell us."

The vicar looked confused. Then caught Fanshaw's meaning. "Not a one, upon my oath, at least before this time, Master Fanshaw."

"That is one too many, since it is my wife's body we speak of." Fanshaw swore a lengthy and vile oath that appeared to shock the vicar, and then drew away.

"But in the Resurrection, all will rise," the vicar called after him.

"I trust that will not be today, sir," Fanshaw replied over his shoulder.

William took a last look at his friend and waved. Kempe smiled and gave William a sign of encouragement by clenching his fist and raising it to his shoulder. It was a gesture they had used at the university that encouraged a common effort. It spoke of unity of purpose. It cheered one on, especially when defeat was in the offing.

31

It was late afternoon when they entered the City, near dark when they crossed the great London Bridge to Southwark, passed the gatehouse, and entered a part of London where William had never been. He did know Southwark by reputation. London had a dozen or more prisons, some of which were in Southwark, there planted among thatched-roofed hovels, ramshackle tenements, taverns, brothels, alehouses, and other resorts of ill-repute. It was an unsavory neighborhood, fit for a prison house. Now fit for him.

Broward had told him where he would be confined and gave the prison a name, but William didn't remember what it was and didn't care. Broward said, "That's where they put the debtors, more particularly those who owe money to the Crown. You would have been sent to the Marshalsea where they keep the hard cases, but it's brimming over these days. Count yourself fortunate, Doctor. The other inmates are mostly former decent types like unto yourself, though they did no murder as you have done."

"I have done no murder," William said. Broward shrugged.

They wound their way down an unpaved street, lined with shabby wooden houses with smoke curling from holes in the rooftops, since the inhabitants lacked the wherewithal to build chimneys. Then they turned a corner and at once came upon a long, high brick wall above which William could see a large building with small, barred windows.

Presently they arrived at an iron gate with a guard house, from which emerged two square-faced, heavy-set officers who appeared annoyed at being called to their duty at such an hour. One of them carried a bottle from which the both of them had obviously been imbibing, for their walk was unsteady and their eyes unfocused. They evidently recognized Broward. They acknowledged him by name and immediately opened the gate.

The company entered into a paved courtyard, beyond which was the building William had seen from the street. Upon closer inspection he saw that it was an oblong edifice of three stories and barred windows starting on the first of the floors above the street. There was no grand entrance as there might have been in some public building or great man's house and no name above the door to tell what manner of building it was. The barred windows made its purpose plain.

One of Broward's men helped William down from his horse. His manacles were removed. He massaged his wrists, which were sore from the iron, and looked up at the building before him. A wave of hopelessness swept over him. One of the barrel-chested guards from the gatehouse came forward and took him by the elbow, squeezing it so tightly William winced with pain.

Broward looked down at him and said, "I'll leave you now, Doctor, and wish you good fortune in your new accommodations, which I trust will meet with your approval."

Broward smiled grimly and gave William a kind of salute. William took the smile to mean that Broward was only doing his duty, that nothing personal was intended against the doctor. Broward's duty was to pursue and capture, not to judge. That would come later, perhaps in a month or two. That's what Broward had told him. Given the severity of the charge against him, there would, in the meantime, be no chance of bail. The warrant Broward had read made that plain.

His guard, who maintained his hold on William, escorted him inside the building where there was an ill-lit vestibule and a long, darkly-paneled corridor at the end of which was a single door. The guard steered him toward it and gave three sharp knocks. William heard a muffled voice within.

It was a small office of sorts, where a stern-faced man wrapped in a heavy black cloak and cap stood staring into a fire, seemingly lost in thought. When this man became aware of William and his guard, he turned slowly, scowled, pulled his coat around him the more, pointed William to a chair and sat down opposite him.

"And who may this be?" the cloaked man asked the guard, who remained standing at attention.

The guard unbuttoned his doublet and pulled out a piece of paper. He handed it to the cloaked man, whom William assumed was the warden of the prison. The warden, who was a small figure with heavy brows and a narrow face marred by pox, began to read, squinting as he did so, for the room was lit with nothing but a single candle and the light from the fire.

"William Gilbert? Of Colchester, Essex?"

William nodded.

The guard said sharply, "Prisoner will answer. Say *yes, Master Warden,* that is who you are."

"That is who I am," William said.

"Prisoner will say *yes, Master Warden,*" the guard repeated shrilly.

William said what he was told to say.

"You are a doctor, sir?" the warden asked.

William said he was.

"And a graduate of our distinguished university at Cambridge?"

Again, William said he was.

"Well," said the warden. "I would be impressed by those attainments were we standing before St. Paul's, rather than here."

The warden began to read the words of the warrant as William first heard them, but unlike Broward, who had read the whole document, the warden seemed interested only in the charges against his prisoner. He looked up at William from under heavy brows.

"I see you are a doctor, sir," the warden said, although that fact had already been established. "We have more than one of your kind here, though they be debtors, not murderers."

William did not deny the charge this time. What was the use?

"I pray you will commit no more murders while you stay with us," the warden said drily. "You will not practice your craft here, sir. Do you understand me, sir?"

The warden's voice changed with this injunction. Before he had spoken softly. Now he bellowed as though he were giving orders to seamen in a storm. It startled William, although the command did not surprise him. Broward, who had become quite talkative on their journey to London had warned him that he could not expect to play doctor, as he put it, inside one of Her Majesty's prisons. William had not known whether that was true or merely Broward's odd humor. The warden's command confirmed what Broward had said.

"I will neither diagnose nor heal, whilst I am here, Master Warden," William said.

William looked around the room. It was plain and featureless with white-washed plaster walls. There were no paintings or wall hangings. He remembered this was a prison. He thought the beginning of one's punishment was deprivation of visual delights. Such things were afforded those who obeyed the law, not accused criminals like himself.

"You will be imprisoned here, Doctor, until your trial, and perhaps after if you are convicted and not hanged for your offense. Until then I recommend you follow all rules of the prison strictly, obeying every command, causing no disturbance by violence or loud noise. In other words, Doctor, keeping your nose clean."

"I will, Master Warden."

"See that you do," the warden said. "Oh, yes, there is one other thing."

The warden paused and stared up at the ceiling as though what he was about to say was hanging there, like a bat in a corner. "Prison is not free, Doctor," the warden said, turning back to William. "There are certain charges—for food, for books or pamphlets, should you desire them. Some of our cells are more accommodating than others. Should you wish to correspond with anyone outside of the prison, there may be a fee. And naturally a small fee is exacted for visitors ... should you have any. Many prisoners do not."

William was tempted to ask why having a visitor or sending a letter should require a fee but thought the better of it. Now was the time for feigned compliance, not the impudence to which he was more naturally given. He did not want to appear combative, to get off on the wrong foot with this man who, William knew, would now control his life for what future remained to him.

The warden went on for some time with the schedule of fees, and it came to William that the prison was not merely a prison, but a business, like a draper's or grocer's. Every service had its price. William thought of the money in his shoe. It could not be more than a few shillings and, yes, a half-crown. How far would such a paltry sum go? Even the money he had in his satchel at the inn, the money Orlando Kempe had promised to bring him, might quickly be exhausted unless he was sparing in his expenses.

The desk at which the warden sat was devoid of objects. There were no books, papers, blotter, inkstands, or pens. So bare was it that William

199

wondered that the warden should want or need a desk at all. But then the warden reached beneath it and pulled, perhaps from a shelf or drawer, a large, flat book—a kind of ledger like the ones used to keep accounts. This he opened and spent a few minutes searching what William could see was a list.

After a while the warden looked up and said, "I think I have a cellmate for you, Doctor. Someone whose interests are akin to yours. His most recent cellmate has died. You have long legs, Doctor, but there's an empty bed that may fit you, though the air there wants something of sweetness, as you will presently learn." He laughed. It was a cruel, joyous laugh, merciless, William thought, with little humanity in it.

The warden asked William if he had any questions, but it was a perfunctory request, and William understood that he was expected to have none.

"Each cell has a chamber pot, Doctor. Use it. It must be emptied daily. By you, Doctor. You have no servants here. There is also a privy in the yard below. Use it, Doctor. This place reeks enough as it is from sweat and rotting garbage."

The warden continued in this vein for some minutes, specifying certain practices that within the prison were strictly forbidden, such as theft, assault, buggery and other perversions, slandering the Queen, or spreading heretical religious opinions. Here, the warden made reference to several sects, some of which William had never heard, although he assumed they were as damnable as any other in the warden's mind.

"We feed you here, Doctor, but it is hardly better than a mouse's portion and unworthy of the wee creature as well. Most prisoners buy food from the vendors who come each morning to the prison gate. At least, those prisoners who can afford it. I assume, Doctor, that you have family or friends that can aid in your support?"

William said he did, but did not specify whom, and the warden did not ask. William knew a few people in London, most his father's friends. There was Kempe, of course, who was on his side and wealthy enough to at least lend him money, if not give it outright for old times' sake. He had resolved earlier to say nothing to his father or stepmother about his troubles. They would be appalled and shamed, and he doubted anything he could say by way of explanation would diminish their sense that he had disgraced the family name. Besides, his circumstances admitted no simple explanation.

"Very good, then," said the warden, apparently satisfied with his introduction to prison life.

William understood this was a regular script for the warden. Each new prisoner would hear the same thing, with only minor variations according to their peculiar circumstances. Now he was just one among many, distinguished in no way, his academic achievements and scientific expertise cast into the balance and found irrelevant.

The warden rose from his chair, yawned, and nodded to the guard, who seized William from behind and pulled him up to standing position. He was roughly steered toward the door, a demonstration of force William suspected designed more to impress the warden than to control the new inmate, who had offered no resistance nor intended any.

"One final matter, Doctor Gilbert."

"Sir?"

The guard held William in place and turned his head to view the warden.

"I forgot to tell you one important rule. Indeed, I cannot say why it slipped my mind."

The warden paused, looked up at the ceiling again, and then leveled his gaze to meet William's. "You may leave this place when you are by lawful authority discharged or, should you die within these walls, borne off to your grave. But not before. I repeat, Doctor, not before. Do not attempt to escape, in other words. It is true attempts have been made, yet all have failed. Every one."

He uttered this last fact with particular satisfaction, as though it were the hallmark of his tenure as warden. His pock-marked face broke into something close to a smile, although there was neither joy nor merriment in it. He paused to let his words settle in the prisoner's mind before continuing.

"You will find no friends in this neighborhood to aid you. On the contrary, the great quantity of them are poor folk, beggars, common laborers, vagabonds. They wait expectantly for your effort so they may be rewarded for fetching you back, alive or dead. And once back, should you live, your accommodations are changed to the depths of this building where there is no light, little air, and a solitary existence I would not wish on my worst enemy. All privileges hitherto afforded you are canceled, permanently. But I doubt I need to tell you that. You seem an intelligent man, Doctor, with a good imagination."

201

The warden asked William if he understood this. William said he did.

"Welcome then to your new home," the warden said. And then he added with a mocking solemnity, "And may God have mercy upon you. Few others here will."

32

His cell was on the highest floor of the prison block and accessed by a stairway of such narrowness that the guard had to climb after him, prodding William from behind as though he were a dumb animal. William's joints were stiff and the climb was arduous but the guard kept him moving. The walls on either side, rough plaster, were marred with handprints and crude drawings of a libidinous sort. Names were written there too— William assumed they were those of current or former inmates—arcane messages, appeals to heaven, and crude obscenities. The stairway had been designed, William imagined, to prevent more than one or two persons going up or down at the same time, thus making it easier to apprehend prisoners should they endeavor to use the stairs as an escape route.

Along the walls of the corridor were doors, a great many of them, each with a number above the lintel. The doors had heavy locks, and all had little portals through which he assumed the guards might observe the inmates within. The rough planked floor creaked as they walked. From within the cells, William could hear muffled voices and occasionally cries of anger or despair.

Even before he came to the door of his cell, he smelled a strong odor of chemicals, some of which he recognized as the recipe employed by many of the alchemists he had encountered in Cambridge and even in his own town of Colchester. His inference was confirmed when the guard pulled the door open to reveal a room not more than eight- or ten-feet square with walls covered with paper, drawings, diagrams, and charts.

There were two straw mats there, one occupied by a scraggly-bearded, long-haired man who seemed to be asleep. The other was piled with books and papers, manuscripts, bottles, and vials. At the room's center was a small square table—crudely made, like the first effort of a joiner's apprentice.

Upon the table sat an alembic—a gourd-shaped glass container with a long beak, half-full of a bubbling, dark, odiferous liquid. All about it were bottles of other liquids of various colors and densities. The alembic sat upon an iron grill, under which were pieces of glowing coal.

The combination of odors emanating from this operation was nearly overwhelming. Among them, William recognized a few ingredients of typical alchemical operations and urine, although as to the latter he wasn't sure whether it was an ingredient in the alembic, or an odor from a far corner of the room where the present occupant had relieved himself for want of a chamber pot.

Behind William, the guard cursed and covered his nose and mouth. "Jesu, what a stench is here. And that fire. If it does not burn down the prison, it will be a miracle." The guard whispered to William that a fire in one of the inmate's cells was against the rules of the prison, but this inmate paid him three shillings a month for the privilege. He winked, suggesting that William might also avail himself of special privileges, at a price.

The guard approached the sleeping man and shook him until the prisoner awoke, looked about himself with alarm, and then, seeing who it was that had awakened him, laid his head back on the bed and glared at the guard. "What do you want?" he snarled. "May a man not sleep the sleep of the just in his own cell but be awakened every hour to do the Devil's bidding?"

"I am not the Devil," responded the guard, smiling wryly.

"Nay, you are not, yet you do his work," the prisoner said.

William looked at the guard to see how the man took this evident insubordination and was surprised to see no anger in the guard's face. "You have a new mate to share with," the guard said, nodding toward William.

"What must I do about it?" the prisoner declaimed. "Shall I rejoice in company if it means less room for my work?" The man waved his hand about him, as if to display the fruits of his labors, and indeed to William the room looked very much like a scholar's den, though somewhat more disorganized than he was used to, with books piled willy-nilly and paper scraps of every size scribbled upon as though the writer thereof was in a frenzy of composition. Certainly, it was not what William expected to find in Her Majesty's prison, this display of learned industry. He wondered at the abundance of books, some of which he now saw were in Latin and other foreign languages as well.

The bearded prisoner looked at William up and down. He asked how old William was.

"I am twenty-six," William said.

"Time then to grow a beard," the prisoner said, and leaped from his bed and began removing the books and papers from the pallet opposite and dumping them on the floor. As he worked, he asked, "Are you yet another debtor, who must be confined, even though it is difficult to see how you can relieve your indebtedness in here? There is naught more irrational than a debtor's prison, and it is a testimony to human folly that this truth is not widely acknowledged. How much, sir, do you owe and to whom?"

"I am an accused murderer," William said, too weary to lie.

The prisoner stopped and looked up abruptly. The guard laughed loudly and slipped from the room, shutting the door behind him.

"What did you say, sir?" his cellmate asked.

"I am a doctor, charged with murdering his patient," William said.

The older man's eyes opened widely. He stroked his beard, which came almost to the middle of his chest. "And are you guilty as charged?" he asked.

"I am not guilty," William said, he thought perhaps for the tenth or twelfth time that day. He was surprised when his fellow prisoner laughed uproariously.

"Not guilty, are you? Then you will have much company here, young sir, for many of us here are innocent as babes. Even those who have the misfortune to owe money we cannot pay. I pray you consider me, for instance. I worked ten years at my trade, gave good value for my goods and services, called no man a thief, treated every man as God would have me, yet I end up impoverished. Why? Because my partner in the business whose charge it was to keep accounts paid himself as often as he paid our joint obligations. He fled to Scotland or some other heathen land, taking his ill-gotten gains with him. I ended up as you see me here, not happy in my wife and children and good house in the City, but in this vile and unnatural habitation, from which I pray God deliver me before my death and my children have children of their own. Oh, Doctor, 'tis an unfair world, is it not, this kingdom of England?"

William knew it was a question he was not expected to answer. But he nodded in agreement. It was an unfair world, there was no denying it. Had it been fair, William knew he would not be in what his new cellmate had called a vile and unnatural habitation.

The man had a nervous manner, and his eyes darted around the room as though he suspected the guard or perhaps William had stolen something while he slept. Seeing evidently that nothing was amiss, he rose from the bed and extended his hand.

"Since we shall share a cell, let us be friends one with another," he said. The man's hand was soft and moist, as though he had been dipping it in one of the many liquids around him. William was growing accustomed to the odor. He had been in many an apothecary shop that had smelled as bad, and in not a few alchemists' dens that smelled worse.

"Let us then make our names known, that we can freely converse. My name is Clement Dockery. I am by trade a glover but as you can see, I pass my days here conducting various experiments for the good of mankind. Welcome to your new lodgings. Would that it were the Queen's table, for the quality of food we obtain here leaves much to be desired. By the way, when did you last eat?"

"I think it was breakfast," William said.

"You have little meat upon your bones, lad," Dockery exclaimed. "That's a poor beginning for prison life, though few grow fat in this place. In faith, they are lucky they don't starve. It's common for an arresting officer to ignore the more basic needs of a man—like food, for example. He is only concerned with his prisoner's need to be incarcerated."

Next to the alembic and the bottles on the table was a small chest. Dockery lifted its lid and pulled out a half a loaf of bread, broke off a part of it and handed it to William. He busied himself around among the bottles and found one, poured a brown liquid into a cup, and handed that over as well. Seeing William's reluctance to drink, Dockery said, "No fears, Doctor. It won't poison you. It's not a bad ale. I buy it from a vendor on Wednesdays and Fridays. You'll find him a useful person to know here. You shall get to know him tomorrow."

William told Dockery his name.

"William? That's as good an English name as there is. 'Tis the name of kings. I don't know any Gilberts, I confess. You're a doctor, are you? Shall I call you Doctor, or will William suffice?"

"William will serve, and if you permit, I shall call you Clement."

"No, call me Dockery," the man said pleasantly. "My father gave unto me that name, Clement, hoping I would go eventually into the church and have my name as polestar for the virtues of mildness and mercy.

Merciful I may be, especially when it comes to my own sins and iniquities. But mild? I confess I was never such, but a scrapper from birth and a controversialist by temperament."

Dockery broke into a hearty laugh that made his whole body shake. "I would rather be called a dog than Clement."

William finished his bread and drank all of the ale and was still hungry, but he decided it was all he was going to get in the way of supper that night.

"We'll talk tomorrow," Dockery said. "I will tell you my story, you may tell me yours, but only if you wish. An hour with our warden, from whom you just came I assume, is enough misery for any man. But now, for sleep."

A sheet covered the pallet and there was a single coverlet. Both were stained by chemicals or other things William forbore imagining. He didn't care. It was a joy for him to lie down, for he had never been so weary in his life. He removed his shoes, determining that his money was still concealed within. He stretched out his legs, which extended beyond the pallet, and having done so, he immediately fell into a dreamless sleep.

33

Breakfast in the morning was the remains of last night's loaf, and from somewhere Dockery brought out some moldy cheese. He used a spoon to divide the cheese in equal portions. He said, "Our schedule here is quite simple, Doctor. You will soon become accustomed to it and loathe it as much as I do. About eight of the clock a bell is rung at which time we march in good order from our cells, those of us on this floor, and descend to the courtyard at the far end of which is the foulest-smelling privy in Christendom. There we do our business, as we need and please. After, we have the freedom of the yard till mid-morning."

"Freedom of the yard?" William asked.

Dockery laughed. "We are permitted to walk about and exercise our bones and joints, breathe in the lovely Southwark air that does destroy the lungs with chimney smoke. At the gate various vendors approach and sell us food, drink, books, and so forth, offer to take our letters to the post, or bear messages to friends or family on the outside. For those of us who have them, that is. Preachers come and call us to repentance and thereby give us news of the world without and occasionally pamphlets, composed by distinguished divines, reminding us of our sins. Most of these learned divines are howling lunatics, in my humble opinion. Oh, yes, and there are women too; ladies of the night who of necessity also work days and allow our grasping hands liberties through the bars. For a price, of course."

"Surely they are not allowed within the prison walls, these women," William said, astonished at this view of prison life and imagining the prison as a bawdy house.

"Usually, no," Dockery said. "But there have been instances. The guards here are not overly scrupulous. They are poorly paid for their services to

208

Her Majesty and wisely supplement their income with bribes and other surreptitious offerings. Therein they do but imitate their betters who are as corrupt as they. All of this you will learn by experience in due course, as does every new denizen of this place."

"The warden mentioned the prison fees to me yesternight."

"And so he would, since he enriches himself by taking a part of each guard's fee. His name is Miles Prychett, and a greater scoundrel you will not find. They say he secured his position by bribery of a certain merchant of the City not scrupulous in his own business dealings and eager to be rid of Prychett's threats to him. Of course, that may all be gossip, slander by his enemies, or it may be true. I confess I belong to the party who believe him guilty as charged."

When he had finished eating, William heard the bell ring and he passed out of the cell into the corridor. He followed Dockery down the stairs and into the yard between the building and the wall that enclosed the prison. It was neither wide nor open, but a long stretch of rough cobbles that seemed something that the old Romans had built and the new structure of the prison had conveniently used as a foundation.

He counted at least fifty or sixty men walking about; some conversing, others solitary and staring upward at the gray sky or at their feet, lost in contemplation. He had been told most of his fellow inmates here were debtors, honest men who had borrowed beyond their ability to repay, or like Dockery, victims of their partners or family members who had robbed or cheated them. He saw few among them who by their appearance or demeanor were what he would have called the criminal class—common thieves, cutthroats, robbers, assaulters, pimps or—worse—murderers. Some, if not well-dressed, were at least decently clothed. And the conversations he overheard as he walked touched upon matters ordinary people of the City might converse upon—news of the City or the Court, views about this issue of the day or that, plays seen or books read, written, or exchanged. For he understood that booksellers did a brisk business at the prison. Prison inmates, after all, had so much time to read.

William had withdrawn sixpence from inside his shoe and with Dockery as his guide, negotiated with a grocer's man who was selling salted herring, cheese, and a strong beer Dockery claimed was the best he had ever drunk.

Then they returned to their cell, where William said, "I see by your equipment here that you are an alchemist. Is that some branch of glove making that I overlooked? Pray tell what the connection might be, for I sit at your feet to learn."

Dockery chuckled and stroked his beard. "Call it a mere hobby, though I suppose this cramped chamber testifies to my devotion to it. Like others of my kind, I hope to find the *alembra*, the philosopher's stone, which men have sought time out of mind, and without success, at least not that anyone knows of. You have heard of the great goal of alchemy, that to which all distillations and operations aim?"

"Who has not?" William said. "It is to take a common substance, say iron or copper, and by the distillation of certain chemicals and elements turn that base metal into gold. It is spoken of by the ancient and modern authorities." He then began to recite the names of a dozen or so alchemists whose work he had read because they touched upon his own obsession, magnetism.

"I see you are informed truly," Dockery said, his eyes alight with pleasure. "I see too that Warden Prychett has finally done me a service for which I owe him more than a curse. That being, he has put you in the same cell with me. A man I can converse with about my work." At that, Dockery rushed toward William and embraced him. "God be thanked, a friend indeed. Yet not only a friend but, God willing, a colleague and collaborator."

William started to protest. He had no interest or belief in the alchemists' efforts to turn base metals into gold. To him it seemed a futile enterprise, when the real object of human effort should be more broadly the understanding of nature and thereby the devising of instruments for beneficial use—the compass, the astrolabe—not to mention a more perfect understanding of the stars and planets, their constituents and motions.

Dockery must have detected a skepticism in William's response, for he said, "You know, of course, that the philosopher's stone will yield more than a precious metal. It also has the power to restore to its original and perfect form and function that which is diminished or diseased. I speak of a medical application, which should interest you, Doctor."

"It will interest me more when I see proof thereof," William replied. "Whatever the ancients have said ought to submit to experimentation and verification."

Dockery made a pretense of being shocked. "You doubt the wisdom of the ancients? Are you so disrespectful of their writings, their collective wisdom?"

"Not disrespectful," William answered. "I do honor and respect them and their efforts. Yet they too often do little more than echo one who

210

came before, whose name is renowned and reputation assured, fearful of offending their ghosts. The alpha and omega of their studies is tradition. All sit at Aristotle's feet, worship at Galen's altar. They build on a foundation of myth and scientific hearsay with a sprinkling of gossip and old wives' tales. Simply a perception of nature which is not verifiable or real. It may accord with theory but not with experience. Why, in so doing, should they not be disappointed in their efforts?"

"Myth and scientific hearsay?" Dockery said good-humoredly. "Why, my new friend, you are impertinent, are you not, eager to dispose of the past—like yesterday's news?"

"Not dispose of it, sir," William said, "but rather see it as it is; primitive, tentative, speculative. It falls to us and our age to confirm through experiment."

For a few moments, Dockery was quiet, thoughtful. He stroked his unkempt beard, a gesture William had already seen as a peculiar habit of his. William feared he might have spoken to the older man too strongly, offended in his zeal, but the issue before them was paramount to him. If the foundation of early science was too often myth and hearsay, easy acceptance of authority, and blind obedience to old ways of understanding and doing, the foundation of *his* science was the belief that truth evolved from experiment. Truth, moral or scientific, was verifiable in experience.

Dockery did not seem offended, and William was glad. He needed a friend in the prison, not another enemy, and like Dockery he was pleased in having been placed with someone of like intellectual interests.

"Tell me about your work, your method," William urged. "I promise I will listen, not play the critic."

William said this truthfully. He was interested in that substance distilling in the alembic, odiferous as it was. He owed it to his cellmate, and he realized that he might find out something that he hadn't known before. New information always had potential value, he believed. One simply could not know when or where it might prove its utility.

For the rest of the morning Dockery discoursed on his method, a discourse in which he took evident delight. William realized that although an amateur, this glover by trade had acquired considerable learning—not from tutor, school, or university but from his own reading and notetaking, the evidence of which was not only in the substance of his lecture, for that

211

is what it was, but manifested plainly throughout their narrow confines of their cell. William came to understand that in his own way, his new friend was also an experimenter. Dockery talked of chemicals and their combinations, of the use of what he called human properties—blood, bile, urine, phlegm, even feces and perspiration—dead animals, and thousands of plants and herbs.

William was acquainted with all of these, as they were commonly employed by physicians and apothecaries and generally supposed to have medicinal uses by the public general. Not that he credited it all, but then who knew what rare herb or plant or animal, obtained from the Indies or even America, might prove a miraculous healer of disease or an element in the transmutation of metals. For William did not disapprove of the fundamental premise of alchemy—that one metal might be turned into another. After all, that was the way iron became steel, the way copper and zinc became brass.

And all of this, instructive as it was, he knew benefitted him by pure distraction. Were it not for his learned friend, William would do nothing but meditate on his perilous situation and the mystery of its cause.

Dockery said he was most indebted to Africanus, an Arab alchemist living in Spain, whose writing he had stumbled upon quite by accident. "In what language was it written?" William asked.

"In Arabic originally, then translated into Spanish, from there to German, and finally to English, but poorly done, I think, by some German who knew our language little."

He said this man had come close to the discovery of the philosopher's stone but stopped when he lacked one element, a rare substance only found in Egypt. "I have started my work where he left off," Dockery said. But then added, "Yet according to you, I have erred in this. I should not have assumed as a true foundation another's work. I should have started from the beginning."

"And what would the beginning be?" William asked.

Dockery thought for a moment. His arms fell to his side in a gesture of surrender. "That is my dilemma. I don't know what the beginning should be. I have tried and tried, a thousand distillations with as many chemical combinations. And all yield nothing but a noxious smell. Perhaps I should offer it to the public as a poison for rats—or base politicians."

William was tempted to say that the distillation would surely achieve that end but did not want to cause greater dejection in his new friend. Again, he had cause to regret his assertiveness. It had made him few friends at Cambridge, among his teachers or his fellow students. He had been put down as arrogant and disrespectful. Perhaps that was true.

He considered how he might lift his new friend's spirits, but it wasn't an art he had developed in his youth or early manhood. Besides, he was becoming dejected himself.

William and Dockery spent the rest of the afternoon of that first day reading, Dockery a book by a French alchemist, William one by an English explorer recounting his meeting with natives of some remote island in the Pacific. Dockery had uncovered it for him from a stack of books in the corner.

Suddenly, the door of the cell opened, and a new face appeared. It was a guard but not the one from the night before. Here was a new face, a younger and more kindly face. He said, addressing William, "If you be the doctor that's here, there's a visitor for you." The guard held out his hand. William went to his pallet and reached beneath it for a coin. "Is that enough? he asked. The guard eyed the coin and took it.

The guard led him down the stairs into the yard where he and Dockery had walked that morning. At the end of the yard, sitting on a bench in the shade of the only tree, appeared Orlando Kempe.

William could see that Kempe had brought William's satchel. Kempe held it under his arm, as though it were as dear to him as to William. Seeing William, Kempe waved and smiled broadly, just as he had done on the day he had first come to Colchester to change William's life forever.

34

What was left of the money Thomas Fanshaw had given William was in the goat-skin satchel, along with a two linen shirts he had bought in Amsterdam, an English translation of a German work on metallurgy, his notebook with its carefully lined pages, a razor—which he used once or twice a week—a bar of scented soap wrapped in a handkerchief, two quill pens and a bottle of ink, half full. There was also a little chest in which William kept various medications—powders and ointments—in case his medical services should be needed.

"I am even more in your debt, good friend," William said, embracing Kempe as though he had not seen him in a month, although it had been but a few days.

Kempe wanted to know how William was dealing with the ordeals of prison life. He said he knew three other gentlemen of the City who were incarcerated for various offenses, and their account of their sufferings had given him nightmares, in which he too was behind bars for a crime he did not commit nor even understand, brutalized by other prisoners and corrupt guards. He said he had known many a man who, like William, had been falsely accused. Some were exonerated at last. Others remained in prison or were hanged—or worse. William knew what *worse* was. Evisceration, emasculation, decapitation, dismemberment; the sequence of horrors sickened him.

"This is a fearsome place," Kempe said, looking around him, although to William, Kempe seemed more curious than fear-struck. But then he remembered that shortly Kempe would walk out of the prison as Kempe had walked in, a free man.

Kempe said he had brought some things for William. He reached into his own satchel and withdrew a bottle of Rhenish wine, a slab of

214

cured ham wrapped in an oilskin, and some apples and pears. For these, William also thanked him.

"Now," Kempe said. "I will do more for you. I know people in the City, important people who can act on your behalf, and gladly. They may be able to work your release, at least until your trial, if I can convince them that you will do no harm, perhaps suspend your practice until your name is cleared. Has the warden told you when that might be, your trial?"

"A month, maybe two," William said. "None here knows for sure, nor cares. But I am fortunate in my cellmate, who is an alchemist of sorts."

"Of sorts, you say? Is he an alchemist, or no?"

"He is, by inclination and practice," William said.

"Will his alchemy have you out of here?" Kempe asked.

William laughed. "I may be undone by the odor of his chemicals, in which case they may carry me out to the boneyard. But, to speak truth, he is a good man, I think. His name is Clement Dockery."

"Never heard of him," Kempe said.

"He is Intelligent, somewhat of a wit, and he has been helpful to me since my arrival. It is not easy to navigate prison life. It is full of hidden shoals and dangerous tides."

Kempe shook his head. "Your metaphor brings an unpleasant subject to my mind."

"Pray tell, what unpleasantness might that be?"

Kempe's handsome face darkened. "Fanshaw's anger has not been tempered by your arrest and present confinement. That I have from his own mouth. If anything, he is more outraged since he is convinced you know where his late wife's body lies and will not say. You do this, he thinks, to vex him the more. He is encouraged by Sir John Parmenter in his discontent. Both have sworn you will not live to be judged by any court."

"What do you mean?" William asked, although he feared he knew.

"Both men, and Fanshaw in particular, have long arms that can reach beyond the borders of their estates into the very heart of London itself. Even into this prison, the high walls notwithstanding. They know people, people who owe them favors and would be pleased to find a way of repayment by doing you in."

"Doing me in—that's an odd phrase," William said when he could speak, for his friend's warning instilled a great fear within him. "Is it an Italian expression Englished, something you learned whilst abroad?"

"In God's name, believe it, William," Kempe urged, ignoring William's question. "Any one prisoner here may be more than he seems—as can any man, whether he be confined or no. I mean no wretched inmate, but someone hired to avenge Alice Fanshaw's death. Both Fanshaw and Parmenter are equal in their hate and nearly equal in their power to do you harm. Therefore, I beseech you to watch your back, William, else you may find yourself victim—not necessarily of a direct assault, say by knife or club, but by some devious means that can be written off as an unfortunate misadventure."

"Unfortunate misadventure?"

"Say, a tumble down the stairs," Kempe went on. "Or a loose brick falls from the wall above you, or … I know not what manner of accident might be contrived by some hireling and therefore appear no one is at fault, but your death is an act of God. By such a means, neither Fanshaw nor Sir John could be held to account for private justice. Their reputations would remain unsullied, the grieving husband and father. Oh, what a mockery it is, William. I know you are innocent."

"For that I thank you, Orlando. That someone believes me gives me hope. I seem otherwise surrounded by enemies."

Then Kempe said he must go. He rose from the bench abruptly, clutching his own satchel as though he feared it might be taken from him. He said he had a new patient in Holborn, the wife of a certain illuminatus of the Court who he could not name out of respect and caution. "I've heard she's a great beauty, but hypochondriacal to the extreme, with more complaints than a dozen of her friends whose malign conditions she does imitate, I hear, so as not to be left out."

"Neither you nor she can hardly hope for a cure, then," William said. "Since she is more devoted to her illnesses than to finding relief from them."

"A delay in cure will only increase my fees," Kempe said happily.

"You think too much of money, my friend," William chided.

"You think too little of it—and to your detriment."

They talked together for another hour until it seemed neither had more to say. Kempe promised to return soon. He asked William to make a list of what needs he had and present it to him upon his next visit, which he thought might be toward the end of the week, or perhaps sooner. "Ask for what you need, my friend. Think not of its expense. Trust that I am on your side in this and will be an instrument in your hands. I will also invoke the powers of heaven on your behalf."

216

"You offer too much, Orlando, and make me doubt you. Besides which, I thought you had given up on religion," William said.

"Not entirely. Some seed my righteous father planted lives within me still. Call it faith, what you will, or a mere desire to believe. In either case, I will pray for your present safety and your ultimate release, both from this place and from the strictures of the law."

"And from the vengeful men who hate me?" William added.

"From them as well," Kempe said. "I have no great love for either man, Fanshaw or Parmenter. They are both corrupt men who love money more than life and advancement more than honor."

"You are a man of principle, Orlando. I'm right glad you're my friend."

"And I am happy in your friendship as well," Kempe said.

William said, "Many thanks for the food, for bringing my satchel, my money, and—"

William hesitated. It was the most important thing his friend had brought him. "And for your warning, which I promise I will take to heart. My aim is to survive these present miseries and live a long and happy life."

"And see justice done." Kempe said.

"And see justice done," William answered.

35

Orlando Kempe did not return as he had promised. He sent a message saying that the great quantity and quality of his patients prevented it. Still, William did have another visitor, one he did not expect to see again and who came in good time, for William had written letters to Pieter Weinmeer in Amsterdam acquainting his Dutch friend with his present circumstances and needed someone to convey them to the postmaster on Lime Street.

"You look surprisingly well, given where you are and why," Julian Mottelay said.

"The surprise is mine in seeing you again," William answered. "I have now had two visitors since my confinement. You and Doctor Kempe."

"I trust he was not here in his professional capacity," Mottelay said, casting his eyes over William—looking for symptoms of some malady, William supposed.

"I am well enough off, despite my confinement," William said.

There was nothing about Mottelay that suggested he was anything but an ordinary Englishman, perhaps a well-heeled merchant or secretary to some lord. He had no priestly air now nor priestly garb, which would have made him subject to immediate suspicion by the prisoners, as well as the guards.

"Orlando brought my satchel I had left behind at the inn. It contained what money I had, which I desperately need here, since fees are imposed for everything. We talked a bit about old and better times. He warned me about dangers from Fanshaw and Sir John."

"What dangers?"

"He said the two gentlemen want more immediate justice for the wrongs I have done them than to wait upon a jury's verdict. He said I should

218

watch my back. Be careful where I walked. He said my death might be made to look like an accident, a misadventure."

"And how does the good doctor know this?" Mottelay asked.

"I assume he learned it from the two gentlemen themselves. He talks to the both of them. He has been a physician to both households, as you well know. They trust him implicitly, although he swears he loves neither man."

"I cannot affirm their threats from my own association with Sir John," Mottelay said, "although I know Fanshaw well enough to believe he would so threaten you. He is not of a forgiving nature. Take your friend's advice. Be very careful, Doctor, where you walk."

"Believe me, I will."

"But I do have news that will interest you; not about Parmenter but about his former secretary and factotum, whose dead body you discovered."

This conversation was taking place in William's cell, which out of courtesy his cellmate Dockery had vacated so that William and his visitor could talk in private. At that hour—it was early morning—the prison yard below was busy with prisoners pressed against the gate with arms and hands extended and a great throng of peddlers supplying their wants and needs. Mottelay had been impressed by William's quarters, as he had called the cell, as though they were a barracks rather than a prison, or—perhaps more appropriately, given Mottelay's secret vocation—a monk's retreat.

"I see scholarship thrives even in this cursed place," he remarked, looking around the walls and seeing how many books and charts there were. He recognized at once the alchemist's alembic and remarked on it. "It is a foolish quest to my way of thinking, to search for an elixir to substitute for God's grace and present help."

William pointed out that the same objection could be made to medical science. But before Mottelay could respond, William said, "You told me you have news of Simon Gresham. Tell me, I pray you, for his death, or the manner of it, surely ties in with that of Alice Fanshaw's, although I know not how."

"Listen then and tell me what you think," Mottelay said. "Gresham was a useful tool for Parmenter. He kept his books, managed his tenants, often recommended investments. He was a clever fellow who wormed his way into the hearts of his master and mistress."

"All this I already know," William said.

"Then you may be interested to learn that with Gresham's death it

219

became necessary for Parmenter to secure the service of a successor to his office. That man arrived the day of your arrest, and in the several days since has been pouring over Sir John's accounts with a close eye. He has discovered certain irregularities therein."

"What irregularities?"

"Certain obligations owed to Sir John that were not conveyed to him but to Gresham himself."

"You mean Gresham had his hand in Sir John's pocket?"

"So it would seem," Mottelay said.

"How much did he take?"

Mottelay shrugged. "This new man, his name is Daniel Staples, says hundreds of pounds, perhaps more. Sir John and Lady Elizabeth are beside themselves with rage, for their trust in Gresham was long-nurtured, and they feel betrayed by one they considered a part of the family, not merely a servant. Their anger at Gresham has quite displaced their grief at their daughter's death and their hatred of you. For that reason, and with all due respect to your learned friend, I do think Sir John is unlikely to be plotting any hurt to you, at least not at this hour."

"But what of Fanshaw? He has no unjust steward to rage at."

"Perhaps he has his own distractions," Mottelay said. "That I don't know. I am not privy to Fanshaw's business or concerns. Parmenter's, yes. But there is something else about Gresham. It was he who negotiated the marriage of their daughter, Alice."

"I had heard that," William said.

"Yes, but did you know, William, that not only did he negotiate on his employer's behalf, but it was he that proposed it as a solution for Parmenter's financial difficulties in the first place?"

"I did suppose Fanshaw met the lady Alice at some event in the City, was smitten with her, and then sought her father's blessing."

"I think not," Mottelay said with a laugh. "After her first fall from grace they kept her a close prisoner. I had that from Alice herself, who complained sorely of it. Not in her confession, I hasten to add. She sometimes talked to me quite casually, as a friend, so to speak. The truth is that Gresham made the first move, on Sir John's behalf. He acquainted Fanshaw with the beauteous features of Alice, praising her to the hilt, speaking openly about the Parmenters' financial need and probable willingness to surrender their daughter to the joys of matrimony."

"For a price."

"Yes," Mottelay said.

"And Alice did not object to being so used?"

Mottelay said, "I think she was happy to get out of Parmenter Hall, even if it meant being bound to an old man. Besides, she was the daughter, bred to obey her parents' will."

"Which I have been told she never did—obey, that is. I suppose Gresham did not tell Fanshaw about his future wife's unseemly past?"

"Of that we can be sure," Mottelay said. "Fanshaw is no model of Christian rectitude, but certainly he would have balked at taking Alice Parmenter to wife had he known her history. Her beauty would have made no difference to him."

"It seems, then, that Gresham is at least in part responsible for the difficulties faced by the Parmenters, and therefore the marriage was in his own personal interest as well as his employer's. I think Alice's, as well, since she was already pregnant before the marriage."

Mottelay said, "Lady Parmenter is ambitious. She desires her husband's elevation at court. She's from an old family herself and married down when she accepted Sir John's offer. It has never since sat well with her, her husband's lack of ambition."

William said, "So Gresham urged the marriage, negotiated all whereby money was received not by the groom, as dowries usually afford, but a large sum to the bride's father."

"And there's still more, which I did hear from this new steward. Gresham took a part of the bride price, as a commission for his services."

"How much did Fanshaw pay?"

"Five thousand pounds. From which Gresham took a tithe."

"So, five hundred pounds? Good God, what did the man do with the money? He could have lived royally."

"Apparently, he had plans to leave Sir John's employ and strike out for himself."

"For the Americas?

Mottelay laughed. "Not quite so adventurous. London, I think, was his aim. Some money-making scheme there."

"By whose mouth did you hear this?"

"One of the gardeners, fond of gossip," Mottelay said. "I don't think Sir John and his lady wife were aware of Gresham's plans. Gresham might have been rattled by Alice's murder, given his involvement in her marriage. Or maybe he had a premonition that his embezzlement would be discovered, and it were better he get out whilst he might."

William considered all this. Given Gresham's criminality, any number of persons might have wanted him dead, certainly including Fanshaw, who had good reason to hate him for deceiving him about Alice's virginity and tricking him into a marriage. Gresham must have known about Alice's more recent pregnancy. By her parents' account, she and Gresham were close. The peat-cutter and his wife had denied Gresham was the father of Alice's child, but how could they know? They were hardly privy to her bedchamber, much less secrets of her bosom, and it was unlikely that Alice would have confessed to them her lover's name when she withheld it from everyone else she knew.

Still, William could not overlook the similarity in the wounds of Gresham and Alice Fanshaw. It was unlikely they were administered by different hands, and he was convinced that Fanshaw had murdered Alice, despite his claim that she was already dead when he discovered her. Fanshaw might well have stolen into her bedchamber earlier, stabbed her, and then returned later to feign amazement and outrage, just as he had pretended to be grieved at his wife's tomb when he believed that she had planted cuckold horns firmly upon his head.

The two men talked for another hour, leaving the question of the murders behind. Mottelay was interested in the conditions in the prison, how the men lived in confinement, how they were treated by the warden and their guards—whom Mottelay described as rude, vile-looking fellows, worse than the inmates themselves. He wanted to know about the spiritual state of the prisoners, whether they were visited by clergy, for he said surely the powers of heaven could give solace in a man's dire straits more readily than in his freedom and prosperity.

He also asked about William's work. He had noticed the book of metallurgy on his bed and marveled that he had presence of mind under the circumstances to think of anything but his perilous situation.

"It is a dependable distraction," William said. "When my head aches from thinking about what happened to me or what may happen still, I open this book, and in a moment I am removed both from troubled thoughts and this place of pain."

"You know, I once was in prison myself, for a year's time," Mottelay said. "I committed no crime beyond ministering to a scattered flock in Norfolk as a fugitive priest. In a prison worse than this, I spent my days in meditation and prayer, and when I was released—well, not released, when I slipped away at first opportunity—I felt somehow my life was the less, my regained freedom notwithstanding. I pray you may make good use of your time here, since you have no alternative. Perhaps in this solitary state, the answer to these mysteries will come to you."

"Like a divine revelation?" William asked doubtfully.

"Not unlike, though I would not expect a sudden flash of light, a booming voice from heaven, or an apparition —Alice Fanshaw or Simon Gresham come from the dead to point the finger at their murderer. But keep the faith, my friend, whatever you do."

"What, will you now in exchange for your companionship desire that I convert to Rome?" William asked.

Mottelay laughed. "No, for me, you can keep your heretical views. I have not the mind of a missionary at this time. Later, one day, perhaps we can reason together over an ale or two … or three."

"That would be more pleasant than this place, surely," William said.

"I only mean that you are a clever man, my friend, and learned in the direction of practicality. If anyone can discern what happened to these dead persons, it is you. I will visit you again, upon my honor. In the meantime, I will keep my ear to the ground regarding Gresham and his secret life. I do think there's a clue there somewhere in his larcenous machinations. Indeed, it would be a wonder if the two deaths were not connected, even if the wounds you describe were not so similar."

"Identical," William said.

"Very well, Doctor, as you say. Identical."

William said he was grateful for the priest's help. Mottelay put on his cap and rose to go.

"Wait, Father, will you do something for me?"

"Gladly," the priest said.

William took the letter for his Dutch friend from inside his book and gave it to Mottelay. "On Lime Street, there is a Dutchman named Van der Kamp. He's the postmaster for the community of his countrymen living in London. Give it to him, I pray you. He will know how to get it to my friend."

The priest looked down at the paper that had been thrice folded, sealed, and bore the name *Pieter Weinmeer, Amsterdam.*"

"Will it find him?" Mottelay asked. A lone man's name and a city which, whilst not as large as London, is hardly a village."

"Pieter Weinmeer is well known in Amsterdam and corresponds regularly with his countrymen in London. Have no fear. The letter you bear will reach its destination."

"I'll treat it as though it were my own," Mottelay said.

"Wait. Here's tuppence for the post," William said.

"Save your money, Doctor. You'll need it here—and a great deal more."

36

For all the companionability William enjoyed with his cellmate, Dockery had never asked him the facts of his alleged crime, nor had William offered them. The two men conversed incessantly—about alchemy, about chemistry, about magnetism, about medicines—but not about William's legal troubles. William thought it might be some sort of rule or prison etiquette: What unfortunate circumstances brought a man to his confinement were a private matter, no business but his own unless he decided to share them.

But he had overheard in the yard other prisoners conversing freely about past crimes and misdemeanors, comparing notes as to their arrests, their captors, their debts and creditors, what they had gained and lost. He decided it was more likely a peculiarity of his companion. Dockery was a discreet man, no gossip or blabbermouth. Yet his new friend must have been curious, William thought. Who wouldn't be? Murder was a hanging offense, no trivial matter.

So, one evening several days after the priest's visit, William confessed, beginning not with the facts of his case, but the state of his mind. Dockery had been busy with his alembic, measuring chemicals into a boiling glass. He paused and looked at William. "You were going to say something, William?"

"I was, but am half afraid," William said.

"Afraid of what? We're safe enough here, the two of us," Dockery said.

"Did you ever wonder what it was I did, to bring me here I mean?"

"I remember you said you were accused of murder," Dockery said matter-of-factly, as though William had inquired about the weather, or that the charge against him was trifling.

"But I never said what I did to bring such an accusation upon me."

"No, you didn't," Dockery said, and waited.

"I think constantly of the reasons I am here," William said. "I wrack my brain about it but find no smooth and ready road to the truth of things."

"Ah, my friend, it is so for most of us," Dockery said. "It is part of the life of a convict or any other held against his will. Freedom is the natural state of man. Deprived of it, all body and soul rebels and cannot rest content."

The room had neither chair nor stool. The two men sat down cross-legged on their pallets, facing each other.

"I was living in Colchester in my father's house," William said. "I went to Cambridge and earned degrees and distinctions, studied physic and healing arts, and returned from there to practice medicine. An opportunity came my way to secure a wealthy patron. He was an old man with a young and comely wife. He distrusted the wife, who was with child when the banns were posted. He did not know about that, her secret lover. I later confirmed for myself that his suspicions were true. This is where my magnets came in."

William recounted his story simply and smoothly. By this time, it was a practiced rendering, like a poem or scripture verse he had by heart, or a tale told to children by the fire. Except this was not by any means a tale for children, being that it involved gross deception, adultery, and murder.

During William's account, Dockery was silent, and William felt that his companion was not only taking in information but assessing William's truthfulness, even his character. William understood this. Sometimes when reciting to himself his recent experiences he imagined how they might sound to another. He did not always find his own account credible. It certainly had not proved credible to the Parmenters. They thought him a brazen liar, a killer and graverobber. Even his friend Kempe seemed to doubt his account of finding dead corpses in St. Mark's churchyard, suggesting he was delusional. At times William wished that he were, and that he could wake up from his supposed delusion and find himself back in Colchester dealing with his stepmother and patients who paid him in chickens and garden vegetables.

He related all the new information he had heard about Simon Gresham from Mottelay, not telling Dockery that his visitor was in fact a Papist priest, and himself a fugitive from the law. Dockery was a good listener. He did not interrupt. At times he looked perplexed. William's account had become complicated with perhaps too many characters to distinguish and with too many motives. Or perhaps Dockery had progressed from mere absorption of information and validation of William's truthfulness to figuring out things for himself. But William really didn't want Dockery as an interpreter of events. That was William's business. He *did* want Dockery to understand who he was and what caused him to be where he was and why he feared not only for his career but for his life.

When William had finished his account, Dockery said, "Surely the two were slain by the same hand, this faithless bride and treacherous steward."

"So do I believe," William said. "There are a hundred ways to end a life and a thousand instruments to accomplish it. That two murders should occur in such proximity of time, involve persons who knew each other and were involved in this same deceptive practice, and whose wounds were identical as to device and position and not be the work of a single hand defies belief and reason."

"Then you know the truth you seek," Dockery said, with what appeared to be something between relief and satisfaction. "This Thomas Fanshaw killed them both, enraged by her betrayal of him. After all, no man wants to be a cuckold, to discover his wife has a lover."

"But what of Gresham?"

Dockery thought for a moment, stroking his beard. "As your friend who came here lately disclosed to you, Gresham was an intermediary in the marriage arrangement. A sort of pimp, since he made the match, thereby condemning Fanshaw to the very cuckoldry and public humiliation he so feared and hated. That would have inflamed Fanshaw the more. His bride sinned, but Gresham set Fanshaw up for the betrayal. Ergo, the old cuckold has ample motive for both murders. Indeed, they complement each other since they both pertain to the bride's adultery."

"I don't know," William said. "I go over and over these facts, these details, and draw the same conclusion as you have just now done, and still I think I am uneasy with what I logically conclude. I do fear men and their motives are more complicated than my science."

The two men sat silent for a few moments. Then Dockery said, "When on that day I explained to you my method of achieving, or trying to achieve, the philosopher's stone, you talked to me about what you called a foundation of myth and long-venerated authority, each unexamined, untested in the crucible of experience. I understood you, Doctor. To many of us who delve into nature's secrets, men like Aristotle or Galen or Pythagoras are veritable gods whom it is sacrilege to question. To many these authorities are right, even when they are wrong. I took your words to heart, considered what you said, and realized that it was true. I had taken the practice of the ancients as the gospel truth, not to be questioned, only to be followed. This you said was the danger of the casual assumption or unexamined premise."

"I do well remember," William said, "and I am heartily sorry at being at times so impudent in my manner like unto one who knows all and must teach others when it would be more beneficial were he to listen and thereby learn. Humility must be a virtue in science, even as it is in daily life."

"No, no," Dockery said, waving his hand as though he were swatting away a fly. "I say this not that you should be ashamed, my friend. You were in the right to tell me what you did. My work was based on too many unexamined assumptions, too slavish a dependence on authority. What kind of foundation is that for discovering something that is true as well as merely new? But let me ask you, William, consider this: what you have concluded from all these various facts is not unlike my fundamental error."

William asked what he meant. Dockery continued.

"You assumed from the beginning, and not unreasonably, that he who most wanted the faithless wife dead was he whom she had most wronged, that is to say, her husband."

"I suppose I did. I disliked Fanshaw from our first meeting. I thought him arrogant and abusive. The more I learned of him, from others and my own experience, the more I disliked and feared him. When his wife Alice died, I knew in my very soul he murdered her, despite his telling me he was prepared to forgive her if she proved unfaithful."

"Which then became a fixed idea," Dockery said, "an unquestioned assumption, like an ancient edict that it is impious to deny."

"Yes," William said, beginning to sense where his companion's reasoning was going.

Dockery continued, "And having concluded his guilt—for his wife's death and for this man Gresham's—you did not look beyond that fixed mark, but held your gaze there, content to look no farther. In any case, my friend, I thank you for your candor. You might have kept all you disclosed private. It's your business, none of mine."

Their conversation ended, both men returned to their work, Dockery to his reading, William to yet another attempt to write a letter to Katrina. But he found himself unable to get beyond the first several sentences, which when he read them over seemed stilted and cold. Something stood between him and his thoughts of Katrina.

It was Dockery's observation about a fault in his own thinking, which at first hearing William had dismissed but now considered more seriously. Perhaps what Dockery said was true. He had been convinced he was right about Fanshaw, and his conviction, being as an iron post planted firmly in its place, could not be moved. Thereafter he sought no alternative explanation or motive or person. Even though Fanshaw had evidently killed the second of his wives, as proved by the decayed body William had discovered, it did not follow that he killed both women. Or even that Gresham died by Fanshaw's hand.

The truth of this settled into his mind—the problem with his method. He had not been a fool, or a simpleton. He had merely been a victim of comfortable certitude. It was no crime in law, but certainly one in science, at least as he had committed himself to practice it.

"I must start afresh," William said, as much to himself as to Dockery, "setting all presuppositions aside. Personal bias as well. It's easy to suspect of evil-doing someone you dislike."

"And by the same token, easy to be blinded by someone you love," Dockery said.

37

William was drifting off to sleep when he heard the door of his cell creak open. He was aware of someone looking in. A face he didn't recognize. Not one of the guards.

In the next moment he was blinded by a flash. Dockery's collection of chemicals was alight—some exploding, some only burning like little candles and making popping noises. In an instant the cell was filled with acrid smoke, choking him. He could barely breathe, his chest burned. He thought he was going to die.

He looked to see where Dockery lay. He could barely see him for the smoke. His cellmate was choking too, grasping his throat, wild-eyed and asking him what was happening. "Fire," William cried. "Fire".

He grabbed Dockery by the arm and pulled him up and toward the cell door.

The corridor was filled with smoke and terrified men, awakened either by the smoke or cries of alarm from fellow inmates, who were bursting from their cells and running toward the stairs, stumbling, falling over each other, pushing other men out of the way and cursing them. All around William were cries of "fire, fire" and "Get out, get out." Some appealed for help—from their fellows or from God, or from the guards who were nowhere to be seen. Some of the men were screaming. William could not make out the words, if there were words at all and not just shrieks of alarm dumb animals make.

William half-carried, half-dragged Dockery until they reached the head of the stairs to the floor below. Dockery complained he could not see and kept rubbing his eyes. Then, William was nearly knocked to the floor by a single, deafening blast so strong that it seemed to shake the prison house to its foundations. He thought it must be Dockery's alembic. Dockery had begun a new process with different ingredients, some of which William knew were highly combustible.

By the time they reached the main floor and found the entrance portal locked, there was general panic and protest. A hundred or more men stood about crying for help and pleading that the door be opened. Some kicked at it, others beat upon it or applied all the strength of their shoulders. All effort was futile. The door was made of sturdy oak, six inches thick, designed to hold prisoners as reliably as iron bars. A battering ram might have breached it or a cannon ball. But not bare hands, no matter how strong or resolute.

There was no light in the entryway, no torches or lamps or even candles. All was darkness and confusion, the smell of smoke and terror and desperation. William thought that if ever there was an image of hell on earth, surely this was it.

William held Dockery up, assuring him that his sight would return, that the blindness was temporary. In truth, William wasn't sure it was, but could not bring himself to predict the worst. As for Dockery, he did not seem to know whether to mourn the loss of his sight or the destruction of his books and manuscripts and charts.

And then William heard a tolling bell. It was the same bell that sounded the hours, the same bell that signaled the time the inmates of the prison should rise from their beds and retire to their cells.

But now it tolled without ceasing. William had hope. Surely this was an alarm that would bring half of Southwark's denizens to their rescue. He knew a fire in one house could easily spread to another. Within minutes there might be a conflagration so intense as to engulf every house and tenement south of the Thames. It had happened before. He feared it would happen now, and he and all about him would be consumed in it.

Suddenly, the door to the building swung wide, and William and others were treated with a rush of fresh air and the anxious faces of their guards. Crying to heaven and appeals for help changed to cheers as the inmates poured into the open air, trampling the two guards who were their rescuers.

William dragged Dockery through the doorway and across the yard where the fleeing prisoners were gathered, urging Dockery to run, for there was no way of knowing what would go up in flames next and the ignited chemicals might indeed prove poisonous, the noxious smoke and ash killing them all.

Now more guards, awakened by the bells if not the explosions, came running with buckets to put out the fire. These were presently joined by townspeople, who had been admitted through the main gate to aid in the effort and were greeted by cheers from the inmates. A well in the yard provided water, and a chain was formed with buckets passed hand to hand, into the building and up the narrow stairs. Within the hour, men, their faces blackened with smoke and gasping, came down to report that the fire was out, although it seemed confined to the third floor where great billows of smoke had poured from the barred windows and filled the sky above them, hiding the moon and stars.

Prychett, the warden, who had come wearing only his nightshirt somewhat late to the scene, now commanded with an authority belied by his short stature, directing the guards and the volunteers from the town to continue to water down every wall. He seemed experienced in this role, acquainted with fire and its extinguishing, and William, who had disliked the man on their first and only interview, found himself admiring his courage and handling of the emergency.

Later, the warden thanked and commended all and sundry for their heroic effort, in a short speech that Cicero, the famous orator of antiquity, might have approved.

William thought the firefighters heroic indeed. He had inhaled the noxious smoke after the first blast and he knew how deadly it was, how insidiously it could fill the lungs and extinguish life. But these brave men had gone up willingly to save the building, despite the smoke and the possibility of other explosions and a flaming inferno.

Some of the inmates had joined in the effort, perhaps motivated as much to save their few possessions as to save the prison house, but most were too stunned and frightened to do much more than gape at the scene. Some lay down to sleep upon the cold ground. Others prayed. Some squatted on the cold pavement as did William and Dockery, both subdued by the heavy knowledge that the conflagration had begun in their cell and spread outward, endangering all about them.

Dockery had recovered his sight, although he said his eyes still burned. He bewailed the loss of his books and manuscripts, his alchemical tools. His precious alembic for which he said he had paid a goodly sum.

William grieved with him. He doubted much could be salvaged from the ruin. Nothing on earth was quite as destructive as fire. William knew that from his own experiments.

Dockery asked, "What happened, William? Do you know? When I awoke the room was already aflame."

"Your chemicals caught fire, exploded."

Dockery rested his head in his hands. "Is the fault mine, then, my alembic to blame?"

"No," William said, putting his hand on his cellmate's shoulder. "The fault is not yours."

William decided not to tell Dockery about the mysterious intruder and the device that had begun the fire. He would tell Dockery later, when his cellmate was more composed and could take it in. Now, it would only add to his confusion and grief.

Then William remembered Kempe's warning that William might meet with an accident. But the fire was no accident. It was deliberately set, and he was the cause of it, at least indirectly. He thanked God no lives had been lost. Later, he would learn that the most seriously injured were the handful of guards who had opened the door to allow the prisoners to escape. They had been bruised and broken by those they sought to rescue.

At dawn, the inmates were herded back into the building. It was thought by the warden that the third floor was still too smokey for habitation. Its residents were sent to join inmates on the second floor, resulting in cells being occupied by four or five persons where, by custom and warrant, they might provide habitation for two or three.

William and Dockery found a place, but not a bed, in a second-floor cell occupied by a bricklayer and a clothier, both bankrupt debtors. So far, other than William, no one knew where or how the fire began—except, of course, the one who ignited it.

38

Before noon next day, William learned the source of the fire had been discovered by guards searching through the rubble and ashes. To them it was clear who was at fault, the alchemist Dockery. They said Dockery had been warned that his alchemical experiments could cause a fire. He had defied the prison rules. Nothing was said about the guard who had taken bribes to keep silent about this infraction.

Now it was believed that the second and greater blast had worked to extinguish lesser fires. The walls of their cell were blackened with smoke. The crudely-made table upon which alembic and chemicals had sat was mere ash, as were their pallets. Nothing burned faster than old dry straw.

William found his money just as he imagined he would, but as Dockery had feared, not a book or manuscript remained, and all the charts, graphs, designs, and notes suffered the same fate. Dockery had talked about the virtues of starting from the beginning of things. Now both would have that opportunity. They were told it would be a week before their cell could be occupied again, unless the two of them were willing to aid in the removal of debris and make repairs themselves. They both said they would, and gladly. William agreed to pay the cost of paint for the walls, to procure new and more comfortable beds, and to find a table more ample and stable than the one lost in the fire. As for books, Dockery insisted that since the fire resulted from his chemicals, he would pay for them. "Some were nonsensical anyway. Perhaps the fire was God's judgment on them all." Dockery's native optimism had risen like the Phoenix from the flames.

Then, William told his friend what he had seen the night of the fire.

"You're certain you weren't dreaming?" Dockery asked, shocked by what William had told him.

"I know the difference between sleep and awake," William answered. "I was awake, as awake as I am now."

Dockery nodded gravely and said he believed him. "Can you describe the man?"

William shook his head. He said the intruder was a man like other men, his face in that instant before the explosion a pale blur illuminated only by the hot coals beneath the alembic. Besides, he had only been half awake when the door opened.

"Did he speak, threaten, curse?" Dockery asked.

"He screamed, as if in pain," William said. "He might have burned himself. He was gone by the time we got ourselves into the passageway and were running for the stairs."

"You got me into the passageway. I might have died else. You saved my life, Doctor William Gilbert—for which thing I thank you."

"I could hardly let you burn."

"Yes, you could, my friend. Many would have. Especially in this place."

"But I am a doctor," William said. "I have taken an oath to do no harm."

"The harm was not yours, but the devil you saw in the doorway."

"Nonetheless," William said. "Say no more about it. It's all past now."

"I will say no more then, but I will not forget," Dockery said. "Nor should you. And when I am able, I will do for you what you have done for me."

Early the next morning a guard came to take them to the warden. William was not surprised by the summons. He knew the warden would have received a report of damage and been told where the fire had begun. But William was determined that his alchemist friend would not bear the blame, although he worried that his own account of events might not be believed. Even to him, his story sounded false and self-serving, a way of avoiding accountability by blaming the fire on a mysterious intruder. Already he imagined the warden's skeptical response. He might not even let William get the whole story out before cutting him off and denouncing his account as a blatant lie.

But he resolved to try. It was, after all, another true story he was prepared to tell. He owed it to himself, and he owed it to Dockery, who would not be in his present difficulties or have lost his books and precious alembic had it not been for William.

In the warden's office, both William and Dockery were made to stand

235

before his desk, already tried and convicted, or so William feared. At first, the warden just glared. He did not speak. Then he shook his head, more in disgust than sadness. He said:

"Doctor Gilbert and Master Dockery. I must put down the blame for this conflagration on one of you. Which shall it be, the alchemist or the physician?"

Before his friend could answer, William said, "The fault was mine, Master Warden. Dockery had naught to do with it, save his chemicals were ignited in the process."

The warden studied the faces of both men, then he fixed his gaze on William. His eyes narrowed. "Doctor, if you have a story to tell, say, that the fire was an accident, the work of an enemy, or from some mysterious source in the heavens, I pray you tell me. I am an open-minded man, and I do love a good story whether it be truth or fiction. But take care, Doctor. I assure you I am able to tell the difference."

William decided he might as well speak plainly. He could hardly be in more trouble in telling the truth than he was now and having a higher opinion of the warden since the night of the fire, he considered the possibility that truth would prevail.

He told the warden what he remembered, the opening of the cell door, the shadowy figure in the doorway, a glimpse of a white face, and then a flash, some manner of explosive that set the room on fire. He said he also heard a cry of pain at the same moment and had thought first it came from his cellmate, but then recognized that Dockery was just coming out of sleep.

The warden turned to Dockery. "You were asleep and did not see this intruder the doctor reports?"

Dockery said he did not, but that he swore by his beard that everything that William said was true. "The doctor would not lie, Master Warden."

"We shall see about that, Master Dockery," the warden said. He turned back to William. "You are saying that this fire was deliberately set—not by you or Dockery here, but by some mysterious figure at your door that wished both of you harm?"

"I do believe I was the intended victim, Master Warden, not Dockery. Indeed, I do know it."

The warden studied William again, as though there might be something in his face he had missed in his earlier scrutiny. "And why, Doctor? Have

236

you made enemies here since your arrival? Have you so offended your fellow inmates that one would want to kill you? Pray what offense did you commit and to whom?"

"None within the prison I think," William said. "I was warned by a friend that the husband and parents of my dead patient wanted revenge."

"What friend?"

"Another doctor, with whom I studied at the university and who knows I am innocent of these false charges. He came here to visit me and warned me to take care where I walked in the prison. He said I might suffer what he called an accident, though it would be none."

"He might better have warned you against the dangers of falling asleep," the warden said drily. "So let me see if I understand you, Doctor. You see this fire as an act of revenge, a sort of private justice?"

"So I believe, Master Warden."

"And in exacting such revenge the arsonist was willing to kill your cellmate and put in jeopardy all the rest of us. If that is it, I would say their thirst for vengeance is extreme, for the responsibility for your patient's death is yours, none other's, and yet the fire might have consumed us all."

William did not answer this, but he knew the warden was right. The whole prison might have been destroyed, along with a good part of the neighborhood round about. Hundreds of lives might have been sacrificed.

For a while, no one talked. William waited. He exchanged glances with Dockery, who seemed nervous, as though he had been the one whose story the warden was evaluating.

Then, to William's surprise, the warden asked, "Doctor, do you know an inmate here named Roger Martins?"

William said he did not.

"You've never heard his name?" the warden asked. "He was a bricklayer before. Gambling proved his downfall. He ended up owing money to many a lender in the City."

"No, Master Warden, upon my oath, I don't know the man, nor have I ever as much as heard his name," William said.

"Well, I believe he knew you, Doctor, for I do think he was the man who entered your cell and flung an explosive device within."

William was astonished—first, that the warden seemed to believe his account, then that the warden already had the name of the arsonist. He breathed a sigh of relief. It seemed to him almost a miraculous deliverance.

"I swear by heaven, Master Warden, that I have never known this Martins, or heard tell of him. But I would gladly speak to him to learn by whose orders he did what he did to put me and the prison in such jeopardy."

"I'm sure you would, Doctor, as would I," the warden said. "Sadly, that opportunity has passed us by. Martins is dead. This very morning one of the inmates, this man named Martins, was found on the floor of his cell. His face and neck and shoulders were badly burned. His pain must have been such that he wished for death, rather than endure it. When he was discovered, he was near gone. I don't think even your salves and lotions would have spared him, Doctor, for he writhed in agony. Indeed, it was his screams that alerted others to his distress. In his cell, which he had occupied alone for several weeks, were found materials for making explosives; principally, black powder. Where he might have obtained such, God knows, although the street vendors sell almost everything to the inmates, as I am sure you have observed."

"It might have been smuggled in," William said.

"Yes, that's possible. In any case, do you know, Doctor, what a grenade is?"

William said he did. He had heard former soldiers tell of them and their devilish consequences to body and property.

"We found one made of clay among Martins' things," the warden said. "It is crudely wrought, nothing worthy of a good soldier's use. It is more likely to blow up in one's face than not, which is what happened in Martins' case. Whether he made it himself, or it was made for him, we cannot tell and may never know, now that he's dead."

"Did this Martins say anything before he died, say who hired him to kill me?"

"Had he done so, that would have been to your advantage, Doctor, although his confession may only have satisfied your curiosity. After all, what could you have done against these persecutors you describe? How could you have proved from a poor bricklayer's word the complicity of the high and mighty? It is certain they would have an intermediary to do the hiring of Martins. They that are rich and powerful ever have servants to do their bidding. They do little for themselves, and certainly no common crimes like arson and murder. Besides which, sometimes ignorance of the truth is better if there is no way to act upon it."

William said he believed it was always better to know the truth whether one could do anything about it or not.

The warden shrugged. "Well, Doctor, you are the philosopher, not I, so I will grant you your point. Yet we did find another thing, which I believe for you is more important."

The warden reached across his desk, where earlier William had seen a small slip of paper. It had not aroused his curiosity before. The warden handed it to William.

The writing on the paper looked somewhat familiar to him. Each letter was formed with a unique flourish, as though the author regarded his penmanship not merely as a substitute for speech but as an art—an art to be admired by the reader, not merely understood.

What was written there was only a name.

It was his own.

William was at first amazed, but then as suddenly relieved. This was indeed evidence of the truth of his story. The warden said, "I think this— the grenade and your name here—bears out your account, improbable as it first seemed. I believe, Doctor, you were indeed the target of Martins' enmity. I would invite you to examine the arsonist's face, to see if it was the one you say you observed before the first explosion, but, sadly for purposes of justice, the man was badly burned. There is not much of his face discernable. The question before us now is, assuming Martins was not the prime mover in this attempt but a mere tool or hireling—say, of this outraged husband or grieving parents, or some other person—will there be a second attempt, and if that does not succeed, even a third? I say this, you understand, not merely out of concern for your safety, Doctor, but for the safety of us all."

It was a question William had been considering since the night of the fire. Why *wouldn't* his enemies try again, find another hireling to accomplish what Martins had failed to do? The prison was full of desperate men eager for release, desperate for money, and doubtless with few qualms about killing a fellow prisoner.

"It would seem you are a marked man, Doctor," the warden said.

39

William knew the warden was right. He was a marked man, and he now understood he had been so since his first and fateful interview with Thomas Fanshaw. He suspected that rumor of Martins' failed effort would get out among the other inmates, and he would become the object of curiosity and even fear. Some would shun him. Others would be waiting for the next attempt on his life—perhaps even hoping for it, if only for a relief from the monotony of prison life.

As it turned out, he and Dockery had been assigned a new cell and given new pallets, water bucket, chamber pot. All else, necessities or luxuries, were theirs to pay for. William gave Dockery money to buy a new table. Dockery had already bought several books to rebuild his library. He told William that although he was forbidden more alchemical experiments, he had not been forbidden to read of them, to think of them, to dream of them.

"I will start again, from the beginning," Dockery said happily.

William decided not to leave the cell, which was a bit larger than the old one and on another floor of the prison house. He commissioned Dockery to buy food for the both of them and whatever else they needed. "They're after me, not you," he told his cellmate, who did not seem particularly comforted by that assurance.

Then, two days after their meeting with the warden, a guard came to the cell door to tell William he was summoned a second time to the warden's office.

He followed the guard across the yard, alert on all sides for anyone who might threaten him. His passage drew stares from other inmates as he walked, or perhaps he only imagined they were staring at him.

When they came to the warden's door, William was at once ushered in by the warden himself; not into his office as before, but to an adjoining room that, given its more commodious furnishing, was the parlor for the warden's residence. The warden shut the door behind him as he left.

Julian Mottelay stood by a window. The priest's face wore a reassuring smile.

William was about to ask what the priest was doing in the warden's quarters rather than meeting with him in the yard or in his cell, but the priest anticipated William's question.

"The warden was at one time a parishioner of mine, before the great divide and his faith and my vocation got us both in trouble. Do not be surprised, Doctor. For every knee that bows to the Queen's new religion, another remains faithful to the old, but in secret. Yes, Doctor, in secret. Your warden is one who keeps his worship to himself. He doesn't want to lose his lucrative appointment as warden any more than I want to lose my head. I beseech you to keep his secret as much as you keep mine and I, yours."

William promised he would. The two men sat down.

"I told the warden you were one of the faithful. He believes I have come to hear your confession."

"And have you?"

Mottelay laughed. "Not today, my friend. In truth, I have come to give you more news of Parmenter Hall and the mysterious Stephen Gresham. I have also brought you some things that will satisfy your bodily needs." He pointed to a canvas bag William hadn't seen upon entering, which appeared to be full of foodstuffs.

"I thank you for both," William said.

"You are quite welcome, Doctor. But to my most pressing business. For if your confession takes too much time the warden will grow suspicious and think our conversing deals with something sinister. Therefore, to the point. Since my last visit and the discovery of Gresham's treasonous embezzlement, Lady Parmenter has been more open about his history."

"And you have learned what?" William asked.

"I have learned, for example, that it was he who recommended a friend of his from his university days as the doctor to their daughter prior to the marriage."

"Orlando Kempe?"

"The same," Mottelay said. "Not only that, but according to Lady

241

Parmenter, your friend Kempe visited the Hall some several years past. Twice he came, according to her. She remembered him as a handsome, charming young man, who spent almost a month there, after which he left to continue his medical studies in Italy, she believes. When he returned, Lady Parmenter secured his services as Alice's physician, again upon Gresham's commendation, which she took readily, she being quite infatuated herself by his manly charms. When Alice married, Kempe followed her to Maldon House."

"Which seems quite reasonable," William said. "After all, if Alice was satisfied with him as a doctor, why should she find another?"

"You mean *if Lady Parmenter was satisfied*," Mottelay said. "She ruled her daughter's will."

"Save in the matter of Alice's lovers," William reminded him.

"Perhaps true," Mottelay said. "Gresham was born on the Parmenter estate. His father had been a groom, a rather ordinary fellow who was often drunk and disorderly. When his son proved to be more clever than his humble birth suggested he might be, the Parmenters paid his way to Cambridge. There he stayed but for a year."

"Long enough to make a friend of Kempe," William said.

"Yes. And then he returned to Parmenter Hall where he quickly made himself indispensable to Sir John and his lady. You know the rest of the story. Now their love for him has turned to hate, given his treachery. Though he now is dead and buried, their hatred has not ended."

There was a pause, then Mottelay said, "William, how well did you two really know each other at Cambridge, you and this Orlando Kempe? Were you fast friends, or merely acquaintances?"

"More the latter, now I think upon it," William answered. "When he appeared on my doorstep a month ago to offer me the prospect of Fanshaw's patronage, I didn't recognize him. At least, not at first. We shared, if I remember, a lecture or two, studied under the same professor of anatomy. Once he came with me to dinner at the house of my Dutch friend, Pieter Weinmeer, whilst he lived in Cambridge. We were not in the same college, St. John's. He was in another, I don't remember which."

Mottelay did not respond to this but continued to look at William thoughtfully.

"He has proved his loyalty since," William said, as much to himself as to Mottelay. "He diverted my pursuers when I left for Amsterdam, telling

Fanshaw I went to Wales or Cornwall. He hid me in his house when I returned and came to visit me here to warn me that I was in danger, that Fanshaw and Parmenter plotted to kill me even before my trial, not willing to let the law take its course. And his warning proved true. I was nearly killed."

"Yes, the warden told me. And he who did it is now dead."

"He will never be more so. The attempt came near to blowing his head off."

"His just deserts, I think," Mottelay said.

"I don't know how to explain this," William said. "I weigh Kempe's acts of generosity and goodness to me in one hand, and this questionable relationship with Simon Gresham in the other."

"I have found something else, about Gresham," Mottelay said. "Apparently, he and your friend Kempe were doing some business together, an investment. I found among his papers which he left behind him, this agreement."

The priest handed William a single-page document. Written on heavy parchment, it was indeed a partnership agreement of sorts, though sparely and plainly worded as though no lawyer had a hand in its drafting. It bound Simon Gresham and Orlando Kempe, wherein they agreed to divide profits from a mining venture in Wales and each offered a similar payment of two hundred pounds, share and share alike. Both men had signed at the bottom.

"This explains what Gresham was doing with the money he embezzled from his employers." William said. "Yet I wonder that Kempe had so much to invest. He is successful in London and lives in a fine house with servants and the rest. But two hundred pounds to invest in a Welsh mine?"

"Perhaps he has income of another source," Mottelay said. "Is his family well-to-do?"

"His father is a poor vicar somewhere, I think, nothing more. Kempe spoke ever of him disparagingly when he said anything at all. Kempe puts on a guise of affability, but in fact he is a very private person."

"Then perhaps he has a generous patron?"

"He always boasted of the great number of his patients but never named them," William said. "There was, of course, Thomas Fanshaw, and before him Sir John."

"Perhaps Alice was his only patient," Mottelay said. "And all the rest imagined or invented to impress."

243

"And Fanshaw paying him enough to buy his London house and dress as he does? That's hard to believe, Father."

William read through the agreement again and then noticed what he should have seen at first view.

It was the handwriting of him who drafted it. Its elegant flourishes and curves were identical to that of his would-be assassin's note. Either Kempe or Gresham had drafted the agreement. One of them had also written his name on the note: a virtual death warrant.

It could not have been Gresham, since he was floating in the pond, dead even before William was sent to prison.

Which left Kempe.

His heart raced. He felt sick. Why had he not seen it earlier, even when Kempe first approached him with the offer of a rich patron? When he realized what Fanshaw really wanted of him? All of Kempe's professed friendship had been a self-serving deception. The magnitude of the betrayal dumbfounded him. Despite this new evidence, he struggled to believe it.

"The handwriting on the note and this on the agreement is the same," William said, when he could finally find his voice. "It is the same, I tell you. If it is not, I will forsake science and turn court jester. Mark me in that and hold me to it."

"But if true, why warn you of the very evil he intended?" Mottelay asked.

"I don't know," William admitted. "I don't know. Yet the handwriting is the same, I have no doubt about that, and it is my name written upon the paper found in Martins' cell."

"Martins?"

"He who blew himself up in endeavoring to do the same to me."

For a moment, neither spoke. Then Mottelay asked, "What are you thinking, my friend?"

"Dark thoughts, Julian, dark thoughts," William said. "Was Kempe the principal in this plot, or only an intermediary? That he is at least the latter is now certain. That he acts on another's instruction rather than his own malice remains to be proved."

For a few moments, the two men were silent. Then Mottelay said, "Pray to God for clarity of mind and direction." Mottelay took William by the shoulders as though he were one of his own flock.

"You urge that of a heretic, as you suppose me to be?" William asked.

"I would so advise any man, be he heretic or no," Mottelay said. "God opens the door to him who knocks."

"And what of human reason?" William asked.

"What is it but a gift of God?" Mottelay returned. "Use the reason God has given you to ferret out the truth of these matters that so bedevil you and have brought you to this pass."

A knock came at the door. The warden looked in. He wanted to know if they had finished their business.

"Yes, Master Warden, we are done here," Mottelay said, standing.

"And was it a good confession?" whispered the warden, looking satisfied that he had participated in the redemption of one of his inmates.

"A very good confession, Warden," Mottelay said, smiling at William. "And an act of contrition, promised henceforth at least."

The warden made a quick sign of the cross. "Then I shall wish you both a very good night."

"Good night to you, Master Warden," Mottelay said.

When Mottelay and William were alone, William said. "Pray tell, what act of contrition have I promised you, sir priest?"

Mottelay smiled. "A good supper in the City, for which you pay the account. My choice of place and hour."

"Done," William said absently. His thoughts were elsewhere. He could think of nothing else but Kempe and his betrayal.

The bag Mottelay had brought with him contained several green apples, a pigeon pie in a wooden bowl, some fresh carrots and parsley, and a loaf of black bread. There were also two bottles of Spanish claret, one for him and one for his cellmate. Dockery could eat it all. William had no appetite. But when William returned to his cell, Dockery was gone.

A guard came by and opened the door. "You'll have this cell all to yourself, Doctor, at least for the time being. "

"Where's Dockery?" William asked.

"Oh, he's gone, probably gone for good, save he gets in the same trouble as before with his creditors. Some friend of his paid his debts and sent a coach for him. A coach, would you believe? He left us like a great gentleman." The guard laughed.

"Did he say anything before he left?" William asked.

"He said, *farewell*. He said farewell to us all. And he said, *God save the Queen and them that serve her.* And to be honest, Doctor, he said not another word."

"He said nothing about me? Left no message as to where he went?"

"Not that I remember, Doctor. No, not that I remember. But his face lit up, Doctor."

"What do you mean his face lit up?"

"All smiles, he was. All smiles, as though he just found gold in his hat, as though his alchemy finally worked."

40

William ate none of the carrots, little of the pigeon pie and bread, but he drank both bottles of the claret. He was too besotted after to think much of what he had learned that day from Julian Mottelay about Kempe and Simon Gresham, whom he now thought of as twin devils deserving eternal damnation for their crimes. He slept restlessly, awaking every time he heard a voice or squeak and in the meantime dreaming terrible dreams, in which once again he struggled to get Dockery out of his bed and to safety. But sometimes it was not Dockery he struggled with but Orlando Kempe, who instead of being terrified at the prospect of death kept mocking William's efforts like a trained monkey William had seen once at Colchester on market day.

Come morning, William kept to his cell as had been his practice since the night of the fire. He thought over the new evidence. He found a new discrepancy of fact that he determined to add to the roster of evidence of Orlando Kempe's complicity, but wasn't sure how it fitted in. He remembered that when he visited the vicarage at Maidenstowe he had impulsively given his name as Orlando Kempe to the vicar to disguise his identity. But when he returned to Maidenstowe with the Parmenters, they had addressed him by his true name. How had the vicar known? Who had informed him? Was that addled old man also a part of the plot against him, or had the remover of the bodies—Fanshaw himself, or perhaps Kempe as his tool—informed the vicar of William's true name? The latter seemed the most probable.

Scientific investigation, as William saw it, began with a clearly phrased question. It proceeded successfully when it maintained a sharp focus. It concluded successfully when it answered the same question. But here William felt almost overwhelmed by evidence. His task was to sort it out.

247

Yet he was sure now that Kempe wanted him dead, but not whether Kempe acted for himself or for Fanshaw. That he should be a tool for Fanshaw was simplest to understand. Fanshaw was the wronged party, or so he professed. And Fanshaw wanted revenge for the supposed murder of his wife. But even if Fanshaw were the guilty party and used Kempe as an intermediary, that still did not explain Kempe's motive for betraying William. Was it money? Was Kempe so corrupt, so devoid of conscience and honor? What had William ever done to Kempe that he should want to entrap him, torment him, kill him?

And why should Kempe have warned him? Was the warning sincere, or was it designed merely to torment him with the prospect of death like the mythical Sword of Damocles of which William had read as a child?

All William knew seemed muddled, the evidence vague and contradictory, pointing in too many directions and incorporating into a web of guilt too many persons. He badly needed a hypothesis or two, and experiments that would clarify and resolve. But now his head ached too much from the claret and the sound sleep that had eluded him. Why had he drunk it all? He had not the habit of drink when he was at Cambridge, where his reputation was that of a dull and sober youth, preferring his books and experiments to petty vice and debauchery. Doctor Magnetic, he was called. Whatever else it suggested, the cognomen did not describe a lover of pleasure.

During the morning he continued to go over the events of summer until he wished for Dockery to be there, at least for a diversion. He had liked Dockery, and he considered him a friend for all his eccentricity and obsession with alchemy. He was happy that Dockery, his debts paid, had been released. Paid by whom? His wife? A rich uncle? A patron of science? The guard had said he left in a coach. What did that mean? Perhaps it did not matter. Dockery was gone, and William was alone.

Until he was assigned another cellmate, one who might prove more successful than Martins had been. Perhaps this time it would not be an explosive device, but something simpler and even more deadly—poison, a knife in the back, a garrote about his neck, a needle-like blade inserted deftly beneath his breast.

At midday, William received yet another surprise, the last thing he expected and a thing that came both as a relief and as a threat. Again, he was summoned to the warden's quarters. He arrived to find the warden in an unusually jovial mood, as though he had just received an unexpected gift as perhaps, William later suspected, he might have—given how little was done in the prison without a fee.

"Well, Doctor Gilbert. It does seem your stay with us has been fore-shortened. You are a fortunate man. At least fortunate in your friends."

"Master Warden?"

"This gentleman here has worked your release from this place. You are to accompany him."

William looked behind him. It was Captain Broward, the officer who had brought William to the prison and wished him well in what Broward had called William's new home.

William asked where he was to be taken. Broward said that he would find out for himself soon enough. He was told to ask no further questions. They were to leave immediately.

"But what of my things in the cell?"

It was a foolish question, William admitted to himself as soon as he uttered it. What little he had, had been destroyed in the fire. His precious notebook was ash, along with the letter from Katrina. The only clothes he had were those on his back.

41

William had never in his life ridden in a coach. His few travels to London with his father and from Colchester to Cambridge had been on horseback. For shorter distances, he walked. The door of the one in which he was invited to take a seat bore armorial bearings, but William did not recognize them. Broward sat in a seat across from him and looked from the window as the coach left Southwark and crossed the river into the City. Within an hour they had left London behind and were speeding through the countryside.

All this, while William had a single thought. The attempt on his life had failed. Was this now not a release from prison but an abduction in which he would be carried to some remote place and summarily executed? After all that had happened, this did not seem a remote possibility to him. Rather, it seemed his likely fate.

During his tumultuous ride he could think of nothing else. Mottelay had advised him to pray to God for clarity and direction. At the moment that did seem the proper course of action. Given his imminent demise, the complexities of his case now seemed irrelevant. Standing before Deity, he would inquire into what happened to him and why. God knew. Even if William did not. Perhaps God would make all plain.

The journey lasted for hours it seemed, although later he understood it was in truth much shorter. They stopped once to rest the horses and relieve themselves behind a tree, Broward standing close to William as though he feared his escape. During the journey Broward never spoke. He sometimes seemed to sleep even though the coach jostled dangerously over rutted roads at a breakneck speed.

William did not sleep. Even with the tumult of the night before, the alarming dreams, the banging head in the morning, he did not sleep. He could not.

Finally, in the late afternoon, William looked from the window to see a rise and beyond it as large a house as he had ever seen. It seemed more like unto a king's residence than a gentleman's manor house. It covered acres of land. It rose three stories in height with a central tower and dozens and dozens of mullioned windows that must have employed a hundred glaziers in their making. William imagined it as a house that the Queen might visit on one of her summer progresses, a visit like the one that had bankrupted Sir John Parmenter before his debts were paid in the fateful marriage settlement.

"That is Theobalds," Broward announced in a gravelly voice, breaking his silence at last.

"Theobalds," Broward repeated. "It is one of the houses of Lord Burghley. It is his lordship's residence."

William's heart sank. He knew that the secretary, William Cecil, had just that year been raised to that honor. It had been broadcast throughout England and was widely praised as a suitable commendation for one whose counsel to the Queen was indispensable for her happiness and security.

William also remembered that it was the same Lord Burghley who had signed the warrant for his arrest. His worst fears had been confirmed. He had gone from prison to a worse state, directly into the hands of his chief prosecutor.

The coachmen drove them around to the rear of the manor where there was an entrance William supposed designed for servants and tradesmen although it was larger than the entrances of most manor houses and far grander. He imagined the staff to serve such a house must number in the dozens, if not hundreds. Theobalds was not merely a lord's home. It was a village, a small city.

One of the coachmen came around and opened the door to help William down. It was help he needed, for his feet and legs were severely cramped by the uncomfortable journey and at first, he walked awkwardly, like a mariner finding his land legs again. He was not led into the house, but suddenly, coming out the door was another surprise, one that gave him a glimpse of hope.

William could hardly believe it. It was Dockery. Was he dreaming all of this?

Then Dockery spoke his name. The men embraced, as though it were a month rather than a day or two since they had seen each other last.

Broward, having apparently done his duty in bringing William here, went inside leaving him unguarded. William and Dockery were alone.

"Why are you here?" William asked of Dockery, when at last he found his voice. "I supposed you went home to your wife and children, to enjoy their company and return to your trade."

"Ah, not yet that," Dockery replied. "Soon, perhaps, if my good wife will have me back. But to answer your question, I am here by the beneficence of Lord Burghley, who despite our difference in degree, I do account a friend."

"You do have friends in high places," William said.

"We corresponded with each other whilst I was in prison," Dockery said. "We share an interest in alchemy, about which his lordship is surprisingly learned. Indeed, Lord Burghley is interested in all scientific inquiry. His library, which I trust you will have opportunity to peruse, is a wonder of the age. For friendship's sake, he paid my debt which to him was a mere trifle. I was released, and he fetched me here, even as he fetched you."

"But why me?" William asked, still unsure that all that was happening around him was truly real and not a dream.

"Because I told him of you, my friend."

"Told him what of me?"

"Your study of magnets, the excellence of your thinking and work. I told him you were at St. John's College at Cambridge, which pleased him, since it was his own college whilst there."

"Did he remember my case?"

"Oh, yes. The warrant he had signed, your imprisonment. I told him I believed you innocent of every charge made against you. I said you were good and honest and a great doctor and scientist, though but a young man. I sang your praises, my friend, until my throat was raw, whereupon his lordship bid me cease. He said he had heard enough of this Doctor Gilbert and all that remained was that you must appear before him straightway to answer for yourself."

William made a little bow to his former cellmate and said, "I owe you, Dockery, a thousand thanks and more. You do not know how you have set my mind at ease. I did think my fate was sealed when I learned this was Lord Burghley's house."

"His lordship said he did not know whether you were guilty or no, but he was intrigued by what he called your *experiments magnetical.* He said

252

if you were to languish in a cell, you might more profitably languish here to tell him of your work. And so here you stand, a guest at Theobalds. Do tell me, what did you think of Broward?"

"Think of him?"

"He who brought you here, by his lordship's orders. The eight-foot, sober-faced gentleman with the sword as long. He commands his lordship's personal guard, and a more grim personage you have yet to meet. He does outdo his lordship in that department each day of the week."

"Broward was the officer who brought me to the prison. He was no stranger to me, or I to him. He said not a word the whole of the journey here, although he was talkative enough when he conveyed me to prison."

"True, he is somewhat melancholic and aloof, but a deep thinker I assure you, and a most dangerous enemy. He has nicked his sword with the number of men he has killed, or so they say."

It was then they were interrupted by a rush of men and maid servants emerging from the house to greet an old, white-bearded fellow wearing a wide-brimmed hat and riding upon a donkey. William, who had turned to look at this strange apparition, said, "It would seem Father Time has come home again."

Dockery began to laugh, almost uncontrollably. Then suddenly he ceased and became quite serious.

"Bite your impudent tongue, William. And be ashamed. That is Lord Burghley, once your prosecutor, now your benefactor. He prefers his donkey to a stallion and rides regularly in late afternoon for exercise."

42

William still thought himself caught up in some dream, strolling as he now was through the immense gardens of Theobalds, his guide arguably, as Dockery had said, the most powerful man in England. A man who had the ear of the Queen but also her affection. A man who was both lawyer and scholar, loyal to his royal mistress, yet a shrewd politician, a stern moralist, a most dangerous enemy.

He was also the man who had signed the warrant for William's arrest, and that thought never left William's mind.

William Cecil, Lord Burghley, whom William had first taken as an old man, was upon closer inspection a gentleman in his early fifties, of middle stature, with a fine, white beard and a high broad forehead, which ever marked superiority of mind.

He said, "Doctor Gilbert, I signed the warrant for your arrest, taking the word of Master Thomas Fanshaw, with whom I have done some business in the past. Whether you be guilty as sin, or innocent as a lamb, I thought I would leave to the judicial counsel. As for now, you are my guest, and, more, my instructor, for your study of magnets and their powers I understand touches on more than mere attraction but speaks to the very nature of the earth."

"It does my lord, it does indeed." William started to explain how the poles of the earth, north and south, displayed the same characteristics as magnets. How the earth itself was a giant lodestone. It was his favorite topic. But Burghley bade him stop.

"Well, then you may demonstrate your mighty proofs, but not now. We can talk together later, perhaps tomorrow when you and I are fresh in mind and in body. Now, while we have an hour or more left of the light of day, I want to show you some specimens of plants and herbs brought to me by our doughty seamen, and more particularly Sir Francis Drake, of whose wondrous voyages I trust you have heard.'"

"Who has not, my lord?"

Burghley said, "Some praise Her Majesty's seamen for the new lands they discover, in the Americas, India, and far Cathay, but to me it is not so much where they go to plant our flag as what they bring home to us that causes me to celebrate their achievements. I mean not merely riches, gold and silver, but new species of plants and herbs. As you are a doctor, I think that should interest you as much."

"It does, my lord," William answered. "I do pray in time to come every human ailment or affliction will find a corresponding cure, perhaps in some remote clime that no man has yet set foot upon."

The garden at Theobalds was laid out with marvelous symmetry that would in itself have required a skilled architect. Everywhere there were signs of artful design, rather than the cultivated wildness common in English gardens. All along the paved path, William observed plants he did not recognize. Plants with strange stalks and multicolored leaves and some with berries or fruit unlike any he had ever before seen. Cecil gave a name to each, describing their character, their place of natural origin, speculating on their medical use, even describing how some could be safely and healthfully eaten and how others were a deadly poison. In nature, Burghley said, even poison has its utility. "In protecting the plant from creatures that would use it for food, even as the porcupine does discourage larger and more voracious animals from making it their supper."

"Yet I have heard, my lord, for those who study such creatures that even the porcupine with all its quills is eaten by wolves and like predators."

"Have you?" Burghley said, looking at William in such a way to suggest that William's correction was unwelcome. Burghley resumed discoursing on poisoned plants about which he seemed to know a great deal. "These we hope to keep from the Italians, who use poison as a political instrument. We English are not so, preferring to sever heads under the cover of law. In love or war, there is something unmanly about poison, don't you agree, Doctor Gilbert?"

William, fearing he might have offended in contradicting his host, rushed to agree. "I do think poison is unmanly. The victim thereof may be dead before he realizes he is in the presence of an enemy. He may be poisoned by him thought to be a friend. Friendship is the best disguise of villainy."

Smiling, Burghley said, "Better advice for a man in public life could hardly be given, Doctor. I pray I may have permission to quote you, for I assume your statement is original. I don't think I have encountered it in my classical studies."

Flattered, William said Burghley could use the statement wherever he wished and was welcome to it, for he said he had had some bad experiences that confirmed its truth and a truth, even a sad one, was always worth repeating.

"Those experiences, Doctor, we may find time to discuss before you depart from here."

Burghley said he had three apothecaries in the house whose duty it was to examine each plant or variety thereof for its virtues and potential use and twenty gardeners whose purpose was to cultivate and nourish them.

"They live in terror of any specimen failing to flourish" Burghley said. "They know I walk among the plants every day whilst I am here at Theobalds. I think of all as my children, and should anything mar my pleasure, they would endure my wrath. In truth, I do think I am more tolerant and merciful than that, but it serves my purpose for them to think me more a tyrant in the garden than I truly be."

Burghley laughed at this, and William joined because he saw it was expected of him to approve of his lordship's humor.

In the garden William also saw long ranks of flowers of various sorts, roses of a hundred varieties. Frequently, they stopped, so that Burghley could invite William to inhale a perfume or admire a particular shade of color. He was invited, too, to admire the statues of mythic figures that stood among the plantings. These Burghley identified, although William recognized most. They were celebrated figures of the classical pantheon, Pan with his pipe, Cupid with his bow, and Priapus, with his enormous member, menacing a sylvan nymph.

On the latter, Burghley commented. "Priapus, as you undoubtedly know from your classical studies, was the Roman god of horticulture and viticulture. The Romans used his statue in gardens to scare away crows and other birds that do harm to gardens. Yet he represents fertility as well, as his strong and conspicuous erection does proclaim. Our ladies walking here often pause in admiration of such wondrous virility. What think you, Doctor?"

256

"I have never seen the like in my medical examinations, but then perhaps the ancients were built differently from those of us who now live. It is thought by philosophers that we are lesser creatures than were in ancient times, that there is a great falling off in every way."

"And what is your opinion of such a notion?" Burghley asked, with an expression of genuine interest that gave William confidence to respond boldly.

"I think it is nonsense, my lord. If anything, man is getting better with time, stronger in intellect and doubtless in body as well, for we are now taller, for example, than the Romans were. We are more judicious in our tastes, more subtle in art, and moral in our religion. Certainly, we are more diligent in our science, for we are not content to merely parrot the so-called wisdom of the ancients, but we put such principles to the test. We experiment. We learn for ourselves."

"Ah, Doctor, you speak with the passion of an evangelist," Burghley said.

"I am sorry, my lord, if I get carried away. I know it is a fault in me."

"No fault in you, Doctor. A thinker without passion is no thinker at all."

They must have walked a mile or more before Burghley said they had seen all that was to be seen. But William was not tired, not now. The exercise of his limbs had done his whole body good and his mind as well. Perhaps, he thought, it was the freshness of the air, or the expansive view. After the visual deprivation of the prison, Burghley's wondrous garden was a delight to his senses, reminding him of the natural beauty of the world, especially given his uncertainty as to how long he would enjoy it.

When the light began to fail, one of the servants who had been following Burghley and William at a politic distance ran forward to place a cloak upon his master's shoulders. "Let us go inside now," Burghley said. "You will want to inspect my library. There you will see my interests range beyond botany and horticulture. If I read the time aright, we still have a good hour before supper."

They proceeded then indoors to a splendid interior that William thought made the manor houses of Thomas Fanshaw and Sir John Parmenter modest cottages by comparison. The house swarmed with menservants and maidservants, and other persons William took to be clerks and secretaries, attendants and grooms. From somewhere in the great house he could smell the aroma of meat cooking and it filled him suddenly with a deep hunger, for he had not eaten all day, or well since he had been confined to prison. He saw other persons—of clearly higher station, by

257

their dress—whom he assumed were members of his lordship's family or guests, for he knew that such great houses as Theobalds were often as bustling as inns.

In all this he kept looking for Dockery, as a kind of anchor to the reality he had known, as bleak as that reality was. Now he was in a different world, elevated beyond his wildest imagination. Still he knew it was an illusory world as well, doubtless as replete with false friends and perilous alliances as the world he had lived in his youth and young manhood when he had taken far too much in his life at face value.

Burghley, continuing his role as William's guide, explained that Theobalds was no ancient seat from Norman or Saxon times, but a house he himself had conceived and designed. He said it was several years in the building and had occupied the talents of the finest architects, stonemasons, glaziers, and carpenters in England. He said it was as much a tribute to English workmanship as it was to whatever status he himself had achieved in service to his queen, and that he would gladly give it to her, should she ask it of him. "Although I do think for the time being Her Majesty has palaces sufficient for her needs. She has been my guest here more than five times in the past few years, she and her entourage. She loves the house, I believe, more than I, were that possible."

They came presently to a wide double door that when opened revealed a darkly paneled interior with a high-beamed, decorated ceiling and an array of more books than he had ever before seen, even more than at the library of his Cambridge college. They covered every wall and rose a dozen feet or more so that some were only accessible by ladder. "I understand from your friend Dockery, that you were at St. John's college whilst you were at Cambridge."

"I had that honor, my lord."

"I spent many a pleasant hour in the library there," Burghley said. "This would have been, of course, before your time. When my fortunes improved, through judicious investment and government service, I sought to match the splendor of that library."

William said, "I do believe, my lord, that you have gone quite beyond it, for never have I seen so rich a collection or in such a variety of languages."

William had gotten close enough to the shelves that lined each wall, save where there was a large window looking out upon the garden, to note titles in Latin, Greek, French, Spanish, and German, although the bulk of the collection seemed to be in English. He wanted to ask whether his lordship had mastered all these tongues, but he thought the better of it. The last thing he wanted was to give offense to this mighty lord by implying that such a library was for show, as Mottelay claimed the Parmenter collection was, especially when his life depended on maintaining his lordship's good graces. For to this moment Burghley's manner had been more than friendly, it had been companionable. He was an English lord and William only an impoverished doctor and accused felon, but there had been no superciliousness in Burghley's manner toward him. Rather, Burghley had been the soul of courtesy. And all that was for the good.

Like Lady Elizabeth Parmenter, Burghley had his collection of curiosities in a smaller chamber adjacent to the library. "I confess I am a compulsive collector," Burghley said. "My friends who travel abroad insist on presenting me with souvenirs of their travels. What can I do but accept? My acceptance gives them as much pleasure as it does me."

Inside glass cases William saw what Burghley had called *souvenirs*. If there was ever a display of variety, it was surely before his eyes now. In cases of glass—and there must have been a dozen of them—he saw what appeared to be old Roman statuary, Greek vases, Spanish and French coins, as well as human skulls, and a display of jewels that a king might have prized. He saw a pearl as large as a goose's egg, and a petrified owl, fully feathered as though alive. There was indeed more than a man could take in, had he several hours to contemplate.

While William looked in awe, Burghley pointed out this curiosity and that, estimated the value of each were he capable of it, for he insisted that some items in his collection were invaluable. "They are one of a kind, so that no man can say what they be worth."

After a while a servant entered to say that supper was served, and William was now led into what Burghley called the great hall. And great it was—with a ceiling reaching thirty or forty feet, William estimated, and long tables arranged as in his Cambridge college, sufficient to seat every student and master. William noted from the crowded tables that Burghley observed the older custom of seating the whole household, master and servants, at a table, with His Lordship and his lady, and the children thereof, along with high-born guests, at places of lesser honor and distinction.

At this point, Burghley motioned to a plump younger servant standing

259

in the corner. "I give you, Doctor, into the custody of Peter Fellows, who has served me well these dozen years and I trust will serve you well while you are a guest at Theobalds." Having said this, he turned to the servant. "Peter, show Doctor Gilbert every courtesy, and do see he has a fresh change of garments while he is here."

William blushed at this reference to the state of his clothes, which had gone unchanged and unwashed since the prison fire, but was grateful for the promise of new ones, although he did hope they would fit.

Peter Fellows proved to be a pleasant young man, who conducted William to a place in the middle of the great hall where he occupied a bench next to him. What Burghley had described as supper turned out to be a feast, with at least six courses of fowl, beef, and pie, good ale and wine to drink. William ate ravenously, and Peter said, "I think you have not eaten in a year, for you are, Doctor, a very thin sort of man. I imagine you have not taken a wife to feed you."

"I have no wife to serve, or to obey," William said. "My thinness is an inheritance from my father."

"A better inheritance than fleshliness, which as you see is my father's legacy to me," Peter Fellows said. "I would I were half the man I am, and were I so, I would still be enough." Peter Fellows laughed at his own joke, and William, well-filled, grew merry with him.

While he ate, he looked around for Dockery, finally spying him on the other side of the cavernous chamber. They exchanged glances, smiled, and Dockery mouthed something that William could not interpret but which he imagined was satisfaction that William, like himself, was being well treated by their host.

Finally, and for William thankfully, the evening was done, the guests and servants slowly dispersed either to bed or duties, His Lordship and his lady, a distinguished-looking woman with finely molded features and magnificent gown, disappeared into another region of the immense house, and Peter Fellows led William up two flights of stairs to a narrow corridor lined with doors. For a moment, the memory of the prison house flashed before his eyes. But these doors had neither locks nor little widows for peering eyes. They enjoyed a delicious privacy, for which William had hungered more than a full belly or clean garments.

Within he found not a cell but a commodious chamber, well furnished with a real feather bed, not a straw pallet, solid, well-made furniture, and wall hangings depicting shepherds in what he assumed were French or Italian countryside. A fire had been laid in a hearth and several oil lamps illuminated the interior.

Best of all, already laid out on his bed were the fresh clothes Burghley had promised him. There were even shoes, although because he had large feet, he was doubtful they would fit. A bowl with warmed water, a towel, and a bar of scented soap lay by to his delight, for he longed as much to wash his body as to don a new suit of clothing. When Peter Fellows had bid him good night and left, William stripped naked, washed from head to toe, and dried himself by the fire. Then he fell into bed. He luxuriated in the freshness of the sheets and was asleep before he knew it.

It was another night in which he did not dream, but slept as though dead, and when he awoke, light was already streaming in his window. For the first time in weeks, he felt a kind of joy. He was alive, at least for now, and in a good place.

Whether it was a safe place as well, was yet to be seen.

43

William dressed quickly, pleased to find the clothes set out for him fit him well, although the shoes provided pinched his toes a bit. They were well made and new, rather than hand-offs, so he supposed he might work them in with time. It was the garb of a higher servant of the house, a clerk or secretary, which pleased him too, for he had no desire to present himself as a courtier or one whose sole merit was displayed on his back to make an impression on those lower than he. His own place in the hierarchy of man now perplexed him. He was gentry by birth since his father enjoyed that distinction, but for the past month he had been on a downward spiral as fugitive and accused felon. Which left him what, and where?

He waited a long while, expecting someone to come for him, to convey him downstairs, for he still felt himself a prisoner, restricted in his movements, subject to another's orders. But when no one appeared, he ventured forth to find the passage without unguarded. When he came to the head of the stairs, he met Peter Fellows coming up.

"Have you seen Master Dockery?" William asked.

"Why, your Master Dockery has long gone abroad," Fellows said.

"What do you mean abroad?" William asked, fearing that his friend had taken flight again.

"Master Dockery is in the garden. His lordship sent him forth to pick what specimens of plants he chooses for some experiment he intends. He rose early this morning to meet with his lordship, who enjoys beginning his day long before dawn and would sooner keep company with a scholar than a prince. He told me last night to let you lie abed as long as it pleased you. He thought your ordeal in prison was probably exhausting."

"That was very gracious of his lordship," William said.

"Will you have breakfast, Doctor?" Fellows asked, taking him by the arm and escorting him downstairs before he could answer.

That William was hungry after last night's feast surprised him, but it was true, and he was glad to be conveyed straightway to the kitchen, where a kindly cook provided him with bread and honey and a large bowl of oatmeal and cream. He was still eating when Dockery appeared, bearing a basket full of leaves and berries. Seeing him, William said, "I thought you were an alchemist. Have you converted to botany that you pass the hours harvesting rarities from his lordship's garden?"

Dockery laughed. "I have many interests, my friend, beyond the philosopher's stone. In prison there was a poor supply of plant life, English or foreign. Here, there is an abundance."

Dockery joined William at the table. "Tell me, William, how do you find Lord Burghley?"

William told him about the bedchamber he had been given and the new clothes. He said, "His lordship is interested in my magnetic studies. He said that I should come to him today and tell him all I know about magnets and their properties and powers, which I will gladly do."

"Did he say he would hear your case? When I told him about your science, I took the opportunity to sing your praises. And I said you had been falsely accused."

"And pray what did he say to that?" William asked.

"Nothing, I regret to say," Dockery answered. "But neither did he say he would not hear it. Have confidence in the man, my friend. He's sharp as a needle's point. Even when he seems inattentive, distracted by some other concern or voice, he is listening and assessing. There is no man in England more discerning of truth or zealous in its pursuit."

"You seem to know him well," William said.

"We have exchanged letters for years, and in those letters I have discovered his character as well as his noble thoughts. I know him also by reputation. In the City he is admired and respected even by his enemies."

"You are lavish in your praise of him."

"He is most deserving," Dockery said.

"I believe I am the more likely to find exoneration in his hands, than in any officer of the court," William said. "He seems a judicious man, not easily misled or gulled by falsehoods and preconceptions."

"I do believe in all of England you could not find a better judge of your case," Dockery said.

It was not until the afternoon that Peter Fellows appeared again, to escort William to the grand library, which William now realized was not only a repository of books but also a laboratory for the study of nature. He found Burghley sitting in a great chair pulled up before the fireplace, where a roaring fire was presently producing a great deal of heat. Nonetheless, Burghley had a thick woolen cloak wrapped around him and wore a soft round hat of a style William had never seen.

Noticing him, Burghley asked him to be seated. "Good day to you, Doctor."

"Good day, my lord. And many thanks for the clothing, for supper, and for the bedchamber, which is more commodious than ever I've had. I pray I may deserve all this."

"If you do not deserve it now, Doctor, yet you shall deserve it, for you must sing for your supper."

"My lord? William was about to explain that he could not sing, at least not well enough to avoid ridicule and scorn but then realized what Burghley meant. "As it please you, Your Lordship. I and my science are at your command."

At that moment, the door opened and into the library walked a well-dressed boy of seven or eight with a hunched back and a somewhat awkward stride. His face was not unhandsome, and his eyes had a thoughtful gaze of a youth curious and quick to learn. William rose instinctively.

Burghley said, "Doctor Gilbert, this is my youngest son, Robert. He is a bright young man according to his tutors, and in his father's judgment. When I told him of your knowledge of magnets and their miraculous powers, he prayed that he might attend your lecture."

"Lecture, my lord?" William said. "I fear I have not prepared so formal a presentation that it might be called a lecture. But I can tell you what I have learned in my experiments, and I do trust this young man will not be disappointed." William nodded toward Burghley's son, who returned a thin smile. The boy sat down in a third chair, in front of which was a low table with a bare top.

"Robert, fetch your magnets for the doctor." At this the boy rose and went into the adjoining room, where the night before William had been fascinated by the number and breadth of his host's collection of curiosities. "And bring also something of iron, say a sword or chain."

Presently, the boy returned, his hands full of an assortment of metal objects. "Here, Doctor, are my magnets."

Burghley explained that these were things Robert had played with while younger. "Mere toys for children, though, you, sir, represent them as correspondents to our Mother Earth."

"I do, Your Lordship. Though they be useful to delight the young, still in the mature mind they present the attraction or coition mirroring the world itself and explain the deviations by which our brave seamen navigate."

Robert Cecil sat down opposite his father, with William between them. He quickly identified the magnets. There were two, one shaped like a disk, the other oblong and about six inches in length. The metal objects were a long carpenter's needle, a knife, and what William recognized as a clump of iron ore.

William had never taught his specialized study in such surroundings, although in conversation he had held forth on the properties of magnets at length, often to the bewilderment of his friends for whom his scientific interest was no more than a hobby horse, as they called it. He had been called "Doctor Magnetic" not because his learning was respected, but because his eccentricity was recognized and mocked. Now, faced with a demand for a description that would have the character of a lecture, that is, organization and sufficient details, he was suddenly rendered almost tongue-tied.

Oddly, he was not so much intimidated by his mighty host as by the son who was watching him intently. The boy had a piercing gaze, and a demeanor that belied his age. Burghley's interest in matters scientific was well allowed and indisputable. But could William hold the attention and satisfy the expectations of this boy? His father had praised his son's precocious intellect, as many a father does in a son whose curiosity is confined to no more than the tennis court or bowling alley. But here William was faced by the real thing, a young mind quick to detect the fraudulent and the superficial.

"Doctor Gilbert, we are waiting for you to begin," Burghley said, with obvious impatience. "Pray, do not disappoint us."

William felt a tightening in his throat. His face reddened. He did not know where to begin. In the brief conversation about his peculiar interest it was evident that Burghley was no novice in natural science but conversant with many aspects of physics and metallurgy. Surely, William would insult his host if his demonstrations and description of principals were too elementary. He would be seen as condescending. He was anxious as well because he knew that Burghley's willingness to consider his innocence and quash his indictment depended on gratifying his lordship's scientific curiosity. A disappointing presentation would result in Burghley's sending him packing. By tomorrow he would be back in the prison, not merely facing his upcoming trial, but vulnerable to another attack by one of Kempe's hirelings.

"Doctor Gilbert?" Burghley said.

And so he began, tentatively at first, speaking of magnetite, the naturally occurring magnetic ore, and where in the world it was to be found, then proceeding with its relationship to iron. He quoted ancient authorities only to dismiss them, defending his impudence by calling attention to the contradictions and nonsensical myths associated with magnets. When young Robert Cecil laughed at some of these and William saw that Burghley was pleased by his son's interest, William's confidence grew. He hit his stride and moved methodically through the mechanism of attraction. He described the circumstances wherein magnetic power was diminished. He analogized the magnetic poles with the north and south poles of the earth. He explained the operation of the compass's needle, the direction it pointed and the significance of variation in its elevation. He explained, in brief, how the compass was used in navigation, both for the determination of latitude and longitude, and was pleased to see Robert Cecil's face alight with interest when William turned to that practical application.

William's excitement grew. He had never had so receptive an audience. Before, his explanations always aimed at justifying his obsession to those who believed him eccentric or even mad. This was different and liberating. Both father and son listened with what seemed genuine interest. Even Dockery's attention paled by comparison. William talked until he was breathless, until Burghley bade him stop because he had grown alarmed by William's zeal, which Burghley said he feared might be prelude to brain sickness.

Besides, Burghley said, he had questions. As it turned out, so did his son.

A manservant brought food and drink into the room. He looked at the array of metal objects on the table before his master and his guest and shrugged. He was used to his lordship's obsession with learned men and their toys and demonstrations.

It was now late in the afternoon. William sipped a good wine, munched a raisin biscuit, and ate an apple, the most delicious he had ever eaten. Father and son bantered with each other, their relationship obviously an affectionate one. William felt ready to begin again.

William answered the questions put to him, the more knowledgeable and sophisticated questions of Burghley, the more basic and yet practical questions of his young son. In this exchange, he did not hesitate to say he did not know when he did not, for he despised the teacher who loses face when he must admit he does not know. Humility, he believed, was as essential in a man of science as it was in a man of God. Foolish pride was the enemy of both and a great barrier to the pursuit of truth.

The conversation that followed was now easy for him. He felt at ease with father and son. He recognized that Burghley, for all his vaunted seriousness and gravitas, did not lack humor, although it was a dry, witty humor, often pointed and sometimes even cutting like a razor's edge. Further, Burghley's grasp of principals, operations, and the role of the hypothesis in experimentation was solid. William thought he had found kindred spirits, both in father and in son. Some of his morning's joy returned to him.

44

By late afternoon, William's voice had become dry and raspy. He had never before discoursed at such length or with such fervor. "I think that's my magnetic science in a nutshell, your Lordship," William said. "I could go on at greater length about my experiments and what I have concluded therefrom."

"Perhaps on another occasion," Burghley said and smiled. "I think you have done well, Doctor, and enough for this day of our Lord. I can sit just so long in this chair before my buttocks burn and my legs lose their strength. When I stand, my knees protest it. I lack not interest to hear more, but the flesh is weak, as the scriptures observe."

Burghley rose with some difficulty. "We dine at eight. You may in the meantime want to refresh yourself, or remain here in the library if you will. I trust you will find something to read in this collection. It contains over three thousand books and is one of the largest in England." Burghley had evidently forgotten that he had told William this the night before.

Father and son turned to go, but then Burghley stopped, as though possessed of an afterthought. He smiled again. "I believe, Doctor Gilbert, that my son and I both have benefitted from your tutelage this day. You have opened a new world to us, no small gift to an aging man, and more especially to my son, who will no longer regard his magnets as mere toys, to cast aside when he becomes a man."

"It was my pleasure, my lord, and put myself and my knowledge at your service," William said.

And then Burghley added, "Oh yes, a final question of you about the power of these magnets. Tell me truly, Doctor, do they have the power to detect moral good or evil within a person, say to discern that a person lies, or cheats, or thinks ill of another, or is possessed of the Devil, or plots against the state? Or in any other way views what is within the soul of man or woman?"

268

William paused before answering—although he did not hesitate because he was uncertain of his answer, but that his words might receive their proper emphasis. "Not that I have learned, Your Lordship, though there are myths and some silly commentary among ancient writers that would affirm the contrary. The magnetic power is physical and material, not spiritual. At least, as I comprehend it. Nothing in my experiments has suggested otherwise."

"You mean what God may read in the human heart, when you speak of spiritual?"

William answered, "I am no theologian, my lord, yet I do believe only God can see within a man what he is made of. A physician can dissect the body and give a name to every part and function. But the soul is invisible to the physician's eye. Had magnets that God-like power it would be indeed a wonder, and every statesman would want a magnet in his pocket that he might determine the fidelity of those who keep him company, distinguish the traitor from the patriot, the faithful wife from the faithless. But, alas, no magnet has that power. Were it otherwise, magnetism would be a sort of witchcraft, a damnable heresy, although more often a palpable fraud."

"And can magnets do physical harm to the body?" Burghley asked.

William knew this was the question that undergirded all else in Burghley's interrogation. He resolved to speak plainly and unequivocally.

"Neither do they have that power, my lord. I assure you. There is some little iron in the blood, but the strongest magnet lacks the ability to extract it from its natural channels or from the heart itself. For that, we have the emperor leech."

William saw that the mention of leeches did not amuse his host. Burghley's expression remained serious. An awkward silence followed. Then, Burghley gave a little nod of his head, a kind of abbreviated bow, which William took not so much a tribute to him as a mark of respect for his science.

"I thank you, Doctor Gilbert. My son thanks you. And for your pains, tomorrow at this same hour, if you can forgo your enthusiasm for magnets and think of other matters, we will discuss your case at law."

45

Next morning, Burghley sent for William before the time appointed. This unnerved the young doctor. Did Burghley change the appointment because, having reconsidered William's case, or having taken counsel in prayer, he had concluded the indictment was sound and the warrant should stand? Or because he had decided otherwise, perhaps moved by Willliam's insistence that his magnets were neither perceptive of evil nor physically harmful?

As before, Peter Fellows had been charged with escorting him to the meeting place, which his guide said would not be the library, but his lordship's garden. Arriving at the appointed place, William found Burghley sitting on a bench beneath a broad-leafed tree of a variety William had never before seen. Ahead, was a small lake into which a waterfall poured, making a pleasant gurgling sound.

"Come sit by me, Doctor Gilbert," Burghley said as William approached. William sat down and took in the view. It was a pretty prospect, carefully designed to delight the eye and calm the spirits—although at the moment William was still uneasy as to what Burghley would say and do. Peter Fellows turned to walk away, even before Burghley could signal to him to do so.

Burghley said that this was one of his favorite places in the garden. "I do like the sound of running water on a day such as this. It stimulates the brain, I think, and stimulated brains are important to the both of us at this time, do you not think, Doctor?"

"I do, my lord," William said.

Burghley said, "You may be interested to know that the last person who sat beside me on this bench was Her Majesty, when in early May of this year she made Theobalds the first stop on her progress north. You know that when the Queen travels, she leads like Moses a great multitude, accompanied by lords and ladies of the court, servants for each, wagon loads of baggage and supplies. Think of a city moving, Doctor, not just a train of wagons. Along the way, she is greeted by her adoring subjects, who line the roads to catch a glimpse of her. She loves her people, and they love her back. Yet I do think she loves their adoration more than all the bowing and scraping and noxious flattery that comes from her courtiers, myself included."

Burghley chuckled. He seemed to William to be in a good mood. "But like unto the rest of us, she sometimes enjoys a few moments of solitude. I showed her this place, this sylvan retreat, which delighted her and at her command left her alone for an hour, her only companion a book she had brought with her."

"I can see, my lord, why it delighted Her Majesty," William said, looking about him. "For the air is wholesome here, and the shade invites contemplation. May I ask what book she read, my lord?"

"You may ask without offense, Doctor, but I do not recall. Her Majesty is a great reader, as you may know. She reads Latin and Greek, and therefore it is not unlikely that what she read was in one of those learned tongues."

Burghley reached over and patted William's hand, a surprisingly intimate and fatherly gesture he thought, and one he counted as a promising sign, for although it might be viewed as a gesture of consolation that William must return to prison, he thought it more likely assurance that all would be well.

"Now then, let us contemplate your case," Burghley said, "even as I have promised. Begin then at the beginning, with your version of events. By *version* I do not mean to say that it is not true, but only that an opposite view is responsible for the warrant for your arrest and the indictment. I pray you then, proceed. You will forgive me, however, if during your narrative I interrupt from time to time. "

"Please, my lord. Interrupt as pleases you. I can hardly object, for I want nothing so much as to tell truth."

"And have it believed," Burghley said.

His case, as Burghley had called it, had become for William the principal story of his life, although he realized now that he must revise it, for Orlando Kempe's role had changed. Kempe had, in an earlier version, played friend and confederate. Now he was liar and betrayer.

271

"I had finished my studies at Cambridge and returned home to Colchester, where my family lived. My medical practice there was struggling. I had few patients, and they were poor paying. I had competition that I found difficult to overcome, for so many there prefer the attendance of herbalists and cunning women whose practice is but one step up from witchcraft."

William paused to see if Burghley was listening or had fallen asleep. It was cool in the shade and Burghley had told him he often napped while in the garden. But Burghley was very much awake and alert. He leaned forward toward William, his eyes bright with intelligence and perception, his elbows on his knees. He was as engaged as he had been the day before when William had talked of magnets and nothing else.

Dockery had told him that Burghley studied both theology and law at Cambridge, that his powers of discernment were not merely an innate gift but the result of training and long experience. Why shouldn't William's case intrigue this man? It was about the law, and it was a mystery, as much for him as it was for William.

William continued. "One day I am visited by a former acquaintance, a fellow student, named Orlando Kempe." William said *acquaintance*, not *friend*, a word he had used in earlier accounts of his history. *Acquaintance* put a proper distance between them, that he now understood to be a truer description of his relationship. "Kempe had left Cambridge before me, under a cloud, I think."

"What manner of cloud? Burghley asked. "I presume you use a metaphor and are not speaking of the weather."

"It was said about the college that he had had some trouble with a local girl, a maid."

"A maid no more, I assume," Burghley said drily. "I remember Cambridge. It was even so in my day, and perhaps worse. More lechery than learning, at least for some of the boys, and boys they were, often as young as thirteen and fourteen."

William did not say that he himself was of that age when he first entered Cambridge. His own academic history, he believed, was blameless, but he was not interested at the moment in drawing an invidious comparison with the false friend whom he now considered his worst enemy.

"In any case, Kempe went abroad, to Italy, to finish his medical studies.

When I met him again, he had a thriving practice in London, on Lime Street. He had somehow heard of my distress and out of friendship offered to connect me with a wealthy patron."

"Master Thomas Fanshaw, I presume."

"The same, my lord. I was invited to come to his house near unto London for an interview. Kempe had arranged it. Fanshaw's wife Alice was with child. They had only been married a few months, and Fanshaw feared the child had been begotten by another and that she had been with child even before the marriage, so that he had been deceived both by Alice and by her parents, who had misrepresented their daughter as a virgin. Master Fanshaw is an old man, near seventy I should think, and his bride was but twenty or twenty-one."

"And naturally he was suspicious," Burghley said. "It is often thus in marriages when age and youth wed. It is ever an invitation to mischief. How did the bride answer her husband's suspicions? I assume he accused her to her face."

"She insisted that Fanshaw was the father."

"As perhaps he was," Burghley said. "Old men have been known to procreate."

"Perhaps, but unlikely, my lord. Fanshaw is impotent, or so he claims, and what man would confess to such a thing were it false? His bride said he was not so on their wedding night—he was as virile as a stallion, she claimed, but he was too cupshotten to remember what he did, and how."

For the second time that afternoon, Burghley laughed. It was a deep mocking laugh. His eyes twinkled. "And did he believe that? It does seem an improbable tale."

"Master Fanshaw wanted to put his wife's virtue to the test," William said. "He had heard an old story of how a magnet could cause a wife to leap from her bed, should she be an adulteress. He had also heard another wherein magnets, woven into a blanket, should cause the faithless woman's flesh to bruise on all her private parts by drawing the blood to the surface of the skin to be a perfect sign of her infidelity. I see now that that was why my services were procured. Kempe had told him of my interest in magnets, how I was even called Doctor Magnetic at Cambridge."

"Doctor Magnetic?" Burghley laughed again. "Well, as nicknames go, you could have done much worse, Doctor. I would tell you what they called me whilst I was at St John's, but I still, after all these years, bear the shame of it.

273

I haven't even told my wife. By the way, where did he learn these so-called myths, I mean this nonsense about magnets? I know Thomas Fanshaw. I have done some business with him over the years. He's a silk merchant, a wily trader and negotiator. But scholar? I think not, sir. That he can read the Queen's English surprises me. I haven't told you before, but Lady Burghley and I attended his wedding, and I do remember the feast, after which the bride-groom had to be carried to the marriage bed. He was so besotted that he could not walk. Nay, so undone that he could not crawl."

"I fault Kempe for this," William said. I suspect it was he who told Fanshaw about the way to prove his bride's honesty and then commended me as her physician that I might administer the test. I have found here and there recorded stories of magnets being employed in such a way, but I do think Kempe invented the particular method. I know of none among older authorities that affirm such a nonsensical thing."

"Yet you consented," Burghley said.

"It was a condition of my employment," William answered. He made no defense of his decision. He had grown weary of hearing himself repent of what he had done.

"That was a mistake, I think, Doctor," Burghley said sternly. "If you believed your treatment was useless, you should have refused and let Master Fanshaw find another way of detecting his wife's infidelity. You are an intelligent lad, well trained in your art. You would have found another patron, even a wealthier and worthier one than Fanshaw."

William shrank under the older man's gaze. Burghley had spoken the truth that William himself had come to accept. That Burghley recognized it too only confirmed the shame he felt. He said, "My lord, I do rue the day when I consented to that which I knew was a foolish undertaking, for as I said yesterday, magnets have no power to work what Fanshaw wanted."

"But why do you think your sometime friend—or acquaintance, as you described him—invented the story of the magnetic blanket?"

"I think, my lord, as a cover for murder, for I did later at the place of her burial examine her body and found a puncture made beneath her right breast that might be easily missed in the deep bruising of her flesh. It was not the blanket and the magnets that caused such a wound, but some sharply pointed instrument."

"And so not the magic of magnets, but the mischief of an ordinary weapon or tool."

"Of that I am certain, my lord," William said.

"And you believe Thomas Fanshaw murdered his wife for her infidelity, stabbed her with some knife or poniard or needle and then blamed you for her murder?"

"So I believed, my lord, at the first, for he had spoken to me of forgiveness for her betrayal. He said he wanted only certainty, the want of which was driving him mad. I never believed a word of it, I mean about what he wanted. Fanshaw was not a forgiving man. The thought of being betrayed by his bride, their parents—he was obsessed with it. He would have rather been hanged than a cuckold."

"Jealousy is a curse," Burghley said, turning away to look into the distance as though he himself was possessed of it. "It does seize the heart and mind of many a man, and not a few women. The question is whether it drove Thomas Fanshaw to murder."

William told Burghley about finding the body of Fanshaw's earlier wife and also the murder of Simon Gresham.

"You saw these bodies with your own eyes, examined the lady's wound?"

"I did, my lord."

"And the body of Sir John's steward?"

"I did, my lord. The wound was of the same sort."

Burghley nodded, sat silent for a moment. Then he said, "I am puzzled by this Kempe's motives. If what you say is true, Doctor, he is certainly the principal mover in your eventual incrimination. Without him, you would not have been accused, nor imprisoned, nor be here talking to me in this pleasant bower. Alice Fanshaw might still live, her child born, Fanshaw appeased when he does think the child resembles him and concludes, perhaps mistakenly, that he is indeed its father. What a prodigious concatenation of events proceeds from a single meeting. Do you believe Kempe murdered her on Fanshaw's orders?"

"I think it likely, my lord."

William told Burghley about Kempe's visit to the prison, his warning about Fanshaw's desire for vengeance, the deliberately set fire that nearly cost his and Dockery's life, and the discovery of his name written on a paper in handwriting he recognized as Kempe's on the body of the arsonist.

"I agree, Doctor, that all this is consistent with Kempe's being Fanshaw's tool," Burghley said. "But you admitted you now had doubts about Fanshaw's guilt."

William paused. This was, for him, the hard part. It was true he now had doubts, but not only concerning Fanshaw's guilt but Kempe's motives. Kempe was, he recognized, obsessed with money. It had caused him, among other reasons doubtlessly, not to follow his father's footsteps into the church. It supported his lavish manner of living on Lime Street. But would he sell his soul merely to please Fanshaw?

"I do have doubts, my lord, for this cause. Fanshaw said his wife was already dead when he found her. Her body was bruised, by which signs he assumed the magnets had done their work."

"Proved her guilt," Burghley said.

"Yet he insisted he did not wish his bride dead, but only exposed for her betrayal. Hence, his rage against me, for I assured him that the magnetic blanket would produce no harm. If indeed he speaks true, if there are witnesses to support his claim among his household servants that his wife was already dead when he discovered her, then as bad a man as he is, he is not the murderer."

"Could it have been Kempe acting on his own?" Burghley asked.

William said, "In light of other evidence, possibly. Yet I do not know his reason. My false friend might have taken money to supply me as a cover for the murder on Fanshaw's behalf, but if he acted alone, what had he against Alice Fanshaw that he should wish her dead?"

"And why such malice against you? Surely, he knew that you would be blamed, your reputation ruined, your freedom in jeopardy," Burghley said.

Burghley turned away briefly to look at his garden. For a moment he seemed lost in thought. Then he said, "Tell me more about Fanshaw's bride," Burghley asked. "A fairer creature I have rarely seen."

"By rumor she had an unruly childhood and ran off with an unknown lover. She returned, with child, was sent off to an uncle's house to give birth in secret. She returned, abandoned by her lover but with her child. I met and attended that same child when she was sick. She is a young beauty, her mother's glass. Her name is Perdita. She is now about six or seven and lives on Parmenter land, raised by a peat-cutter and his wife, the Digbys. Villagers believe she is their child, but she is nothing like them."

"Do these Digbys know who she is?"

"They do, my lord."

"So the child she carried when she was murdered was her second child, also by an unknown father?"

"Yes, my lord, I examined Alice before her death. By finger and eye, I surmised that she had before given birth. Besides the unlikeness of the miraculous restoration of Fanshaw's potency on his wedding night, she seemed too far advanced in her pregnancy to have her new husband as the father."

"And no one knows the true father?"

"Not even her confessor, apparently."

"Confessor?"

William thought quickly. Mottelay's role had slipped from William's tongue without his intending it. Yet it was essential to the narrative as he now understood it. Here he realized he must tread softly so as not to expose Mottelay, whom he now considered not only a confederate, but a friend. He knew that Burghley was a zealous Protestant and therefore no lover of the Papist clergy—and more especially the priests who serviced in secret the Catholic families of England.

"Alice was sick during her pregnancy and knew her husband suspected her of infidelity. It was a cause of great grief to her. She also had terrible dreams, premonitions of an early death. Her early religious instruction came to her as a consolation, but confessing her sins to achieve forgiveness was hard for her. She was in the way of doing so when she died."

Burghley said, "This confessor then, whom I assume was a Papist, would not reveal what we should very much like to know: the father of these children of hers. But Alice Fanshaw might, as condition of her repentance, admit her crimes to her husband, naming her lovers and whatever other mischief she might have done in her short life."

"Orlando Kempe might have been her lover," William said, speculating now and remembering how Kempe had boasted of his prowess with women, and how he had called Alice Fanshaw a veritable Venus. Kempe had practically salivated at the thought of her.

William was going to continue, to relate more of what Kempe had done to him, but he stopped suddenly. He had a new thought. The idea struck him like a sharp jab.

In his excited brain, he knew the answer. He had been wed to his assumption of Fanshaw's guilt, bound and committed to it to the exclusion of other possibilities. Fanshaw's character, his confession of malicious intent, invited if not demanded that he be first in line among the suspects. Perhaps that he be the only suspect. But what if

Kempe had acted alone, from motives that had nothing to do with Fanshaw? It seemed to him as an inference from what he knew of Kempe's earlier history.

What Kempe loved as much as money was women—and more as objects of his lust than adoration. Mottelay had learned from Lady Parmenter that Kempe had spent a month at Parmenter House years earlier. Orlando would have met Alice Parmenter and being as he was handsome and clever and witty, older than she and wiser in the ways of the world, she might have found him irresistible. Surely, he would have been attracted to her. Like iron to a magnet.

Perhaps, this relationship might even have been the cause of Kempe's abrupt leaving of the university. Surely it was more likely that he would flee from the wrath of an outraged father, a landed knight, than from some barmaid he had violated or her kinfolk. Why had William thought that was the liaison that was referred to in Cambridge gossip? The answer was simple. Because it was a commonplace offense, where punishment was easily evaded and responsibility even easier to deny. It was always easier to take the most likely interpretation of events.

And from this William established a new hypothesis, as he thought of it. Kempe got Alice with child during that summer month, ran off, taking with him a chest full of money. Returned to England, he then established himself on Lime Street, renewed his friendship with Simon Gresham, resumed his affair with Alice, and got her pregnant a second time. Doubtless he worked with Simon on the Fanshaw marriage scheme, which would have benefitted them both. He undoubtedly thought to continue his rapport with Alice after the wedding, but had not counted on the suddenness of her conceiving a second time, or, more, the illness and fear of death that led to her desire to confess her sins. Had she carried through with that pious resolve, his conduct might have been exposed to his considerable detriment and inspired the wrath and vengeance of Alice's outraged husband. Not to mention that of her parents.

William's imagination worked quickly, creating one scenario after another. Kempe might have loved Alice with a brooding passion that brought him back from Italy to resume their affair. William thought this unlikely. That simply did not sound like the Kempe he had come to know. Or Kempe may have desired her only because she loved him and was available to meet his needs, an opportune target. That seemed the more reasonable explanation. Maybe he thought she was dying, and that the death stroke was an act of corporal mercy. It was more likely, however, that he killed her and her unborn child to silence her and save his skin. Which would make him an adulterer, a liar, a traitor, and a thief. In sum, had Alice Fanshaw lived to confess all, Kempe would have been ruined.

It was a poor history for a London doctor, especially one who claimed to be so successful in his profession.

All of this came to William as a sudden revelation, and since it offered an explanation of things that he was prepared to defend, he conveyed it all in a rambling outburst to Burghley with his speculations, inferences, and conclusions a complete muddle. William was proficient in explaining the science of magnets. He was not so in explaining the evil that men do, and why they do it.

46

Burghley believed William's story, at least he said he did. But he said that more evidence against Kempe must be sought, not only to clear William from blame but to shore up Kempe's guilt, which he said was highly probable given all of William's facts and reasoning but still wanting a little to make it unassailable.

Relieved, William returned to his chamber. In the retelling of his tale, he had achieved more clarity and more certainty, what Mottelay said he should pray to God for. His new hypothesis put together things that before were disparate and unexplained. And although the knowledge of Kempe's betrayal weighed more heavily upon him than before, he knew now who his true enemy was. He would no longer combat shadows, figments of his imagination. He would no longer be distracted from his purpose—justice and exoneration.

William had hoped what he had said to Burghley would be enough to quash the indictment against him. But he respected Burghley's desire for thoroughness. Burghley's investigation would not reach a conclusion until all evidence had been weighed. William understood that. It was the same for his science. Nothing was worse than a premature conclusion. It was like boarding a leaky vessel. Presently it would sink, taking all down with it.

Burghley proposed a plan of action. He said he would send a troop of officers to London in the morning to arrest Kempe and bring him back to Theobalds. In chains if necessary. "He may, confronted with all that points to his crime, admit as much and save me the trouble of wringing it out of him."

"My lord, may I go with your men?" William asked.

"What, Doctor, and endanger yourself should Kempe resist with violence? He may well do so, if indeed he is so depraved a spirit to kill a most vulnerable woman and the unborn child of them both."

"I put my trust in Your Lordship's men to protect me," William said. "Besides, I can be of use there in ferreting out evidence your own officers may overlook. A notebook of Kempe's perhaps, or letters or other papers that would damn him."

Burghley looked doubtful. "Let me think upon it," he said.

That night, William dreamed he was in Maidenstowe again, standing in the churchyard before the Fanshaw tomb. A thick fog surrounded him and made the monuments appear not as slabs or crosses, but as men, standing as they might have been when alive. He felt no fear of these specters. In his dream-mind, quite different from that of his waking, it was as though nothing was more natural than that the dead should stand upright and stare sightlessly at the living, perhaps envying their vitality, or judging their unworthiness, or calling them to account.

He walked into the tomb without hesitation or obstacle, for the lock had been removed, and saw by the light of the lamp he now realized he carried, two figures sitting upon the coffin. One he saw was Alice Fanshaw as if she were alive, and not only alive but well. The other figure was an older woman he knew was Fanshaw's second wife, Augusta, she who also had betrayed him. Now she was not a much-decayed corpse, but a lady; well-dressed, even elegantly so, her flaming red hair reaching to her waist. The two women looked at him and suddenly broke out in raucous laughter. They began mocking him, shaming him for his stained clothes, his foolish ideas, his thin, boyish body. William started to say that he had discovered who had murdered them, explaining to them that they had been victims of two different persons, a jealous husband and a knavish doctor. But his words came out garbled and his inability to explain caused the women to laugh even harder.

He turned and fled through the graveyard, barely missing the monuments that were no longer revivified dead but moss-covered stones. Then he awoke abruptly, his chest heaving, his face bathed in sweat.

It took him time to remember where he was, to fit the dream in its proper category, as the idle mind at work and not reality, not something to fear, although the mockery in the dream haunted him. He rose and went to the window. He pulled aside the drape that covered it, as though to reveal, as on a stage, the reality without.

There he could see that it was still night. He tried to return to sleep, but sleep would not come. He tossed and turned until it was dawn.

Suddenly he found Peter Fellows standing by his bed and looking down at him. "Best be up, Doctor. His lordship says you are to go to London with the captain and his men."

47

Captain Broward led the troop, which consisted of six other men, all heavily armed with pikes, swords, breastplates, helmets; each one prepared to go into battle as though with a foreign enemy, not a single alleged murderer. William had been alarmed by Broward's severe mien and rigidity on the occasion of his arrest, and again when Broward escorted him to Theobalds. But under the present circumstances William decided these qualities were an advantage to him. Faced with the imposing Broward, Kempe would surrender straightway, and then all would return to Theobalds, where his false friend would be confined in some nether region of the house, a dank cellar or some obscure or filthy and rat-infested outbuilding. Kempe deserved no less. William imagined Kempe confessing all, voluntarily or under duress. At this point he didn't care which as long as the truth was told, and Kempe got what he deserved.

A mount had been brought around for him, a broad-rumped gelding like unto those of the officers, not the docile mares he was accustomed to hire for his occasional use. He climbed up into the stirrup. The horse seemed to sense William's lack of confidence and bolted to the right and then to left, snorted and whinnied in protest, so that one of the officers was at pains to bring the creature under control. All of this caused the officers and their leader Broward much merriment at William's expense. He was relieved that once they had started out, the gelding settled down and kept pace with the other horses.

"Don't be embarrassed, Doctor," Broward said, no more than a quarter of an hour into their journey. "Stalwart always takes issue with a new rider. He's frisky at the beginning just to show his mettle, then settles down and does what he's told. Like the rest of us." Broward laughed.

"His name is Stalwart?" William asked, finding little comfort in Broward's assurances.

"The name was given to him by Lord Burghley himself," Broward said. "Therefore, I dare not change it."

Before noon they were in Lime Street, and William was pointing out Kempe's house. In the light of day, it seemed smaller and less grand than he had remembered it when under cover of darkness he had climbed over the garden wall and taken Kempe by surprise. He remembered how he told Kempe all that had happened to him since their last meeting. It was a disclosure that now made him feel a fool for having put his trust in the man.

"You're sure this is the right house?" Broward asked. "I wouldn't want to frighten an innocent householder if it is not."

"It *is* the right house," William insisted. This was presently confirmed by several passersby, who knew the house was indeed a doctor's for the sign above the door; although none claimed to have used his services or knew anyone who had.

No one responded, neither Kempe nor servant, even when Broward's polite knock became a resolute and angry demand that would have awakened the dead. It alarmed neighbors as well, for some of them came out of doors to see what the uproar was and then, seeing armed men, went prudently in again and shut their doors behind them. William could almost hear the bolts being thrown on the doors, the hushed apprehensive voices within. Meanwhile other entrances were tried; the postern door, the door to the lower floor where Kempe had told him he saw his patients. Frustrated by the prospect of failure, Broward ordered the main door breached. Two of the larger and stronger men came forward and, with evident delight, put their shoulders against the solid oak.

This proved more difficult than it had first appeared. One of the invaders cried that he had broken his shoulder in the effort, but with much cursing and a good deal of sweating, the door yielded. William followed the men into an abandoned house.

Not entirely abandoned, for furnishings remained, along with an unkempt kitchen with nothing but cold ashes in the grate and empty larders. It was apparent that the doctor was not only out, but gone, with little evidence of an intent to return. Broward asked again if William was sure the house was the right one. William said it was. He had been there before, he said, spoken to Kempe himself. It was just as he had remembered it, every chamber in its place, only master and servants had vanished.

Broward snorted with disbelief.

William wondered how Kempe could know of the danger he was in, but then William remembered the warden at the prison might well have disclosed to Kempe William's whereabouts. The warden would have seen no reason not to. That William should have been conveyed by coach under the protection of Lord Burghley did not bode well for Kempe's prospects. He may have had an inkling, a premonition, that his murder had been discovered or was about to be.

Broward cursed long and hard, and some of the men, disappointed at having no one to arrest likewise complained of a wasted time when they might have been doing more profitable things, although none disclosed what these things might have been. They began to search the house, looking not for evidence William suspected, but for things of value they might carry off. Broward saw this and rebuked them harshly. "We be not housebreakers or vandals," he declared, "but officers of his lordship. Do your duty, men, and nothing more nor less."

With this pronouncement, discipline was restored. Broward looked at William for approval. William said that Broward had done well. He said he would convey a good report to Burghley of the expedition, whether anything was found or not.

Broward said he would look for evidence, and the doctor too, but the rest of his men should stand with the horses in the street and make sure no one entered the house or stole the horses, which he had seen done before, he said, to the great disgrace of their proper owners.

William thought Kempe's library and his bedchamber above gave best hope of being a repository of evidence. But he wanted to be the one searching these chambers, not Broward, whom he prized for his military prowess, but not necessarily his intellect. As it turned out, Broward, still grieved that his quarry had fled and he should find no reward or honor in this expedition, found a comfortable chair to sit in and was content that William should look around for himself. He said that Lord Burghley had not told him what crime this London doctor may have committed and therefore he had no idea what thing might be regarded as evidence against the man.

"That makes good sense, Captain Broward," William said amicably. "Rest easy. You have done your part and well in getting me here whole. I will make quick work of my searching and give you credit for your patience."

William began with the bedchamber. His search yielded nothing. Kempe had removed everything, not an article of clothing or other trace of its previous occupant remained. Then William went to the library that after his experience in the grand chamber of that name in Theobalds seemed a modest space indeed, more confined than he remembered. A bookshelf contained several dozen volumes, almost all medical works. Some were in Italian, not surprising since Kempe had studied there. William opened each book and ruffled through the pages looking for slips of paper that Kempe might have used to mark a sentence or passage, but found nothing. Most of the books had not been read, by Kempe or anyone else. Their pages were still uncut.

He proceeded to the desk, which had been emptied of all papers or other items a doctor's desk might contain. Again, Kempe had been thorough, leaving no trace of himself. But to William, Kempe's unaccountable disappearance was damning. Why should a doctor so successful, or so he claimed, suddenly forsake all? That Kempe was wealthy enough to live in such a house and dress in such finery raised the question of the source of it all. His neighbors claimed they never saw patients come in or out of his door. Were these high-born patients figments of Kempe's imagination, or a self-aggrandizing fiction?

Kempe still had a patron in Sir John Parmenter. He was physician to Parmenter's household. But would Parmenter's patronage extend to all of this, so lavish a display of the world's goods?

48

The rest of the day was spent in search of Kempe's missing servants, who by one neighbor's account had been gone for two or three days. The neighbor was a lawyer who had done some business for the doctor and knew him well.

Broward asked what manner of business that might have been. The lawyer was reluctant to say. "It was private business, sirs, and therefore I cannot say what manner of business it was."

Then Broward, throwing his shoulders back and extending himself to his full height, said he was on Lord Burghley's business, and under those circumstances there was no such a thing as private business, and if the lawyer thought otherwise, Broward had a place for him in one of Her Majesty's prisons where the lawyer would be at leisure to change his mind.

This threat, delivered in Broward's great booming voice, caused the lawyer, who was but a little man half Broward's height, to cower and sing a different tune.

"The doctor invests in various enterprises," the lawyer said, appropriately humbled now and seemingly eager to please. "One a coal mine in Wales. I drew up papers for him and arranged for the sale of his share and the share of his partner in the investment, lately deceased."

"The doctor's partner died?" William asked, knowing full well that Simon Gresham was dead.

"Yes, sir, regrettably he did," the lawyer said. "And upon which death, by prior agreement the doctor inherited it all and has since sold it at profit to another. A very large profit, I must say, proving thereby that though he be a doctor, still he has a good head for business."

William ignored this slight to his profession, which he had heard before and partly believed to be true.

"And this partner's name?"

"Why, sir, I do think it was Gorsham or Gerson, or some such name."

"Gresham, Simon Gresham, do you mean?"

"The very man, indeed, sir. Simon Gresham," the lawyer said, his eyes bright. "I do remember the name well, now that you have said it."

But the lawyer knew nothing of the present whereabouts of the servants. One servant was much like another, he said. None was to be depended upon, but all despised as an inferior breed, born to serve them whom God had placed above them. He was beginning a litany of complaints about his own servants, when Broward shut him up, shoved him away, and the lawyer went off—relieved, William supposed, to have escaped Broward's wrath.

It was late afternoon before one of Kempe's former servants was found, a thirteen-year-old girl who had been an upstairs maid and now was serving in a brewer's grand house at the end of the street. William asked her where her previous master the doctor had gone. She didn't know. The doctor had told her and the rest of the household staff that he was going abroad. He said their service would no longer be required. He had given each a little money to sustain them until they found a place in another gentleman's house.

"Doctor Kempe is a very good man, sir," the girl said, looking more than a little alarmed at the armed officers who surrounded her. "He always treated us well, never harshly, and he looked after us, sir, he did. He was a godly man, if ever one was."

William said he was sure Doctor Kempe was a godly man and gave the girl a shilling for herself.

He had turned to go when the girl said she remembered something.

"What was it that you remember?" William asked.

"Something Doctor Kempe said, sir, to me and to the others. He said he was going abroad, as I told you, but he also said he would return. When the weather improves, he said. Which thing I thought was strange, sir, for it was a fair day and one of several we had here in the City. I wondered why he should think on such a day that the weather was bad and that was why he was leaving, because the weather was very good, sir, on the day he left and wished us all well and said God bless to us all."

The girl's gray eyes glistened with tears. She was a pretty girl, buxom, with clear skin and good teeth. William wondered if Kempe had been able to keep his hands off her.

Broward's men had found in the garden of the house a place where a fire had been made. Among the ashes were papers, too badly burned to be read. But it was clear that Kempe had displayed in such wanton destruction a guilty mind. William hoped Burghley would agree. Had his visit to Kempe's house offered anything new, besides testimonies to his depravity and deceit? William already knew about the investment partnership, but therein he thought might lie a motive for murder. Kempe had doubled his investment. Perhaps he had done even better for himself in his inheritance from his quondam partner.

49

It was near dark when they rode through the park of Theobalds and stabled the horses. William and Broward walked toward the house. Broward said, "His lordship will not be pleased that your friend Kempe escaped us. And what you found there seems to me a paltry amount of evidence of wrongdoing."

"But that's not the only evidence there is, Captain," William said. "There's Kempe's disappearance itself, which argues a guilty mind. And by the way, Captain, Kempe is no friend to me, nor was he ever."

Broward nodded gravely but said nothing. Did Broward believe him? William couldn't tell. But it didn't matter. It was what Burghley believed that mattered.

When William entered the house and approached a footman to ask where his lordship might be found he learned that Burghley had already given orders for him to come to the library as soon as he returned. It was urgent, the footman said nervously, perhaps fearful that he would be blamed because the expedition to Lime Street had returned later than expected.

When he walked into the library, the first person he saw was Burghley looking very serious and a little threatening. The great man was standing before the huge hearth, not sitting as William might have expected, remembering Burghley's complaints about bad knees. And then he saw that Burghley was not alone. Sitting before him were Thomas Fanshaw and the Parmenters, Sir John and Elizabeth.

William knew at once this was no dream from which he might awaken himself, such as he had suffered when he dreamed of the churchyard at Maidenstowe and the two dead women who mocked him. From that baleful vision he had awakened.

Burghley regarded him sternly, but the hostile expressions on the faces of Fanshaw and the Parmenters unnerved him most. Suddenly, he feared that if Burghley had defended him before these supposed victims of his malpractice, Burghley, for all his legal expertise, had failed to convince. And worse, perhaps their hostility toward him had persuaded Burghley that William was indeed guilty.

"Doctor Gilbert, you know these gentlemen and this lady, I believe," Burghley said, gesturing toward the last people in England William expected to see in the same room together, given Elizabeth Parmenter's professed loathing of her former son-in-law.

"I do, my lord." William made a stiff bow to acknowledge each of his accusers but tried to avoid their eyes.

"I have invited them here so that they can give testimony about Doctor Kempe," Burghley said. "And by the way, where has the captain put him? Kempe should be here to account for himself."

William took a breath and told Burghley that Kempe had escaped, burned his papers, and not told his servants the cause of his sudden flight or where he now might be found. "His house, my lord, is empty. He was most thorough in cleaning up after himself."

Burghley's response surprised William. He had expected an angry reproof, or at least expression of disappointment. But Burghley seemed to take Kempe's escape in his stride, as though he had expected it. He said, "The man is conscious of his guilt. It gnaws at him. An innocent man would have stayed to defend himself, his honor, his name. He incriminates himself in his very absence."

Then Burghley told William to join them in the circle of chairs, so that he was sitting opposite the Parmenters, who continued to regard him with a mixture of distrust and contempt.

"I was just about to ask Master Fanshaw about the morning of his wife's murder," Burghley said to William, and then he turned to Fanshaw and said, "Tell Doctor Gilbert what you told me earlier."

Fanshaw stiffened in his chair and reluctantly looked at William. "Very well, my lord, but I do resent this so-called doctor being out of prison, where you yourself sent him to await his trial and where he therefore should properly remain."

Burghley responded sharply. "You may keep your resentment to yourself right now, Master Fanshaw. It is true my warrant imprisoned the doctor, but by the same power I can have him released. Proceed with your account, sir, as I have bidden you."

This stern reproof startled Fanshaw. For a moment he said nothing, but scowled like a disciplined child. Then he began his story, keeping his eyes on William as though his facts themselves would condemn and justify his protest at William's release.

"I went into my wife's bedchamber to see how she had passed the night, having been sick the day before, and found this man's blanket with its damnable magnets wrapped around her and my wife dead and cold."

"This was the blanket you requested of Doctor Gilbert that you might prove your wife's fidelity, was it not?"

Fanshaw hesitated before responding; surprised. William suspected that Burghley knew the purpose of the experiment.

"Was it not, Master Fanshaw?"

"Yes, my lord, it was, but—""

"This blanket with its magnets was your idea from the beginning, was it not?"

Fanshaw said it was.

"And Doctor Gilbert told you he was uncertain whether this test, this proof, had any validity. He questioned whether magnets had the power to discern infidelity, or for that matter, any moral fault?"

"Yes, my lord, he did express doubt in the powers of the magnets, yet he agreed at last when I offered him payment for the service."

"Tell me, Master Fanshaw, where did you learn of this method, this means, of determining that a wife was faithless or no? Was it from your own deep study of the ancients? Or was it some rumor? Or was it some manner of witchcraft you were aware of and resolved to practice?"

With the mention of witchcraft, Fanshaw's face paled. William saw Burghley's strategy. Certainly, if witchcraft were the source of his information Fanshaw might be accused of consorting with witches, as much a hanging offense as murder. Now, Fanshaw would be desperate to shift blame, and in so doing tell the truth.

"It was Doctor Kempe who first told me of it."

"And how came he to do that?" Burghley asked.

"I told him I suspected the child my wife carried was not mine."

"Because you were impotent and you and she had only been married a few months," Burghley said.

William had rarely seen an old man blush, but Fanshaw did now. His cheeks blazed, he shifted uneasily in his chair, and William imagined that Fanshaw, at that moment, wished he were anywhere else in the world but where he was.

"She was already showing, my lord. She was very far along, farther than she should have been, had she been chaste when we did marry."

Fanshaw turned to look accusingly at the Parmenters, but neither Sir John nor his wife seemed prepared to defend their daughter's honor as a virgin bride. They sat like stones, neither regarding each other nor seeming to pay much attention to Burghley's questioning of Fanshaw.

Fanshaw said, "My late wife came to me with no dowry. On the contrary, I paid a goodly sum to her father, enough to settle his debts, that I should take his daughter as my wife. I believed she was a virgin. They should have told me, if she were otherwise."

Fanshaw turned to look at the Parmenters accusingly.

"In which case, you would have declined to marry the woman?" Burghley asked.

"I would not marry another man's cast-off," Fanshaw said bitterly.

"We did not know she was with child when she married," Parmenter said.

"I shall be speaking to you presently, sir," Burghley said. "For now, keep silent, if you will. We seek the truth here, not feeble defenses that on their face are self-serving lies. I suspect both you and your lady were well aware of your daughter's condition when she did marry. Thus, the urgency of the marriage. Thus, your willingness to convey her to a man old enough to be her grandfather. The marriage wasn't just about the money. You did not take the possibility of his impotence into your reckoning."

Then Burghley turned back to Fanshaw, who seemed relieved that Burghley's anger was now focused on the Parmenters. But his relief was short-lived. Burghley turned back to Fanshaw. "Master Fanshaw, you said you found your wife dead and assumed Doctor Gilbert's magnets had been the cause. You saw dark bruises upon her breast and belly and assumed that while the magnets had detected her faithlessness, they had by side-effect caused her death."

"That is what I believed then, and what I now do believe, my lord," Fanshaw declared, somewhat recovered from his earlier embarrassment.

293

"Even though these signs were more likely produced by some other means, say a sharply pointed instrument, say a poniard or a stiletto or some medical tool?"

Fanshaw hesitated. Then he said, "I saw no such wound, if that is what you mean, my lord."

"Did you look for one, a wound, hidden perhaps in the folds of her flesh?" Burghley asked. "Did anyone examine her body, beyond the superficial bruises you describe?"

Fanshaw hesitated again. It was clear to William that Fanshaw suspected a trap. If Fanshaw had not been aware of Burghley's shrewdness as a lawyer before, he must surely be aware of it now.

Fanshaw said, "Doctor Kempe examined her body. He said the blanket was the cause."

This was news to William. He remembered Kempe's tissue of lies about the reaction of Fanshaw and Sir John Parmenter, designed—he now realized—to instill terror in him, to cause him to flee and make his guilt manifest. He remembered Kempe's devious assurances to him that William's magnets were not to blame, and he was sickened again by Kempe's perfidy.

"And you took him at his word?" Burghley asked.

"I had no reason not to, my lord. He had been her doctor before we married."

"What business had he at your house that day?"

"He had come to ask if Doctor Gilbert had accepted my offer. I told him Doctor Gilbert had."

"And then?"

"He came with me to my wife's chamber. He wanted to see how she did. It was then we found her dead."

"And his explanation served your interest, did it not?"

"What mean you, my lord?"

"I mean it confirmed what you already suspected—that your wife was unfaithful."

"No, my lord, I protest. it did not serve my interest. I did love my wife and would not see her dead."

"Even though you suspected she carried another man's child?"

Fanshaw made no answer to this. His gaze fell to the floor.

"Let us return, then, to Doctor Kempe, who seems by your account

294

to have initiated this tragedy. You say he offered to you a theory by which you could resolve your doubts about your wife's fidelity?"

"Yes, my lord, he did," Fanshaw said. "And he commended Doctor Gilbert to me as having great knowledge of magnets and their applications. He said Doctor Gilbert and he had been students together at Cambridge. That Gilbert was called *Doctor Magnetic* by those who knew him. He said that he was as well an excellent physician who might tend to my wife in her pregnancy. I took his word for this."

"And why did you so trust his commendation?" Burghley asked. "How did Doctor Kempe come to your awareness?"

"Why, he was commended to me, by Lady Elizabeth," Fanshaw said.

Burghley turned in his chair to face Elizabeth Parmenter, who through most of this interview had maintained her usual rigid dignity and only now condescended to look at her former son-in-law.

Burghley said: "Lady Elizabeth, I assume you did not pick this doctor, Doctor Kempe, out of the air, but knew of him. Knew that, were he to recommend another of his profession, he would not do so save that man were competent, even superior in his learning and skill."

"We had, for some years, a steward in our household, whom we trusted implicitly," she said.

"And that was?"

"Simon Gresham. He died, having before that embezzled money from us, despite the many benefits we had bestowed upon him."

"Benefits?"

"His father was a groom in our household. Simon was a clever lad, quick to learn and apt to serve. We paid his way to Cambridge and after a year there, having wasted his time in ill habits youth are prone to, he returned to us, became my husband's steward and served us well—or so we thought."

"Ah," said Burghley, "the prodigal son, was he?"

"One might say that, my lord," Lady Parmenter said.

"And how did he die?"

"We don't know, my lord, only that he is dead. One of the tenants brought him back to the hall. He was buried soon thereafter."

"Was his body examined, to determine how he had died?" Burghley asked.

"No, my lord. We saw no reason."

"You saw no reason?" Burghley said with a derisive laugh. "Men do not simply die. They die for a reason. They suffer a fall, or endure a blow, or fall ill of some disease."

"We think he drowned, my lord."

"How did Gresham know Kempe?" Burghley asked.

"They were boyhood friends," Elizabeth Parmenter answered. "Doctor Kempe later came to visit Gresham one summer. He stayed with us for two or three weeks. We got to know him, like him. When Alice, our daughter, became sickly before the marriage, I remembered Doctor Kempe from his visit when he was still but a student. Gresham wrote to him, explained our need. Kempe agreed to come, attend upon my daughter. He brought me a gift from Italy where he had been studying. I added it to my cabinet of curiosities."

"What gift was that he brought you, may I ask?"

"It was a blade, my lord. A rare piece he said had been owned by generations of Italian noblemen. He said he had several he had acquired whilst he studied abroad, but this piece was one of a kind and he bought it expressly that I might add it to my collection."

"Doctor Kempe was your daughter's doctor before he commended Doctor Gilbert here in that same role?"

"Yes, my lord. He was, because we had known him in the old days and liked him very much."

"Because he was handsome, charming, easy with words?" Burghley asked.

"I do pray, my lord, that you are not implying some impropriety between us? I mean Doctor Kempe and myself?"

"Not at all, Lady Parmenter. I do believe a man and a woman may be friends without being lovers as well. If I implied otherwise, I humbly beg your pardon."

Elizabeth Parmenter remained silent before Burghley's steely gaze. William could almost read her mind. She had been taken in, gulled. She had not known it before, but she knew it now. And she no doubt saw in her mind's eye what was coming next. Burghley was presenting to her a new narrative of events and inviting her to accept it as truth. Her awareness and guilt were written plainly on the faded beauty of her face.

"Tell me, Lady Parmenter, your daughter Alice gave birth before. There is another child by her body, a child that lives, and is cared for by one of your tenants, is that not so?"

The Parmenters looked at each other and then back at Burghley, who spoke again before they could respond. William knew Burghley's knowledge surprised them.

"Tell me, the both of you, that summer Orlando Kempe spent in your house, did he pay court to your daughter? Did they spend time alone together? Was or is he the father of your granddaughter, whom you have committed to the care of a tenant? And is or was he the father of the child Alice was pregnant with at the time of her death?"

Now Burghley pressed them harder, questioning first the husband, then the wife. The matter of stolen money came out. The return of the daughter, her belly already showing signs of pregnancy, the sending her off to an uncle in Norfolk to give birth discreetly, the assigning of the child's care to the peat-cutter and his wife.

Burghley also drew out from them the details of the marriage bargain and Gresham's part in the negotiation. Yes, they had realized Alice was pregnant again, but she had always been wayward, had always been wanton. As a young girl she had been unnaturally interested in boys, and they had been naturally interested in her. Some were common farm boys. Some the parents suspected were members of the household. They said Alice was beautiful, but there was something within her that was devilish, untamable—until near the end, when she had surprised them by turning to a priest for consolation, confession, and repentance.

Burghley asked them, what priest? Of the Queen's church or the Pope's? There was no point in denying that. But, as before, Burghley set the issue aside. Today, evidently, the case was a case of murder, not of religious nonconformity.

William did not like the Parmenters. They were proud and arrogant, and ordinarily he would have found their exposure and humiliation at Burghley's hands richly deserved. But now he felt pity for them. They had suffered much by their daughter's behavior. They had tried to conceal her sordid history for their reputation's sake and hers. They had been invited to Theobalds to give evidence against William, an anticipated honor. Fanshaw had undoubtedly felt the same pride, the confirmation that Burghley was his friend, a friend he could call upon to issue a summons or warrant or send an enemy to prison.

But it had not turned out as they supposed. William wondered that the Parmenters had never suspected that it was Orlando Kempe whom their daughter had run away with, or Orlando Kempe, having returned to England and renewed his association had also resumed his affair with the woman who was to become the third Mistress Fanshaw. Alice Fanshaw had been a faithless bride, but she had been consistent in her partner in vice. It was a consistency that led to her death. That is how William understood things at that moment. As much as Fanshaw and the Parmenters hated William, they would have hated Kempe more, had they known the depth of his treachery.

As for Fanshaw, that he had not suspected that Kempe was his wife's lover seemed inexplicable to William. William could only imagine how Kempe's guise of professional rectitude disguised his moral depravity in the eyes of the old man. But he should have seen it, as William should have seen it. Neither did. They had been equally blind.

Burghley said, "I do think I have heard sufficient today of this evidence, and I do trust more will be forthcoming that will incriminate Orlando Kempe and exonerate Doctor Gilbert here. I will therefore retract the indictment and warrant against Doctor Gilbert. Subject to receiving the evidence against Kempe that Doctor Gilbert has alluded to, a warrant will be issued for his arrest for double murder and conspiracy to murder Doctor Gilbert whilst he was in prison."

Burghley directed his attention now to Sir John and Lady Parmenter and Thomas Fanshaw.

"I do express my sympathy to you Sir John and Lady Parmenter for the loss of your daughter. While she may have been wanton and as faithless as her husband here suspected, nonetheless she was your blood and there must needs be sorrow at her loss. As for you, Master Fanshaw, you have my sympathy as well. Though a wise man of your years should have known that marrying so young a wife would more likely lead to marital misery than bliss, it delights no man to find himself a cuckold—and shame on him who ridicules another for it. For that, too, you have my sympathy, sir."

Burghley rose from his chair with difficulty. Fanshaw and the Parmenters stood and waited for the great man to speak again. When he did, he told them to go home, to mend their ways. He told them lies would profit them nothing, in this life or the next.

* * *

Fanshaw and the Parmenters quickly departed. There seemed nothing left for them to say. They had not been invited to have supper at Theobalds or stay the night. But William thought it unlikely they would want to, having received such chastisement and so narrowly escaped worse.

Burghley turned to William and said, "Doctor Gilbert, your ordeal now is ended—at least insofar as it pertains to the law. Yet Kempe remains at large. He tried to kill you once. He may try again. Or he may think himself fortunate to escape and exile himself forever. I would recommend that you walk carefully. You are not perfectly safe whilst he is at large."

"I do know it, my lord, and will walk circumspectly," William said.

"A good practice for any man," Burghley said. "For now, sup with us. Stay another night. Take your ease. In the morning you have leave to go wherever you will, but if I could ask for an hour of your time in the morning, no more, before you set forth?"

"Gladly, my lord," William said. "You may have as much of my time as you will, for I have no words to thank you for your gracious disposition of my case. But for you, I might still be in prison, or even dead by another of Kempe's devices."

Later that night, as William drifted off to sleep, he remembered Julian Mottelay. It was possible, even likely, that to Kempe, Mottelay was a possessor of dangerous information. And while Mottelay was forbidden by the seal of the confessional to disclose it, he doubted Kempe would rely on the priest's silence. William resolved to send a message to the priest warning him of the same danger Burghley had warned William of.

Kempe was at large, and he was murderous.

50

Peter Fellows came knocking shortly after dawn. William was already dressed.

"Lord Burghley awaits you below, Doctor. He would speak to you before you leave."

"He told me yesterday he had a matter of business to discuss," William said.

William looked at Peter Fellows, waiting to see if Burghley's servant would say what matter of business it was. But Fellows said nothing, and William concluded the man didn't know, or knew and wouldn't say.

William was unsure what Burghley wanted of him. The night before, Burghley said he believed William's account of Alice Fanshaw's murder, and that he shared his belief that Orlando Kempe murdered her and Simon Gresham. Most importantly, Burghley had withdrawn the warrant and indictment. For that, William felt immense gratitude, both to Burghley himself but also to Dockery whose commendation of William's science had made this happy result possible.

William thought their meeting would again take place in the library. Instead, Fellows led him up to another wing of the house where the family had their personal chambers, as Fellows informed him on the way. They came presently to a door, Fellows knocked, and Burghley's now familiar voice admitted them.

It was clear to William at once that this was a child's room; an older child, given the books, hangings, and clothing tossed casually around. Yet it was no ordinary child who dwelt there but a gentleman's son, a son being prepared to enjoy all the world's goods and much of its power.

"This is the chamber of my son, Robert, whom you have met. He is not here now but will join us presently. In the meantime, we can talk."

"Of what, my lord? Would you know more of my magnets and their powers?"

"No, Doctor, my mind is filled with new knowledge it will take some days to digest. My questions are nearer my heart than my head, if you must know. I want to talk to you about my son."

"Your son, my lord?"

Burghley waited before continuing, as though unsure of how to proceed. He looked pained, an expression William had not seen before in the man. Finally, Burghley said, "You have observed I am sure how my son is disfigured. Not in visage, but in body. He does not grow as children of his age are wont. You have seen him. He is a hunchback. He walks with splayed feet. I do not know that you and all your science can work a cure for him that he might be made whole, but I do wish that you might examine him and give me your opinion of his condition. And a prognosis, if you can. Will his back straighten as he ages? Will he achieve the height of his father and brother? Will he walk as a normal man walks?"

There was only one answer that William could give. "I will do what I can, my lord, and gladly—for your sake and for his."

Burghley said, "He suffers, Doctor Gilbert. He suffers sorely. He is mocked for his disfigurement, which mockery will grow worse. Not only that, but many believe that such disfigurement is a sign of malignancy. They make the sign of the cross as he passes to ward off the evil. Thus, the body is an index to the soul, or so it is believed. But he is a good lad, quick to learn as you have seen, and I do believe he has promise as a statesman when he grows to a good age, though he be but a boy now. We are a people and time that prize beauty and physical prowess in men and hate and even fear ugliness and deformity. I fear my son will be forever excluded from those positions of authority which his talent and training merit. For this reason, I seek your counsel, in your professional capacity. Moreover, I will pay you for this service."

"I will take no pay of you, my lord, either now or at any time. I am always at your service or the service of a member of your family."

At that, the boy Robert appeared, greeted his father and acknowledged William with a stiff bow.

"Doctor Gilbert wants to examine you, Robert. Will you allow it?"

Robert Cecil looked at his father uncertainly, then at William. "Will Doctor Gilbert use his magnets that I may grow as tall as my brother Thomas?"

William laughed a little, to put the boy at ease. "I will not use magnets, only feel your bones, the bones in your back, to prove their strength and solidity."

Robert hesitated a bit, then said, "If it be my father's wish, then it is mine as well, Doctor."

The boy slowly removed his shirt, revealing a pale, sunken chest and thin shoulders and arms. The boy's flesh was white, as though the sun had never touched it, and his body reminded William of his own when he was that age. Although straight of limb himself, he felt his old sensitivity about his own body, which had lacked the well-defined musculature of other boys his age.

He turned the boy around to examine his back. That the boy's spine was curved unnaturally was obvious, and his shoulders hunched. He had a condition William knew as scoliosis. He had seen it most often in older women—women the age of Elizabeth Parmenter, who already was somewhat bent over as she would not have been in her prime. He touched the boy's spine, slowly worked his fingers up from the base to the boy's neck. He could feel the deformity of bone, like a knotted rope. He asked, "Does that hurt, when I touch you there?"

The boy winced. "A little, Doctor, only a little."

"And what of there?" William applied pressure to another disk.

"Somewhat more, Doctor."

William knew the boy was in pain but struggling not to show it in front of his father. He made the examination last longer than needed. There was no mystery to solve here. Nor elusive remedy to be sought or proposed. And certainly, no role for magnets. The boy's condition would be permanent. It would influence his mind, his way of behaving with others as well as his body. When he thought this, William felt a great sadness. He had often felt so when confronted by a condition he supposed congenital. His sense of helplessness was the worst of it.

William motioned to Robert to put his shirt back on. Burghley told his son to leave the room so he could speak to the doctor.

"Can he be treated?" Burghley asked, as soon as his son had gone.

"Many a physician might engage to treat your son, my lord, but none to good effect. It would be a waste of time and money. And also hope."

"You answer directly, Doctor," Burghley said.

"I answer honestly, my lord. Do you know what caused his condition, some sickness in his infancy or accident?"

"Some claimed a nurse dropped him when he was an infant, but I don't know if that is true," Burghley said. "Lady Burghley says she does not remember such a thing and insists that she would, had it ever happened. There are those in the village I have heard who cruelly charge that he was cursed, or victim of some witchcraft that has so crooked his back and stunted his growth. And, of course, my enemies are not without their cruel commentary."

"They are ignorant and cruel indeed who say such things," William said. "That is all nonsense, proceeding from disorderly and unlearned minds."

"I know that's true, yet hate to see my son so maligned," Burghley said.

"His spine does not look as if it were an injury he suffered, but some congenital effect, beyond cure. To speak plainly, as I believe Your Lordship would have me speak, there is nothing I can do for him."

Burghley looked down at his hands and sighed heavily, then he turned his eyes up at William and said, "Thank you for your candor, Doctor. I would have it no other way. Where there is no hope, none must be desired."

"Yet I will say this, my lord, to give you consolation," William said. "This deformity of your son is an act of God, imbued in him from birth and for reasons unknown to us in our mortal state. It is not a sign of evil within him, as some ignorantly believe. Such belief is a superstition. It is an offense to God who gives to each man what he shall have in this life. Your son may be deformed in body and perfect in his mind, just as a man may be endowed with a perfect body but be depraved in his soul."

Burghley nodded in agreement, but his face fell. He seemed older suddenly, as though he had aged ten years in a moment. Then he stood and shook William's hand. "Thank you, Doctor. I had hoped for a different answer. Perhaps even a comforting lie to distract me. But I know lies comfort only for a season. In the end, truth prevails. I do wish you well now and in your future, which I am sure will give credit to you and to England."

While talking of false appearances to Burghley, William had thought of Orlando Kempe, a friend as false as hell. How could he not think of Kempe? He also thought of Alice Fanshaw, whose beauty belied her own lasciviousness. Even her penitence now seemed to him a sham. The world, he now understood more than ever, was full of deceptive seeming, false appearances, hidden motives. Good and evil were easily confused. The truth was never plain on its face, but discovered with great effort, like peeling away so many false skins until one came at last to the core, the reality of things. It was true in science. It was true in one's dealings with men.

Later that morning, Broward came to bring William to the stable, where he was given the same horse he had ridden to London and back—the horse Broward called Stalwart. Broward and two of his men were to accompany William on his way, by order of Lord Burghley. Although William would have preferred to ride unaccompanied, that he might be alone with his thoughts, he saw the wisdom in Burghley's offer. Exonerated by Burghley and hopefully with Fanshaw and the Parmenters too, he still had Orlando Kempe to avoid and Julian Mottelay to warn.

51

Tymperleys, his father's house in Colchester, had never seemed so sweet to William. It was not Theobalds, but then what other house in England was? The narrow streets of his native place, faces he remembered from his youth, the castle on the hill, the sweet flowing river. Even his stepmother's smug self-satisfaction that his effort to become a great figure in London had evidently failed. "Pride, pride, William, has led you to this," she said, and more than once, that week of his return.

During which time, he wrote letters—to his Dutch friends, to Clement Dockery, and, importantly, to Julian Mottelay, warning him of the danger Kempe presented to him—since he now believed Kempe was set to avenge himself on anyone who knew about his treachery and murders, and might convey the same to others and most especially to the authorities. At the same time, William resumed his medical practice, his first patient being the cobbler wanting another blood-letting for a physical condition, the name and symptoms of which changed with each visit. The cobbler had heard William had returned, probably, William supposed, from his stepmother, who would have told her friends and they, everyone else.

But William declined to treat him.

"Is it that you want more money for your service, Doctor?" The cobbler asked, looking at William suspiciously.

William answered that it wasn't about his fee. It was about the method. He didn't believe in blood-letting. "It only weakens the body by taking from it its life-giving substance. It is founded on a false theory of body humors, long credited but now called into serious question. That it does anybody good is an old idea, easily refuted by experience."

The cobbler, when he had recovered from his surprise, protested. He

305

told him he would pay the customary rate and that William was a poor excuse for a doctor if he refused an ailing man's request.

"Before, you complained of the gout," William reminded him with a heavy sigh. "Pray tell, what new sickness have you that letting blood will remedy?"

The cobbler said he wasn't sure. He had pain in his back and sometimes in his head, and sometimes both at the same time, which caused him much grief and kept him from his work. But he was confident that blood-letting would improve his health. His wife and father had said so. "And they know whereof they speak," he said. "They have submitted to many a cure in their lifetimes."

Again, William said no; more firmly this time. "I do not use methods that have no value, that may do harm to my patients."

"But, Doctor, you did it when before you were here—and took my money for the doing of it. You raised no objections then but did apply those creatures to my body until they had sucked up a pail-full of my blood, after which I felt much improved."

"Not that much blood," William corrected.

The cobbler made more protests, which William disregarded.

"How much did I charge you?" William asked, finally growing weary of the debate.

"Two shillings, I remember," the cobbler answered sullenly.

"I remember it was one," William said. "Two is what you would have paid, had you gone to another doctor in this town." He went to his desk, found his purse, and pulled out a shilling. "Here," he said. "Take it." He handed it to the cobbler, who regarded it with contempt.

"Well, sir, it will then cost me a sixpence more if I go to another."

"Indeed it will, and good luck to you."

William ushered the cobbler out into the street, and said, "You may tell your friends and neighbors, and more particularly your wife and father, that I do not employ remedies in which I have no confidence, and which might do harm to my patients."

William was surprised and pleased when what he had declared to the cobbler made the rounds of Colchester. It earned him four new patients, whose complaints he could diagnose and treat with some promise of success. He had not given up his dream of practicing in London, but after his recent ordeal he enjoyed the relative quiet of Colchester and the comfort of being in a house in which he had been a child, despite all the bodies and voices of his younger siblings. Besides, in addition to the threat presented by Kempe's being at large, there were still aspects of his recent experience that were a mystery to him. It was as though there was unfinished business for him to attend to, and he could not do it satisfactorily until he had more answers.

He was sure Kempe had killed Alice Fanshaw, and that he had probably killed his friend and business partner, Simon Gresham. He was sure Kempe fathered both of Alice Fanshaw's children, born and unborn, and had wanted to conceal his part. But it was the whereabouts of the bodies of Alice and Fanshaw's earlier wife that troubled him. He had had another dream about the two women. If anything, it was more troubling than the first. In this dream he had been in his own town and house. A knock had come to the door and there stood Alice and Augusta Fanshaw. They said they wanted him to treat them. "What is your complaint?" he had asked. "We are dead," they said, turning to look at each other and smiling conspiratorially.

At first these spectral creatures appeared as though alive, with flushed cheeks, clear, lustrous eyes, and white, healthy flesh. But then, slowly, in the dream they began to decay as though they were dead—first a week dead, a month dead, then years so.

He woke when they were mere skeletons.

His stepmother had heard him cry out and ran into his bedchamber to learn what the matter was, whether she should call a priest or the constable. "Bad dream, very bad," he muttered, half awake, gasping for breath, his heart still racing. "Don't worry. I am well enough. It was but a dream, nothing for you to worry over."

She looked at him uncertainly.

"A dream. Dreams have no reality," he insisted when she continued to regard him doubtfully. "They are but fruit of a brain made idle by sleep, or something I ate at supper."

But in his heart, he wasn't sure, and he couldn't remember what he had eaten for supper.

A day after, he received a letter from Julian Mottelay. It said he was in Maidenstowe and had discovered the missing bodies. He asked William to come straightway, to see for himself. He said the vicar and his wife had found them.

William thought it strange that Mottelay had not mentioned his warning letter. Or the news of William's exoneration. Was that a bad sign? A cause of suspicion? He considered it had always been Mottelay's manner to be direct, to come to a sharp point of relevance. Perhaps that explained his lack of response to William's letter—if, that is, he ever received it. He considered the dilemma presented by his caution. Should he expose himself to risk in order to find answers?

William knew himself, or at least, had come to know himself better. He could not fail to go. He could not see himself continuing as he now was, treating patients, participating in the town's business, all the while uncertain of where the bodies of the two women lay. He did not believe in ghosts, or even in the predictive power of dreams, but still he wondered if their appearance in his dreams did not represent a duty unfulfilled. Besides, they remained the most convincing evidence of Alice's murder and would be indispensable in Kempe's trial, were he ever to come to it. And without the decayed body of Augusta Fanshaw, Thomas Fanshaw would never see the judgment he deserved.

No, he could not fail to go to Maidenstowe, come what may. He owed it to Mottelay and to Lord Burghley as well—and even to poor Alice Fanshaw. She had been, after all, his patient. She was dead, but he still felt a duty toward her, despite what she was, whatever she had been.

52

William left early the next morning, which caused his stepmother to rail against him. "Just when new patients flock to your door," she said.

He had assured her that his business in Maidenstowe would be brief, that he would return within the week.

"Maidenstowe?" she asked. "Where might that be? I have never heard it spoken of. Is it in England, or some foreign part?"

"It's a village in Hertfordshire."

"But why need you go there? Were it London where you have longed to go, I should understand it. But some village none has ever heard of save those who live there …?"

He had told neither her nor his father about the murders, or even about his imprisonment. That circumstance would not have aroused her pity for him, but rather disdain that he had so disgraced the family name as to be imprisoned. But he told her now about Lord Burghley and his visit to Theobalds. She had heard of Theobalds, as well about the Queen's chief minister, whose house it was. When she learned that William had been a guest of Burghley at his palatial home, her sorrow subsided and was replaced with pride. "Lord Burghley, is it he who you have been consorting with in your London ventures? What a wonder, William. You have reached the pinnacle and will now surely prosper. I can hardly believe it. Your father will be so proud when he hears of this."

"Upon oath, it is true," William said. "I am on his lordship's business in this trip to Maidenstowe."

He did not like to lie to his stepmother. She was a decent woman after all, despite her constant fussing. She had assuaged his father's loneliness after William's mother died. She gave his father a new brood of children, whom William tolerated when he did not love them. She was a Wingfield, a family not without distinction in the borough. No, he did not like to lie to her, but any explanation of his purpose in going to Maidenstowe would open up questions he was not prepared to answer. Besides, he considered, it was not really a lie, his explanation. Lord Burghley continued to investigate the case. And so William's business in Maidenstowe was Burghley's as well.

53

He made good time to Maidenstowe. He rode the horse he had ridden to Kempe's house in London and back and from Theobalds to Colchester. It had been presented to him as a gift from Lord Burghley. William was used to the creature now, and the creature to him, and he appreciated not having to hire an unfamiliar mount for the journey. He called the horse Galen, after the famous physician of that name. The old name, Stalwart, struck William as being too martial. He was, after all, a doctor, not a soldier.

It was the rain that bedeviled him on the road. And though it was still summer, it was cold. When he came at last to the village, he went at once to the vicarage, where Julian Mottelay said he should go and where the priest would meet him. That is what Mottelay's letter had said. It also said that the vicar had found the bodies. He wondered if that discovery had been conveyed to Fanshaw and the Parmenters as well. He prayed it had not. He didn't want another encounter with his erstwhile enemies. He had nothing more to say to them, and what they might say to him, he did not want to hear.

The church and adjacent burial plots and monuments looked bleaker than he remembered them. Perhaps, he thought, it was the ill weather that made all so gloomy, or more likely his memory of what had happened there. He looked all around for Mottelay, but the priest was nowhere to be seen.

When he knocked on the door of the vicarage, the vicar answered almost immediately as though William's arrival had been anticipated.

"Why, Doctor Gilbert," the vicar said, extending a hand. "Come in, come in. You are most welcome, sir."

Behind him, the vicar's wife appeared, looking tired and somewhat wary, as though she still feared this lying stranger.

Suddenly, William was uncertain about the wisdom of his coming here.

The vicar and his wife were smiling, ingratiating themselves, inviting him to sit and warm himself by their fire, to enjoy a hot caudle. When he had departed Maidenstowe last, he had been in manacles, a prisoner, being led off for murder and grave robbing. He remembered the vicar standing on the church porch, watching him leave, witnessing a felon being dragged off to prison. There had been no mercy or forgiveness in that hard face. Not then. But at the moment, William was being welcomed as though nothing of that had been seen by them or understood. They were a couple of mature years, but were they that old and forgetful?

"I have been told, by a friend, a Master Mottelay, that you have found the bodies that were lost, that is, stolen, from the Fanshaw tomb."

"That would be true, Dr Gilbert, so true," the vicar said. "We did find them, after much searching."

William sipped the caudle. It was a sweet and creamy liquid, made from milk and eggs, pleasantly hot and flavored with cinnamon. The interior of the cottage was warm and comfortable. He waited for them to tell him where the bodies had been found, but they did not, and he had to ask.

"Oh, Doctor, we found them where no one would expect," the vicar said. "The bodies had been concealed in the church, which as you will remember none searched on the day you were here because none thought him that stole them would dare to dispose of them so."

"Where in the church?"

"Beneath the floor of the chancel. A crypt lies beneath. Few know of it. The church is an old Norman church, built in William the Conqueror's time."

William thought they would now proceed to the church itself, as seemed to him logical, but neither the vicar nor his wife seemed in a hurry. They encouraged him to finish his drink. The vicar's wife said, "It will warm your heart, Doctor, and you will need warming, for as unnaturally cold as it is out of doors, it will be the colder down in the crypt I warrant."

William obliged her. What could it hurt? He finished the drink. He looked across the table where they were sitting. The old couple were watching him curiously, both of them smiling as though anticipating something or someone. Perhaps it was Mottelay. Suddenly, William felt drowsy. The room was so warm, and he was weary from the journey, very weary. He realized he was falling asleep and tensed his muscles to bring himself around again, but it was useless. He was aware of the door of the cottage opening. He turned to look behind him to see who it was that was entering unannounced. He thought it might be Mottelay, keeping his promise to meet him here, but his eyelids were heavy, and his mind wandered and he began to dream again, right there, sitting up in the chair.

"Who is that?" he murmured, not half awake.

"It's only my son, Doctor," he heard the vicar's wife say.

The last thing he was aware of was yet another vision of the two dead women that according to the vicar and his wife were in the crypt of the church. They were fleshless, old bones, and ….

54

He awoke to the stale sweetness of death and mold. This was no dream, he knew. He was awake, or waking. He knew he had been bound up for some hours at least for his wrists were raw and his back ached terribly, lying as he realized now on hard, cold stone.

There was no light, but somehow, he knew where he was. In the crypt the vicar had spoken of. How had he come here? He had no memory of that. He did remember that he had fallen asleep in the chair in the vicar's kitchen, suddenly overcome with a debilitating drowsiness and then oblivion. He knew what had happened. It had been the caudle, the milk, the eggs, and whatever else was in it. Some soporific to induce unconsciousness. At least it had not been a poison, or he would be in the world to come, not here. He was grateful for that. There would at least be more to learn, more to comprehend—although he now understood that whatever was happening to him, the vicar and his wife were part of it.

He fell asleep a second time, despite the cold, the discomfort of his position and the pain in his back. He awoke sometime later when he heard something—something not far from him. It was a groaning, a man, somewhere near him. Another prisoner? He reached out as much as he could, being as his wrists were bound. He pulled back in alarm when he touched warm flesh. It was a hand. He squeezed it but there was no response. It was another soul, a man by the size of the hand and the hairiness of the back of it.

He called, "Julian? Is that you?"

No answer came.

He waited. He could do nothing else. The groaning stopped, replaced with a soft, husky breathing. Then suddenly there was a light, a lamp, a figure entering the dark space in which he had been imprisoned.

It took a time for his eyes to adjust. His gaze swept the crypt now, largely illuminated. Its walls were stone, and on each side there were long stone slabs, sepulchers he imagined for Norman dead. Over against the opposite wall in a partially sitting position was Julian Mottelay. His eyes were shut as though he were in prayer. His head was covered with dried blood. But not for the slight rising and falling of the priest's chest and the breathing, William would have supposed him dead.

And then he turned to him who held the lamp. It was the vicar, staring down at him.

William said, in a dry raspy voice, "Why have you done this? Why am I here?"

"Because you are evil," the vicar said, holding the lamp closer to William's face as though William were a monster requiring the vicar's most intense scrutiny. The vicar's face registered disgust and horror.

"Evil?"

"You escaped from prison, where you were charged with murder—nay, *two* murders. I myself saw you carried off by Master Fanshaw's men. You returned here to kill me and my wife. It is for that reason you are here, at least for the time being."

"Why in heaven's name should I want to harm you or your wife?" William managed to ask.

"Because we were witnesses to your perfidy, how you stole into Mistress Fanshaw's tomb, how you brought the bodies here."

"I removed no bodies," William said. He started to explain that he had been exonerated, that he had not escaped from prison but been taken under Lord Burghley's orders to Theobalds. Not that that would have made any sense to this old man whose sanity William now doubted.

The vicar's wife appeared, standing behind her husband and looking around him as though she supposed her husband would protect her from their prisoner.

"My son told me all about what you did at Master Fanshaw's house," she said. "He told me you would come here and try to do me and my husband harm, to avenge yourself upon us for what we said and did."

"Your son?" William asked.

"You know him well enough," the vicar's wife said.

"I don't know him."

"Then you lie again, Doctor. You know him well, and he knows you and the evil you are capable of."

"What is your son's name?"

"Orlando. Orlando Kempe."

Her answer seemed to William, at least at first, as more evidence of her madness. But as he looked into the woman's eyes, he saw no evidence of insanity. On the contrary, she seemed to be telling the truth.

But how could that be? Then he remembered that Kempe had always said his father was a poor vicar. He had never said where or mentioned his father's name. Could it really have been the vicar of St. Mark's he spoke of? But the difference in family names ... How was that explained?

The vicar must have seen the confusion written on William's face. He said, "Orlando is my wife's child, not mine. Her first husband, now dead, was once vicar here. I succeeded him both as vicar and husband. Orlando kept his birth father's name. Why he did, I do not know, given how his father died. He should have been ashamed to bear it, after what his father did."

The vicar's wife began to protest, but her husband waved away her objection. "Let this false doctor know the truth," he snapped at her. "The man lost his faith, and I do think his mind as well. He hanged himself in this very church, hanged himself from a beam above the altar, which he climbed upon. Who would do such a thing, commit such sacrilege, save he were possessed? My wife—his, then—was she who found him. It is for that reason few in Maidenstowe will come to the church, believing that it is cursed, or at best stalked by her first husband's ghost. Surely, he burns in hell for that. He is not buried on sacred ground."

The two men, vicar and doctor, looked at each other without speaking. So Orlando Kempe was the son of this old woman and her husband. The revelation was almost too much for William to take in. He hardly believed it. And yet he knew it was true.

It explained much that had bewildered him. The old couple's confusion and fear when, during William's first visit, he had used their son's name. Kempe's private conversation with them during William's second visit to the vicarage. Their enmity toward him, fostered by Kempe in secret as part of his plot against him.

What are you going to do now?" William asked. "And what of Master Mottelay here? It would appear he's alive. His wound needs attention."

316

"Him," said the vicar contemptuously. "He's naught but a Papist priest, as I believe you well know, Doctor. He will be allowed to die, as he deserves. It's what you deserve as well, though you will not die here—but die you shall."

The vicar was old, unsteady on his feet as well as mind. it was difficult for William to take his threats seriously, although caution dictated he should. Mottelay's wound was serious enough to render him unconscious, and William's present condition made him vulnerable to even an inept stroke of knife or sword or club. He had also noticed, lying upon one of the sepulchers, a mound covered with sail cloth.

He knew what it concealed. The vicar had told the truth about that. The missing bodies of Alice and Augusta Fanshaw had indeed been discovered, right where Kempe had put them.

"Orlando told me all about the both of you," the vicar continued, forgetting that he had said this before, but with the added conviction that his son's word was sufficient to incriminate

"Where is your son?"

"My wife's son, he's none of mine."

"Very well, then, be it as you choose, your wife's son. Orlando Kempe, where is he?"

"He will be here soon," the vicar answered, "along with officers to take you back to prison and your much-deserved punishment, and may God have mercy on your soul."

William remembered how often of late he had been so blessed—by Captain Broward, by the prison warden, and now by the vicar. Well, he would need all the mercy he could get if he was to survive this.

William thought it highly unlikely that Kempe would be bringing any officers to take him back to prison or anywhere else, given there was now a warrant out for Kempe's own arrest, but he suspected that is what Kempe had told his parents to justify his and Julian's imprisonment.

"Here, take this," the vicar said, pulling from somewhere beneath his cassock a bottle.

William looked at it uncertainly.

"Don't worry, Doctor. It's only water."

William nodded and took the bottle.

He pulled the cork that stopped it and smelled. It detected nothing amiss, but he would take no chances. He had been drugged once, not again if he could help it. "I'll drink it later," he said.

317

"As you please, Doctor," said the vicar, who left the lamp sitting on top of one of the sepulchers as he went out. William heard the echo of the vicar and his wife's footsteps climbing the stairs that led up to the chancel.

He crawled over to where Julian Mottelay's body sprawled, and used the water to wash away the dried blood so he could examine Mottelay's wound. The priest was still breathing, but it was a shallow breath, such as a dying man makes. The wound was a vicious contusion of the skull, a blow dealt with murderous intent. It was something that might have killed most men, but somehow the priest had survived it, at least for now.

William bent over to listen to Mottelay's heartbeat. It was steady, rhythmical. A sense of relief washed over him. It was Mottelay's loyalty to him that had brought the priest to this state.

Suddenly Mottelay's eyes opened. He looked at William first with a start and then questioningly.

"We're in a crypt, below the chancel floor," William said. "You have been struck upon the head, hard. You're fortunate to be alive, Father."

"A staff," Mottelay said weakly. "It was an oak staff. I saw it before it struck me."

"Who struck you?" William asked, although he knew.

"Kempe. The vicar had just shown me where the bodies lay." He nodded in the direction of the covered mound. "Kempe was waiting here. He was hiding over there." Mottelay nodded toward a recess in the opposite wall. But why are you here?" Mottelay suddenly asked.

"Your letter to me," William said.

"What letter? I wrote you no letter. I would have done so but was attacked before I could."

"Then it was the vicar who wrote it, appending your name," William said. "Or Kempe himself, feigning another's hand that I might not recognize his. All to bring me here."

"To have us both," Mottelay said.

William told Mottelay what he had learned from the vicar, that Orlando Kempe was his wife's son from an earlier marriage, hence the difference in their family names.

"You never knew?" Mottelay asked.

"He always said his father was a vicar, a poor man living in a wretched parsonage somewhere in England. That's all he said, but that they were connected makes sense. Maidenstowe is Fanshaw's native place, Fanshaw is its most distinguished son. Kempe would have known of him at least."

"How interwoven all these relationships are," Mottelay said. "Like a sailor's knot."

William told Mottelay about Kempe's natural father, the priest who had lost his faith and hanged himself in the church.

Mottelay shook his head sadly. "The suicide violates the fifth commandment, thou shalt not kill. What hope has he in the life to come who takes upon himself what only God can ordain? And what son can survive such grief? It is no wonder that Kempe turned out as he did."

"You pity him who nearly killed you?" William asked. "And who seeing his work unfinished may attempt again to end your life?"

"I pity the sinner of whatever stripe," Mottelay said. "It is as much a part of my vocation as is yours, to heal the sick and afflicted."

"I see our confessor has awakened from his slumber," a new but familiar voice said. William looked up.

Orlando Kempe was staring down at them with wry amusement.

55

William had not seen Kempe since that day at the prison when he had warned William of the danger he was in. Then, William believed his old schoolfellow was his friend and ally.

Not now. And Kempe himself had changed. He looked older. His handsome face had made him successful as a wooer and lover of women. Now he looked ravaged and wary, hunted if not haunted. William knew he had murdered Alice Fanshaw and Simon Gresham, his mistress and his best friend. If the course Kempe had set was as William feared, he would kill William and also Mottelay before the day was out.

"I should have hit you the harder, Mottelay," Kempe said, looking down at the priest. Then he flashed an angry glare at William. "And look at you now, Doctor Gilbert. How the mighty have fallen."

William said nothing to this. What was there to say? He could not ask for mercy or even pity from this man, who he knew was capable of neither.

"How glad I am that I may now speak freely to you, Doctor Gilbert. You thought that I arranged matters for you with Master Fanshaw for old time's sake. That I felt pity for your state and was moved thereby to advance you."

"I know now, I have known for some time, that you wanted to use me as a cover for your own murder," William said.

"How I hated you and envied you at Cambridge" Kempe said, smiling grimly. "You were so arrogant, so full of yourself. You and your stupid magnets. No one was as bright as you, as opinionated, as successful in your studies. I cannot say how much joy I had in your misery. At last, there was a state you could not understand, much less master. I watched you struggle, and I confess that I enjoyed the spectacle more than I can say. And you know what they called you?"

"Doctor Magnetic."

"Doctor Magnetic indeed. I coined that name, you know. After that, it caught on around the colleges, mine and yours. As I hoped it might."

"I didn't know that," William said.

"I did it that you should be mocked—derided, William."

"I never thought of it that way."

"No you didn't," Kempe said. "And that made me despise you the more, that you didn't see or feel the mockery right before your eyes."

"And now you are going to surrender me to the officers?" William asked. "That's what your father said."

"So the vicar thinks, as does my mother, which is precisely why I have found in them such useful allies, as you have observed. And by the way, do not call the vicar my father. He's not my father. He is my mother's husband, and as you have seen, somewhat of a tedious and credulous fool. My true father was once vicar of this wretched place. He was a wise man who saw, finally, what a fraud it all was, this business of religion." He spat out the final word in his cruel sentence. He paused and looked scornfully at Mottelay, whose face was expressionless, as though Kempe were invisible to his eyes and he deaf to Kempe's words.

"My father, Richard Kempe, hanged himself here, you know. In this very church, widowing my mother and orphaning me. But in that I find no fault in him. A man must see to himself in this life, this life being all there is. And it was his right to end it when he did, he being the master of his fate, as are we all."

"What of Alice?" William asked. "You were the father of her first child and her second, and you murdered her."

After a pause, Kempe burst out laughing. When he could speak, he said, "Oh, William, you really are a blind, self-righteous fool. You think you know so much. In truth, you know nothing at all. Nothing at all. But I shall tell you one thing, though I doubt you will believe me."

"And that is?"

"I fathered no child upon Alice Fanshaw's body, either before her marriage or after. It's not that I would not have liked to enjoy her, but she was always guarded after she came home again, even up to the time of her marriage. When I attended on her, her father was always present—or sometimes a half dozen of her maids, with Argus eyes. Parmenter knew what she was capable of, and I suppose he knew me well enough that I should not be left alone with her."

"I don't believe you," William said.

"Believe what you will."

"I believe you stole money from the Parmenters, and you stole money from your business partner as well, Gresham."

"Now there, sir, I do plead guilty. Gresham was my friend, it's true, and we did do some business together. He was useful in helping me move the bodies of these two women, but then he made it clear his love of money was greater than his love for me. I have little patience for blackmail, as it is called. As for Fanshaw and Parmenter, what was the loss to either? Sir John recouped his losses in the marriage contract. Five thousand pounds, if I remember, minus what Gresham skimmed off the top. Still Fanshaw got what he wanted, a young bride he could brag of. And the Parmenters, and more especially that old hag Lady Elizabeth, who knew right well her daughter was with child before she married. Well, they got what they wanted, the semblance of respectability and a cloak for Alice's faithlessness."

"Until Alice got with child again. Before the wedding."

"Well, that was not foreseen, but nature will take her course, will she not, Doctor?"

In all this, Mottelay had maintained a steel-like gaze that, had it been real steel, would have penetrated the heart of Orlando Kempe like one of his poniards or stilettos. But he had kept silent. Waiting for what?

William heard steps. It was the old couple coming down into the crypt again. William wondered if they had overheard what their son had said of them, calling his step-father a tiresome old fool. But if they had heard and were aggrieved neither showed it. Both seemed gratified, if not joyful, at the sight of the two prisoners prostrate before their son. For them, William supposed, it had been a good day's work, a Christian act. Orlando Kempe, the prodigal son, had come home again, welcomed by his grieving parents who now saw him as a public benefactor, trapping a fugitive murderer and equally fugitive priest. Might there not be a reward in the offing? Surely such a capture would get them more than a simple thanks from the authorities, perhaps even from the Queen herself. That was what Kempe would have told them. William could read it in their open, hopeful faces.

The vicar started to say something but was interrupted by a thunderous pounding at the church door. Kempe turned abruptly and looked at his mother, whose face broke into a smile. "Oh, my son, that would be Lord Burghley's men, come to take charge of the prisoners. Go up and let them in, I pray you. We locked the church door behind us, as you instructed, that none other come upon us whilst we do our work."

For a moment, Kempe stood his mouth agape, his face ashen, his grin of triumph gone. He seemed to have lost his power of speech. He looked at his mother. "What do you mean, Lord Burghley's men?"

His mother said, "A captain and two of his men, all armed and armored whereby I knew they were officers of the Queen or some high lord of the land. I went to the village to buy thread, and there they were, seeking they said, Doctor Gilbert here, for they said they sought him in Colchester and learned that he had come to Maidenstowe. I told them where he was, at the church, in the crypt below the chancel, and said my son had captured the murderer and the priest and asked them if there was not a reward for their capture. They asked me then my son's name. Orlando, Orlando Kempe, I said."

Above them, the pounding was deafening, like a battering ram of an invading army. Kempe looked at his mother and cried, "You stupid woman, you stupid woman! I am undone because of you."

"What do you mean, my son?" the old woman asked tearfully when she was able to speak. "Should I have said nothing, not have spoken your name, in which there can be no shame, or that you had captured these wretched men who lie at your feet?"

Kempe did not answer. He spit out curses, damning all and his fortune too. He turned to glare at his prisoners. He reached into the loose sleeve of his shirt and pulled something out. To William It looked at first like a large needle. Then William recognized what it was.

A stiletto, like the one he had seen in Elizabeth Parmenter's cabinet of curiosities.

"A pretty device, is it not, Doctor?" Kempe said. "I received it as a memento for my service to the Italian duke and his troops. It is made of the finest Italian steel. It has done me good service on more occasions than one."

Pausing briefly that William might receive the full effect of the weapon, Kempe rushed toward William with fury that in itself was terrifying, thrusting the stiletto toward William's chest.

William hurled himself aside to avoid the point aimed at his heart. It missed narrowly and struck the stone wall with a snap, its needle-like point breaking. Kempe cursed again, distracted now by the pounding above that was growing louder and more insistent. He stared at the broken blade and then cried out something unintelligible, turned, and ran for the stairs.

The vicar and his wife had witnessed all this and seemed now incapable of speech or motion, as though the display of their son's violence and his hurtful words had left them bereft of sense. They looked down where William knelt by Mottelay, who had come around and was reaching up to touch the back of his head. The vicar mumbled something William could not hear. He doubted it was an apology for what they and their son had done. That would have been too much to expect. What was written on the old couple's face now was not pride in their son, not shame or contrition, but confusion and terror.

The awful pounding continued, grew even more insistent. For William, time seemed to stop. Then, the vicar reached down and unbound him. The old man said nothing, but turned, seized his wife's arm and pulled her toward the stairs.

She followed without a word. Within seconds, William heard a cry. It was the vicar's wife. Sharp at first, a cry of surprise, it became an agonizing wail, more animal than human. It chilled William's blood. Whatever prompted it, it was horrible to hear, not for its volume but for its expression of unbearable grief.

William had heard such cries before at the bedside of the dying. It was the worst part of his calling—not the dead, now relieved from the burden of life—but those who survived and suffered the loss that no physician or apothecary could mend.

Suddenly the pounding stopped, although the wailing continued. Now William could hear the voices of men, one of which he recognized. It was Broward's voice. Evidently the vicar had unbolted the door and let them in.

William climbed the stairs to the chancel, uncertain of what he should see there, but fearing some awful thing. At once he saw what had caused the wail from the vicar's wife. She had collapsed in a heap in front of the altar, which before King Henry's reformation displayed an ornate representation of Christ on His cross. It was gone now, but a shadow of it remained on the otherwise featureless wall. The vicar stood silently by her, looking up to the ceiling.

Orlando Kempe had followed in his father's footsteps. He had found a rope, probably left by workmen repairing the ceiling, and tied it deftly in what William recognized as a sailor's knot.

His body swung slightly, as though sensitive to the revolving earth, like the needle on a compass seeking true north.

56

At the apothecary's in the village, William bound up his friend's wound, cleaning it first with water and then applying what he understood as the best remedy to heal a wound of this sort. William was good at wound binding. His mentor in Cambridge had commended him for his skill. He even thought that with the wound bound Mottelay would be able to mount a horse, return with him to Colchester. They would ride slowly with no need to keep up with Broward and his men, who were eager to return to Theobalds and report their success.

Mottelay said he could ride though it were his death to do so and would indeed, for he never wanted to see Maidenstowe again, or hear its name, or have anything to do with the Parmenters. He was a priest, he said, but he had had enough. The Parmenters could find another to minister to their spiritual needs, such as they were, he said.

Broward said he had gone to Colchester at his master's command. Word of Kempe's death in Italy had been reported, and Burghley wanted Doctor Gilbert to know of it at once, so that he would be assured he was now safe from Kempe. When Broward arrived in Colchester, his stepmother told Broward that William had gone to Maidenstowe on his lordship's business. Broward hadn't known what manner of business that was, but he still had his orders to find the young doctor and give him the good news. That had brought him to Maidenstowe, from the village to the church, and finally to the place William and Mottelay had been confined and Orlando Kempe had hanged himself.

The vicar and his wife, stricken with grief, had at once retired to their cottage to beweep their dead son, probably still trying to understand what they had done wrong, why their son had been so angry with them for doing the very thing he said he wanted, to bring two malefactors to justice and deliver them up to lawful authority.

Before they left the church, William had shown Broward the corpses of the two women. Also the wound in Alice Fanshaw's chest and the broken blade that had pierced her heart. William wanted a credible witness to the cause of her death. He knew Broward would do. Burghley trusted him, and in the end Burghley's judgment was what really mattered.

"And this other corpse?" Broward has asked. "She that is well decayed."

"Thomas Fanshaw's previous wife. Fanshaw murdered her years ago because she had betrayed him."

"What shall we do with her, Doctor?"

"Let her rest here for now. She shall be reburied hereafter as befits her."

"And Master Fanshaw's bride?"

"Have her taken back to the Fanshaw tomb from which Kempe took her. Treat her body with respect, Captain Broward. She has been ill-used beyond what she deserved."

William would later discover how true that was.

57

Broward had been eager to push on to Theobalds. He wanted to report what had happened. He was happy now. His journey had achieved the kind of success that meant something to him—a villainous murderer apprehended, an innocent man rescued. Lord Burghley would be pleased and when Burghley was pleased, he was generous.

But William persuaded Broward to go by way of Parmenter Hall. He said Alice Fanshaw's parents deserved to learn what had happened to their daughter's body, to know that it had been returned to its proper resting place. It was only right, William said. Besides, it was late in the evening. They could all spend the night at Parmenter Hall and then make their way to Theobalds the next day.

"Well, there's a good moon and the road's dry," Broward said, agreeing with the plan.

Orlando Kempe's body had been placed across a saddle on the horse he had rode in on and was found loose in the pasture. The body had been wrapped in the same canvas that had been used to cover the bodies of Fanshaw's two wives and looked like a sack of wheat or barley. Broward had ordered the noose to be left around Kempe's neck as a testimony to how he died, his suicide being considered, in his mind, a full admission of his guilt.

When they arrived at their destination, the Hall's darkened windows suggested the lord and lady of the manor had already retired, along with their household. William's instinct was to wait until the morning to break the news, but Broward insisted the grieving parents be informed at once. "Lord Burghley always says that if there be news to be broke, then it must be broke betimes, not sat upon to molder in the mind or vex them that awaits it."

"Then let us do as Lord Burghley counsels," William said.

Broward pounded on the door to the house for some minutes before it opened. Not by the butler who would customarily admit guests, but by two of the maidservants, who obviously wakened by the noisy summons, stared out into the night, their eyes wide with alarm at seeing armed men at the threshold. One, older and more courageous than the other, recognized Mottelay and admitted them. She told them that her master and mistress had already gone to bed, but she had no sooner said this than from behind her, Sir John Parmenter appeared—slippered, gowned, nightcapped, and clearly annoyed by this unexpected visit.

Broward told Parmenter who he was and whom he served, but the introduction was unnecessary. Parmenter obviously remembered the tall, imposing captain well. Now the butler appeared along with two other household servants who were told to fetch braces of candles. "We shall not stand in darkness to hear your news if it is of such import as you claim, Captain," Parmenter said.

Without waiting for more light, Broward gave his report, most of which William thought was accurate. He seemed confused as to the part the vicar and his wife played in his and Mottelay's abduction, which William made no effort to clarify. He had no enmity against the old couple, despite their complicity. They had been duped by their son, even as William had been. Nor did Broward say anything about the weapon used to kill Alice. Broward did get one thing right, the most important thing of all, at least to William. "It was the other doctor, Doctor Kempe, who murdered your daughter, Sir John. He confessed as much to these two gentlemen here."

Broward pointed to where William and Mottelay stood watching. "He was also undoubtedly the father of her two children, the one born and the other yet to be."

For a moment Parmenter seemed too shocked by this revelation to speak. Then he spoke. "And my daughter's body?"

"Found where Kempe had concealed it," William said. "In a crypt in the church, which was not searched when you came there. It has been returned to its proper place, where God willing it will not be disturbed again."

Parmenter nodded. "My wife will be consoled by that. I, as well."

And then Parmenter's manner changed. He suddenly grew angry and demanded to know where Kempe was. He stared wildly at the faces before him as though he expected to see Kempe lurking in the corner. Finally he bellowed, "Where is he? Where is Kempe? Bring him to me. As God is my witness, I will make him pay. We took him into our house, trusted him to care for our daughter, and he murdered her, you say? Got her with child?"

Before Broward could tell Parmenter that Kempe was dead, the knight dashed from the entrance hall into his library and presently came running out again, waving a rapier above his head and screaming that he was going to disembowel Kempe. He said he would not wait for the law to do its work but would have justice if he must administer it himself.

Two of Broward's men had to restrain him, snatching the rapier from his hands and delivering it to Broward. When Parmenter had gotten ahold of himself and was no longer raging but still breathing so heavily William was concerned for his health, Broward told Parmenter that Kempe was dead and that he might see for himself if he doubted it. "His body is sprawled upon his horse."

Parmenter grew calmer now. His breathing became more regular. "How dead? By what means?" Parmenter asked in almost a whisper.

"He hanged himself out of fear of being taken and condemned for what he did, sir," Broward said. "He was a coward at the last, sir, as are all they who take their own lives."

Parmenter murmured, almost to himself, "Then there is some justice in the world."

"He also confessed to killing your steward, Simon Gresham," William said. "They were in a partnership together, each investing half. Kempe, wanting it all, killed Gresham." Since Broward had not done so, William explained that Kempe was the vicar's step-son, and had convinced the vicar and his wife, Kempe's mother, that he was acting on behalf of Thomas Fanshaw and with the authority of Lord Burghley. "Kempe wanted to kill both me and Master Mottelay here, to silence us forever, that his murders should not be known."

Parmenter looked at Mottelay and asked the priest if that were true. Mottelay said it was. "If you doubt it, Sir John, go outside to the stable where you may see Kempe's body for yourself. The noose is still about his neck."

Parmenter said that would not be needed. He said he believed Lord Burghley's officer. He rubbed his forehead and then his eyes as though his sight had been affected as well as his conscience by all he now heard.

"Sirs, this is too much to learn and too quickly," Parmenter said. "I must sit down to make sense of it all." He turned to William again. "You, Doctor Gilbert, to whom I owe such a debt for these revelations and my sincerest apology for ever suspecting you of murder, pray come with me. You can then at your leisure disclose to me more of what you have learned. Come morning, I will be able to convey all to my wife. We shall not disturb her sleep with this news now, being as it is such a mix of good and evil."

Then he said to Broward and his men who were standing by, "All of you shall be quartered here for the night. To travel farther would be foolhardy. I congratulate you all for having done your duty. I have no doubt that you shall receive from Lord Burghley many thanks as well, and perhaps even some greater reward for your diligence."

William followed Parmenter into his library. A servant revived a fire on the hearth. Another brought wine and more candles. Parmenter seemed in a good mood now, at ease, open, companionable. It was hard for William to recognize this Sir John Parmenter, who only days before had seemed so threatening and brutal to him, much less the knight who had within minutes threatened in his rage to disembowel his daughter's secret lover and murderer.

"Sit you down, Doctor," Parmenter said. "Here, across from me. Now do tell me all you know about this plot in which you found yourself enmeshed. Orlando Kempe was your friend, or so you supposed, yet he entangled you in his plan to murder my daughter, tried to kill you by fire whilst you were in prison, hiring some incendiary to do the work that his malice be not known to you. Hated you from the very first."

"He did, sir, and confessed the same to me in St. Mark's church whilst I was his prisoner there," William said. "He said he always hated me, that he was jealous of what I had attained as a scholar and that it pleased him to torment me. When your daughter was found dead, he blamed my magnets, told Master Fanshaw that the fault was mine, although to me he said otherwise, ensuring me that he believed me innocent of any wrong-doing. All this Kempe did and conceived in his heart from the very first."

Parmenter shook his head sadly. "Orlando Kempe was a promising young man and might have proved a decent doctor. You know we knew him before he went to Italy to finish his studies."

"I know he spent several months of a summer here at Parmenter Hall."

"He did. Gresham and he were old friends, boys together I believe. I see now that I suckled two serpents at my bosom, believing them honest when neither was."

Parmenter shook his head and sat silent for a few moments, staring into the fire. He seemed to forget William was there, but this gave William time to think too, for he had just heard something Parmenter said that puzzled him.

Parmenter took another sip of his wine and said he was weary and needed to go to bed. He started to rise. But William said, "Sir John, may I ask a question of you? Concerning some matter never resolved in my mind. I ask not out of mere curiosity, but to understand the whole of what happened and why. To me a mystery is to be explained, not left hidden to bewilder and vex."

"What question would that be?" Parmenter asked, smiling. He sat back down. "What mystery as you describe it, when all mysteries seem now resolved? Speak, Doctor, for I am curious myself."

"Your daughter, sir, Alice. You were wont to say some boy of the village got her with child."

"So I believed before Kempe confessed it was he," Parmenter said.

"No, Sir John, with all due respect, he did not confess it."

"Well, he would not confess, would he, being as he was a liar?" Parmenter said.

William said, "He seemed most open in his declarations to me, thinking I was about to be dead by his hand and unable to reveal it all. He confessed, nay boasted, of his murder of Gresham and your daughter, but denied fathering any child on her body."

"Nonetheless, I do believe it was Kempe," Parmenter insisted. "He was always leering at her, sniffing about her. I suppose, Doctor, you think we were foolish to be so trusting."

"No, Sir John. I trusted Kempe as well. I cannot fault you and your lady for being deceived. May I ask one more question, sir?"

Parmenter sighed heavily and said. "Ask it, but know, Doctor, that I am one who seeks his bed early for my health's sake. We are now well past my usual hour of retirement. You yourself must be weary after such a day in your life."

"I am indeed weary," William said. "And I promise I will be brief. But pray tell me this: Tonight before you learned that Kempe was dead, you wanted

332

to kill him. You had armed yourself with a rapier and with, I perceive, an intent to use it. The Captain's men restrained you. But when you learned he was dead, you seemed relieved. Given your cause for anger, I am surprised you weren't disappointed to learn Kempe was now beyond your reach and thereby the more angry that you had been deprived of your vengeance."

"I think you mistake me, Doctor," Parmenter said with a weary smile. "I was not relieved but much gratified. The man is now burning in hell. No, Doctor, if anything Kempe's death is a cause of celebration. I do hate and despise the man, and when my wife discovers all he did, her hate will match my own. If not be the greater. You do not know my wife well, Doctor, but you know her well enough I think, to know what I say is true."

William nodded.

Then William spoke again, "With all respect, Sir John, I do not think I mistook your response. Relief and gratification are two very different emotions, if I may say so. This is not science, but plain common experience. If you had been content to let God judge Orlando Kempe, you would never have taken up your weapon—to kill him, or perhaps only to cut out his tongue."

"What do you mean, cut out his tongue?" Parmenter said. He looked at William suspiciously.

"I mean so that he might not betray you."

"Betray me?" Parmenter's eyes flashed with anger. His chest began to heave. "What are you saying, Doctor? Are you mad? How betray me? What are you thinking? Are you accusing me of killing my own daughter?"

"You have within these last few minutes made reference to my near-death in prison, for which I thank you. But you also described the nature of the assault, the incendiary himself, the fire in my cell. How would you know that, Sir John?"

"Why, Lord Burghley made mention of it," Parmenter said.

"Lord Burghley made mention of an assault upon my person, but in general terms. You referred to the particulars. Assaults take many forms, Sir John, as all the world knows. There are many ways to kill a man, or a woman, but you knew exactly what had happened, the actor, the means, and the outcome. How would you know that save you were the begetter of it? You used Kempe as your intermediary to hire the man, now deservedly dead. To kill me, to keep me quiet, lest I discover what you had done, your part in all of this."

333

For a moment, Parmenter said nothing. He sat looking at William, his face red with unexpressed outrage. Then anger was replaced by alarm, in his eyes, in a slight tremor in his hands. William was trained to notice these things, symptoms of a disquiet mind, panic.

William said, "No, Sir John, I am not accusing you of killing your daughter, but of colluding with him who did, for reasons of your own."

"Colluding?"

"Of paying Kempe to kill your daughter, even as you paid him to be rid of me."

Parmenter gave out a derisive laugh. "You have lost your senses, Doctor. Why on earth would I want my daughter dead? I was her father, she my child. Kempe killed her because he was her lover and would not have her reveal the same to that pernicious priest, Mottelay. Or, worse, to confess all to her husband."

William said, "So I thought myself for a long while, sir. But there is one who might have an even greater stake in Alice's silence."

"Who? Pray tell who, you who know so much?" Parmenter's eyes blazed with anger, and William thought at any moment he would be attacked, perhaps as violently as he had been attacked by Kempe only a few hours before but with greater success.

"The father of her two children," William said, not sure that it was true yet but feeling in his gut it must be so and willing to invest in it.

"Kempe," Parmenter said.

"Not Kempe. Not Kempe but yourself, Sir John."

58

The dark, horrid thought had come to him suddenly. Not from nowhere, but some place unfinished, a hypothesis unconfirmed but sturdy enough for him to stand upon. Like the insights he sometimes had at Cambridge when during a lecture some enigma suddenly became clear, as though a veil had been lifted and truth stood before him shining like a crystal.

This was like unto it. Elizabeth Parmenter had said her husband was lascivious, not to be trusted by her or any woman. Kempe had said that after the first disgrace Alice was kept under lock and key, to preserve the tattered remnants of her virtue. If Kempe was not her mysterious lover, as he had declared when he had nothing to lose by admitting it, a process of elimination left but one other person who had access to her, though the very thought of it repelled William. It was more a leap of faith than a logical inference.

Now Parmenter jumped to his feet. His whole countenance changed to show righteous indignation, a new look for him yet not entirely convincing. "You lie, sir," he screamed. "You dare say that to me, in my own house?" He looked wildly about him. For what? William wondered. Then he knew. The rapier. But it was gone. Broward had wisely removed it in an abundance of caution. Parmenter turned back to William, his piercing eyes drilling into William's head even as Kempe's stiletto had pierced Alice Fanshaw's heart.

William had said what he had darkly imagined. He could not unsay it now, regardless of Parmenter's threats. He decided he might as well go forward. He raised his voice to match Parmenter's.

"Tell me, Sir John, did Kempe know that is why you wanted your daughter killed, to hide your sin? Was that why Gresham also had to die, because he too knew what you had done. Was this, then, how Kempe

335

made himself rich, bought his London house? It was you that gave him money to keep him quiet, to do your dirty work, wasn't it? Not Kempe's wealthy patients who existed more in his imagination than in fact. And was your lady wife also knowing of your incest, sir? Did she countenance it, or blind herself to the truth of what you did?"

Parmenter retreated into a stony silence. He folded his arms across his chest and stared at William with hatred, as though defying him to prove the outrageous allegation. Undaunted, William pressed on.

"When your daughter turned to religion and sought to confess, you feared she would expose you as the father of her children, which in her pious resolve she might well have done. You couldn't let that happen. It would ruin you, disgrace you, make you a hiss and a byword. Fanshaw worried about being thought a cuckold. You had much more to fear."

Suddenly, William was aware that someone else had come into the room. It was Elizabeth Parmenter. She stood there regarding her husband with dead eyes. She looked stricken with age, her hair fallen around her frail, bony shoulders, her face hard and unyielding. How long had she been standing there? William knew she had overheard, most if not everything. At least, she had heard enough. It was written on her face along with her contempt for her husband.

She said in a cold voice, addressing William, but not taking her eyes off her husband, "In answer to your question, Doctor Gilbert, I did not know, nor would I have countenanced it had I known. What mother would? Had I known about the first child, trust me, Doctor, there would have been no second child by this husband of mine. He would have been, like Thomas Fanshaw, quite unmanned I assure you. I would have carved him up with relish, for though I be but a woman, yet a woman knows better than a man how to avenge wrongs done to her or hers."

Parmenter started to say something to his wife. His face, suffused with anger before, was now pale. But he kept silent, in terror of her.

"In truth, I always suspected it," Elizabeth Parmenter continued. "But thought it was too perverse to credit, a figment of my imagination. Now, I see it is the truth indeed."

She approached her husband until she was within arm's length of him. But his back was to the fire. He could not withdraw, although it was clear to William he wished to. "You killed our daughter," she said. She repeated the accusation. She repeated it again, and each time she did so her voice became lower until it sounded nothing human, like a growl of some voracious beast ready to pounce upon her prey.

The scene was horrible to William. He wished now he had never voiced his theory, even if it was slowly and inevitably being confirmed before his eyes and in his ears.

Parmenter looked at William and pointed an accusing finger at his wife. "She was unfaithful to me, Doctor. You must know that. Alice was not my child. What I may have done with Alice, seduced by her beauty, I did with no blood relation. Call me adulterer, if you will. I freely confess it. But I committed no, no …" His voice faltered. He could not find the word. At least not at first, but then he spoke it. "No *incest*."

Parmenter looked defiantly at his wife, but William knew that it was a false face, a pose. Like Kempe feigning friendship. Like Fanshaw pretending tolerance of his wife's infidelity or grief at her tomb.

"She *was* your child," his wife said, glaring. "And you know it, you devil."

"I heard otherwise from Gresham," Parmenter responded, lifting his head in a gesture of triumph, as though Gresham's word were indisputable proof. But it seemed to William another weak and desperate defense of the indefensible.

His wife gave out a sharp, derisive laugh. "Simon Gresham, who all the world now knows was a thief and a liar to boot. You believed some idle gossip of his? What manner of fool are you, husband, to be so easily deceived? I tell you, sir, you are a man looking to excuse yourself. I say Alice was your daughter. I swear it before God, His sacred mother, and before all the angels in heaven. The babe she carried was your daughter as well. Young Perdita I now know is your daughter too. Daughter and granddaughter both. Pitiful child. Oh, this is vile practice, my husband, truly vile, and were it known abroad, if it were known—"

She stopped, seeming to realize what she had just said. She spat upon the floor, just missing her husband's slippers.

"Oh, this is more than I can bear," she cried, pressing her fists against her forehead as though she were suffering physical pain there. "It is more than any woman should bear. Were our lives different, were I a village woman, I would cast you out, husband, you and every memory of you, like some detestable spider come indoors. But I am not some woman from the village who enjoys such freedom. I have a name in this county. I have a place in this kingdom. But come you to my bed nevermore, husband.

Speak to me nevermore. I don't want to hear your voice. I don't want to see your face. Thank God each night that I do not take you to the law. But it would disgrace me as well as you. When you die, I shall not mourn you, but give thanks to God for my deliverance."

Neither husband nor wife seemed to take note of his leaving. Behind William, the rancor and recriminations continued, growing in a furious intensity. He knew it would end badly for one of them, probably for both.

It was now near midnight, and he felt his physical strength ebbing away. He had begun the day as a prisoner, drugged, bound, assaulted. The shocking discoveries of the evening made all worse for him. He had guessed rightly about Parmenter's guilt, but he had paid a price for his success, a disquiet mind. A glimpse of depravity he would never forget.

He left the house and found some place in the nearby wood to lie, like a fugitive again, but this time not from the law but from life about him. The moon down, he knew he could not travel in the dark. As uncomfortable as the cold ground was, it was better than being in the cursed house he had just fled.

It would have been better had he never known Parmenter's secret, he thought. He could have gone on, thinking Kempe acted on his own, motivated by lust and greed and envy. Vices of which Kempe was surely possessed. But Parmenter's crime was the greater, the violation of his daughter, the destruction of his soul. Even if Gresham's accusation had been true and Alice was not Parmenter's child, it would have been a violation still.

He would tell Mottelay what he had learned. Perhaps it would confirm in the priest his decision never to set foot in Parmenter Hall again. The question now was whether William should tell Burghley. He knew enough about the law to know it would be a hard case to make, the illicit paternity. Unless Parmenter confessed it. William doubted he would. And what proof might there be of his incest? There was no way of proving paternity, at least none that was known of. The victim was dead. She would not rise to point the finger at him who wronged her.

It was another case that might well be left up to heaven.

When he returned to Colchester two days later, he was still thinking about what he should say to Burghley, or if he should say anything at all. But

338

then he received a letter from Mottelay. It was very brief and rendered the issue moot. Mottelay wrote that Sir John Parmenter had died in the night. His heart had failed while he slept. His lady wife had found him, stone cold, staring sightlessly up at the coffered ceiling, which Mottelay said was decorated with flights of angels. Mottelay had heard all of this, of course, from a maidservant in the village. He did not know of it directly but had no reason to believe it to be false.

The funeral would be held in two days, one of which had already passed. William doubted Parmenter's wife would attend.

59

In the late summer of that year, Pieter Weinmeer's glorious garden had begun to fade into muter colors, and the sky above Amsterdam was gray, like unpolished steel. Still, William took delight in it and even more in his company. Katrina, whose father had kept his promise to be silent about William's misadventures, had begged him for news of their young English friend. Now that he was here, she was full of questions. She wanted to know how his practice did in Colchester. What sort of patients had he? What manner of town was Colchester? What was the character of its people?

She knew Cambridge and its venerable colleges well from the time she had lived there but beyond that, the towns and cities of England were mysteries to her, simply names on a map she had seen in her father's library. William described Tymperleys, his family's house in Colchester, although he had done that before when earlier he was her English tutor and she a girl of fourteen. Now he described Theobalds, more palace than house, and to make sense of that he slowly revealed most of his experiences, except for the more gruesome parts—the dead women at Maidenstowe, his near-miss with death in prison, Orlando Kempe's hanging himself, and especially the Parmenter incest, which he felt was much too unpleasant for her ears. He named no names. What did that matter to her or, increasingly, to him?

What came forth thereby was a fragmented and much edited narrative, which she heard with a mixture of pity and dismay, exclaiming from time to time, "Oh, how you endured that" and "What evil you encountered!"

He doubted she could comprehend it all, but not because she was a woman or slow of understanding. She was indeed a woman now, lovely and soft-voiced and, according to her father and his own observation, sound-minded and perceptive. It was, rather, that she had suffered enough.

He could not add to it with his own heavy burden of regret and remorse. Not now. Not ever.

They sat together as they had months before during William's brief exile in her country, neither apparently willing to return to that painful place where they had left off, she confessing the assault upon her honor in Cambridge and both facing the enduring consequences, an unnatural reserve and defensiveness. William had understood her response then. He thought perhaps he understood it even better now. When their conversation drew near that old wound it was she who made it bleed again, not he.

"Since you left, William, I have thought much about our parting. It was sad, and in more ways than one. I was most sorry to see you return to England, but even sorrier that I seemed to rebuff you, your affection, which I do swear I share. I mean when you—"

At this he cut her off, pressing her hand in such a way to indicate that she should say no more about it. "I understand," he said. "You need not talk of it. That is, if you do not wish, which if you do not, I understand perfectly."

Perhaps he had himself spoken too much. He shut his mouth and listened.

"For years I did not want to speak of it," she said. "As I said to you, I never told my father, and I do wish still that he might never know. My pain is a burden my mother must carry, my secret."

"Yet you told me," William reminded her.

"Because I trusted you above any man," she said, fixing him with her eyes as though he were the only one of his kind in the world.

She suggested they walk along the path from one part of which they could view the sea. It was a splendid view. England was so far away, which at the moment was good to him as well. His unhappiness had begun there. He prayed that it had ended there as well.

After they had walked for a while in silence, she said, "I had a dream one night not long ago. It was a frightening vision, by which I mean it caused me fear. No, more than fear—terror. I was in Cambridge again. But as old as I am now. I was walking in the country as I did then to gather flowers and breathe the pure air. I am happy, and I think I am in love."

"In love?"

"With my English tutor, you idiot," she said laughing, and then continued as though her answer surely must have been obvious to him. She grew serious again. "Suddenly, in the dream, I was in a wood, a deep wood, and before me appeared the two men who had attacked me. I know who they are, and I know what they are about to do. But in the dream, they were not wearing masks. Their faces are visible. Two men of about the same years, dressed as students."

"Was either face familiar to you?" William asked.

"No, and thinking back now, I cannot remember their faces save they were young men, not farmers or laborers but dressed as young gentlemen, much as yourself now."

"So your dream was like unto what happened to you, except your attackers were unmasked?"

"I don't remember their faces from the dream. Perhaps because they were strangers to me then. I might not have recognized them even if they were unmasked. In the dream they did not attack me, though I felt apprehensive that they would. Knew that they would, that it would be the next thing, my violation. That was terrible enough."

She said "violation" with a pained expression, as though the very word were the offense done to her. Then she continued.

"I do believe I woke myself so that I would not have to undergo all that pain and humiliation a second time, which certain I am that no woman deserves. But the strange thing is this. When I awoke, I remembered something from the real experience that I had long forgotten, or perhaps hidden away in my mind that I should not think of it."

He waited for her to tell him. He would not demand it of her.

She paused and took a breath. "It came to me suddenly, a memory that I had hidden from my very self. For when I awoke, all came to me of a sudden, as though all had happened that very day. For hours after I lay broad waking, weeping, not for the woman I am now, but for the girl I was then. Innocent and well-meaning, a child really. All that was ended that day.

"Ended?"

"I mean my childhood."

"You don't have to tell more, you know," William said. "Perhaps it is better to bury the experience, since it cannot be undone."

"No it cannot be undone, William. About that you are right. But I will tell you more, and you alone. You may be able to tell me what it all means, this dream and what befell me when I awoke from it."

The interpretation of dreams had not been in his course of study at Cambridge. It was the work of another sort of person, a priest like Julian

Mottelay, a soothsayer or even a witch. But he resolved to help her if he could. He could deny her nothing that she needed.

"I remembered this," she said. "Although the men were masked, they spoke while they assaulted me, and now I do recall their voices, which thing I had no memory of before. Is that not strange, William? How is it that it lay buried in me, the important thing that was said?"

"What important thing?"

"One called the other by name, which I do think was a slip on his part rather than intended. They had every reason to keep themselves unknown to me. One said to the other, taunting him, 'Now she is yours, Gresham. Let us see if you are man enough to take her.'"

William's blood ran cold. He wasn't sure he had heard accurately and asked her to repeat the name and phrase she remembered. She did.

"And the other? Did you hear his name?"

She thought for a moment. "Yes, she said, "when both had finished and were dressing themselves again, he who had called his companion Gresham—"

William didn't need to hear more. He knew the name she was about to utter.

Rage seized him like a physical affliction. It burned and seethed in his head and in his breast. He thought to himself: this is what madness is. But it was more than madness, which only affected the brain. His whole body reeled with what he now felt.

For a time, he could not speak. Katrina asked if he were well. He said he was. But it was a lie. He was far from well. He wanted to kill both of them, Kempe and Gresham, and with his own hands, not some impersonal instrument like that used to kill Gresham and Alice Fanshaw. Avenging Katrina's rape was now beyond his power, even as Sir John Parmenter's death prevented his public disgrace and hanging. He knew God would judge them and punish them, and that was just, but divine retribution seemed too remote to satisfy him, to give him any relief for what he now felt.

Orlando Kempe and Simon Gresham, a pair that were closer than he and Kempe ever were, and a good thing too. He might have been tainted by the same bad blood, the same cruel disposition that bound the two men together until one murdered the other and the murderer killed himself. Kempe had admitted he had envied William while at Cambridge, hated him even, because he was the better scholar, the sharper intellect. Kempe had known William tutored Katrina, the pretty Dutch girl. Kempe had come to dinner at the Weinmeer house. Long before Sir John Parmenter had contrived to set Kempe up as murderer of Alice Fanshaw to secure her silence, Kempe had taken out his malice on Katrina Weinmeer, taken her body and her innocence and egged his friend Gresham on in the effort.

Katrina had suffered this because of William. And once he had thought that, he could not unthink it. His rage was changed to a profound guilt and remorse.

Katrina must have noticed the anguish in his face. Astonished, she said, "Did you know these young men, Gresham and Kempe?"

He had mentioned no names in his highly edited narrative of his experiences. Their names had not mattered. Now they did. He very much wanted to answer her question in the negative, but that would have been a lie. Katrina would see through it, know he was lying, and that would make everything worse. He wanted her to trust him. He needed her to trust him.

"I knew Kempe then," he said slowly, watching her face to see how she was taking this new and terrible revelation. "It was he who later arranged for me to attend on Alice Fanshaw, whom Kempe murdered using me as scapegoat for his crime. We were acquaintances at Cambridge, never true friends. Gresham I did not know whilst there. I learned later just how close he and Kempe were, born and reared in the same village, evil men, Katrina, more conspiring and duplicitous than you can know."

William did not tell her that Kempe had made her his victim out of jealousy of him. That lust was not what drove the assault but a craven envy of her tutor. It was terrible that he should even utter as painful a truth as it was for him to think it. But he remembered what Kempe had boasted of while he still lived, standing proud and arrogant in the crypt with two of his mortal enemies helpless before him and relishing their fear. He had shown no mercy. William heard Kempe's cold, pitiless voice, as though he were present.

"I hated you even then and swore your undoing."

Another heavy silence fell between them. He could not read her thoughts, but her pain was evident in her clear eyes. He wanted to console her, to be a good doctor and ease her pain. Was it not for that purpose he had studied the healing arts? But hers was not a pain of the body. He did not know what to say and feared his very knowledge of these men made him somehow complicit in their assault. Is that how she saw him now—one of those men who used women as they willed? Had he been tainted with the same brush in her mind?

"Both men are dead," he said, knowing this might not console her at all, although he knew it must be said. "One killed the other and then later killed himself."

Hearing this, she regarded him uncertainly, showing neither surprise nor satisfaction. He repeated to her what he had said, but now more emphatically. "I swear by heaven, that your ravishers have paid a terrible price, yet much deserved. They are both dead. I saw the bodies myself. Kempe, who urged Gresham to the act, hanged himself. He had no hope of escape. He was about to be arrested. Lord Burghley's men were at the door. Their arrival saved my life. And Gresham, well, he died too, by the hand of his friend, Kempe. Both received what they deserved."

Katrina said nothing in response. He stopped speaking. She had taken both his hands in hers. Her eyes filled with tears. "Oh William, be done with it, for it is past and over," she said. "It would have been so, were they both still alive in England and thriving as they wished. They hurt me once, and now they can hurt me no more, not because they are dead, but because I refuse to let them hurt me more. God in heaven, I will not have it."

She uttered this resolve in her native tongue, but William somehow understood it, as though it were spoken in the plainest English.

They returned to the house. She said goodnight. This time she received his lips without hesitation. Her own were soft and warm and a delight to him. Katrina was right. It was done, all done. Fortune had turned her wheel.

At least for the moment.

CPSIA information can be obtained
at www.ICGtesting.com
Printed in the USA
BVHW052049190922
647419BV00001B/42